Happy reading!

Pamela Burford

UNDERTAKING

Irene

D1600707

Also by Pamela Burford

Jane Delaney Mysteries
Uprooting Ernie
Perforating Pierre
Icing Allison

Romantic Suspense
Snatched
Going Commando
Storming Meg
A Case of You
Twice Burned (Double Dare book 2)

Contemporary Romance
Rags to Bitches
In the Dark
Snowed
Too Darn Hot
The Boss's Runaway Bride (a novella)

The Wedding Ring matchmaking series:
Love's Funny That Way
I Do, But Here's the Catch
One Eager Bride To Go
Fiancé for Hire

UNDERTAKING

Irene

A Jane Delaney Mystery
Book 1

Pamela Burford

RADICAL POODLE
P R E S S

Paperback edition published 2018 by Radical Poodle Press
Copyright © 2014 by Pamela Burford

ISBN 978-1-939215-86-4
Ebook ISBN 978-1-9392-1584-0

Interior design by Polgarus Studio
Cover design copyright © 2014 Patricia Ryan
Author photograph copyright © Jeff Loeser

www.pamelaburford.com

for Jeff, always

1

Frenemies

I KIND OF hated swiping the brooch. It made a real fashion statement for the corpse, who, need I mention, was the best-dressed person at the Leonard T. Ahearn and Sons Funeral Home.

Nobody *dresses* anymore. Have you noticed? Shorts at the office. Flip-flops in church. In *church*. Okay, so I'm not what you'd call a churchgoer, aside from the occasional paid-mourner gig, but you get my point. It's a matter of respect. I mean, if it were your blue-haired granny packed into that satin-lined box, all decked out in a yellow Chanel suit and Hermès scarf, with a manicure to die for, would you show up for the wake in plaid flannel dorm pants and fuzzy slippers?

Fuzzy bedroom slippers, I kid you not, as if locating an actual pair of flip-flops would have taken too much effort for the grieving granddaughter. The girl, who looked around eighteen, sat slumped in the front row between her pimply younger brother and nose-picking boyfriend, playing Angry Birds on her iPad and whining about missing *Keeping Up With the Kardashians* because she'd maxed out her DVR for that time slot. Your basic sullen Long Island youth.

I shouldn't care. Colette O'Rourke wasn't *my* blue-haired granny, she was an assignment. Which might come across as pretty cold considering I knew her, but it had been years since our paths had crossed. Thankfully, none of our mutual acquaintances were here at the moment.

How was *I* dressed? Glad you asked. Conservative gray skirt suit, crisp white blouse, two-inch black pumps. Strawberry-blond hair pulled back in a French twist. Tasteful faux pearls and just enough makeup to keep my pale brows and lashes from doing a vanishing act. It was my standard funeral-home uniform and had served me well, though if I really wanted to blend in with the mourning crowd nowadays, I should probably buy some of those light-up sneakers. Maybe a housedress and hair curlers.

My name is Jane Delaney and I do things my paying customers can't do, don't want to do, don't want to be seen doing, can't bring themselves to do, and/or don't want it to be known they'd paid someone to do. To dead people.

No, really, it's all legal. Well, okay, sometimes there's a kind of gray area. Like with the brooch. Irene McAuliffe had hired me to salvage her property before it ended up six feet under the lovingly tended sod of Whispering Willows Cemetery. Had I demanded proof of ownership before accepting the assignment? Had I demanded to know why, if the brooch belonged to Irene, it was now pinned to the lifeless bosom of longtime frenemy Colette O'Rourke? No, I had not, but she'd cheerfully filled in the blanks.

Irene was a crusty old buzzard who didn't take crap from anyone. She was also my steadiest client—my very first client, as a matter of fact, from way back when I was in high school. She'd been putting food on my table and pants on my ass for two decades. Irene had money, along with specific ideas about how she wanted that money spent. Most of those ideas had to do with imparting stern lessons to individuals who, due to the fact they'd stopped breathing air, were less than receptive to such teachable moments.

You know that saying about how revenge is best served cold? Irene believed that revenge was best served to those who were cold. A subtle distinction, I'll grant you, and one I chose not to dwell on as I crossed myself and rose from the kneeler next to Colette's casket. I'm not Catholic, but I have the moves down.

The brooch was a cheap bauble, but one with powerful sentimental value. Not that Irene was the sentimental type, aside from the smother-love she lavished on her toy poodle, but she'd known Colette her whole life. They'd grown up in the same grimy apartment house in Bay Ridge and had at one time been closer than sisters. The brooch had been a sweet-sixteen gift from Irene to Colette and had cost all of $4.39 back in the 1950s.

When you have no money, you remember the cost of things. Irene's words. She'd saved up nickels and dimes from baby-sitting for weeks to buy that brooch.

Why, you might ask, if their lifelong friendship meant so much to Irene, had she boycotted Colette's wake? Their relationship, always volatile, had been on a downward trajectory for the past decade or so, the result of an infamous row over the minimum bet in the weekly poker game Irene hosted.

And then there was the brooch itself. Ages ago, Colette had specified in her will that she was to be buried with it. Irene, the repository of an inexhaustible supply of obscure and suspiciously convenient Unwritten Rules, had insisted that Colette, the

Recipient of the Gift, was morally bound to offer the trinket to Irene, the Giver of the Gift, if the alternative was Burial of the Gift.

Colette had greeted this pronouncement with her signature dry cackle and single-digit salute. It was on to Plan B: What better *nyah-nyah* than for Irene to snatch the thing from her erstwhile BFF when said BFF was in no position to do a damn thing about it?

Irene was big on getting the last word.

I know you're wondering what this brooch looked like. It was made of some kind of white base metal, two to three inches long and in the shape of a mermaid holding a mirror and running a comb through her hair. The entire piece was heavily encrusted with fake gemstones of various shapes and sizes. The lines of the mermaid's body were graceful and feminine, from her flowing red hair to the sweeping fan of her tail. The fishy lower parts were done in dark blue and green stones, the human upper half in cubic zirconia or whatever stood in for diamonds back then. Rhinestones probably. The perky breasts were bare and tipped with tiny red nipples—no clamshell bra for this brazen mermaid. Daring stuff for the fifties, but then, I get the sense that Irene and her friend were not exactly the shy, bookish type.

There was something just plain wrong about the sight of that sexpot mermaid in such close proximity to the rosary beads clutched in Colette's cold fingers. Still, I was impressed by the artistry and workmanship of the piece, despite its being worth approximately what Irene had paid for it in her youth. By contrast, she was shelling out three hundred clams, pun intended, for me to snatch the thing from under the very noses of Colette's clueless kinfolk.

The wake was scheduled for seven to nine p.m. My arrival had been timed for the final few minutes when the last visitors would be saying their good-byes and the family would be too tired and distracted to notice me liberating the brooch one-handed and slipping it into my jacket pocket as I executed a slow turn away from the casket. Plus, there'd be scant time afterward for anyone to notice something was missing. I'd practiced the moves at home and had them down. All I needed was a few seconds of alone time with the stiff.

Behind me a trio of Colette's gal pals converged on the occupants of the front row. The eyes in the back of my head saw the old ladies bending over Colette's son and daughter-in-law, squeezing their hands and filling their field of vision in a most fortuitous way. "Lenny Ahearn did such a nice job, she looks so natural," they murmured, and "What a shock, I ran into her just before Easter at Whole Foods," and "Will you be putting the house on the market? I might know someone." What they were no doubt dying to say but didn't have the nerve was, "What in the world possessed you to pin that vulgar brooch to a genuine Hermès scarf?"

Meanwhile Fuzzy Slippers and her brother squabbled like rabid wolverines over the iPad. "It's mine," she hissed, jerking it out of the boy's grasp. "I bought it with my own money." She called him a filthy name and he responded in kind.

It was show time.

I commenced my well-rehearsed sleight of hand, angling my body to conceal my fingers as they darted over the side of the—

Feet shuffled on the carpet directly behind me. I jerked my hand back and turned to see a good-looking, fortyish man waiting to pay his respects to Colette. The man had sandy hair cropped so close it was practically shaved. He wore a black shirt and black pants. And a white clerical collar.

Can you sprain your eyeballs? Because I swear, when mine zeroed in on that collar, they practically dislocated.

A priest. I'd almost been busted by a priest.

My heart attempted to sledgehammer its way out of my ribcage as I wondered giddily which particular circle of hell was reserved for those caught stealing from the dead by a man of the cloth.

"Please." The padre gestured toward the guest of honor and took a half step back. "Take your time. I can wait." The words were indulgent, the body language reassuring. So why did it feel as though that unsmiling blue gaze was boring into my skull, rummaging through my brain, and reading my guilty, guilty thoughts?

"Oh…that's okay." I scooted away from the casket. "You, um, go ahead. I'll just, you know…"

He dipped his head in thanks and approached the casket.

I sank into the chair next to Colette's son and dragged in a deep, steadying breath, nearly gagging on the cloying scent of the floral arrangements. The three old ladies bestowed final cheek-pecks and shuffled toward the exit. Well, that particular window of opportunity had officially slammed shut. I sneaked a peek at my watch. I had a couple of minutes left. I would do this thing. I had to. The funeral was tomorrow morning. It was either swipe that brooch here and now or invest in a shovel and flashlight. I'd never failed a client, and I wasn't about to start now.

Plus, if I had to fail a client, it sure as heck wasn't going to be Irene McAuliffe, who'd recently become even more irritable and demanding than usual. True, we had a long history. She was the grandma I never had—though I'd be willing to bet my real grandmas never planted stinkweed on a grave or mixed an unloved one's ashes into a bag of kitty litter. For twenty-two years I'd managed to keep out of Irene's crosshairs. Return to her empty-handed? I had a better idea. I'd change my name and move to Rangoon. Less trauma in the long run.

Also, I could really use the three hundred bucks.

As the priest knelt and prayed, Colette's son turned to me. He was lean and rangy, wearing a dandruff-specked corduroy sport coat and loosened tie. He looked older than the sixty or so years I knew him to be. "Thanks for coming. Patrick O'Rourke."

The hand I shook felt rough as bark. I'd never met Patrick before, but I'd heard whispers around town, none of them flattering. Terms such as *troubled* and *misfit* and *loser* had followed the guy since adolescence.

He tried to introduce me to his wife, Barbara, a well-nourished bottle blonde encased in a bedazzled stretch-denim ensemble, but she was making her own grab for the iPad and yelling at their kids to shut the hell up and show some respect. "So did you know my mom?" Patrick asked me.

You might think this is where it got awkward, but in fact, I could do this part in my sleep. "Not as well as I would have liked," I said. "I'm Mary Filcher. I just recently started working at the senior center here in Crystal Harbor. One thing about Colette, she could always drum up a poker game."

That produced a half smile. "She was one hell of a player. Never rubbed off on me. I couldn't manage a poker face to save my life."

I always come armed with a factoid or two about the dearly departed. Also, I routinely leave my purse in the car so if I find myself in a tight spot, I can pretend to be an employee of the funeral home. The suit-and-pearls uniform helps to pull that one off, besides being just plain good manners. This evening, though, since I'd been observed in civilian mode actually visiting with the corpse, that particular ploy wasn't an option.

Okay, let's get something out of the way so we won't have to deal with it again. I can hear you thinking, Oh, that Jane Delaney, how does she live with herself? Pretending to be something she's not. For money. Taking advantage of grieving families. For money. *Stealing* from dead people. For three hundred bucks cash money.

Well, I think I explained that last thing. It wasn't really stealing—the brooch belonged to Irene. Kind of. And anyway, this particular job wasn't what you'd call typical, even for Irene. My usual assignments involve activities as benign as placing flowers on graves or scattering ashes at sea. Plus that thing I mentioned before, being a paid mourner, which I'll have you know is a career with a long and distinguished… well, a long history, so don't turn up your nose.

Okay, I'll admit there have been a few assignments over the years that might be described as offbeat, the current one being a splendid example. And for the record, I had nothing to do with the kitty-litter episode. That was before my time.

The bottom line is, I help my clients deal with their grief and loss, and I have a strict moral code regarding what kinds of jobs I'll accept. You think swiping jewelry is bad? You should see what I've turned down. Once word gets around that there's this person called the Death Diva—no, I did not choose the nickname!—willing to perform all manner of chores for grieving folk, at reasonable rates and with the utmost discretion, well, you're going to get the occasional kook slithering out of the woodwork. There's a reason morgues are locked up at night.

I watched the priest as he rose from the kneeler. *Bless me, Father, for I have noticed what a fine, firm butt you have.* You want to know why I don't go to church? How could I pray to a God who lets a swell-looking man like that go to waste? And I don't even care if he's gay. *Someone* should have the pleasure.

Patrick yammered on about Colette's fatal stroke, the EMTs and emergency room, all the gooey details family members seem compelled to share and that no one wants to hear. Meanwhile I kept one eye on the casket, hoping I didn't look as impatient as I felt. I heard a low, Latinate drone as the priest prayed for Colette's irascible soul. I saw his arm move as he blessed her with the sign of the cross.

I assumed that meant he was wrapping things up. Sure enough, within moments he was strolling toward the exit.

Show time, take two. I stood and smoothed my skirt. "I'm just going to say good-bye to your mom one last time."

"We going to see you tomorrow?" Patrick asked. "At the funeral?"

"I wish I could, but I have work in the morning. I'm so glad I got to meet you."

All right, so sometimes I do feel like a heel. Are you happy?

"It's nine," Fuzzy Slippers informed her parents as I stepped up to the casket. "Let's go." Her brother announced that he had stuff to do. From behind me I heard Barbara ordering them, in hushed tones, to park their butts and wait until the last visitor—that would be me—was finished.

I welcomed the bickering. Something to occupy the family while I accomplished my dark deed.

My fingers began to slink into the casket, then froze. I stood paralyzed for an endless moment, staring at Colette's scarf, specifically at the spot on the scarf where a cheap mermaid brooch should have been pinned—the spot where it had been pinned less than two minutes earlier. Abandoning any semblance of stealth, I yanked at the scarf, peered under and around it.

Colette's meticulously lipsticked mouth was curved in a taunting little Mona Lisa smile that I swear was new.

Behind me the boyfriend drawled, "Is that lady supposed to be, like, doing that to your grand—"

"Son of a bitch!" I took off running after the priest.

The pencil skirt and heels slowed me as I raced for the main entrance. I yanked open the heavy door and nearly took a header on the building's rain-slick marble steps. Through the gloom and early-spring shower I spied, in a far corner of the parking lot, a dark figure mounting a motorcycle. I turned on the juice and ran straight for him.

"Hey!" I cried. "Wait!"

He seemed in no hurry, giving me hope that I could catch up to him. In the instant before his helmet settled into place, I saw clearly that it was indeed the priest, now wearing a black motorcycle jacket. With maddening calm he observed my awkward dash through the lot.

"I need to talk to—!" I tripped on a fast-food cup and went down with a screech. Pain exploded in my knee. He was still a good twenty yards away. "Stop!" I bellowed, on all fours now, struggling to rise. *Give me that damn brooch!*

The priest started the motorcycle, executed a lazy turn out of the lot, and disappeared down the street.

2
Heads Will Roll

IT WAS A quarter past nine when I reached Irene's place, located in the snootiest neighborhood of the snootiest town in the snootiest part of Long Island's North Shore. I was twitchy as a gerbil on crack, expecting the cell phone in my pocket to ring at any moment—my impatient client on the other end, exhibiting her usual gracious reserve. *What, did you stop to pawn the damn thing? Get your ass over here, pronto. I want my brooch!* I mentally rehearsed how I was going to break it to her.

The funniest thing, Irene. A priest beat me to the brooch, can you believe it? Is that just too weird or what? In my imagination Irene laughed and laughed. We laughed together, the two of us. Then she insisted on paying me the three hundred bucks anyway because I'd tried and isn't that what really mattered?

I didn't bother jumping in my car to chase down the sticky-fingered priest. What would be the point? In the laughably unlikely event my geriatric Civic caught up with his Harley, I would do what precisely? Sideswipe him? Run him off the road? Club him with a tire iron and ransack his pockets for a hunk of tin worth less than a Caramel Frappuccino?

Okay and yes, I'd managed to deduce that the cute priest was as faux as my pearls. In lieu of a fruitless car chase, I'd hobbled back into Ahearn's on my banged-up knee and quizzed Colette's family about the guy. They'd never seen him before, and once Patrick had recovered from the shock of the bizarre theft, he informed me he had no interest in reporting it to the authorities. The brooch had no monetary value. He hadn't a clue why his mother had wanted to spend eternity with the gaudy thing, much less why some "crackpot" had gone to the bother of snatching it—unless the thief was under the misguided impression it was worth something. Patrick had no intention of putting his family through a tangle of police red tape at a time like that.

I'd tried to change his mind. I wasn't thrilled either about the idea of getting the cops involved, but face it, they were the ones with the resources. How was I supposed to track down the pilfering padre and get a second chance to swipe the brooch myself without the assistance of Crystal Harbor's finest?

And yeah, I know how that sounds and I don't care.

I resisted the temptation to drive at a snail's pace and delay the inevitable confrontation. All it would take was a meandering half-hour motor tour past Crystal Harbor's swankier gated communities in my eleven-year-old beater and I'd be the one answering to the police—though if I had to choose between them and Irene in her current belligerent mood, I might be tempted to take a swing at a cop just to spend the night in the relative safety of a holding cell.

I turned onto the curving, tree-lined drive leading to Irene's brick-and-stone mini-mansion, set well away from its nearest neighbors on five exquisitely landscaped acres. The covered portico was flanked by white double columns. Elegant Palladian windows adorned the three peaked roofs. Every window in the place glowed, top to bottom, and not because she was expecting company. Irene liked to make her house look like a spread in *Architectural Digest*. She thought a low carbon footprint was something you made your housekeeper scrub off your $150-per-square-foot macassar ebony floors.

While we're on the subject of housekeepers, it was Maria's day off, so she wasn't there to answer the doorbell, a chore Irene herself would perform only after an exhaustive hair and makeup inspection. Since the April rain had turned into a serious downpour, I braked in the circular cobblestone courtyard and hauled out the keys Irene had given me two decades earlier when she'd hired me as an after-school dog-sitter.

She prided herself on being able to size up people at first glance, and she must have seen something honest and dependable in my sixteen-year-old self. A few months later when her beloved toy poodle Dr. Strangelove sprinted out of the house and under the wheels of her gardener's truck—no, not while I was watching him!—she began paying me to deliver a weekly bouquet to Best Friend Pet Cemetery. Irene was too busy to do it herself, and anyway, wasn't it the thought that counted?

I still dog-sat a couple of times a week, and I still drove to the pet cemetery every Sunday, only now I brought three bouquets, the other two being for Annie Hall, a sweet-tempered white poodle who'd died of natural causes at fourteen, and Jaws, a plump gray poodle who'd succumbed to a tough wad of prime rib three years ago. And before you ask whether Irene ever paid me to deliver flowers to her husband Arthur's grave, the answer is no. He'd been cremated. So there. Irene is the reason I do what I do. She helped me build my business through referrals, and I'm indebted to her.

I didn't call out to announce my presence. Irene considered raised voices inside the house to be vulgar—unless the raised voice emanated from Irene herself, but of course in those cases there was always a perfectly legitimate reason. I was kind of surprised she hadn't met me at the door, considering how determined she was to get her hands on that stupid brooch. I was just as happy to put off the confrontation for another few minutes while I collected myself.

I deposited my shoulder bag on the console table in the foyer, kicked off my shoes, and bent to examine my throbbing knee. It was beginning to swell and discolor, not to mention the layer of skin I'd left in Ahearn's parking lot. I heard the scrabble of nails on ebony as Sexy Beast—SB for short—came running from the direction of the kitchen.

The shaggy apricot poodle barked up a storm, his tiny body charging straight toward me. It wasn't his usual welcome. SB is the most submissive dog I've ever known. His usual routine is to grovel and scrape his way toward me, head bowed, tail firmly tucked under, his little legs splayed so far he barely has purchase on the slick floor. You'd think he's beaten on a daily basis instead of being coddled like a canine pasha.

"There's my good boy, come to Jane for scritches." I bent to bestow the customary scratches behind his ears and love pats along his little body, but to my surprise, he did a one-eighty and dashed back toward the kitchen.

"You'll get your treat after I pull myself together." I had more urgent business at the moment. I pushed strands of sodden hair behind my ears as I limped across the foyer, past the curving staircase on my right to the powder room tucked beneath it. There I assessed the damage, gulping down a couple of Advil and wiping at my mascara-smeared zombie eyes.

SB followed at my heels, barking nonstop, tail lifted straight up as if he were top dog in these parts. Which he was, but until that moment, he'd never gotten the memo. "You're not turning alpha on me, are you?" Next he'd be lifting his leg on the custom-made sideboard.

He started for the kitchen again but didn't get far. I grabbed him up in a football hold and carried him there myself. "Enough already. I'll give you your treat, then you have to leave me alone." I half expected to see Irene in there, scooping ice into a cocktail shaker for her evening martini. Two drops of vermouth—not an atom more!—with an olive. She wasn't in the breakfast room on the other side of the big granite kitchen island either.

I opened the fridge and rearranged the contents like puzzle pieces, searching. Finally at the back of the top shelf I spied the little jar of Vienna sausages Irene bought just for her pampered pet. Sexy Beast was picky in the extreme. He had little use for lowly doggie treats, preferring to save his appetite for salty, cholesterol-laden human snack foods. I'd never seen SB turn down a Vienna sausage, but that's what he did then, wriggling in my hold and whining to be set down.

I tightened my grip on him and peered into his dark little eyes. "You're not getting sick, are you, boy?" If he kept acting strange, I'd have to take him to the vet in the morning. Irene never took him herself. She couldn't bear to see her precious SB in distress, and you show me a dog that does Snoopy's happy dance when you pull up to the vet's.

Or to the groomer's in the case of Sexy Beast, an aversion Irene indulged by, well, not having him groomed. She refused to listen to reason on this point. As a result, the dog's curly, peach-colored hair hung in long, unkempt mats. The hair on his head had grown so long it draped his eyes. I had no idea how he saw through that mess.

As if the matted coat weren't enough, one of his long fangs protruded beyond his lips when he smiled. Yes, he did so smile! He wasn't a show-quality dog by any stretch of the imagination, but Irene never applied conventional standards of perfection when selecting a puppy. She judged a prospective pet solely on personality, which I always felt said something positive about her.

Once in a great while I'd screw up my courage to trim Sexy Beast's nails and bathe him myself in Irene's kitchen sink. Suffice it to say, I could have charged admission. Sometimes he even ended up clean. At one point in the dim and murky past, I attempted to brush him, but a chainsaw couldn't have gotten through those mats, and Sexy Beast knew just how to pitch his screams to make me stop trying. Not that he was in even an iota of pain—I was very gentle. He'd simply learned from experience that a shrill, girlish shriek would make most humans stop whatever irksome thing they were doing and back away in alarm.

I returned the sausages to the fridge and went in search of the lady of the house. I crossed through the breakfast room and stepped down into Irene's sunken game room—the onetime family room back when her late husband, Arthur, and his first wife had lived in this house. Then on through to the high-ceilinged living room, which, like the rest of the house, was expensively furnished with contemporary, one-of-a-kind pieces in pale, muted tones.

I crossed into the foyer, on the other side of which was the dining room with its striking, one-of-a-kind table, ebony inlaid with birds-eye maple. I proceeded through it and the butler's pantry past the kitchen to the laundry room, where I noticed a wet trail leading from the back door. Irene must have gone outside after the rain started—to accompany SB on a potty break, no doubt. The instant anything wet started falling from the sky, that dog would dig in his little heels at the threshold and struggle manfully to hold it in. Pathetic behavior for an animal billed as a water retriever. If you wanted him to go out in the rain, you had to be prepared to drag him on the leash, cooing encouragement and praise the whole time. The fact that Sexy Beast's ratty coat was currently dry only meant that, as usual, Irene had held an umbrella over the spoiled brat while he did his business.

Next to the laundry room was a bedroom with en suite bathroom that served as a maid's room on the rare occasions when Maria stayed overnight. I didn't expect to find Irene in there, and my expectations were fulfilled. I opened the door to the garage and saw that all three vehicles were present and accounted for: the slick BMW sedan, the big honkin' Lexus SUV, and the sporty little Porsche Boxster. Wheels to match a girl's every whim. Could one of Irene's friends have picked her up for some outing?

No way. She was wild to get her hands on that brooch. She wouldn't have left the house this evening.

Vulgar raised voices were underrated—it was time to get this over with. "Irene!" I hollered as I reversed direction and limped back to the foyer. I trudged up the curved, thickly carpeted staircase, SB still whining and wriggling in my arms. "It's me. Where are you?"

Once I reached the second floor, I didn't pause on the

balcony to admire the dramatic view of the foyer below but headed straight for Irene's master suite. The sumptuously appointed bedroom was vacant, the king-size mahogany sleigh bed unmade, this being Maria's day off. The room smelled of Chanel No. 5, Irene's scent of choice as long as I'd known her. She wasn't in her dressing room or either of the two walk-in closets. Ditto for the huge master bath with its whirlpool tub and thirteen-foot ceiling.

Oversize oil portraits of her last four pets adorned the second-floor hallway, in chronological order from current to deadest: Sexy Beast, Jaws, Annie Hall, and Dr. Strangelove, the names engraved on brass plaques affixed to the heavy gilt frames. I met their vacant poodley stares one by one. *Where's Mommy, fellas?*

I poked my head into the other three bedrooms on the second floor, one of which served as her home office and library, and their bathrooms. No Irene.

Hundreds of skinny fingers tightened on my scalp. I did not like this one bit.

"Irene!" My knee throbbed as I hobbled back down the stairs.

I set SB on the foyer floor and the neurotic little animal charged into the kitchen again. I took my cell phone out of my purse and auto-dialed Irene's number. If I weren't worried about her, I could simply have left her a note—easier than breaking the news in person, certainly—gone home, iced the knee, and self-medicated with a shot of outrageously expensive aged tequila. The bottle had been a birthday present from Irene three years ago, and I dispensed it like the liquid gold it was. Another shot or two and there'd be nothing left but fumes.

I waited for Irene to answer her phone. It just rang. Which didn't necessarily mean anything. Irene didn't always charge her phone, and didn't always remember to keep it with her even when it had a charge. I cocked an ear, straining for the sound of her "Theme from *Shaft*" ringtone, but Isaac Hayes had left the building. All I heard was more barking, from the direction of the kitchen but farther away.

Comprehension dawned as I limped in there. The one place I hadn't checked was the basement, the entrance of which was located between the butler's pantry and garage. The door was half-open and I peered down the stairway to see SB standing at the bottom, staring up at me expectantly. He emitted a string of demanding barks.

More steps. Oh joy.

I took them one at a time, clutching the banister for support, my knee getting stiffer by the second. SB couldn't have expressed his impatience more eloquently if he'd been able to grab me by the lapels and shake me.

When I was halfway down I heard the muted sounds of a movie in progress. Mystery solved. Irene was in her home theater, which shared the basement with her wine cellar and a home gym with a full bath, plus storage and utility rooms. If poker had pride of place in her heart, movies were a close second. Her eclectic collection of films numbered in the thousands.

I let my eyes drift shut on a little prayer of gratitude. I told myself I'd been an idiot to worry. Irene McAuliffe might appear the delicate septuagenarian, but the coiffed and perfumed exterior she showed the world concealed a core of pure, unadulterated gristle. I'd never known her to suffer anything more serious than a head cold.

Then I remembered the bad news I was about to impart, and my sigh of relief turned into a groan of dread. Well, Irene might be spry, and I might have a bum knee, but I liked to think I was still young enough to outrun her. Good thing I'd ditched the heels.

Sexy Beast kept looking behind him to make sure I was with the program as he disappeared through the open door at the back of the darkened forty-seat theater.

"Knock knock," I said as I followed him inside. I could just make out Irene's shape in the front row. "What are we watching?"

She didn't answer, and didn't need to. I saw right away it was *Jaws* playing on the jumbo screen up front, specifically the nighttime scene where police chief Brody and oceanographic researcher Matt Hooper go out in Hooper's boat to see what they can discover about a certain toothy character who's been chewing the scenery. Moody music helped set the tone.

I performed a mental head-smack. Of course! The Prime Rib Incident that had carried little Jaws to Poodle Heaven had occurred three years ago that day. How could it have slipped my mind? That very morning Irene had had me deliver an enormous, poodle-shaped arrangement of white roses to the pet cemetery. Whenever one of her beloved dogs died, she honored its memory by screening the film it was named for every year on the anniversary of its demise—or as colorful Captain Quint pronounced the word in the action-packed flick du jour, its *de-meeze.*

I'll tell you how it had slipped my mind. If I hadn't been so distracted by the craziness at Ahearn's and trying to devise the best way to broach the subject—yeah, broach, another lousy pun, I'm not proud—I would have realized that of course she'd be down here watching *Jaws,* and saved myself all those flights of stairs on a banged-up knee.

Onscreen, Brody and Hooper discover an abandoned boat in the misty gloom. Hooper decides to go into the water to investigate. Brody is not down with that. More moody music.

"Hey, Irene?" I said, gimping my way toward her. "Think you can pause that for a minute so I can, um…" Can what? Get ready to make a run for it? This scene was less than halfway into the film. If I had to sit through the rest of it before breaking the news, I'd be a gibbering wreck by the time the credits rolled. Plus, where was her sense of urgency? Earlier she'd been wild to get her hands on that brooch.

"Did you hear me?" I reached the front row of cushy upholstered theater seats. Irene's silhouette was eerily lit by the flickering image of Hooper, now wearing a wetsuit, slipping into the water and snorkeling under the abandoned boat with a handheld light. The music is now more ominous than moody. Whaddaya know, there's a ragged hole in the bottom of the boat. Better poke around there, Hooper thinks, see what I can find.

I expected to see Sexy Beast curled up on Irene's lap. Instead he paced in front of the two of us, whining piteously. "SB's acting weird," I said. "Has he been like this all day?" She ignored the question, and no wonder. Her favorite *Jaws* movie moment was fast approaching, the part where Hooper gets a head in his research, so to speak. Even though she'd seen the film countless times, even though she knew what was about to happen, she jumped and screamed every time. Okay, so did I. Then the two of us would collapse in girlish giggles.

I dropped into the seat next to hers and began to formulate my story as Hooper pried a ginormous shark tooth from the edge of the hole. *See, Irene, the thing is, I had the brooch in my pocket, but then this cute fake priest wrestled me to the carpet…*

Which naturally led to thoughts of lying under Father Faux, struggling in vain as he runs his hands over my clothing, leaving no pocket unturned. My jacket lacks an inside breast pocket, but he doesn't know that, and he valiantly gropes around for one. Hmm… maybe I slipped the brooch into my bra…

The shrieking musical score snapped me out of my reverie as, right on schedule, a severed, one-eyed human head floated out of the hole in the boat.

I was proud of myself—I jumped this time but didn't scream. Chuckling, I turned to Irene and saw that she hadn't so much as blinked.

Then I screamed.

3
Winner Take All

"HOW CAN YOU be sure it was a heart attack?" I asked.

"Let's take a look at this knee first." Jonah Diamond turned his breakfast-room chair to face mine and opened his black medical bag, the same one he'd carried down to the basement after my frantic call to him more than an hour before.

Naturally, my first call had been to 911. Then, almost as a reflex, I'd phoned Jonah on his cell. He happened to be a few blocks away, driving home after attending to one of his patients in the emergency room of Harbor Memorial Hospital. He was more than Irene's doctor, he was her friend and a longtime member of the infamous Poker Posse, the group of well-heeled players who got together at Irene's every Thursday evening for a high-stakes game.

Jonah had arrived first and verified what had become clear once I'd turned off the movie and flipped on the overhead lights in Irene's home theater. I'd seen plenty of dead people in my line of work, but always after processing, if you know what I mean—lying peacefully in a box with their eyes glued shut. There was no mistaking the absence of life in Irene's blank stare. Nevertheless, I'd checked her still-warm throat for a pulse, prepared to perform CPR if there was even a chance.

Once the paramedics and cops had left, I crashed. I felt as if my legs could no longer support me. Sexy Beast was in a similar condition. He dozed on his plush doggie bed in a corner of the breakfast room. Now we were waiting for Ahearn's Funeral Home to send a hearse. I'd wanted to wait downstairs with Irene. Jonah gently vetoed that idea.

"Ow!" I gripped my leg above the knee, trying to be a grownup as Jonah swabbed the abraded flesh with battery acid. Sure, he *said* it was some sort of antiseptic, but all I know is, if battery acid doesn't feel like that, it shouldn't be called battery acid.

"How did this happen?" He produced a pair of tweezers and commenced to plucking gravel out of the raw meat of my knee. I looked away.

"It's a long story." One I was trying to mentally suppress, even as my subconscious insisted on playing connect the dots between what happened at Ahearn's and Irene's death. Two striking events are allowed to occur in one evening, aren't they? There's no rule that says they have to be connected. Yet my mind had a, well, mind of its own. "So it was definitely a heart attack?" I persisted.

"All the signs point that way." Jonah was in his early forties and athletically built, with light brown hair and a short, neatly trimmed beard. That evening he wore a forest green polo shirt and custom-made khakis.

"It just seems so…" I shook my head. "That woman was as strong as an ox."

His mouth twisted in a wry smile as he fished ointment, gauze pads, and tape out of his bag. "That's the image she projected, but I treated her atrial fibrillation for years. The truth is, she should have gotten a pacemaker long ago but kept putting it off. You know how she felt about hospitals."

Did I ever. Irene's horror of hospitals was simply a more extreme version of how she felt about doctor's offices. She rarely went to Jonah's office. More often he came to her, especially for routine matters such as blood-pressure checks.

Jonah was a concierge physician, catering to a limited number of wealthy patients who could afford his hefty retainer and fees—no insurance accepted. In return, each patient received the kind of time and attention that was almost unheard-of in most medical practices. Dr. Diamond was available twenty-four seven by cell phone and email, and yes, he cheerfully made house calls.

"But… how could it have happened so suddenly?" My eyes stung. "I spoke with her a couple of hours ago, around eight. She sounded fine."

He looked up from my knee. "I know how hard this is for you, Jane. Here." A crystal cookie jar filled with homemade chocolate-macadamia biscotti sat on the table. I recognized the handiwork of Nina Wallace, another member of Irene's Poker Posse. Nina loved to bake and always brought a sinfully delicious dessert to their weekly games. He pushed the jar toward me and lifted the lid. "You could use a little sugar."

It should have been a dream come true: a man of medicine prescribing cookies. I shook my head miserably.

"Do it for me." He handed me a biscotto.

"Yes, Doctor." I let out a soggy chuckle and bit into it. At that particular moment, it tasted like cardboard.

After Jonah had pronounced Irene and things had quieted down, I'd made one phone call, to her longtime lawyer and poker pal, Sten Jakobsen, who was also the executor of her estate. Irene had never discussed her blood relatives, but I assumed she had some somewhere. Sten would get in touch with them, as well as her estranged stepsons. Irene never had kids of her own. I told him I'd notify her closest friends, but those calls could wait until the morning.

"I guess I just want to make sure." I set my half-eaten cookie on the table.

"Make sure of what?" He tore off a strip of first-aid tape.

"You know. That that's what it was. Natural causes." I looked at Jonah, willing him to understand my misgivings. Hell, *I* didn't understand my misgivings. It just didn't seem right, this diagnosis of death by cardiac infarction in a woman who'd always seemed so full of life.

"What else do you think it could have been?" he asked.

"I don't know, but…" I shrugged. "Well, isn't it possible… I mean not likely but possible that someone, you know, did something to her?"

He frowned. "You think someone murdered Irene?"

"Not really, I just…" I scrubbed my hands over my face. "Okay, I just think it's something that should be considered, that's all. Irene rubbed a lot of people the wrong way. Maybe one of them just, I don't know, snapped. And anyway, aren't they supposed to do an autopsy? Why is she going straight to Ahearn's?"

"Because you had the good sense to call me, and as her personal physician, I was able to ascertain cause of death, based on my examination and her medical history."

I hoped I only imagined the impatience underlying his words.

"If I hadn't been here," he added, "they would have had to call the coroner and an autopsy would have been required.

Believe me, it's better this way. More respectful to Irene."

"I don't know…. She was acting different the past few days, Jonah."

"Different how?"

"Irritable. Cranky."

That elicited a bark of laughter. "I'm sorry," he said, "but that differs from Irene's usual state how?"

"More irritable," I said. "A different kind of irritable. Like something was bothering her."

"Like she wasn't feeling well?" His knowing look spoke volumes. "Like her heart condition was getting worse and she didn't want to admit it to anyone else or even herself?"

I found it hard to meet his eyes. "You think I'm being immature. Self-delusional. Something."

"I think you've had a shock tonight and you're not seeing things in the clearest light. I think a good night's sleep will help." He patted my bandaged knee and started repacking his medical bag, offering the usual instructions: rest and elevation, ice then heat, yadda yadda.

"When's the last time you spoke with Irene?" I asked.

A pause while he fastened his bag and considered the question. "Not since last week's game."

"Did she tell you then that she was feeling poorly? Did she make an appointment or anything?"

His calm hazel eyes locked on to mine. "No. As far as I knew, she felt no better or worse than usual. These things happen, Jane. She was seventy-seven."

I shook my head. "Irene just turned seventy-two."

His eyes crinkled at the corners.

"Really?" I said. "She lied about her age?"

"What a shock." He rose and walked around the large kitchen island toward the fridge.

"But to me? I can see her fibbing about her age to other people, but…" I trailed off, realizing how pathetic I sounded. Okay, so maybe I didn't know every last thing about my longtime client, friend, and surrogate grandma. Like that her health was deteriorating and she hid how sick she was even from her doctor.

I sighed. "There's something else. Something happened earlier tonight."

Jonah rooted around in the freezer. "What?"

"Well, it was at the funeral home. At Colette's wake."

"I was there last night." Colette had been his patient too. He returned with a bag of frozen mixed berries, which he wrapped in a clean dish towel and placed on my knee.

"Yeah, well, you should have been there tonight," I said. "That's when all the cool kids showed up." I told him about my aborted attempt to retrieve the brooch for Irene and how the pilfering padre had swooped in and made off with the prize. "That's how I got this." I indicated my knee. "Running after the guy."

Jonah gave a little shake of the head, as if struggling to make sense of my story.

"I know," I said. "I can't figure it out either. It's not as if the piece of junk were worth anything. Colette's son didn't even bother reporting the theft."

"The mermaid brooch?" He leaned back against the kitchen island, arms crossed. "You're kidding, right?"

A crawly feeling tickled my scalp. "What do you mean?"

"That brooch is a McAuliffe family heirloom. It's worth over a hundred grand."

His words stunned me into silence.

"I saw it on Colette at the wake," he said. "I just assumed it would be returned to the family. It never occurred to me it was going into the ground with her."

Belatedly I realized my mouth was hinged open. "No," I said. "No, it's a costume piece. That's what Irene told me. She bought it for Colette when they were kids. For a few bucks."

"Well, I'm not sure why she told you that, unless she thought you might run off with it."

"I would never!"

Jonah held up a hand. "I know that. I'm sure Irene knew it too. So probably she said it to keep you from balking at the assignment. If you knew it was worth a fortune, would you have agreed to steal it?"

I hesitated.

He nodded. "She knew you, Jane. She wanted that brooch and she knew how to get you to steal it for her."

"I wish you'd quit saying 'steal' like that. It wasn't stealing, it… it belonged to her. I mean, not, um, legally maybe, but…" I dropped my head into my hands and cursed my dumb, trusting self. "Wait a minute." I raised my head. "You said it was a McAuliffe family heirloom. Colette wasn't a McAuliffe. Irene was."

"Well, Irene's late husband was. Arthur. I never met him. He died about twenty-five years ago." He reached for my partially gnawed biscotto and popped it into his mouth.

"Twenty-two years ago," I said. "Right before I started dog-sitting for Irene. So the thing is, the brooch probably did belong to Irene. Originally anyway." But not as far back as the fifties, as she'd claimed. It had to have come to her decades later through her marriage into the McAuliffe family. "How did Colette get ahold of it?" I asked.

"She won the brooch from Irene in a poker game."

My mouth dropped open again—such a good look for me. "You can't be serious."

"Serious as a heart atta—" He winced. "Sorry. I was there, Jane. It was the regular Thursday night poker game, right in there." Jonah pointed toward the sunken game room, visible over the half wall separating it from the breakfast room where we sat. The centerpiece of the game room was a custom-made professional poker table with six matching chairs.

"When was this game?" I asked.

"Ten years ago?" He frowned, thinking back. "It wasn't long after Rachel and I moved to Crystal Harbor and I started my practice. No, closer to nine years, I guess. Right before Christmas. I remember Irene had the tree up. Colette and Irene got into it that night over the minimum bet. Colette wanted it lowered, wanted Irene to dial back on the whole high-stakes thing. That's when The Harbor Room was starting to lose serious money."

"I remember." The Harbor Room was a waterfront restaurant owned by Colette's husband, Burt O'Rourke. The place had been a local landmark since the1840s and boasted a colorful history. During Prohibition, rumrunners steered their boats between the stilts supporting the restaurant and passed crates of smuggled booze through a secret trapdoor behind the bar.

Burt had died almost a year ago. Rumor had it that Colette was never the same afterward, that her husband had been her emotional rock, keeping her grounded during all their years together. She'd become impulsive and unpredictable since his death. Quitting the church choir. Redecorating the house in Crayola colors. Signing up for senior Zumba classes. I didn't pay much attention to the gossip. New widows tended to find themselves under a magnifying glass. So what if Colette let loose a little after her stuffy hubby was in the ground? You only live once.

Okay, to be fair, Colette's selling the ailing Harbor Room too soon and for too little, practically before Burt was cold, could legitimately be called impulsive. Not that anyone expected her to turn it over to their son, Patrick, who would no doubt have run the restaurant into the ground. But that's one decision that probably should have waited until she was in a clearer frame of mind.

"I mean, we all knew about their financial troubles," Jonah continued. "Irene knew it better than anyone. And Christmas was coming. Colette's grandkids were little. I'm sure she wanted to buy them some nice presents."

I thought about Colette's grandkids, whom I'd seen earlier at the wake: Fuzzy Slippers and her brother. A couple of self-absorbed teens too preoccupied with their gadgets and their TV shows to give their grandmother the respectful send-off that was her due.

I sighed. "Irene could be stubborn."

"Colette loved that weekly poker game. She was part of the very first Poker Posse, going back, what, almost twenty years at that point. But it was Irene's game and her decision to make, and she wasn't budging. Anyone who couldn't stomach the action was free to leave and not come back."

But Colette was her oldest friend, and she was experiencing hardship. I cringed inwardly at Irene's insensitivity, her skewed priorities. I was embarrassed for her.

"Colette did leave the Posse," I said. "Because of that very fight, from what I was told."

He nodded. "But not until she'd gotten back at Irene."

"By winning the brooch, you mean. How on earth did that end up for grabs?" Absently I reached into the cookie jar for another biscotto, my lack of appetite forgotten.

"I thought Colette would take a hike after Irene's ultimatum," Jonah said, "but she pulled up a chair and anted up. I don't know whether it was plain dumb luck or that their argument had sharpened her wits or what, but it was like she couldn't lose. The rest of us folded one by one and then it was just Colette and Irene, your basic Texas Hold 'Em one-on-one death match. Colette cleaned her out and we all thought that was that, it's going to be a good Christmas at the O'Rourke homestead, and then Irene says don't anybody move and she runs upstairs. Comes back with the mermaid brooch and slaps it down." He smacked a palm on the table in demonstration.

"How did you guys know it was valuable?" I asked. "I didn't." Which meant precisely zip. What did I know about real jewelry? Dom had been too poor to buy me a diamond when we got hitched eighteen years ago. Of course, now he was rolling in it and could afford to put a garish four-karat boulder on fiancée Bonnie's finger to commemorate her ranking in the ever-growing pantheon of Dominic Faso's Wives.

Me? Bitter? Just because my poor but adorable high school sweetheart, whom I'd loved to distraction and regretfully divorced after seven months of marriage because he was dead-set against having kids and I wanted them real bad, is now the proud father of three and is filthy stinking rich?

Guess how many kids I have at age thirty-nine with my

biological clock pounding a frantic but increasingly faint jungle drumbeat every twenty-eight days. Here's a hint. None.

Did I mention he's rich now?

"Irene had this appraiser's certificate," Jonah continued, "and she shoved it under Colette's nose. Diamonds, rubies, et cetera, it says. Platinum. The thing was made at the turn of the twentieth century by some famous Scottish jewelry designer. Worth a hundred four thousand and change. Colette's pot is worth maybe eighteen, twenty grand. You and I go all in, Irene says. Five-card stud. Winner take all."

I found myself sitting wide-eyed, my hand over my mouth.

"Well, you could just see the wheels turning in Colette's head," he said. "She's eyeing that mermaid and thinking how sweet it would be to win that thing from Irene, after the humiliation Irene just put her through."

"I can't believe Colette didn't just walk away," I said. "Keep her winnings and call it a good night's work."

"You're assuming she was thinking the way you and I do. If she'd been playing against anyone else, she probably would've done just that. But these two had…" He shook his head. "They had a really warped way of dealing with each other. It infected all their interactions."

"Do you think Colette considered herself unbeatable that night?"

He shrugged. "Irene didn't, that's for sure. She never thought for an instant she was going to lose the brooch. You could see it in her eyes, that cocksure attitude of hers."

I knew that look well.

"We all held our breath." Jonah's eyes got a glassy, inward-gazing look, as if the clock had turned back nine years. "Judge

Ivie dealt. It was over in less than a minute. Irene had a full house."

"And Colette?" My voice was strained.

"Four of a kind. Sixes."

I blew out a breath. "God."

"I stuck around to keep an eye on Irene," he said. "She looked like she was going to stroke out any second."

"She flipped out?"

He shook his head. "If anything, she was too calm. Like it didn't mean anything to her."

"Yikes." I knew that look of Irene's too. *Danger! Danger!* "How come I never heard anything about this? I mean, I can understand why Irene wouldn't have told me. She was too proud to advertise this kind of defeat."

"Exactly," he said. "Which is why she swore everyone there to secrecy, once Colette had gathered up her winnings and left the house."

Never to set foot in it again. "Who else was there?" I asked.

"Let's see… the judge, of course. He died five or six years ago. And Stan Golden. Stan and Maggie moved to Arizona last year to be closer to their daughter and her family. And Dom."

My head whipped up. "Dom was there?" Well, of course Dom was there. My ex had always gotten along famously with Irene. He's so damn personable, he gets along with everyone. During Dom's brief interludes between wives, Irene was always scheming to get the two of us back together.

At the time of this momentous poker game, Dom's little smoothie shop, Janey's Place, which he'd established at age nineteen with financial backing from Irene, had already morphed into the biggest health-food chain in the New York metropolitan area. He'd bought fancy digs in Crystal Harbor eleven years ago when he and Meryl got married—nothing but the best for Mrs. Faso Number Three—and had sweet-talked Irene into letting him join the Poker Posse.

It was Meryl's idea. Irene's game room on Thursday evenings was the most coveted invitation in Crystal Harbor. Dom's then wife saw it as a way for him to indulge his love of poker and make important business connections at the same time. Which had made me roll my eyes until Dom expanded his chain of Janey's Place shops into New Jersey and Connecticut with the cooperation of fellow Posse member Stan Golden, a major real estate developer in the tri-state area.

"I can't believe Dom never told me about that game, about Colette winning the brooch," I said.

"Why would he? You guys were long divorced by then, right?"

"Right, but we remained friends." Sad to say, my ex was still my best pal. Which I suppose says something about me, right? Something kinda sad about my ability to adapt to changing circumstances, to form new and satisfying relationships?

Don't answer that.

"Listen," Jonah said, "once you're in the Posse, the last thing you want is to be ejected from it for any reason. That kind of thing gets around, you're a pariah. Irene says don't blab about what happened here tonight…" He mimed zipping his lip.

"Until now."

He executed an eye-shrug. "No more Poker Posse."

"Hey, you can all reconvene in my one-room basement apartment in Sandy Cove," I said. "I'll borrow my landlord's card table and rip open a bag of Cheetos."

He grinned. "I'll bring the Bud Light." Jonah was the kind of guy who made you forget he was good-looking until he turned that hundred-watt smile on you, then you had to remind yourself of his happy fifteen-year marriage to the lovely Rachel.

"Listen," I said, "I know Irene was the backbone of the Posse, there's all that history associated with this place, but she wouldn't have wanted the game shut down just because she wasn't around anymore."

He wore a skeptical smile. "Are you sure about that? With her ego?"

All right, maybe he had a point. "But that doesn't mean you have to disband. Who's in the Posse now? It's you, Dom, Nina Wallace… who else?"

"Sten Jakobsen and Sophie Halperin."

"Well, I can't see Sophie just letting the Posse fade away," I said. Sophie Halperin is the mayor of Crystal Harbor, a well-padded fireplug of a woman with a big personality.

"She's the reason I was in the ER this evening," he said.

I frowned. "Nothing serious, I hope."

"She's fine." He waved it off. "She had a scare, but it turned out to be nothing."

"Glad to hear it." I liked Sophie. She was one of the few people in Crystal Harbor who could be counted on to call them as she saw them.

Nina Wallace was the newly elected president of the Historical Society, having replaced Irene, who'd held the position for years. It had been a contentious election, with several of Irene's longtime pals in the organization squirming out of her camp to throw their support behind Nina. I suspected that even Irene's most loyal friends were weary of her heavy-handed style and more than ready for a change in leadership. Irene had been bitter about it—she wasn't accustomed to losing—and privately there was no love lost between the two women, but publicly they both put on a good show.

"I don't get it," I said. "If Colette and Burt needed money so badly, why didn't she sell the brooch?"

"Because she cared more about keeping Irene from having it." Jonah reached over to adjust the makeshift ice bag on my knee. "The first thing Irene did was try to buy it back. When Colette refused, she upped the offering price. Irene's mistake was letting Colette know how badly she wanted it. Colette knew that if she sold it to anyone else, anywhere on the planet, Irene would find it and get it back, and that she would never allow."

"Did she hate her old friend that much?"

He took a deep breath. "Their relationship was a series of little humiliations for Colette. That's the way she saw it anyway. For one thing, Irene never let her forget that she'd married better—if the definition of marrying well is landing a wealthy husband, which for their generation it was."

While Irene had held out for a man who could support her in the style to which she was determined to become accustomed, Colette had married for love. She'd been barely seventeen when she'd exchanged hasty wedding vows with handsome young Burt, fresh from Korea with a Purple Heart. It wasn't long before Patrick arrived, and Burt spent the rest of his life struggling to support his small family.

I refrained from mentioning that Jonah hadn't done so badly for himself in the "marrying up" department. His wife, Rachel, came from serious money. The fortune she brought to the marriage was the only reason they were able to raise their family in this exclusive neighborhood. It was the reason Jonah was able to book exotic adventure vacations, collect rare wines, maintain cripplingly expensive country-club and elite gym memberships, and bet so extravagantly during Irene's poker games. No internist—not even a concierge physician in swanky Crystal Harbor—made enough on his practice alone to afford that kind of opulent lifestyle.

Thinking of the Chanel suit and Hermès scarf Colette was being buried in, I said, "I do know that any really nice things Colette had—the designer clothes, all that—were hand-me-downs from Irene when they were still on speaking terms." Back when The Harbor Room was doing well, Burt had bought a modest home in the least fashionable area of Crystal Harbor. Later he'd refinanced it to try to keep the restaurant afloat, and succeeded, barely.

"Colette must have told her family that the brooch was worthless so they'd honor her decision to have it buried with her." Jonah shook his head. "It wasn't just Colette and Burt who could've used the money. Their son Patrick has always struggled to support his family. The guy has a troubled background—I don't know if you're aware."

"I heard some things," I said. "I take it Patrick was a hell-raiser in his youth. There was an arrest?"

He nodded. "Drugs. He did a couple of years, then tried to join the army, but they wouldn't have him. Eventually he got himself straightened out, but by then it was too late to go to college and really make something of himself. It's been a string of lousy jobs. But Barbara works too, so they've managed."

I thought of the used-up-looking man I'd met earlier at his mother's wake, struggling to salvage a decent life for himself and his family after a perfect storm of bad decisions.

"The point is," he continued, "Colette adored Patrick, adored his wife and kids, and not even for them did she sell the brooch. That's how strong her feud with Irene was."

"Which is why Colette didn't brag about winning the brooch," I said. "Her husband and son would have found out she was sitting on something worth a hundred grand. Talk about cutting off your nose to spite your face."

"In the end," he said, "Colette and Irene's relationship was all about revenge and one-upmanship."

"How do you know all this?"

He offered a crooked smile. "People tell things to their doctors."

"Well, I for one can't imagine the tournament this weekend without those two in it," I said. Every year the Crystal Harbor Historical Society sponsors a poker tournament to raise funds for the work it does. It's held on the first Saturday in April and is the biggest event on the village calendar. The five-thousand-dollar buy-in is hefty enough to discourage casual players. Needless to say, Irene and Colette entered every year, and one or the other of them was usually the first-place winner.

"At least now I know why the fake priest stole that brooch." I rubbed my fingers together to indicate filthy lucre.

"Are you sure he's a *fake* priest?"

"Well, there is that whole vow-of-poverty thing," I said.

"Maybe the poor celibate guy was so taken with the naked mermaid, he couldn't help himself." Jonah's grin was crooked. "She's pretty hot stuff."

"Doesn't it seem like too much of a coincidence, though? I mean, at the very same instant that I'm steal—" I raised my palm

"—that I'm *retrieving* Irene's brooch for her, this guy shows up to swipe it himself."

"Coincidences happen," he said. "Didn't you say you went at the very end of the wake? Less chance of being caught? The thief was probably thinking along the same lines."

"But he came right up behind me, got in my personal space, you know? Just when I was making my move. It got me so flustered—a *priest*, for crying out loud!—that I backed right off. It's almost like he planned it that way. Like he wanted me to remember him, wanted to rub my nose in it."

Jonah's expression was one of exaggerated patience. "How could he possibly know you were after the same thing he was? Did you or Irene tell anyone else about your plans?"

"Of course not."

"Coincidence, Jane."

"Maybe," I said. "But how did he even know where the brooch would be? Wasn't it this big secret that Colette even had it?"

He frowned, thinking. "What are you saying? That Irene told him about your plans?"

"I know *I* didn't," I said. "And think about it. She wouldn't have just volunteered that kind of information. What if he somehow forced her to spill the beans and then… you know, did something to keep her quiet."

"Like what?"

"Smothered her? Strangled her? I don't know." I could tell he wasn't buying it.

"Jane, there's no physical evidence that anything like that happened. Irene had a heart attack, a massive one that killed her quickly. Who knows? Maybe the stress of waiting for you to come back with the brooch, of not knowing whether you'd be successful, maybe that was the trigger."

A weight sat on my chest. Was Irene still alive when I entered the house? Did she hear me clomping around overhead, looking for her? If I hadn't wasted precious minutes searching the whole damn place, was there a chance I could have saved her?

"Plus the timing doesn't add up," he said. "It's clear that Irene died shortly before you got here. I don't see how your priest could have killed her and then made it to Ahearn's in time to steal the brooch."

Since he'd brought up timing, there was the movie to consider. "The scene in *Jaws* that was playing when I found her, it's less than an hour into the film," I said, "maybe forty-five minutes. I got here around nine-fifteen. I didn't find her till about ten minutes later. That means she started the film around eight-thirty, eight-forty."

His eyebrows lifted. "And you've got this guy, what, sneaking in, forcing Irene to spill the beans about the brooch—good luck with that, by the way—and then killing her without leaving so much as a mark." I tried to interrupt, but he plowed ahead. "Now it's around a quarter to nine at the absolute earliest, if he arrived right after she started the movie. And *then* instead of racing straight over to Ahearn's to beat you to the brooch, the murderer takes the time to dig up a priest's getup and change into it. Maybe he keeps one in the trunk for just such emergencies."

"He was riding a motorcycle. Maybe he dressed as a priest before he got here?"

"Okay, fairy-tale time is over," Jonah said. "Are you familiar with Occam's Razor?"

"Umm…"

"It's the principle that says if you have competing theories about something, the simplest explanation is usually the right one."

I fiddled with the bag of frozen berries. "The simplest explanation in this case being a heart attack."

"Exhibit A," he said, tapping a finger. "An elderly woman with a heart condition. Exhibit B." He tapped a second finger. "Scary movie."

"Oh, forget Exhibit B." I waved away the outlandish suggestion. "Irene's seen that movie countless times. She's immune. Was," I corrected myself. "And your cramped timeline doesn't hold up. Think about it. You're Irene. You just started watching your movie. A strange fellow barges into your home theater."

"Exhibit C," he said. "Scary home invasion."

"All right, all right. Jeez. So anyway, she pauses the movie. See? Or he does. They're not going to sit there chatting about the brooch or whatever with *Jaws* blasting from the speakers. After he kills her, he turns the movie back on, turns off the lights, makes it look like his victim died of natural causes. If he got here shortly after the film started…" I crunched the numbers in my head. "He'd have had thirty, forty minutes to get to Ahearn's, which is about an eight-minute drive from here. Maybe five on that Harley of his."

Jonah just stared at me, letting his bland expression say it all.

I threw up my hands. "I'm just saying it's not outside the realm of possibility, that's all. If that guy hadn't shown up at Ahearn's to steal Irene's brooch on the very same night that she died, I wouldn't even be thinking along these lines. Oh!" I bolted upright. My ice bag slid onto the floor. "The footprints!"

He frowned. "What footprints?"

"In the laundry room." I pointed toward it as he bent to replace the ice bag. "There's a wet trail from the back door. Go look. Someone came in that way after it started raining tonight, which was what, around eight, right?"

He did indeed go look. I yelled, "At first I figured it was Irene because, you know, SB won't go out alone in the rain." When he refrained from yelling a response, I added, "But now I'm thinking it could be the guy. You know? He sneaks in the back door, picks the lock or whatever—" He reappeared and I lowered my volume. "Well?"

"The floor's wet." He shrugged. "So what? Irene took SB out to do his business, like you said."

"But there are no distinct footprints," I said. "No way to tell if it was a man or an old woman with a little dog or… or Sasquatch."

"Occam's Razor." He resumed his pose against the kitchen island, arms crossed. "Nothing better for shaving Sasquatches."

"Enough with Occam and his razor. The simplest answer isn't *always* the right one. And what about SB's feet?"

Jonah glanced at the hirsute pooch snoozing in his little bed. "SB has feet?"

"I noticed he was dry earlier, when I saw the wet streaks in the laundry room. Which makes sense because Irene's not going to take him out without an umbrella—*but* now that I think about it, his feet and legs are as dry as the rest of him."

He shrugged again.

"When that animal goes out in the wet grass," I said, "he comes back with his legs sopping wet, umbrella or no umbrella.

I mean, the poor little thing is basically a mop with a nose. It takes him forever to dry out. Oh! The umbrella!"

I jumped up and walked as fast as my gimpy leg would allow into the laundry room. "Jonah, come look at this!"

He took his time returning to the scene of my imaginary crime, and when he did, his expression spoke volumes on the subject of Occam, his razor, and wet dogs. "Jane, you're getting yourself worked up—"

"Look at Irene's umbrella. Look at it!" I plucked the object in question out of the umbrella stand by the back door and shook it at him.

"I give up."

"Dry." Another shake. "It's bone-dry, Jonah. Irene didn't take SB out in the rain. These aren't her footprints. Someone else came through this door after the rain started."

He didn't have a ready answer for that. He scrubbed a hand over his beard, and I saw the strain behind his hazel eyes. It couldn't have been an easy thing for him to rush over here after my panicked call, to pronounce Irene, more longtime friend than patient, dead.

"Maybe Irene dashed outside after it started coming down," he finally said. "Without dog or umbrella. Just to cover something out there, or to bring something in out of the rain."

My mouth twisted as I pondered this. He had a point.

"You done?" he asked.

I sighed. "I'm done." I replaced the umbrella in its stand. My adrenaline high of a few moments ago had fizzled, leaving me wrung-out. "Thanks for being my sounding-board." We returned to the kitchen. "You know, even if I'm full of it about… about how Irene died, there's still the theft of the brooch," I reminded him. "The fake priest is definitely guilty of that."

"Didn't you say Patrick already decided not to report it?"

"That was when we both thought the thing was a junky piece of tin," I said. "When he finds out it's worth a cool hundred grand…" I raised my palms and let my expression state the obvious.

"Let him get through the funeral first," he said. "There's nothing more you can do tonight. I can give you something to help you sleep."

"The guy looked me straight in the eye, Jonah. The fake priest. It's as if he wanted me to remember his face." I shivered.

"Now, does that make sense if he'd just murdered Irene? Knowing that anyone in your position would draw a connection between her death and the brooch?" After a moment he asked, "Could he have disguised himself?"

"Aside from the priest getup, you mean?" Reluctantly I shook my head. Between the dearth of facial or even head hair and the close fit of his clothes, I could state with near certainty that the padre had made no effort to fudge his appearance.

His raised eyebrows drove home the point. Yet one more strike against my murder-and-mayhem version of events.

The doorbell rang and I jumped.

"That's Ahearn's." He squeezed my shoulder. "Go home, Jane. I'll take care of this. Do you want some Xanax?" He indicated his black doctor's bag sitting on the table.

I shook my head. My eyes stung. "I—I should be with her when they—"

"No. You shouldn't." He steered me out of the kitchen toward the front of the house.

In the foyer, he handed my shoulder bag to me and reached

for the doorknob. I stopped him.

"Jonah, do me a favor," I said. "Irene… well, you know she had her pride. Appearances meant a lot to her. I don't think she'd want everyone knowing the details—you know, that she was watching a movie when she died, and especially which movie. I think she'd consider it undignified." It would be morbid grist for the Crystal Harbor rumor mill: *Did the scary movie kill her? Which scene? Did she choke on a piece of popcorn?*

"I understand," he said. "And you're right. The world isn't entitled to all the details."

"And as for what I was doing at Ahearn's tonight…" I let my pleading expression say the rest.

He gave a mock-baffled look. "You were at Ahearn's tonight?"

I gave him a relieved smile. "Thanks."

He opened the door to two young men in dark suits who nodded and politely identified themselves. I recognized one of them from my earlier visit to Ahearn's. Behind them I spied a black hearse parked in the circular courtyard behind my Civic and Jonah's Audi. It had stopped raining.

Jonah took them aside and quietly began to fill them in on the who, what, when, and where. I heard the words "death certificate." I heard one of the young men suggest that the lady relocate to a distant part of the house while they worked. At first, crazily, I thought the lady he was referring to was Irene. Jonah assured them I was on my way out.

I felt ridiculously grateful for his take-charge attitude. The truth was, I didn't want to see Irene again the way she was, didn't want to see these polite young men wrap her in a sheet and remove her from her home like a worn-out sofa.

I felt little paws on my legs and heard a familiar whining. I looked down to see Sexy Beast trying to climb me.

"Oh! The dog," I said. "What am I thinking? I can't leave him here." I scooped him up and nuzzled his raggedy head. SB licked my cheek. My eyes filled. Through an effort of will I managed not to break down right then and there. "Mommy's gone," I whispered, "but you have me. I'll take good care of you."

"You're taking him home?" Jonah asked, as the men from Ahearn's returned to the hearse for whatever equipment they'd need.

I nodded, not trusting myself to speak without blubbering. Irene had no doubt made arrangements in her will for some friend or relative to take Sexy Beast. I tried not to think about how it was going to feel handing him over.

"It's just as well," he said. "I don't think he and Daisy would get along." Daisy, the Diamonds' Great Dane, could snack on SB and have room left over for a Labradoodle. He placed a warm palm on my back. "Go home, Jane. Get some rest."

"Okay, I'm going. I just need to get some things for SB."

I stepped aside as the men brought in a wheeled cot with a fitted cloth cover. The cover was dark green with *Leonard T. Ahearn and Sons Funeral Home* stitched in white on one end. While Jonah led them to the basement, I returned to the kitchen and placed a bag of kibble and some mini cans of gourmet wet dog food into SB's bucket-shaped bed. I tossed in his harness and leash. He warehoused his favorite fuzzy toys in the bed, so that was covered.

I opened the fridge and retrieved his Vienna sausages, then peered inside for more of his favorite snacks. I reached into the back for a block of cheddar—SB loved cheese—and accidentally knocked over a half-filled, pint-size takeout cup that bore the apple green logo of Janey's Place, Dom's health-food chain. The lid popped off, spilling a creamy, pale orange concoction on the glass shelf. I cursed and poured the remaining smoothie down the drain, then tossed the cup in the under-sink garbage. I opened the other side of the cabinet and shoved aside scouring powder and wasp spray to get to the glass cleaner.

"Just what I need right now," I muttered, as low voices drifted up through the open door to the basement. Despite everything, a smile tugged at my mouth. Irene's idea of health food was an extra olive in her martini because you should never drink on an empty stomach. Dom was forever trying to convert her. No doubt he'd brought her this smoothie when he was here for the last poker game. That was Thursday, six days ago, which meant this drink was well on its way to becoming a science experiment. I was surprised Maria hadn't jettisoned it already.

I grabbed paper towels and started wiping the refrigerator shelf and the items that had been in the path of the orange flood: a bowl of leftover crab dip, a bottle of vermouth-marinated "drunken" martini olives, and a slice of frosted layer cake in a plastic clamshell. All the essential food groups, present and accounted for.

I asked myself what the heck I was doing. Irene was gone. The fridge and its contents would be cleaned out soon enough. There was no need for me to do this now in the state I was in. I abandoned the task.

SB was in a sniffing frenzy, standing between my legs and cataloging the contents of the fridge with his turbo-powered schnoz. I finally managed to push him away and grab the block of cheddar.

My gaze landed on Irene's favorite cozy cardigan, draped on the back of a chair. It was a practical wool garment, light blue, an unfashionable thing she'd never have worn out of the house. I recalled her wearing it as she sat in the living room cuddling Sexy Beast and his predecessors. She'd had this thing a long time. I lifted it from the chairback and brought it to my nose, inhaled the faint scent of Chanel No. 5. I knew SB would be able to detect not only the familiar perfume but the comforting smell of his "mommy" as well. I tossed it into the dog bed.

From the basement came the sound of something being wheeled toward the stairs, then the clank of metal on metal. I pictured the nice young men collapsing the legs of the transport cot to carry it and its burden up the stairs. The urge to flee overwhelmed me. I knew the sight of Irene's dead stare would haunt me for a good long while. I had no desire to add another unwelcome mental image to the mix.

"Come on, Sexy Beast, let's go home." I hefted the loaded dog bed and hightailed it to my car.

4
Over My Dead Body

I KNOW YOU'LL be stunned to learn I didn't get much sleep that night. I dozed fitfully, occasionally snapping awake with the realization of what had happened, my mind whirling. Sexy Beast slept better than I did, curled up next to me in bed.

At one point around three a.m. my eyes flew open as I realized I hadn't called Maria, Irene's housekeeper. She'd be at the house at nine. Maybe it was better that I hadn't called her. Breaking the news by phone might be easier on me, but Maria had been with Irene for twenty-eight years. She deserved to be told in person.

Which is why I dragged my exhausted butt back to Irene's house at a quarter to nine the next morning, hoping to get there before Maria. As I entered the house, the lemony scent of furniture polish told me she'd arrived early. If I'd driven around to the parking area near the garage instead of leaving my car in front of the house, I'd have seen her blue Forester.

I took a couple of deep breaths and automatically reached down to stroke SB, reclining in a straw bucket tote hanging from my shoulder. I'd arranged Irene's sweater in the bottom of the tote, which was essentially a stiff basket with shoulder straps, and he seemed content to get a free ride in his mommy-smelling nest.

This was not going to be easy. Maria Echevarría had been a nineteen-year-old bride when Irene had hired her as a full-time housekeeper. She'd managed to raise three children to adulthood while working for Irene nine to five, five days a week, rarely taking a sick day.

I found her in the kitchen chopping cilantro on a cutting board. The herb's pungent aroma filled the room. She'd set out avocados, limes, a white onion, and a tomato. The dishwasher was humming. She appeared mildly surprised to see me. "Are you limping?"

"Oh, it's nothing. I fell and banged my knee." It was stiff this morning, but I'd popped a couple of Advil and changed the dressing. I'd live.

"Mrs. M isn't up yet," she said. "I'm making guacamole for tonight's Poker Posse. The mayor loves my guacamole." Her gaze lit on SB's head and paws perched on the edge of my tote. Her eyes widened. "I thought the dog was upstairs."

"Maria, I have something to tell you." My pulse banged so loudly in my ears I could barely hear my own voice. "Sit down." I pulled out a breakfast-room chair.

She stood her ground, her eyes wide and fixed on me, the kitchen knife still in her hand. "What is it?"

"It's Mrs. McAuliffe." Giddily I asked myself where that "Mrs. McAuliffe" had come from. In all the years I'd known Maria, I'd always referred to her employer as Irene, even as she'd always called her Mrs. M. "She... I came here last night to... well, anyway, I was here last night and I... There's no easy way to say this."

Slowly Maria set the knife on the cutting board. "She's dead."

I gave a little nod. "I'm sorry, Maria. I know what a shock this must be."

She said nothing for a few moments. I watched conflicting emotions chase one another across her plain face. At least that's how it seemed to my sleep-deprived brain, which detected something more complex than simple grief behind her dry eyes.

I can't say what response I'd expected to see. Maria had never been what you'd call the warm and fuzzy type, but she was dependable, trustworthy, and took initiative in maintaining the big house and seeing to her employer's needs. For Irene's part, she'd paid her housekeeper a more-than-decent salary with benefits, topped off with a generous Christmas bonus.

But I'd been around those two enough to see what few casual visitors picked up on: Irene's dismissive and condescending treatment of Maria, her lady-of-the-manor routine meant to keep her longtime housekeeper in her place. I'd been embarrassed by Irene's attitude and wondered where a poor girl from Brooklyn had learned to put on those kinds of airs. Her beloved movies probably.

Finally Maria said, "What was it? Her heart?"

I nodded again. "That's what Dr. Diamond says. He came over and, you know, pronounced her."

"She took pills, but… I didn't think she was that sick."

"Neither did I," I said. "I found her a little after nine last night in her theater downstairs. Dr. Diamond says she hadn't been gone very long. He says it was quick and that she didn't suffer." I figured a little embellishment wouldn't hurt.

Sexy Beast pawed my side and gave a demanding little bark, asking to be put down. I set him on the pale marble floor and watched him stretch languorously, followed by a vigorous shake—always a spectacle, considering the ratty condition of his coat.

Maria looked down at the ingredients she'd amassed for her guacamole, then without comment took a small plastic bag from a cupboard and scooped the chopped cilantro into it. She opened the refrigerator to put it away and clucked her tongue when she spied the spilled smoothie residue. She grabbed a sponge.

"Oh, that's my fault," I said. "I knocked it over last night. Here, let me—"

"I have it."

As I watched Maria scrub the orange goo, something about the interior of the fridge seemed off. I'd moved the contents around last night looking for treats for SB, and now my subconscious detected that something was missing. It bugged me, yet I couldn't say why.

"Maria, did you get rid of anything that was in here?" I asked. "You know, since you got here this morning?"

"No. Why?" she asked. "What are you looking for?"

"Nothing. I just… Never mind." Yeah, that's what this difficult situation called for—me obsessing over the contents of a dead woman's fridge. As emotionally wiped out as I was last night, how could I trust my memory? And what difference did it make anyway? I ordered myself to get a grip.

Maria tossed the sponge in the sink. "He's always bringing those orange-colored drinks for Mrs. M. Supposed to be good for her stomach. Supposed to be better than my cooking, I guess."

I was tempted to remind Maria that Dom only brought the smoothies because he cared about Irene, and that it wasn't a rebuke of Maria's cooking, but I let the subject pass. I'd called

Dom last night as soon as I got home. I'd sobbed into the phone and he'd let me, had listened patiently and said just the right things. He'd always done that, always known what I needed.

Well, not always, not when it came to the family I needed to have with him, but that issue was long settled, and there was no sense rehashing it.

Can you see how mature I am, how I resist rehashing long-settled issues?

I'd heard Bonnie in the background asking Dom who was on the phone, followed by subtle changes in the ambient noise as he walked out of whatever room the two of them had been in together—their bedroom? I heard a door close. Even in that moment of unalloyed grief, I couldn't help wondering whether Mrs. Faso the Fourth would put down her foot after the wedding and demand her husband end his cozy friendship with Mrs. Faso the First. He was pretty chummy with ex-wives two and three, also, but after all, he shared kids with both of them, and wasn't it better for all concerned if the parents got along?

Maria was on a roll about the smoothies. "I poured a little into a glass once and tasted it." She pulled a disgusted face. "Worse than medicine. Why do people drink those things?"

"Maria, I need to ask you something," I said. "I know you were off yesterday, but did Irene have any visitors in the days just before?"

She spoke to the cabinet as she pulled out a red porcelain bowl. "Sure. Almost every day friends come. They stay in, they go out. You know."

"Right, but I mean… well, the man I'm thinking of is about forty, maybe six feet tall, supershort buzz cut."

"No."

"Riveting blue eyes. Strong, chiseled jaw," I continued, before halting my runaway tongue with a mental bitch-slap. "Are you sure?"

She glanced over her shoulder at me, and in the instant before she schooled her features, I saw twenty-eight years of being treated like milady's servant. "I'm sure."

"Of course you are. I just meant… well, maybe he was here yesterday when you were off," I said, more to myself than Maria.

"*Someone* was here." She placed the avocadoes and other vegetables in the bowl.

"What? When?"

She shrugged. "Maybe yesterday, maybe Tuesday evening after I went home." She routinely prepared Irene's dinner, then skedaddled at five p.m. "When I came in this morning there was a beer glass in the sink along with Mrs. M's dishes."

Irene drank only vodka martinis—no wine, beer, or other spirits, though she kept it all on hand for guests.

Maria scowled. "There were messy rings on the glass coffee table in the living room."

Irene's guest hadn't used a coaster. The fiend!

I heard the jaunty opening bars of "Tequila" and retrieved my cell from the pocket of my suede jacket. I checked the screen. It was Sten Jakobsen, Irene's lawyer. My gut tightened. Of the many unwelcome thoughts that had kept me up all night, one of the most unwelcome was the question of what would become of Sexy Beast.

The dog was Irene's only dependent, and Sten was responsible for seeing to his disposition in accordance with whatever instructions she'd left. Which no doubt meant delivering him to whichever well-heeled friend or relative was best equipped to support him in the style to which his pampered little self had become accustomed.

Why else would Sten be calling except to request that I deliver SB to his next owner, who wouldn't give a rat's ass about him or know where he likes his scritches or how many hard-boiled eggs to put in his chopped liver.

Answer: two eggs for every pound of liver. And don't skimp on the chicken fat.

I dumped the call. I was in no hurry to help Sten check that one off his to-do list. That conversation, which would likely include the words "over my dead body," could wait until I was more rested or at least had a gallon or three of black coffee coursing through my veins.

"Maria, I lost an earring last time I was here. I'm going to go look for it." I touched her arm and searched her eyes. I could read nothing in her closed expression. "Are you okay? Why don't you go home. I'll be in touch."

"I'm fine." She waved me away. "I'll finish tidying up, take out the garbage. Then I'll go."

It wouldn't be easy for a forty-seven-year-old grandmother to get another job in this economy—yet one more worry that had kept me up last night. "Listen, um… if you need references," I said, "you know, to get another job, maybe they'll accept a letter from me. I mean, I wasn't your employer, but under the circumstances—"

"No need. I'll be all right." I must have looked dubious, because she added, "Mrs. M took care of me in her will."

"Oh. Well… good. I mean, I'm glad to hear that." Irene never mentioned the contents of her will to me, not once. I assumed she had relatives somewhere who would inherit all her worldly goods, but apparently she'd also had the foresight to make provisions for the person who'd seen to her care and comfort for nearly three decades. I guess the lady-of-the-manor thing included a healthy dollop of noblesse oblige.

"Well, if at some point you decide you want that letter," I added, "just give me a call."

My first stop was the laundry room, whose floor was now dry. I looked in the recycle bins next to the big upright freezer. Sure enough, I spied, along with a spent bottle of premium vodka and a few empty food jars, a brown Guinness bottle. I picked it up, peered inside, shook it. The heady perfume of Irish stout cut through the cloying scent of fabric softener that always permeated that room. A drop or two of liquid remained. So this bottle had probably been tossed in there in the past couple of days.

Maria must have heard the clinking of glass. "Did you lose your earring in the recycling?" she called.

"I'm checking everywhere."

I hope you've already figured out the lost-earring bit was a big fat lie. My intuition was shrieking like the Bride of Frankenstein. Okay, in all probability the beer drinker was a regular pal of Irene's—didn't Sophie Halperin like a brewski or two?—but the whole thing didn't feel right. Throw a larcenous padre with impeccable timing into the mix and I figured there was a better than even chance said padre had been sitting in Irene's living room in the past day or two, sipping a cold one and working the conversation around to a certain McAuliffe family heirloom, one with a fishy tail and perky, ruby-tipped tatas.

Had he come here dressed as a priest then? Was that how he'd gained entrance? Irene was raised in the faith but had long ago slipped into your basic A & P routine: Ash Wednesday and Palm Sunday. Would the clerical collar make her easier to manipulate, or would she be quicker than I was to see through it? Knowing Irene, my money was on that second thing.

A plausible scenario was beginning to take shape in my overtaxed brain.

Okay, first of all? I know what I said last night about the guy forcing Irene to talk, but Jonah was right. Torquemada with his rack and thumb screws couldn't have gotten her to spill the beans about that brooch. This was one stubborn, headstrong broad. But let's say the padre was just as determined to learn the location of the brooch, or even to leave here with the thing in his pocket. After all, if Jonah was correct, no one outside of the Poker Posse knew that it was no longer in Irene's possession, and they weren't blabbing. How many people even knew of its existence? For that matter, how did the padre know?

Anyway, let's say he's wrangled an audience with her ladyship and has nothing more to show for his efforts than a bellyful of good Irish beer. Maybe she's booted him out on that nice, tight butt of his and commanded him never to darken her door again. But he refuses to accept defeat. What then?

My guess? He returns Wednesday evening with a more aggressive plan of action. There's no talking his way through the front door this time, so he picks the back-door lock, locates the lady of the house in her home theater, and leans on her hard. We're talking threats, coercion. Maybe he waves a weapon at her.

I still couldn't see Irene giving in. Well, maybe if he threatened Sexy Beast, but let's assume he didn't go to that extreme—mainly because I didn't want to think about it.

What I *could* see Irene doing in that terrifying situation is suffering a fatal heart attack. Jonah's *Exhibit C: scary home invasion* was gaining credibility by the minute. The padre might not be a murderer in the technical sense, but if he scared her to death, if he stood there and watched her expire without attempting CPR or calling for help, then you tell me where you draw the line.

So now Irene has gone and died on him and he's no closer to the mermaid brooch than he was before. Yet somehow he finds out not only where the darn thing is but that if he intends to beat me to it, he'd better get the aforementioned butt over to Ahearn's pronto.

I'd gone back into the foyer and started up the curved staircase before I realized I was headed there. I took the steps more slowly than I wanted to because of my knee. Irene's library, at the end of the hallway, doubled as her home office. She kept meticulous records, all of which were of the dead-tree variety and resided in an expensive lateral wooden file cabinet. A state-of-the-art laptop sat on her desk, but it was reserved for email, shopping, and of course online poker.

The bottom file drawer contained household paperwork, everything from A for art purchases to W for warranty info. The top drawer was for sensitive stuff such as medical records, investment statements, and invoices from Jane Delaney, your friendly neighborhood Death Diva and dog sitter.

Irene kept the file cabinet locked at all times, yet when I tried the handle, it slid open on well-oiled tracks. My nape prickled.

Delaney, Jane, was filed between *Credit Cards* and *Dentist*. I pulled out the extra-wide hanging folder bulging with copies of every piece of paper that had been exchanged between Irene and myself during our long association. She was a stickler for formal record keeping and insisted on presenting me with handwritten work orders before each job and receiving a detailed invoice upon its completion. If Irene had qualms about paying someone to lift a valuable piece of jewelry from her former friend's corpse, you couldn't tell from the top item in the folder. It was a copy of the most recent work order, the particulars of the assignment spelled out in cringe-inducing detail, including precisely when and where I would nab the brooch.

But that's not all that was there. My heart pounded so hard, I nearly stumbled. Irene's visitor had left his calling card, all right.

No, literally, he'd left his calling card, paper-clipped to the work order. It was a stark white card, a little smaller than a business card. Printed smack-dab in the center, in elegant raised black ink, were the words *Mr. Martin Kade McAuliffe*.

I'd never been formally introduced to the man, but his reputation preceded him. The black sheep of the family had some explaining to do.

5
Bad Bad Black Sheep

"THIS IS YOUR lucky night, Jane. Ladies drink free on Thursdays." Mr. Martin Kade McAuliffe slapped a small square napkin on the bar in front of me. "What'll it be?"

So much for ambushing him at his place of work. He hadn't looked at all surprised when I claimed a barstool. I could have been one of his Thursday-night regulars. The man who'd left the calling card wore a black vee-neck sweater with the sleeves pushed up, displaying his lovely shoulders and pecs to better effect than the priest's shirt and collar I'd last seen him in.

He'd recognized me instantly, though I, too, looked different than I had at Ahearn's. My hair was down, for one thing, the reddish blond waves falling unrestrained past my shoulders except for the front pieces, which were loosely pulled back in a charmingly messy bun, though some strands had escaped to curl artlessly around my face and my big hoop earrings. And yeah, it had taken me twenty minutes in front of a mirror to achieve that level of casual perfection, what of it? I wore a dark red top and suede jacket over skinny jeans.

The internet is a wondrous thing. Within two seconds of typing "Martin Kade McAuliffe" into the search bar, I'd discovered that he tended bar at Tierney's Publick House in Southampton. I knew little else about the black sheep of Clan McAuliffe, aside from the fact he was the illegitimate grandson of Irene's late husband, Arthur, and had done bad, bad things that had alienated him from his family.

Tierney's was an upscale Irish pub in Southampton, oceanfront playground of the rich and famous and more than an hour's drive from my Hobbit hole in Sandy Cove. After Memorial Day this bar would be crammed with the wealthy folks who summered out here, as well as working stiffs with weekend house shares and day-tripping tourists. But it was a Thursday night in early April and there were a handful of locals, most in their twenties, schmoozing at the tables, drinking, and playing darts. At the end of the bar a hipster couple were enjoying a quietly intense conversation over Irish coffees.

The décor featured the usual dark wood with Gaelic posters and tchotchkes, but the place was clean, the lighting refined, and the faint aroma of beer within a range I considered acceptable. The classic rock emanating from the speakers wasn't too loud, and the TV over the bar, now showing a soccer match, had been blessedly silenced.

"Nothing for me," I said. "I'm here to talk, not drink."

Martin produced a cognac snifter and a bottle of high-end añejo tequila. The brand happened to be my favorite, the one I dispensed like a miser at home, the one that would run you well into the double digits for a single shot at your better watering holes. Not that I ever ordered it outside the house or even found myself in your better watering holes on a regular basis.

"How's the knee?" he asked. So he had been paying attention in Ahearn's parking lot.

"Hurts like hell." Okay, not really, it felt a lot better today, but he didn't need to know that.

"This should help." He dispensed a generous pour and made a show of glancing around for his boss. "The free drinks are supposed to be from the well. I won't tell if you won't."

"Shucks, Padre, I'm honored," I said, and was rewarded with a little scowl, which made the bastard look even sexier, damn him. "How'd you know?" I lifted the glass. "About this."

"I know a lot about you, Jane."

"Which isn't really fair, is it, since the only thing I know about you is that you have a gift for breaking and entering." I tossed his calling card on the bar. "Oh, I do know one other thing about you. I know your drink is Guinness."

"Second choice. Irene doesn't stock Jameson's."

What I knew about Martin McAuliffe did not, in fact, end there. I knew he wasn't a murderer. Well, unless he happened to be the dumbest killer on the planet. People who do very bad things do not, as a rule, advertise the fact by placing darling little calling cards at the scene of the crime. For the same reason, I was fairly certain he hadn't witnessed Irene's death by natural causes and failed to call 911.

Finding that card had shot my carefully crafted theory all to hell.

He was, however, indisputably guilty of grand theft mermaid. It was that troublesome mermaid that had brought me here.

Martin gave me a quick once-over. "Take off your jacket. It's warm in here."

"Nope. I'm good."

He was right, it was warm, and getting warmer with each sip of tequila. However, I couldn't remove the jacket without taking my straw tote bag off my shoulder, and I couldn't take the tote off my shoulder without revealing the presence of a scruffy seven-pound stowaway, currently snoozing in the bottom of the bag on his sweater-nest. My hope was that Sexy Beast would remain asleep and undetected until I was out of there.

Well, what was I supposed to do? Leave him all alone in my shabby little basement apartment? I could be gone for hours. He'd just suffered the loss of his mommy and needed the reassurance of a warm, familiar body.

All right, so maybe that reassurance went two ways and it felt good to have SB's slovenly little self curled against my side when I went to confront the big bad wolf in black sheep's clothing. It didn't mean I was insecure. Or a wimp. Or…

Oh, shut up.

A burly young man with a goatee sidled up to the bar, checked me out, and pushed an empty pitcher toward Martin. "Again, dude."

"You got it." As Martin set the pitcher under the beer tap he told me, "You made a long drive for nothing."

"Oh, I don't know." I raised my glass. "I'm sitting here with a tasty free drink and enjoying a scintillating conversation with a mysterious stranger. Beats sitting at home watching *Seinfeld* reruns."

Beer and money exchanged hands. Martin watched the young man saunter back to his buddies. He turned to me. He was not smiling. "Tell Irene she can forget about the mermaid. She's never getting her greedy mitts on that brooch again."

His words were a punch to the gut. I wasn't surprised he hadn't heard. He was, after all, estranged from his entire family.

While I groped for the right words, he braced his impressive forearms on the bar and leaned over to stare at my tote. In a bored tone he asked, "Seriously?"

I looked down to see Sexy Beast peeking over the top of the bag. He yipped and I tried to shush him. My affection for this little animal and my feelings about Irene swirled into a confusing amalgam of love and grief, and at that moment I just wanted out of there. My eyes stung and I kept my head directed down at the dog, horrified that this man might glimpse my weakness.

"SB, hush, now," I whispered, trying in vain to push the dog down into the tote before anyone else noticed him. "Be a good boy for Jane."

"Get that thing out of here," Martin said, and something burst inside my chest.

"I will!" I snapped, getting in his face now, letting him see it all, the grief, the tears. "But not until I finish what I came here for." I cursed and rummaged in my pocket for a tissue, cursing again when I came up empty. SB chose that moment to leap from the tote onto the bar. He's quite the little acrobat when he puts his mind to it.

Martin seized the poodle's harness and handed me a fistful of bar napkins. He stood watching as I mopped my damp eyes and blew my nose. I happen to know I could lead Santa's sleigh when I've been crying. So much for Jane Delaney, drop-dead-sexy Death Diva. Meanwhile SB was in an orgiastic frenzy of sniffing, straining against Martin's hold to get at the beer taps and their fascinating malty, hoppy smells.

Well, the cat—or rather, the dog—was out of the bag. I shucked off my jacket and tossed it onto the barstool next to me. From his table behind me the burly beer drinker said, "Yo, what is that thing, some kinda hairy rat?" His buddies laughed.

Martin said nothing, just watched me with his unreadable blue gaze as I got myself under control.

I cleared my throat and looked him in the eye. "Irene died last night. Heart attack."

If I hadn't been watching him closely, I wouldn't have noticed the slight widening of his eyes.

"I just saw her," he said. "Tuesday evening."

Well, that was one question answered.

"Tequila" started playing in the recesses of my tote bag. What now? I dug in the bag, ignoring Martin's smirk at my choice of ring tone, and discovered the phone had fallen out of its sleeve and was caught in the folds of Irene's sweater. I yanked the sweater out of the bag and watched something drop out of one of its pockets and roll onto the wooden floor. I snatched up the phone, glanced at the screen, and groaned. Sten Jakobsen again, doing his lawyerly thing. *Not a good time, Sten.* I did my SB-loving thing and dumped the call.

I bent to retrieve the object that had fallen out of Irene's sweater pocket: a half-used roll of antacids. In all the years I'd known Irene, I'd never seen her take an antacid. She'd bragged about her cast-iron stomach, even in her eighth decade of life. So what was she doing with these? I shoved them into my jacket pocket where SB couldn't get to them.

Martin lifted the bottle of añejo tequila. I held my hand over my glass. "No more for me, I'm driving." He brushed my hand away and poured, then produced a bowl of peanuts. As if a few goobers would undo the effects of a couple of shots once I was behind the wheel. I let the excellent tequila sit there untouched, and wished I could take it home and pour it into my nearly empty bottle.

SB's nails scraped the bar top as he changed course and fought to get near the peanuts. With his free hand Martin picked up a nut. "Does he like these?"

"He likes anything that qualifies as people food. It's dog food he turns his nose up at."

"Wouldn't you?" He offered the peanut and watched SB chew, the little mouth gaping wide open with every smack of his lips. Martin looked closer. "What's wrong with his fang?"

"Nothing's wrong with his fang. It's a perfectly functional fang."

"The left one." He peeled up SB's lip on that side. "It sticks out over his bottom lip."

"So?"

"So it's a bucktooth. A buckfang," he said. "I've never seen that."

"Big deal," I said. "It's not like it hinders his eating or anything."

"No, it just makes him look even more special."

I scooped SB off the bar and tried to wedge him back into the tote. The little demon braced his legs on the rim of the bag and refused to cooperate.

I surrendered and held him against my chest. "So," I said. "You were at Irene's Tuesday evening."

Martin arranged glassware in silence. He wouldn't have revealed even that if I hadn't surprised him with the news of her death.

"Had the two of you met before? Maybe when your grandfather was alive?" Metaphorical crickets chirped. I was curious about their connection, but more than that, if I could break the ice, if I could get him to warm up to me even a little, he might be in a more receptive frame of mind when I brought up my real reason for being there.

"Beat it, Jane."

Or not.

"And waste all this quality tequila?" I pulled my drink closer, though we both knew I had no intention of finishing it. I popped a couple of peanuts into my mouth and fed another to Sexy Beast. I had to be careful how many I gave him. It was a long drive back to Sandy Cove.

"There's only one reason you'd have bothered to track me down here," he said. "Tough luck. You had your chance and you blew it."

Thanks for rubbing it in, jerk. "I'm thinking you returned in the middle of the night Tuesday—well, Wednesday morning," I said. "After Irene was asleep. You picked the back-door lock, disabled her sophisticated alarm system. Quite an impressive skill set, by the way." When he failed to acknowledge the backhanded compliment, I plowed on. "You came looking for the brooch, but it's a big house and you figured you'd start with Irene's home office—her files. Like if you learned the thing was in a bank safe-deposit box, you'd have to give up."

His derisive snort said, *Like that would ever happen.* Well, at least it was a response.

"What you found was my latest work order," I said. "It told you where Irene's brooch was and precisely when I'd be going to Ahearn's to retrieve it."

"*Irene's* brooch, huh?" He gave me a flat stare. "You believe everything that malignant old bitch told you?"

So much for not speaking ill of the dead. "Colette O'Rourke's brooch then," I said. "If it matters so much which deceased old woman you stole it from. Have you sold it yet?"

Martin exchanged good-nights with the hipster couple, now heading for the exit. "You've been doing Irene's dirty work for a long time, Jane. She paid pretty well from what I've seen."

"Because if you haven't gotten rid of it yet," I said, "there's something you need to consider. Just hear me out."

"And you have other clients too, right?" he asked. "You know, I've been thinking of trying my hand at that—doing sick things to dead people. You make a decent living at it?"

I sighed in exasperation. "Okay, for the record, I do not do sick things. I provide a valuable service to griev—"

"Is that what you call loading my grandmother's ashes into shotgun shells and giving them to a hunter during turkey season? A valuable service?"

"Wait, what?" I shook my head. "Your grandmother? Your grandmother was…?"

"Anne McAuliffe. The woman whose husband Irene stole."

I knew Irene was Arthur's second wife, but I'd never heard anything about her stealing him away from the first Mrs. McAuliffe. I'd always assumed he was a divorced man when they'd met nearly thirty years before.

That thing with the shotgun shells had been my first assignment from Irene way back when. Well, my first assignment that didn't have anything to do with dog-sitting or the pet cemetery. But it was for a close friend of hers, she'd told me, an avid hunter who'd requested that particular disposal of his cremated remains. People ask for all kinds of weird stuff. I once arranged for a ceramic artist to incorporate the ashes of a client's deceased boyfriend into a lifelike dildo. The client provided the artist with a plaster cast of the real thing to use as a model, and reported that she was more than satisfied with the finished product. Or to be more precise, that she was satisfied multiple times in quick succession.

"Okay, so you came across that work order, too," I said, "when you broke in to Irene's home. But trust me, that was someone else in those shotgun shells. It had nothing to do with your grandmother. I don't know where you got that idea."

"From Irene herself. She taunted me with it when I saw her Tuesday. Grandma loathed firearms and hunting. She was an anti-gun activist. That's the last thing she would have wanted her remains used for, and Irene knew it."

Something squeezed in my chest. "You're lying. How would Irene even have had access to your grandmother's ashes? Anne was already divorced from Arthur when she died."

"Of a broken heart." His jaw tightened. "Not a year after he left her for that conniving bitch."

I was surprised to hear the big, bad black sheep use such a quaint term. *Broken heart*, that is, not *conniving bitch*. I was fairly certain Anne McAuliffe's death certificate said nothing about a broken heart, but I kept that to myself.

"Grandpa never stopped loving her," he added, "and after she died, he realized what a colossal mistake he'd made."

"How do you know this?"

"He told me. I was eighteen, nineteen. He died a year or two later." He didn't repeat, *of a broken heart*, but the implication was clear.

"He was devastated by her death," Martin said. "When he asked my dad and my uncles if he could keep her ashes, they didn't have the heart to say no. He hid them from Irene, but she found them after he died." He leaned over the bar toward me. I managed not to flinch. "And that's where you come in. Irene paid you seventy-five bucks to desecrate my grandmother's remains. Must have seemed like a lot of bread at the time."

I took a deep, calming breath. I shook my head, but it was a hollow gesture. I knew Irene a lot better now than I had twenty-two years earlier when I was a gullible teenager. I found it all too easy to imagine her doing that to her husband's first wife. But lying to me to engage my cooperation? That, I didn't want to believe.

A pair of pretty twenty-somethings entered the place and made a beeline for the bar. They trilled greetings to "Marty" and leaned over the bar to bestow cheek kisses and give him a good long look down their plunging necklines.

"The usual?" he asked. They giggled, which apparently meant yes. He produced a couple of margarita glasses, salted the rims, and began dispensing ingredients into a blender, including a measured pour of cheap well tequila, so bite me, Barbies.

One of the girls noticed Sexy Beast. "Omigod, how cute!" she squealed. "What is it?"

"A poodle," I said.

She giggled again. "No, really, what is it?"

"It's a rare Mongolian chinchilla." Martin raised his voice to be heard over the whirring blender. "They mate them with wire-haired guinea pigs to get just that kind of matted fur. Then they skin them to line billionaires' underpants."

"No! Omigod," the second girl said. "I'm, like, so against fur. You're not going to skin him, are you?" she asked me.

"I rescued this one from the fur breeder," I said. There are times when 'tis noblest, or at least easiest, to tread the path of least resistance. "He gets to spend his days eating kibble and playing fetch."

"Almost like a dog!" Her friend showed her perfect dimples. "Can I pet it? Does it bite?"

I assured her my chinchi-pig was tame. He accepted their adoration and responded with strokes of his long tongue. More giggles.

Martin wiped the bar top and admired the view as the two turned and carried their frozen green concoctions to a table, where they immediately snagged the attention of the goateed one and his cohorts.

"I have to admit," I said, "I'm surprised to hear you talk about your grandparents with such affection. Irene told me you wanted nothing to do with your family."

His flat, hard stare made my breath catch. "Most of them wanted nothing to do with *me*, the bastard son of a married deacon."

"Your father is Arthur and Anne's middle son, yes?"

He gave a curt nod. "Hugh McAuliffe. My mom was an exotic dancer he was screwing on the side. I mean, could I be any more of a cliché? To everyone but Grandma and Grandpa, once they found out I even existed. I was eleven then."

My eyes widened. "Your father kept you a secret for eleven years? From his own family?"

Martin lifted the calling card I'd dropped on the bar. He turned it in his fingers, something close to an actual smile on his face. "These were a gift from Grandma McAuliffe when I was fourteen or fifteen. She'd been telling me about the old traditions, how a proper gentleman would never have stopped by someone's house without leaving his card. She thought it'd be fun for me to have some of my own."

Martin's tender expression told me that Grandma McAuliffe's

unspoken message hadn't been wasted on him: *You are a gentleman and have every right to hold your head high.* I got a sense of how devastating her death must have been for him.

"What the hell is that thing doing in here?" The gruff voice belonged to a portly middle-aged man now joining Martin behind the bar. The owner of the place, by all appearances. "You know better than that," he told Martin. "No pets."

Before I could respond, Martin said, "That's not a pet, Tommy, it's a service animal—like a Seeing Eye dog. It keeps her calm when the psychotic hallucinations start to take over."

I struggled to keep from rolling my eyes. First the chinchi-pig, now this. For his part, Tommy frowned with the effort of processing this information. His nervous gaze flicked between me and my "service animal" as if he expected me to start bouncing off the walls at any moment. "I dunno…"

Martin shrugged. "Nothing we can do about it, man. It's the law. You can't keep it out."

Tommy poured himself a bourbon on the rocks and retreated to his office, shaking his head and muttering to himself.

I bribed SB with another peanut to get him back into the tote. "Okay, so here it is," I said. "I'm hoping you haven't sold the brooch yet because I want you to consider doing the right thing."

Martin looked at me steadily. "Which is…?"

"Giving it to its rightful owner. Patrick O'Rourke. Colette's son."

"What a coincidence," he said. "I had a similar conversation with Irene on Tuesday evening. I told her she should do the right thing and return the mermaid to her rightful owner. I didn't know then that she'd sold her to the O'Rourke woman."

"She didn't sell her. Colette won her in a poker game." Now he had me calling the thing *her*.

"Seriously?" He shook his head. "Crazy old bats. Irene didn't tell me that. She let me believe she still had her."

"Who do you think the rightful owner is?" I asked.

"I'm tired of this conversation." He picked up my glass of tequila and tossed it back.

"Oh, I know." I tapped my head as if just now figuring it out. "That brooch is a McAuliffe family heirloom, so it should go to a McAuliffe, right? You have any particular McAuliffe in mind?" I picked up Martin's calling card from the bar top where he'd dropped it and tucked it into my jeans pocket. "The police take a dim view of burglary."

He raised his hands as if to show how empty they were. "Burglars take things."

"Breaking and entering, then."

"Irene invited me into her living room and served me a beer. I assume I left a few fingerprints, as invited guests tend to do." He shrugged. "We had a conversation and I left."

And returned hours later in the middle of the night armed with gloves, lock-picking tools, and the skills of a seasoned thief.

"How about the fact that you stole a valuable piece of jewelry from a dead woman lying in her casket," I hissed, careful to keep my volume low. "Right in front of her family."

"Only because you didn't steal it first." He tucked the handset of the bar phone against his ear and touched the keypad. "Sure, what the hell, let's call the cops. It'll be fun. We can tell them all about the mermaid, sort of a he-said-she-said. The he-said part will include the long and colorful work history of a certain local Death Diva."

Remember when I said that everything I do is legal but that sometimes there's a sort of gray area? Well, has this ever happened to you, that you'll be looking at something dark gray, like pants or something, and you'll be wondering hey, are these pants really gray, 'cause they look kinda black, and you just can't tell, and you'll turn the pants this way and that and carry them to the window and squint at them real hard and you still can't tell? But it doesn't really matter because no one's going to get hurt even if it turns out they're kinda sorta black?

Well, I've worn a few, you know, pairs of pants like that. And my conscience is clear and all, but I wouldn't necessarily want to invite the whole damn Crystal Harbor Police Department to paw through my wardrobe.

This also explained why Martin had felt free to leave his calling card as a kind of *gotcha!* for Irene. He knew she couldn't report him for swiping the brooch from Colette's casket without turning a spotlight on her own plan to do the very same thing.

He might have won this round, but I couldn't stand for this smug bastard to get the last word.

Oh, stop it, you know what I meant by *bastard*.

I leaned across the bar, got right in his face. "You're full of it with that 'rightful owner' crap, Padre. You stole that brooch because you could, and you're going to sell it if you haven't already, and you're going to keep every penny for yourself. I know about you."

"I thought all you knew about me was what kind of beer I drink."

"If you have any sense of decency, you'll turn that brooch over to Patrick," I said. "Something like that could really make a difference for him and his family."

"Don't worry about Patrick O'Rourke. He's going to be fine, mermaid or no mermaid."

"I'm sure telling yourself that helps to soothe your conscience, if you have one." I slid off the barstool and settled SB's tote against my hip. "Thanks for the drink and have a crappy life."

6
Kids. You know?

I ADMIT IT, I always get a little thrill when I pass Janey's Place and see my name up there on the apple green awning. Even now, almost twenty years after Dom opened the original store—which just happened to be the one I now found myself standing in front of—and seventeen years after our divorce, the words *Janey's Place* with their cheerful chalkboard font, separated by a tilted cross section of an apple, makes a little something inside me glow with secret pleasure.

My ex's flagship store was located in the busiest section of the busiest commercial block in downtown Crystal Harbor. It was a quaint, high-end shopping strip, with a pottery gallery on one side of Janey's Place and UnderStatements, a high-end lingerie boutique, on the other. The morning was chilly and overcast, and as I entered the welcome warmth of the store, I inhaled the homey scents of hot soup and fresh greens and fruit. I hadn't been there since the previous summer, but it was always a comforting place to walk into.

The interior of the store was decorated in a pale palette, predominantly light beige and more of the signature apple green, with blond-wood and chrome accents. The food-service counter and cold case ran along the left, with a colorful wall menu offering a selection of healthful salads, sandwiches, soups, vegetable juices, and smoothies. Most people ordered takeout, but a handful of wood-and-chrome tables were arranged in front of the big picture windows overlooking Main Street. An older woman sat at one of the tables, sipping a Kermit-colored smoothie and reading *Mother Jones*.

The remainder of the large space was a natural-foods grocery store. One whole wall was taken up with clear plastic self-serve hoppers filled with all manner of organic nuts, seeds, dried fruits, rice, beans, oats, granolas, and fair-trade coffees. The shelves were packed with every variety of nutritional supplement, protein powder, alternative baking mix, whole-grain cereal, organic snack and convenience food, healthful cooking ingredient, and bottled juice your little heart could desire. Well, maybe your little heart, but not mine. The place might be named after me, but my taste in vittles runs more along the lines of pizza, ice cream, and McAnything. I give the folks who shop at Janey's Place credit, I really do, but please.

I'd timed my visit for late morning when I knew business would be slow—too late for the breakfast-smoothie crowd and too early for the lunch-salad stalwarts. I'd scheduled a job in New Jersey that would gobble up the rest of the day and probably the whole evening as well, so I'd left Sexy Beast in the care of my mom and dad, with exhaustive written instructions and a carload of supplies. I could only imagine new parents experienced the same temporary insanity when leaving a newborn with the sitter.

And before you think, how sad, she's at Janey's Place to see her ex, who has long since moved on—and on and oh yeah, on some more—let me just tell you I did not come here looking for

Dom. This isn't where he works anyway. He runs his health-food empire from offices on the other side of town. He does, however, pop into his flagship store on a regular basis, so I half expected to see him behind the counter, throwing together a vegan panino with hummus, avocado, and all manner of life-giving rabbit food. He likes to take breaks from the big-business side of things to serve the customers and get back to his roots and remember why he opened this store in the first place and so on and so forth.

Which always sounds to me like a load of horse poo, but hey, Dom is a nice guy. Everyone says so. All his ex-wives, for example, think he's swell. I'm sure he's never late with a child-support payment, although I personally can't attest to that.

And for the record, Dom isn't the only one who's moved on. I date. I just haven't found anyone who comes up to my standards. Okay, my "impossibly high" standards if you listen to my gal pals, who claim I'm pining for my ex-husband and that until his exact clone miraculously drops into my bed, I'll remain a lonely and emotionally needy ex-wife. What do they know?

Anyway, I was there to see Patrick O'Rourke. Imagine my surprise when I phoned his home that morning only to have his wife, Barbara, inform me he was back at work that day—as manager of this very store. Dom had never mentioned hiring him, not that he kept me informed of business matters.

But it wasn't Patrick I spied behind the counter. It was Fuzzy Slippers, his daughter, diligently pretending to wipe down the food-prep area. Today she wore an apple green Janey's Place tee-shirt tied at the midriff over skintight orange leggings and high-heeled animal-print ankle boots. She probably thought she looked like a million bucks in the outfit. Unfortunately it was more like a million and change, the excess taking the form of a muffin over her waistband and cottage cheese below. Her lank, highlighted hair was pulled back in a ponytail for hygiene's sake.

The girl looked up and noticed me. After a moment I saw recognition dawn, though she made no effort to appear welcoming. Her eyes were red-rimmed and puffy. "What can I get you?" she asked.

I smiled for both of us. "I'm Jane Delaney. We kind of met Wednesday evening at your grandmother's wake. We didn't really get to speak then. I'm so sorry for your loss."

She excavated her ear canal and examined her finger.

"I'm afraid I didn't get your name the other night," I said.

It took her a few seconds to realize I was waiting for a response.

"Cheyenne," she said.

"That's a pretty name."

"What can I get you?"

"I really just came in to speak with your dad, Cheyenne," I said. "Is he around?"

"In the back."

I waited. "Um… can you let him know I'm here?"

"Daddy!" she bellowed, making me jump. *"Someone here to see you!"*

The customer at the table gave Cheyenne a disapproving look. The girl responded with a flat, hard stare until the woman returned her eyes to her magazine. Cheyenne turned to me. "What can I get you?"

Resigned, I scanned the menu offerings on the wall behind her, each accompanied by an appetizing photograph. I recognized the pale orange smoothie from Irene's fridge, the one

Maria had said tasted worse than medicine. I was curious, and heck, I was no fan of any of this stuff, so why not try the kind Irene had favored?

"I'll have a papaya-ginger smoothie," I said.

"What size?" Could the girl look more bored?

"Um, small, I guess."

All the smoothies were accompanied by florid descriptions of the wonders they performed, from boosting your immune system to scouring your colon to promoting mental serenity to bringing up hairballs. Okay, you got me, I made that last one up, but to me it sounds no more outlandish than the other claims. I mean, come on, they're fruit shakes. And yes, Dom believes every word of it. He would never knowingly misrepresent a product he sells. I might not buy in to all this health-food stuff myself, but I've always found his sincerity endearing as hell.

And yeah, kind of sexy too. So sue me.

I assumed most customers purchased these sweet drinks based more on taste than their purported healing properties. The description of the papaya-ginger smoothie said it was good for digestive problems and helped settle the stomach. I frowned, thinking of the antacids I'd found in Irene's sweater pocket.

I was watching Cheyenne toss ingredients into the blender— and before you ask, yes, she'd put on gloves—so I didn't notice Patrick until he was right next to me.

"It's Mary, right?" He smiled. "You were at Mom's wake."

A great big wad of dread lodged in my throat, rendering me mute. I swallowed, took a deep breath, and said, "Patrick, could I drag you away from your responsibilities for a couple of minutes? We need to talk."

His smile faded as he took in my expression. "Sure, no

problem. Cheyenne can handle the counter. Heck, she could just about run the place single-handed. Right, hon?" he asked his daughter as she handed me my smoothie. Her response was a sullen shrug. She took my money and managed to make change, then Patrick and I took a table out of earshot of the other customer.

"At least you're not limping anymore," he observed. "Your knee looked pretty bad the other night."

"It feels better," I said. "A little sore is all."

I'd made up my mind during another long night in which I'd gotten a scant three or four hours of shuteye. Patrick deserved to know the truth about the brooch. Despite Irene's attempt to rewrite history, Colette had won the thing fair and square—nobody had forced Irene to toss it onto the poker table—and I had to assume Colette's only son was meant to inherit everything that was hers. It didn't get much more cut and dried.

The fact is, I was ashamed of the part I'd played in Irene's scheme to get it back, although ironically I wished I'd succeeded, for the simple reason that then I could have handed the brooch over to Patrick. There would have been an awkward conversation, though not as awkward as the one we were about to have.

Diffuse light from the big picture window found every line in his face and emphasized the weariness underlying his features. I looked him in the eye. "My name isn't Mary. I lied to you the other night."

His gaze sharpened. He waited.

My mouth felt dry as dust. I licked my lips. "I'm Jane Delaney. I went to your mother's wake because Irene McAuliffe asked… because she hired me to."

I watched realization dawn. "You're the one they call the Death Diva," he said.

I cringed inwardly and nodded. After two decades, the detested moniker wasn't going away. Heck, I even thought of myself as the Death Diva. Maybe I should stop fighting it and add it to my business cards: *Call the Death Diva for those ghoulish chores that really creep you out.*

"You're Dom's wife," he added, then corrected himself. "His ex. Janey's Place is named for you."

I managed a weak smile. "That was a long time ago."

"Yeah, but you're really raking it in now." He grinned. "With twenty-seven stores and three more opening before summer."

Here we go again. Every time I had this depressing conversation, I wanted to go home to my cramped basement apartment, scrub the rust stains out of the tub, slip into a nice warm bubble bath, and open my veins. "Yeah, well, they're Dom's stores, not mine."

His smile faltered. "But you musta got a piece of the action, right? In the divorce?"

"Well, you see, Patrick—and this is actually pretty funny— Dom offered me a fifty-percent share when we divorced because, you know, we kind of started it together and Dom always does the decent thing. It was just this one little shop then, the one we're sitting in now, and it hadn't really taken off yet and I thought, hell, who needs this? It's a money suck that'll tie me to my ex forever. I'm my own woman. I want no encumbrances. And stuff like that." I cleared my throat. "So instead I asked for this little antique student desk we found once at a flea market."

There was a long, painful silence while I watched Patrick digest this. Finally he said, "That's not actually such a funny story."

It was a nice little student desk, the one-piece kind with chair and desktop bolted to a metal frame. It was pretty old, made of real tree wood and with a depression for an inkwell. I still had it. It served as combination writing surface and snack table in my Lilliputian apartment. I could just manage to fold myself into it and, more important, wriggle myself out of it. I was one sack of White Castle sliders away from a lingering and ignominious end. *Mystery surrounds the grisly death of a Sandy Cove woman found trapped in a charming antique kiddie desk. Nearby pile of hamburger wrappers offers no clue.*

"Honest to God," Patrick said, "I thought that Death Diva thing was just some kinda weird hobby."

"More like a weird way to feed myself."

"About the wake," he said. "I know that Mom and Irene weren't on speaking terms lately. Well, for years, right? I'm guessing Irene figured she wouldn't be welcome at the wake, so she sent you in her place. It isn't true. We would've been glad to see her there. Her and Mom meant something to each other at one time. I, uh…" He cleared his throat. His eyes were shiny. "I was sorry to hear about Irene." His grief was more for his mother, I knew, than for Irene, whom he probably hadn't set eyes on during the past decade.

How easy it would be to accept his assumption without comment, to let him believe my presence at Ahearn's had been that benign. "It's not that simple, Patrick. I wish it were. Irene hired me…" My palms were damp. "She hired me to steal your mother's mermaid brooch before it was buried with her."

He frowned and reared back a little. "The thing that priest took? That cheap trinket?"

"The thing is… well, it isn't a cheap trinket, as it turns out. I thought it was at the time. It turns out the brooch is worth over a hundred thousand dollars. Your mom won it from Irene in a poker game nine years ago."

He opened his mouth to speak, then closed it. He shook his head. "Is this some kinda joke?"

I raised my hand. "It's all true, Patrick, I swear. We could get into why your mom kept the true value of that brooch secret, why she wanted it buried with her, all that. It comes down to her relationship with Irene, which basically ended with that poker game. But right now we have something more urgent to discuss."

"For real?" he asked. "A hundred grand?"

"A hundred and four, actually. Well, that was the figure back when Colette won it. Who knows? It could be worth more now. I doubt it's lost value."

I let him sit and digest that for a few moments. Finally he looked down at my untouched smoothie. "Have you had that before? It's one of our more popular flavors."

"I haven't. I've, uh, heard about it, though." I unwrapped my straw and poked it through the opening in the cup's lid. If this thing tasted as hideous as Maria had claimed, I only hoped I could keep from barfing it back up, considering my current agitated state.

I took a tentative sip. The bright flavors of papaya, ginger, and yogurt erupted in my mouth, along with notes of lemon and mint. It was delicious! I drew deeper on the straw, taking a nice big gulp. I shared my verdict with Patrick, who beamed as if he alone were responsible for the recipe. Maybe Maria had an aversion to ginger.

The customer at the other table slipped her magazine into her shoulder bag, placed her trash in the bin, and strolled into the grocery section of the store.

"So the something more urgent we gotta talk about," Patrick said. "That'd be the priest that ran off with Mom's brooch."

"Right. Well, he isn't really a priest, of course."

"Yeah, no kidding. A damn ghoul is more like it, stealing from the dead." His expression morphed from outraged to sheepish. "I didn't mean you."

"No, you're right. I should never have accepted that assignment. It's just that where Irene was concerned… I mean, I knew her for a long time and…" I shifted my gaze out the window, ambushed by my feelings, the conflicting whirl of emotions that had assailed me since Irene's death. I struggled for composure.

Patrick's rough hand patted mine where it rested on the table. For a couple of seconds only, long enough to offer more understanding than I deserved.

"Well." I cleared my throat. "I was able to do a little digging. I managed to find out who the thief is." I withdrew the padre's calling card from my purse. The corners were getting a little battered. I'd never be able to look at that card again without thinking about his grandma McAuliffe and their special relationship. I pushed it across the table toward Patrick, who picked it up and examined it.

His eyes widened. "The guy's a McAuliffe?"

I nodded. I told him about Martin's family connection to Irene. I told him where he worked.

He tossed the card onto the table. "I should've guessed that pin was worth something when you came back into Ahearn's the other night and told me what he did. I mean, only a crazy guy would take that kind of risk for a piece of junk jewelry."

"Well, this crazy gal took the risk for the three hundred bucks

Irene promised me." I took another long pull of the smoothie. Was it my imagination or was the drink actually settling my nervous stomach? I blotted my mouth with a little napkin from the old-fashioned dispenser on the table. "She claimed its only value was sentimental. And gullible Jane bought it." My mouth twisted.

"Hey, don't be so hard on yourself," he said. "If it weren't for you being there Wednesday night, I'da had no idea the thing was even missing. So maybe it's just as well Irene sent you. You know what they say—things happen for a reason."

"Which I assume means you're going to share all this with the police?" I tried to sound supportive. This was why I'd come looking for Patrick, after all, to get him up to speed on the worth of his stolen property so he could make an informed decision.

The thing is, once Martin came under police scrutiny, he would almost certainly follow through on the threat he'd made last night at the pub. He'd retaliate by entertaining the cops with fun facts from the two-decade work history of Jane Delaney, Death Diva, culminating in my failed attempt to make off with the brooch myself. It wouldn't matter that I wasn't the one who'd turned Martin in. He'd know who was behind it.

"I guess I have to, huh?" Patrick tucked Martin's card into his jeans pocket. "I mean, how can I let the bastard get away with it?"

I got the feeling that voluntarily engaging with the police was not in this man's experience or comfort zone.

"It's not about the money," he added, avoiding my eyes. "I don't really need it."

"Well, that's good." I tried to sound as if I believed him. The man had his pride. "I think you're doing the right thing, Patrick."

"Don't worry. I won't tell the cops what you were doing at Mom's wake."

"I appreciate that," I said, "but I have a feeling they'll have some questions for me anyway. For one thing, I was a witness to the theft." For another, the thief was going to do everything in his power to bring me down with him. I only hoped whatever criminal record Martin possessed would make me look like Mother Theresa by comparison.

"It's been, what, a day and a half," he said. "If the guy's smart, he already fenced it."

"That's what I'm afraid of."

"Unless he had a buyer lined up," he said. "Someone that wanted that brooch real bad and hired him to get it. Like Irene hired you."

I liked to think the two scenarios were worlds apart, but he was right. I'd become a thief for hire. The thought made me queasy. I sucked down more of the smoothie and it had the desired effect. Next time I'd get a large.

The first order of business was damage control. I intended to return to Irene's home office at the earliest opportunity and make all gone with the more, shall we say, arresting work orders currently residing in Irene's file cabinet. The most problematic work order was, of course, the most recent one, the very document to which Martin Kade McAuliffe, Victorian man about town, had affixed his gentleman's calling card. Of the folks who knew what I'd been up to at Ahearn's that night, I wasn't worried about anyone except Martin ratting me out. Both Patrick and Jonah had promised to keep my secret. Sadly, the originator of the document was in no position to tell the tale.

The paranoid part of my brain worried that it was too late for damage control. In my mind's eye I saw Martin whipping out his cell phone and photographing the juicier work orders during his middle-of-the-night not-burglary session. The rational part of my brain told the paranoid part that it had been watching too many of Irene's spy flicks. Burglars don't do stuff like that in real life.

Do they?

Bottom line: I'd do my best to stay under the cops' radar, but I was prepared to take some heat if it came to that. Ditto for hits to Irene's reputation. I simply couldn't live with myself if I kept my yap shut and let an inheritance like the mermaid brooch slip through Patrick O'Rourke's fingers. That kind of money could spell the difference between a college education for Fuzzy Slippers— I mean for Cheyenne and her brother, or a lifetime working the same kinds of dead-end jobs their dad had held.

Not that managing the Janey's Place flagship store occupied that category. It was a good job and he took justifiable pride in it.

"So how long has Cheyenne been working here?" I watched the girl ring up a purchase for the Kermit-smoothie customer. The woman asked a question about the vitamins she was buying. Cheyenne responded with the same glum shrug I'd witnessed earlier.

"Almost two months." Patrick lowered his voice. "She graduated high school last June. I figured she'd start looking for a job, but all she wants to do is sleep late, watch TV all day, and stay out all hours with those no-good friends of hers." He shrugged. "Kids. You know?"

The smile I gave him said, *Yeah, I get it, heh heh. Kids.* But I didn't get it. At Cheyenne's age I'd been working after school for

Irene for two years. After graduation I scrounged up every bit of work I could find to pay for college. Between work study, pet-sitting for Irene, and my budding Death Diva business, I managed to get my degree. It took me six long years of juggling work, classes, and all-night cramming sessions, and I can say with all honesty that at no point during that time did I consider chilling on my parents' sofa to be a viable lifestyle choice.

I groped for a neutral response. "It must be hard raising children nowadays."

"Hell, I was no better at that age," he said. "Worse, you wanna know the truth." He glanced at his daughter, now leaning against her work station and texting on an expensive-looking smart phone. "Finally I laid down the law. She comes to work at the shop where I can keep an eye on her or she's out on her ass. What they call tough love, you know?"

"Nothing wrong with that."

"Only, it doesn't seem to be working," he said, "if I'm reading the signs right."

"Signs?" I said. "You think she's involved in… um…" Did I know Patrick well enough to have this conversation? He seemed to have no such qualms.

"Drugs," he said without hesitation. "Same as me at that age. Okay, I know about the weed. I don't care about that. Everyone does it and it's never going away."

"You don't think she's into anything harder, do you?"

Cheyenne's customer passed us on her way out of the shop. Patrick exchanged have-a-good-days with her, then leaned closer to me. "It's not that, it's when I see her buying stuff and I don't know where the money came from. Not from me or her mom, that's for sure. And she won't tell us."

I looked at Cheyenne with her fancy phone and remembered the iPad she'd been playing with at the wake. Those toys don't come cheap. "You think she's dealing?" I said.

"She denies it." His expression was eloquent. It spoke of the love, frustration, and never-ending worry that was parenthood. "I only wish that when I was her age, someone would've stepped in and knocked the stupid outta me. My folks loved me, but they didn't see what was going on till it was too late. I'm not gonna make the same mistake with my kids."

Now I was patting *his* hand. "She's lucky she has you for a father," I said, and meant it.

The door swung open and Nina Wallace entered the shop. She spied Patrick and me and made a beeline for us. Perfumed air kisses all around.

Nina swanned around Crystal Harbor as if she owned the town. She didn't, of course, but her great-grandfather had—or close enough. Hank "Hokum" Hannigan had been a notorious gangster and partner in crime of Dutch Schultz during the 1920s and '30s. Hannigan made his fortune during Prohibition, bootlegging and running booze from Canada and the Caribbean to Crystal Harbor's shoreline, where most of it made its way to the speakeasies of New York City.

Most, but not all. The town had supported at least two thriving speakeasies. The current Town Hall had been a four-story hotel back then, with a secret saloon and gambling den on the top floor. The building that now housed the Historical Society had been a boardinghouse and brothel, with an illegal watering hole located in the basement. Both buildings had been owned by Hannigan, whose family had donated them to the town after his death. According to less-than-reliable local lore, there was an old tunnel connecting the two buildings, to store and transport booze and as an escape route during raids. I'd heard it was in danger of collapsing and that the entrances had long ago been sealed.

Far from being embarrassed by her notorious relative, Nina basked in her connection to the town's shadier past. She was rumrunner aristocracy, as it were. Several years ago she'd turned the Historical Society's basement speakeasy into a Prohibition museum, displaying such charming period pieces as a battered still, antique whiskey bottles and beer taps, a tommy gun, and framed newspaper articles about Hokum Hannigan—a blowhard with a fondness for spewing pretentious BS, hence the nickname. The display was set against the background of the original crudely painted wall murals and scarred mahogany bar. I had to wonder how many of the "historical artifacts" had been lugged out of her parents' attic.

"I was so sorry to hear about Irene." She patted my hand and gave Patrick a sympathetic shake of her elegantly coiffed head. "First Colette, now her."

Nina was always impeccably dressed, even to run errands around town. Today it was a pink cashmere sweater set and pinstriped slacks. Her glossy black hair was cut in a stylish shoulder-length bob with bangs, and her makeup defined understated elegance. She was at least my age but looked a good five years younger. Nina Hannigan Wallace always made me feel like I should be living under a bridge, eating billy goats.

"Well, I gotta get back to work." Patrick rose and offered Nina his chair. "Can Cheyenne get you something, Nina?"

"I just came in to pick up some almond flour, but you know, maybe I'll have a cup of veggie chili—it's so raw out." She parked her trim butt as Patrick joined his daughter behind the counter. I watched Cheyenne ladle chili into a small stoneware bowl on a saucer.

"I need the almond flour for gluten-free cookies I'm making for the poker tournament tomorrow," Nina said. "What is it about gluten nowadays? It seems like half the players are claiming allergies. Anyway, Maia Armstrong is taking care of everything else," she added, naming a popular local caterer. "You know, I so used to enjoy baking for the Poker Posse."

She shook her head again, and I wondered whether she grieved more for the regular Thursday-evening game or its dead hostess. Certainly there was no love lost between Nina and Irene after last week's gladiatorial election for president of the Historical Society, and it was no secret that Nina and Colette had been bosom pals. Privately I'd wondered how long it would take Irene to find an excuse to revoke Nina's membership in the Posse.

"I saw in Irene's obit that her memorial mass will be held at the end of the month," she said. "The thirtieth."

"She wanted to be cremated," I said, and wondered whether that process had already been completed. In truth, I didn't want to know precisely when it would happen. As many cremated remains as I'd handled in my career, still it was hard to think of that lively, crabby, autocratic woman being reduced to ash. "So there's no need for a speedy funeral." I tipped my cup to suck down the last of the smoothie.

"At least she died doing something she loved," she said. "Watching *Jaws*, of all things. I for one can't see the appeal, but if it gave her some comfort at the end…"

I lowered my cup. Feeling a frown trying to form, I

sandblasted my expression with a deep, calming breath. "Where did you hear that?"

"Hear what?"

"About *Jaws*." No one knew that except me and Jonah, and I couldn't see him going back on his promise not to spread it around.

Nina drummed her nails on the table. Her hands always appeared freshly manicured, the nails invariably painted a tasteful sheer beige-pink. "I don't remember who told me." She placed a hand on my arm, deftly redirecting the conversation. "I know you're the one who found her, Jane." Her tone oozed sincerity. Or something. "That must have been terrible for you."

I murmured something appropriate.

"I hope Irene didn't suffer too much," she said. "That kind of death can be quite painful, from what I understand. And the poor woman was all alone. Well, except for that ugly little dog— *Ah!*" Nina leapt out of her seat with a yelp of pain.

Cheyenne's hand had slipped as she'd set down the cup of steaming veggie chili, and half of it had landed on Nina. I pulled a wad of napkins out of the dispenser and glared up at the careless girl, prepared to see her usual sulky puss. What I saw brought me up short.

Never before had I witnessed such raw, soul-crushing misery. The girl trembled, eyes brimming, features contorted by an anguish too overwhelming to hold in. I sat paralyzed for a long moment, transfixed by the unexpected sight. My cell phone chose that moment to ring.

Nina frantically wiped her sweater and pants. "Get me some water at least!" she barked at the girl, without so much as glancing at her.

Patrick was nowhere in sight. I stood and touched Cheyenne's shoulder. "Honey, what's wrong—"

My hand might have been a cattle prod, the way she jerked from it. She turned and bolted for the door to the back rooms, overturning a chair and knocking down a display of rice crackers.

"This is just great." Nina tossed the soiled napkins onto the table. She stood with arms wide. "Where did that girl go? Is she bringing water?"

"I don't think so." I glanced at my ringing phone. Sten again. I dumped it. "The ladies' room is over there." I pointed.

"She did it on purpose," Nina hissed.

I didn't agree. The accident looked like just that to me, a result of Cheyenne's inexplicable emotional turmoil, perhaps, but in no way a deliberate act. I said nothing, not wanting to get Nina even more riled. She stomped into the john as Patrick emerged from the back. Noticing the spilled chili, he grabbed a towel and joined me at the table.

"What happened?" He lifted the dishes and started wiping up the mess. "Cheyenne ran out to the car and took off. She was bawling like a baby. Wouldn't tell me anything."

"To tell you the truth, I'm not sure." I picked up the scattered boxes of rice crackers and restacked them. "Nina and I were talking about Irene. That seemed to be what triggered it."

Patrick pondered this. "Could be it made her think of her grandma. She didn't seem all that broken up at first, but at the funeral yesterday, that's when it hit her. Maybe I shoulda let Cheyenne stay home today, but I thought it'd be good for her to get back to her regular routine." He sighed and returned to the counter.

Could it be that simple? A delayed reaction to Colette's

death? If so, it was the most dramatic emotional turnaround I'd ever witnessed, and in my business I'd witnessed a few. I'd seen Cheyenne at her grandmother's wake. If she was suppressing her grief, she did an outstanding job. To go from that to her current crippling despair… Something about it didn't ring true. I saw no reason to share my observation with Patrick.

A pedestrian on the sidewalk held the door for a young mother pushing a twin stroller the size of my Civic. Okay, my Civic had a bigger trunk. One of the toddlers snoozed peacefully while the other bucked against his restraining straps and screamed for carrot juice. Carrot juice, I kid you not. Had this poor kid even tasted Coca-Cola? I thought they both looked burly enough to stroll into the store under their own steam, and maybe laugh at the *No Smoking* sign and light up a couple of stogies, but nobody asked me. Hey, wouldn't you ride around in a souped-up rickshaw all day if some poor schmuck was willing to do the grunt work?

I recognized the good Samaritan who'd held the door for her. I should, I was married to him for seven months a million years ago.

7
Got Serial Monogamy?

DOM WALTZED INTO the store like he owned the place. That's a joke.

Patrick greeted him and began juicing carrots for the screamer. Dom's expressive features softened when he saw me, and I got the same stupid, giddy thrill I'd experienced in his presence since I was thirteen and he was the new boy in Mr. Bender's eighth-grade Spanish class. *Buenas tardes, Dominic Faso, usted es muy guapo.* Before that first class bell rang, my overstimulated young mind was rolling around the words *Jane* and *Faso*, just to see how they sounded together.

In truth, Dom was never classically *guapo*, then or now. His strong, pleasant features got an aesthetic boost from the fact that his natural facial expression was a smile. And not just any smile, but a smile that made you feel as if you were the center of his universe—at least at that particular moment. His bottomless brown eyes were the same dark shade as his thick, curly hair. And he had height in his favor, being a quarter inch shy of six two. Today he wore jeans and a white dress shirt, open at the throat, under a casual sport coat.

He hugged me. "How are you doing, Janey? Better?"

The last time I'd spoken to him had been the night Irene died. I was tempted to say no, no better, just to prolong the hug. Instead I nodded and stepped back. I glanced at Patrick and led Dom to the table I'd recently vacated. We sat.

I lowered my voice. "How long has Patrick O'Rourke worked here?"

"I hired him six months ago. He's doing a great job."

"Since when do you personally choose store managers? I thought your human resources department took care of that."

"Well… this one was a favor for a friend," he said.

"You're such a soft touch, Faso." I gave him a crooked smile. "Who's the friend?"

"I'd rather not say. It was kind of hush-hush."

"What, you can't even tell me?" Colette was the only person I could think of who'd make such a request, and to my knowledge, she and Dom hadn't kept in touch after that fateful poker game nine years earlier.

I could see the mental debate being waged behind those expressive dark eyes. "Well, what could it hurt now?" he said. "Irene's gone."

I blinked. "You don't mean that Irene asked you to hire Patrick? Why on earth would she do that?"

"Mine is not to wonder why…"

"But it makes no sense," I said. "That would be like doing a favor for Colette, and Irene would have moved heaven and earth to avoid doing a favor for Colette. Did you ask Irene why she wanted you to take him on?"

"The man needed a job," the nice guy across from me said. "He's had a lot of bad breaks."

"No, I know that. But why Colette's son? A lot of people have had bad breaks. What made her choose him?"

"That, I can't tell you."

Clearly Dom did not share my ferocious curiosity about the matter. "And I see Patrick hired his daughter," I said.

"Yeah, where is Cheyenne?" He craned his neck to look around the store. "I thought she was working today."

"I think she's doing something in back," I said, unwilling to rat out the kid to her boss. I didn't think Dom would fire her, but her departure in the middle of her shift would be a mark against her, and this job seemed to be a key component in Patrick's plan to keep his daughter out of trouble. "She seems to know what's what," I added. "She made me a really yummy smoothie."

"You're kidding me, right?" Dom's signature grin was out in full force. "Jane Delaney willingly consumed a beverage with zero caffeine, artificial coloring, or high-fructose corn syrup?" He grabbed my wrist and pretended to check my pulse. I made a *Ha ha, very funny* face but didn't pull my hand away.

"I ordered the same flavor you were bringing Irene," I said. "Papaya-ginger."

He looked bemused. "What would Irene do with a smoothie? I could see her rubbing it on her face as a night cream, but drink one?" He pretended to consider the matter. "Maybe if it had enough vodka in it."

"No, really, Maria said you were bringing them to her."

He touched his chest. "She said *I* was bringing them?"

"Well…" I thought back to my conversation with Irene's housekeeper. "She said something like, 'He's always bringing her those orange drinks.' I guess I assumed it was you."

"Wasn't me." His grin widened. "She must've had a secret

admirer with exceptional taste in smoothies."

Nina exited the ladies' room, wearing a murderous glower and an elegant ensemble that was now wet as well as stained. She made a beeline for the counter, obviously intending to give Patrick an earful, but changed course for the exit when she saw him juggling several customers who'd just arrived. I was grateful Dom had his back to her. If she'd noticed him, I have no doubt she would have demanded he fire Cheyenne. She left without the almond flour she'd come in for. The players at tomorrow's tournament would have to live without homemade gluten-free cookies.

"So what brings you in here today?" Dom asked me. "Dare I hope we're winning you over to the dark side? Today a papaya smoothie, tomorrow a tofu scramble wrap."

"Stop, you're going to make me upchuck." In fact, the mental image his words conjured put me in mind of something that had already gone up the down staircase. "I had to talk with Patrick about something." I leaned in close. "Why didn't you ever tell me about that poker game where Colette won the mermaid brooch from Irene?"

Dom's dark eyebrows rose. "You know, I hadn't thought about that thing in years, then I go to Colette's wake on Tuesday—for old times' sake, the Poker Posse and all that—and what do you think she's wearing. The mermaid pin!"

"Yeah," I said glumly, "I know."

"I didn't see you there."

"I, uh, stopped by for a few minutes on Wednesday. Answer the question, Dom."

"How did you find out Colette won it?" he asked. "Irene made us take blood oaths."

An image of Irene slicing the palms of her Posse pals flitted through my mind. Dom's words were hyperbole, but a part of me wouldn't put it past her.

"Never mind how I found out," I said. "I can't believe you'd keep a juicy tidbit like that from me. You know you can trust me to keep my mouth shut."

I suspected he was only half joking when he said, "I was scared of that woman. We all were. She says don't any of you blab…" He shrugged.

I shook my head in disbelief. Irene McAuliffe had been a little old lady living in the suburbs. To hear big, strong guys like Dom and Jonah talk about her, you'd think she was in the cement-overshoes business.

"Who's watching Sexy Beast?" he asked.

"At the moment, my folks."

"I stopped by their place last week," he said. "Brought them an Easter gift basket."

"I saw." The thing was gigantic, more like an Easter gift bathtub. What kind of man kept in touch with his ex-wife's parents, for decades and with no grandkids in the picture, bringing them birthday and holiday gifts, sitting and chatting for hours, fixing the occasional leaky faucet? Oh, and? Inviting them to all his subsequent weddings.

Only the Nicest Guy in the World, that's who. A guy whose deep sense of family connection didn't evaporate with the end of a marriage. I couldn't help but wonder whether he did the same for Svetlana's and Meryl's parents. Where did he find the time? But I knew where. Dominic Faso does not rest. He doesn't believe in it.

"So now that Irene is gone," he said, "you can finally get that dog groomed."

I groaned. "SB's not ready for that. It's too soon since he lost his mommy."

"It's unhealthy, Janey. It's bad for his skin, for starters. What does the vet say?"

That it's unhealthy and bad for his skin, for starters. "Nothing."

His smile twisted. It's so inconvenient that he can read my mind. He pulled out his phone, a state-of-the-art smart phone like Cheyenne's—I should think about getting myself one of those, perhaps when I win the lottery—and tapped the screen a few times. He turned it toward me.

It was a photograph, a side view of a dog. And not just any dog, but a big, tall standard poodle, a majestic-looking beast with a shiny, even coat of curly hair that was disconcertingly close to my own reddish blond. The ears were long and sleek, the snout neatly trimmed, the undocked tail long and feathery. This was the Nina Wallace of dogs. Or it would be if it were a bitch. Clearly this was a boy poodle. Which made me realize I'd never even glimpsed SB's little winky beneath all that matted undergrowth.

"This is Frederick." Dom handed me the phone. "He belongs to Bonnie."

Well, that was just perfect. Dom's fiancée owned a poodle that was the polar opposite of my poodle. I mean Irene's poodle. Oh hell, I didn't even know whose poodle SB was now. Frederick's imperious top-dog stance said, *Sniff my princely butt, mongrel hordes. Your alpha has arrived.*

"Very nice." I tried to hand back the phone. He made me hold it and watch while he scrolled through shot after shot of Frederick.

He paused at a picture of a little girl hugging the dog. "Frederick chased off a pack of feral dogs that tried to attack Bonnie's niece. He saved her life."

Of course he did.

"Oh, and here's Frederick at the agility trials." Dom glowed with pride. "He came in first place."

I hated Frederick. When the next photo appeared, I brought the phone closer to my face. "Is that a *pheasant* in his mouth?"

"Frederick is a champion retriever. You should see him take off after game."

Dominic Faso was the only person I knew who was both a committed vegetarian and an unapologetic hunter. He donated the meat to soup kitchens, natch.

"Are you finished playing 'my dog can kick your so-called dog's ass'?" I skidded the fancy phone across the table. Fortunately for my ex and his expensive toys, he has quick reflexes.

"My point," he said, "is that this is what a properly groomed poodle looks like. Sexy Beast should be a miniature version of Frederick. I'm going to put you in touch with the groomer Bonnie uses." More tapping on the screen.

"No. Wait a minute." I made a grab for the phone, which he easily evaded.

"Rocky has a waiting list," Dom said. "It takes a year and a half to get an appointment as a new client, if you can believe it."

"Shucks, that's too bad."

He brought the phone to his ear. "But for Bonnie he'll move you to the head of the list."

The last thing I wanted was to be beholden to the next Mrs. Faso. And what kind of name is Rocky for a dog groomer? Rocky sounded scary. Rocky sounded like a scowling, tattooed bodybuilder who wouldn't be at all gentle with my poor little Sexy Beast, who went apoplectic at the sight of shampoo, never mind clippers.

I listened as Dom asked his fiancée to use her persuasive powers on Crystal Harbor's most sought-after dog groomer. He called her "honey." I hated Bonnie, too.

I never said I was mature, so you can just stop, you know, thinking whatever you're thinking.

Dom signed off with Bonnie and said, "Done. She'll have Rocky's assistant call you to schedule an appointment."

I blew out a defeated sigh. "Irene's going to haunt you for this." Then I scraped up enough good manners to say, "Thanks."

"You're welcome. Want to see pictures of the kids?"

Why, I can think of nothing that would make this day more perfect. I pasted on a cardboard smile. "Of course!"

More screen tapping and then I found myself sitting through a slide show of Dominic Faso's offspring, starting with the older two, ages fifteen and sixteen. Their mother was Svetlana Khorkov Faso, a Russian-born endocrinologist whom he'd met and married within weeks of our divorce.

"How are young Boris and Natasha?" I asked.

"Ivan and Karina are doing great, thanks for asking." He showed me a picture of Ivan onstage in a school play. "He played the Stage Manager in *Our Town*. He's not really interested in theater, he just does it 'cause that's where the girls are. A Lothario at fifteen."

"Like his dad. He really shot up in height. Looks like you." Studying his son's photograph, I was transported back in time to those heady first years with Dom. A knot of unwelcome emotion constricted my throat. I swallowed it down and gritted out a smile through a seemingly endless stream of images of Ivan, Karina, and ten-year-old Jonathan, Dom's son by Meryl Hanover Faso. He'd met and married Meryl, hotshot poet and darling of the literary set, shortly after divorcing Svetlana.

What's that, you say? You detect a pattern here? Why, how perspicacious of you. Dominic Faso is not a man who's comfortable with his own damn self. He needs a woman to complete him, as the sappy saying goes. He does not, however, require that it be the same woman till death do them part. Dom could be the poster boy for a "Got Serial Monogamy?" campaign.

For what it's worth, I've never suspected him of cheating. He waits for the amicable breakup, then immediately reels in a replacement. In the good-news department, each of his marriages has lasted significantly longer than the preceding one, which means he just might be getting this thing down.

That was good news for Bonnie Hernandez, a local police detective. If it were up to Dom, Bonnie would already be Mrs. Faso the Fourth. She took a good, hard look at her fiancé's marital history and demanded a two-year engagement, much to the groom's frustration. He did, however, persuade her to move in with him.

"Rocky charges a fortune, by the way." He slipped the phone back into his breast pocket. "And for Sexy Beast it'll be a fortune and a half. No worries, I'm paying for it."

"No." This was my knee-jerk response to Dom's frequent offers to pay for stuff. I had my pride—as misplaced and self-defeating as that pride was, considering the anorexic condition of my wallet.

"Stop it, Janey," he said. "I know you can afford it now. I'm doing this for Irene."

"What are you talking about?"

"I know how much she loved that dog. It's just something I want to do for Sexy Beast, even if she didn't see the need—"

"No, I mean the other part. About how I can afford it now."

"Well, maybe not right this instant," he said, "but once the inheritance comes through. I'm going to get a grilled-veggie pita. You want something?"

He started to rise. I yanked on his arm to reseat him. "What inheritance? I didn't inherit anything."

He opened his mouth to speak but then just kind of froze like that while he ruminated on my words. Finally he said, "Hmm." He snagged his bottom lip in his teeth, a sure sign he had something up his sleeve.

An electric charge rippled up my body and buzzed my scalp. "What, Dom? What do you know?"

"Hasn't Sten called you yet?"

Sten. I grabbed my phone and checked to see whether Irene's lawyer had left voice mail. Yes, one message, just a few minutes ago after I'd dumped his latest call. I punched in my password and listened to Sten's leisurely, basso profundo delivery. He always spoke slowly, weighing each word, which invariably caused young, inexperienced attorneys for the other side to underestimate the old warhorse. When they learned to their detriment how wrong they were, it was usually too late.

Sten's message began, "Jane, you are a hard woman to get ahold of." In my agitated state it seemed to take Sten an hour and a half just to get those words out. My heart was a wild thing in a cage. He felt the need to add, "This is Sten Jakobsen." I slapped my forehead. *For the love of God, Sten, get to the point!* Clouds roiled through the skies, day turned to night, the stars winked out and the sun rose high in the sky once more while Sten drawled, "There are issues you and I need to discuss with respect to the disposition of Irene's assets, and also with respect to guardianship of that little dog of hers. If you would do me the kindness of phoning me at your earliest convenience—"

I cut off the message and searched the contact list in my phone with shaking hands. I went through the *J*'s twice looking for Jakobsen before it occurred to me he might be under *S*.

"Janey." Dom commandeered my phone and pushed a couple of buttons. "Just dial the missed call. Here."

Add cell phones to the list of things I hate. Even the dumb ones are too smart for me.

While I waited for Sten's secretary to pick up, I asked Dom, "How do you know I inherited something?"

He shrugged. "Irene told me."

"How could you have kept something like that from—"

"Jakobsen and Keller," came the female voice on the other end.

I identified myself and said I was returning Sten's call. He came on and I apologized for having missed his calls. Busy, busy, that's me, just too busy to answer my phone. My palms were so slick with sweat and my grip on the phone so fierce, I half expected it to shoot across the room. "You wanted to discuss, um, Irene's will?" I said.

"Yes. If you would be so good as to come down to the office," Sten said. "Are you free at two-thirty?"

"I'm not, unfortunately. I have a job in Jersey today. I actually have to get going soon. I can come in another time, but meanwhile can you just, um, give me the gist of it over the phone?"

Okay, no exaggeration, I watched Patrick take an order for a tofu Waldorf salad, dish out the glop, and make change for the customer before Sten got to the end of, "I suppose I can do that, yes, although if this conversation goes the way I anticipate, you and I will need to meet in person to process the paperwork."

I wiped one palm on my jeans, switched the phone to that hand, and wiped the other palm. Dom watched my face the whole time, waiting for me to react to whatever the lawyer was about to tell me. "Well, this certainly sounds, um, intriguing," I said.

"Intriguing, yes." Sten allowed himself a nice, leisurely chuckle. "I am sure you know how very special you were to Irene. She loved you like a granddaughter."

I cleared my throat. My eyes stung. I still couldn't quite fathom that she was gone. No good-byes, no period of illness to get used to the idea. Just gone. I shoved my free hand in my purse and rooted around. What happened to all my tissues? Dom pulled a napkin from the dispenser, and I flashed on Martin McAuliffe doing the same thing when I'd teared up at his bar last night. I dabbed my eyes. "You know I felt the same way about her."

"I know that, Jane," Sten said, "and Irene knew it, too. Now, to get to the gist of the matter, as you put it, there is the issue of her beloved pet."

I held my breath.

"Understand you are under no legal obligation to accept, but Irene wanted you to have full guardianship of her three-year-old toy poodle, Sexy Beast."

A gusty cry erupted from me and I clapped a hand over my mouth. The tears came then, tears of joy and relief, and I let them. Dom gently stroked my back. In a quick aside I told him, "SB's going to me."

"I know." Dom handed me more napkins. "You have the phone on speaker."

"What?" Mortified, I examined the device. My ex calmly touched a button bearing a speaker icon. I glanced around to see if any of the nearby customers had overheard my conversation with the lawyer. If they had, they were polite enough to pretend they hadn't.

"Jane?" Sten's deep voice continued. "Are you there?"

"I'm here, Sten, sorry."

"She wanted him to live with you because, aside from Irene herself, you have been his primary caretaker—a dependable and loving one, by all accounts. Sexy Beast has known you his whole life. Do you accept this responsibility?"

"Yes, of course," I said. "I'm thrilled to be his guardian."

"That is what I expected you to say, and I am glad you did, because Irene's other bequest regarding you hinged, as it were, on your accepting the guardianship role."

I frowned. "What does that mean?"

"She was determined to avoid, to the extent possible," he said, "any and all disruptions to her pet's life and routine."

"Well, I can tell you that he's already gotten settled at my apartment, no problem. He sniffed every corner of the place and made himself right at home."

"I am not surprised to hear it," Sten drawled. "In my experience, dogs are generally adaptable in situations like this. Irene did not agree, at least not where Sexy Beast was concerned."

A pause. "I must say, I feel a little foolish every time I say that animal's name."

Dom was making "get to the point" gestures, aimed not at me but at the slow-talking lawyer on the other end of the line.

"Okay, so when you say the other part of Irene's bequest is dependent on my taking Sexy Beast," I said, "that means what precisely?"

"Irene gave you her house."

That was funny. It almost sounded like he said, *Irene gave you her house*. "Excuse me," I said, "could you repeat that?"

"You have inherited the property situated at Three Rugby Place, Crystal Harbor, New York. You will need to come in to the office so that I may transfer the property to you by deed."

I sat dumbstruck. Dom said, "Don't faint on me, Janey," and took my free hand. I clutched his fingers with bruising force, but he didn't flinch.

"I—I—" I shook my head to clear it. "Are you serious, Sten? Irene left me her *house*?"

"There is a second condition," he said, "aside from the primary requirement that you first agree to be guardian of her pet, which you have met. While Sexy Beast is alive, you are required to occupy the property and are prohibited from selling it. To this end, your ownership will be subject to a life estate held by Sexy Beast."

"What does that mean?" I asked.

I had to hand it to Sten. He managed not to crack up as he said, "Essentially it means that Sexy Beast is the owner of the property until his death, when it will revert to you. I will explain in more detail when you come in to sign the documents."

My mind raced. "This was, well, astoundingly generous of

Irene, but I don't see how it can work. I can't afford to maintain a house like that. My annual income won't even cover the property taxes."

"Irene provided for all expenses related to the property. You will receive one million five hundred thousand dollars—"

For the second time during our conversation, I clapped a hand over my mouth. It's not a gesture I can recall having made before in my life. Dom chuckled. Apparently he'd known all this for some time.

"—to be applied to taxes," Sten continued, "utilities, repairs, maintenance of the grounds and house, and of course all expenses related to Sexy Beast. His food, veterinary care, and so forth."

"I don't know what to say," I breathed.

"One point five million might sound like a lot of money," Sten soberly intoned, "but it is expected that you will spend only the investment income it produces. If you invest conservatively and leave the principal untouched, you should be able to enjoy a comfortable life in that house until the end of your days, should you so choose."

"I…I wish I'd known all this before she…" My voice was raspy with emotion. "I wish I could thank her."

We said good-bye and he transferred me to his secretary to make an appointment. I hung up and in a tone of wonder said, "I'm a millionaire."

8
Grope, Grope, Grope

OKAY, I KNEW I wasn't a *millionaire* millionaire. I was in no position to, say, cart half a mil to the track and put it on Lucky Mermaid to win. I did the arithmetic. Sten was right. The best way to ensure that my million and a half would support 3 Rugby Place for decades to come was to put it to work earning interest and dividends and stuff like that—can you tell I know squat about investing?—and to spend only the interest and dividends and stuff like that. That took care of SB and the house, but I still had to feed and clothe myself and pour gas in my Civic. Quitting my day job was not an option.

Which is why I spent the rest of the day in West Orange, New Jersey, pretending to be the Mysterious Other Woman in the life of one Theodore Marcus Seabrook, recently deceased. I tarted myself up with big hair, a slinky green halter dress, high-heeled do-me pumps, and, God help me, false eyelashes that felt like a family of caterpillars had nested on my face.

Ted had engaged me for this assignment around Thanksgiving after learning he had at most six months to live. The prospect of dying didn't frighten him—he'd lived a long and fruitful life and had few regrets. One of those regrets was having remained faithfully married for twenty-two years to Margaret Seabrook, a self-absorbed dumpling of a woman who, once she realized her husband was strolling toward the exit sign, couldn't resist taunting him with the revelation of her myriad cheap affairs, starting with a three-way involving a pair of virile croupiers during their Las Vegas honeymoon. *Jackpot!*

I was to remain conspicuously weepy during the funeral and graveside service, then take my act back to the home Ted had shared with Margaret, where family and friends would gather to get ossified and mourn the dearly departed cuckold.

I'd met with Ted again shortly before his death, and he'd laughed himself silly imagining the look on the Widow Seabrook's doughy mug when she came face-to-face with his hotsy-totsy longtime mistress. See? I do so help people find peace and closure.

Ted got his money's worth, let me tell you. Yours truly was the talk of the funeral. During most of the reception I sat surrounded by a cluster of his inebriated buddies, and received more sympathy, tequila shots, and phone numbers than I knew what to do with. By the time the shindig wound down around two in the morning—these guys knew how to party a pal into the afterworld!—Margaret looked like she wanted to kick someone down the stairs. Well, me. Ted had assured me she was too well bred to start a catfight in front of all their friends and relatives, and he was right. Altogether, it was one of my more enjoyable assignments. I only wish my client could have been there to witness it.

I slept late the next morning, as millionaires are wont to do. In my case it was because I didn't get home until after three. I drove to my folks' place to check up on SB, who was curled up on my dad's lap and too absorbed in *Meerkat Manor* to pay me much mind. I decided to leave him in their capable hands while I went to Irene's house—I doubt I'll ever stop thinking of it as Irene's house—to execute my damage-control plan.

The day was cold and windy, with flurries expected. Snow in April always ticks me off. Mother Nature teases you into thinking it's spring, then sucker-punches you the instant you lower your guard. I left my car in the parking area around the side of the house and let myself in through the garage. It was so strange to walk through the house and realize it belonged to me now. I assumed the contents were included. I'd find out the details when I met with Sten on Friday.

I headed straight for the file cabinet in Irene's home office. I pulled it open and zeroed in on the file labeled *Delaney, Jane*. That is, I would have if the file had been there. *Credit Cards* now rubbed shoulders with *Dentist*. Could I have misfiled it last time I was there? I pawed through the drawer and then for good measure checked the bottom drawer, though I didn't see how it could have made its way there.

My file was gone. Twenty-two years' worth of work orders, including a handful that could be considered questionable or even—and yes, I was thinking of that final one—downright incriminating.

The padre hadn't left his card this time. He hadn't needed to. Martin McAuliffe was the only person with both the motive and the requisite skill necessary to break in to this house, for the second time, and have his way with Irene's file cabinet.

What an idiot I was. I should have gone directly here from Janey's Place yesterday and grabbed that file, even if it meant being late for Ted's funeral. I'd underestimated Martin. He'd made it clear he was prepared to drag me along for the ride if I made trouble for him. This was obviously a preemptive strike, yet another instance when he anticipated my move and swooped in to beat me to the prize.

I wondered if Patrick had already gone to the cops. I might find myself having some interesting conversations with the local gendarmerie before this day was through. On the plus side, there was no way Martin could know about sketchy assignments I'd taken on behalf of other clients besides Irene. And trust me, those clients would be the last ones to volunteer information to the cops. *Yes, Officer, I paid Ms. Delaney to surreptitiously grind my brother's ashes into the coffee-stained carpet of the Crystal Harbor police station.*

The brother in question had had what you might call an unfulfilling relationship with the Crystal Harbor PD. How, you ask, did I accomplish this audacious feat without getting caught? Have you ever watched *The Great Escape*? The guy who thought up those dirt-dumping pants was a certifiable genius.

Well, chalk up another win for the pilfering padre. Speaking of unfulfilling relationships.

A thick file folder marked *Poker* caught my eye, reminding me that the annual Crystal Harbor Historical Society Poker Tournament was being held that day. Out of curiosity I briefly flipped through the contents of the file and found handwritten notes on all of Irene's Poker Posse members, going back nearly three decades to the birth of the Posse. She'd cataloged her friends' betting habits, skills and weaknesses, the distinctive tells that revealed when they were bluffing—in short, anything and everything that might give her an advantage at the poker table.

I supposed I shouldn't be surprised that a player as formidable as Irene McAuliffe would take this kind of obsessive approach to the game. I replaced the file without reading it. I didn't anticipate testing my pitiful poker skills against any of those folks.

I started to slide the drawer shut when the word *Will* jumped out at me. Holy cow, here it was. Well, of course Irene had kept a copy of her own will. If I ever found reason to make a will myself, I'd probably store a copy in this very file cabinet.

Well, I guess I'd have to make a will now, right? Isn't that what women of property do?

I slid the document out of the folder and scanned the first page, hoping to see my name pop out at me. Pop it did, after the first part authorizing the executor to pay all just debts and funeral expenses. Irene had indeed bequeathed to me the property situated at 3 Rugby Place, including the entire contents of the house, with the exception of the automobiles. And no joke, her beloved toy poodle really did hold a life estate in the property. She'd also set aside $1.5 million for upkeep and SB's care. It was right there in eye-crossing legalese.

In the back of my mind was the knowledge that when and if I ever sold the house, I'd be a millionaire in the for-real sense, this place being valued conservatively at close to four million simoleons. But since that sale depended on Sexy Beast no longer being in the picture, I chose not to think about it.

I stood there with a goofy grin on my face, drinking in the black-and-white proof that I hadn't dreamed the whole thing. I read and reread the clauses, then read them again just to make sure the words hadn't evaporated. Out of curiosity, I flipped to the next page. The name printed there didn't so much pop as catapult itself.

Patrick Edmund O'Rourke.

What was Colette's son doing in Irene McAuliffe's will? When I read further and saw what he was doing there, I took a wobbly step backward until my knees connected with the cream-colored leather swivel chair, which I sank into like a sack of spuds.

Irene had left everything else to Patrick: all her moola except for what she'd set aside for property upkeep, and I happened to know that my one and a half mil represented a small fraction of her assets. I had just assumed the rest would go to relatives—maybe to charities, too, although in life she'd always been a stingy donor, given her wealth. The only regular recipient of her largesse had been the Crystal Harbor Historical Society. If I was now a millionaire, Patrick was a multimillionaire. Plus he got all three luxury cars and the contents of a safe-deposit box.

But why? He and Irene weren't connected except through Colette, and to my knowledge, Irene hadn't set eyes on her ex-friend's son since before the big rift nine years earlier. I thought about my conversation with Patrick yesterday when he'd told me he didn't need the hundred grand the brooch could bring him. I'd assumed it was his pride talking. Yeah, pride and about sixteen million pictures of George Washington.

Then I remembered what Dom had told me. Six months ago, Irene had gotten him to give Patrick a job. I couldn't help wondering whether Colette had known about that favor, or this unfathomable bequest.

I continued reading and discovered a third beneficiary. If the last one made me gape in astonishment, this one made me cringe. Irene had left Maria a hundred bucks. As in *one* followed by two, count 'em two, zeroes. After twenty-eight years of loyal service. Jeez, if she'd wanted to insult the woman, why hadn't she just left her the contents of her junk drawer? Irene had promised her housekeeper she was being taken care of in her will. Maria obviously thought she'd be able to retire on the bequest. I closed my eyes and gave a sad little shake of the head. *Irene, would it have killed you to do the right thing?* Okay, bad choice of words.

I'd risen and started replacing the will in its folder when a noise downstairs paralyzed me. I listened intently. There it was again. Someone was walking around in the house. The footfalls sounded too heavy for Maria. I went to the window, which overlooked the parking area near the garage. I saw only my car. Maria always parked there, never out front.

Naturally, my first thought was to call 911. It would have helped if I hadn't left my purse with my phone in it on the dining room sideboard as I passed through from the garage. And unfortunately for me, Irene had been a modern woman with no land line in the house.

On reflex I looked around for anything that could serve as a weapon. My gaze landed on Irene's antique brass letter opener. Okay, no. That kind of thing might work great in old movies, but there was no way I was confronting a burglar with a flimsy thing like that. Then I remembered reading somewhere that a shot of hairspray in the eyes could be an effective self-defense weapon. What the heck, it was better than nothing.

I slipped into the master bath next door and quickly located Irene's hairspray. I shook it to make sure my weapon was loaded, then crept across the hall to one of the guest rooms overlooking the front of the house. Peering down from the window, I spied an old-looking blue sedan parked in the circular courtyard. From up there I didn't recognize the make.

I asked myself what kind of burglar parked right in front of the place, in plain sight. As far as I knew, no one besides Maria had keys. Well, except for Jonah, for evening house calls when Irene might not feel like answering the door. And Jonah's ride was a new-every-year Audi A8.

Whoever it was, he made no effort at silence. He probably assumed the place was vacant, since Irene was gone and my car was parked out of view. If he was a burglar, he would figure out he wasn't alone as soon as he came across my purse. At that point, one of two things would happen. If he was a nice burglar, he would leave. If he was a not-nice burglar, he would find me in whatever hiding place I'd crawled into, in which case I doubted a can of hairspray would do me much good. My best bet was to sneak downstairs, get to my purse—my car keys were in there, too—and get the hell out of the house.

And yeah, I know what you're thinking, because I was thinking it too. The padre. Last time he'd taken only paperwork. The time before that he'd not only gone away empty-handed but had actually left his gentleman's calling card behind, the politest version in recorded history of a raised middle finger. Not that larceny was beyond him. This was the guy who'd boldly swiped a piece of jewelry worth a cool hundred grand, after all.

Could he have returned for more jewelry or perhaps Irene's art collection? Somehow I couldn't picture the Harley owner I'd traded verbal barbs with at Tierney's Publick House behind the wheel of the beater currently parked out front—unless he needed the beater's trunk space for whatever he intended to carry out of the house that day.

I figured there was an eighty to ninety percent chance it was the padre down there. For what it was worth, I hadn't gotten a sense of physical danger from him. He might take pleasure in cutting me to ribbons verbally, but he didn't seem the type to do so literally.

I held my breath and tiptoed onto the balcony overlooking the foyer, hairspray at the ready as if it could possibly be effective from up there. I heard the person moving around the kitchen. Quiet as a cat, I descended the curved staircase and inched through the foyer. To get to the dining room and garage, I'd have to pass the entrance to the kitchen. I gripped the hairspray, my finger on the nozzle, and gingerly peeked inside.

My view of the intruder was blocked by the open door of the refrigerator. I heard the contents being shifted around. Was he looking for a snack? Before I could slip into the dining room, the fridge door banged shut and he saw me.

Patrick O'Rourke and I hollered in unison. My finger tightened reflexively on the nozzle, shooting hairspray directly into my face. I squeezed my stinging eyes shut and barked out every cuss word I knew, then started over at the beginning of the list.

"You about gave me a heart attack," Patrick said.

"I gave *you* a heart attack?" I heard water running and then he placed wet paper towels in my hand. I scrubbed my eyes and face, and said, "What are you doing here? How did you get in?"

"I used my keys."

I shouldn't be surprised he had keys to Irene's house, considering the last will and testament I'd just read. "There's a doorbell, Patrick," I said. "You might not be aware, but this is my house now."

"Sten told me," he said. "I didn't think you'd be here."

Yet he chose to let himself in anyway. Why?

Now that my vision was clearing, I saw that Patrick looked

like anything but a man who'd just inherited a fortune. Dark bags hung under his eyes. His skin looked gray and he was unshaven. He didn't look like the same man I'd spoken with yesterday at Janey's Place.

"Aren't you supposed to be at work?" I asked.

"I called in sick."

"What about Cheyenne?"

His tired gaze sharpened. "What about her?"

"Well, you know, she was so upset yesterday," I said. "I hope she's okay."

"Oh. Yeah, she's fine." After a moment he added, "Female trouble. She gets emotional."

Something about the way Patrick cast about for that explanation made me think Cheyenne had not, in fact, been suffering from The Worst Period Ever, but I let it go. I offered congratulations on his inheritance, and he murmured something that sounded like thanks.

"Listen," I said, "you can tell me if I'm sticking my nose where it doesn't belong, but I didn't think you and Irene had anything to do with each other. Especially after that big falling out with your mother. And yet, wow. She left you nearly everything."

He looked even more uncomfortable, if that was possible. "I'd rather not talk about it." He rubbed his bristly jaw. "Out of respect for Irene's wishes. She wanted to keep certain things private."

"Fair enough." My mind raced. Patrick was around sixty, a lot younger than Irene, but an affair wasn't outside the realm of possibility. But with Colette's son, of all people?

What was it Martin had said at the bar Thursday night? *Don't worry about Patrick O'Rourke. He's going to be fine, mermaid or no mermaid.* Which meant the padre's snooping hadn't been confined to those work orders. He'd read Irene's will and probably every other sensitive document in the place. He'd known about Patrick's inheritance, and mine as well. Before I did.

"I have to say, Patrick, if I came into a windfall like that, the first thing I'd do is quit my job."

He shrugged. "The best thing for me is to keep working. I need the routine, someplace to go every day. It's not a bad job."

"I guess it's good for Cheyenne, too," I said, "for the same reason."

He shrugged again. His gaze slid away. For someone who'd been completely open about his daughter and her problems not twenty-four hours earlier, he was surprisingly closemouthed now.

"Have you gone to the cops yet?" I asked.

His face paled further. "What do you mean?"

"About the brooch? To report the theft?" Maybe he really was sick. I prayed it wasn't drugs. I'd assumed all that was behind him. "Patrick, are you okay? Do you want to sit down?"

"I changed my mind. I'm not involving the cops." He pulled Martin's calling card out of his jeans pocket and handed it to me. The thing was creased and one corner was torn. It was really getting a workout.

"Why?" I said. "I mean, I know the brooch is a drop in the bucket compared to what you inherited, but yesterday when we talked, you seemed determined to pursue this guy." I wagged the card.

"I did some thinking." He kept glancing toward the doorway, clearly eager to get away. "It's like I said at Ahearn's. I'm not gonna put my family through all that. I better be going."

"Did you get what you came for?"

He flinched. "What?"

"You must have had some reason for dropping by." I nodded toward the fridge. "What were you looking for in there?"

"Nothing. I… I was thirsty. A bottle of water."

Wordlessly I pointed to the ice and water dispensers on the outside of the refrigerator door. "What were you really looking for, Patrick?"

"I wasn't looking for anything." He tried to smile. It was painful to watch. "Not sure what you're getting at."

The hard drive in my head automatically sought a connection between Patrick O'Rourke and the refrigerator belonging to Irene McAuliffe. Bingo! "You were bringing her smoothies from Janey's Place," I said.

He looked like I'd kicked him. He shook his head. "No. That wasn't me. I mean… Irene didn't go in for that health-food stuff."

"I know she didn't, but she was having indigestion or something and you brought them to her as a favor." I smiled, trying to put him at ease. "Did they help?"

He shook his head again, edging away. "I gotta go. I don't know anything about that."

I stood in the front doorway and watched him take off in his blue Hyundai. The instant he was out of sight I mentally kicked myself. I hadn't asked him to return the house keys. I'd been too distracted by his inept fibbing. No wonder he'd ended up behind bars during his hell-raising youth. His guilt flashed like a beacon before he even opened his mouth. His words during the wake came back to me. *I couldn't manage a poker face to save my life.*

I made a mental list of the folks besides myself who had keys to my new home: Patrick, Maria, and Jonah. And they were only the ones I knew about. Then there was the guy who seemed to be able to stroll through locked doors whenever the mood struck him. The padre needed his lock-picking wings clipped. Okay, lousy metaphor, but you get my point.

I went into the dining room, retrieved my phone, and called information for the numbers of the local locksmith and the home-security company Irene used. A few minutes later I had appointments for later in the day. All the doors would be refitted with state-of-the-art, unpickable locks, and the security system would be similarly upgraded. For now, I'd slap it on a credit card. I hoped that by the time the bill came, I'd have access to the property-upkeep funds.

I made one more call, though I dreaded it. Maria picked up on the third ring. Her tone turned frosty when she heard my voice. I had no doubt she knew what Patrick and I had inherited. She'd probably demanded the information when Sten gave her the news about her own pathetic bequest.

"Maria," I said, "I need to know something. Do you remember on Thursday morning when we were talking about that orange smoothie and you said he was always bringing them to Irene?"

A long pause. I could almost hear her wondering why I was bothering her with something so piddling. "What about it?" she finally asked.

"I need to know who that was. Who was bringing the smoothies?"

She sighed. "Patrick O'Rourke."

I nodded to myself. "When did he start bringing them?"

"About a week before Easter. A fresh one every day. Why?"

"I just want to… thank him." So the smoothie deliveries started about ten days before Irene died. "Do you know why Colette's son would have been visiting Irene? I mean, since she and Colette hadn't really been—"

"Not my business," she said.

"Okay. Well. Thanks—"

"Two weeks." Maria's voice was tight. "That's all she let me take."

"Excuse me?"

"I had three babies," she said, "and each time Mrs. M gave me two weeks maternity leave, like she was doing me this big favor. And let me tell you, she resented it. When little Joey came along… oh, he was so tiny, you should have seen him, five weeks early… I asked Mrs. M could I take a little more time, or at least change my schedule, like flextime, you know, not nine to five. You know what she said? She said, Maria, you'll have plenty of time off, 'cause if you do that, you'll be looking for another job."

Before I could formulate a response, she added, "She paid me for the two weeks, but that's not the point. My sister raised my children along with her own. Once, I heard Joey call her 'Mama.' I locked myself in the bathroom and cried."

I closed my eyes and resisted the urge to apologize on behalf of her dead employer, for this and all the indignities Maria had endured for nearly three decades.

"She told me I would be well taken care of after she was gone," Maria continued. "That's how she put it. 'Well taken care of.' I thought that meant I could retire, get to enjoy my grandchildren while they're still little." She spat the next words like a foul taste. "One hundred dollars. Everything went to you and Mrs. O'Rourke's good-for-nothing son."

I took a calming breath and said, "Maria, I want you to know that my offer still stands. I can write you a referral, maybe ask around to see if anyone needs a—"

She hung up on me. I blew out a gusty exhalation. Could I blame her?

I certainly didn't need or want a full-time housekeeper, and I doubted she'd agree to work for me in any event, but maybe one of Irene's friends needed someone. I made a mental note to see what I could do.

I returned to the kitchen and stood staring at the contents of the refrigerator. Again I got that nagging sense that something was missing, that some item had mysteriously disappeared after I'd shifted things around in there gathering treats for SB and spilling that smoothie. I concentrated hard for a few seconds, then gave a disgusted shake of the head. Not a good time to get sidetracked by my imagination.

There was only one fridge-related question I needed to concern myself with: Why had Patrick lied about bringing Irene smoothies? On second thought, make that two questions: Why had he snuck into this house to search for that last one, the one I'd accidentally knocked over? I had to assume that's what he was looking for, considering he lied about having brought them.

I reached into the fridge for a can of orange soda and grabbed a couple of biscotti from the cookie jar. Not my number-one choice for breakfast, but Irene didn't stock Fruity Pebbles, so I had to make do. I sauntered through my game room and into my living room. I crossed my mosaic-patterned silk rug, opened my hand-woven silk drapes to let the sun stream through my towering Palladian window, sank back into my oversize sofa upholstered in mushroom-colored linen, and propped my feet on my glass-topped coffee table with the burl-wood cube base. My my, I could get used to this.

Outwardly I was the picture of indolence, slumped into the cushions sucking on my soda and chasing errant cookie crumbs. All the action was occurring inside my cranium, where pieces of a jigsaw puzzle bumped and shoved and jockeyed for position. An image was beginning to form, and it was an ugly one.

I'd never known Irene McAuliffe to suffer a stomachache, yet in the days before her death she'd started chewing antacids. She'd also been exceptionally irritable—because of stomach pain or, as her personal physician seemed to think, a worsening cardiac condition? Maria had told me the smoothies Patrick brought were supposed to be good for her stomach but tasted terrible. Yet the one I'd had at Janey's Place was delicious.

Was it possible the ones Patrick had brought Irene diverged in some significant way from the original recipe? As in a secret ingredient meant only for the woman whose death would make him a multimillionaire?

And for that matter, had Patrick known he was going to inherit her wealth? Had she told him ahead of time or had he learned about it only after her death when Sten called him? I couldn't ignore the fact that he had a sketchy past which included run-ins with the law.

In any event, the smoothie he'd come searching for was long gone. I'd rinsed the dregs down the kitchen sink myself and tossed the cup in the garbage.

Abruptly I sat up and was rewarded with an epic soda belch, the kind that erupts violently via your nostrils and makes your eyes water. Yeah, that's me, Lady Jane Delaney.

I slammed the soda can onto the coffee table—no coaster for

Lady Jane—and ran back into the kitchen. The under-sink garbage can was empty. What had Maria said last time I saw her? She was going to tidy up and take out the garbage. I experienced a moment of panic as I tried to recall the garbage-collection schedule for this neighborhood. I was pretty sure it was Thursdays and Mondays, around six a.m. Which meant the last pickup would have been a few hours before Maria tossed the kitchen trash, which meant the bag with the smoothie cup should still be in one of the two big garbage cans by the side of the house.

I went out through the garage and stood in the blowing snow flurries, gloomily considering the hulking garbage cans and their contents before returning to the kitchen to locate Maria's rubber dishwashing gloves. I buttoned my suede jacket and pushed up the sleeves, went back outside, and set to work searching for that last Janey's Place cup. I pulled out the first white garbage bag and tried to untie it. No such luck. I tore a hole in it and peeked inside. Papers and bathroom trash. I set it aside and repeated the process with the bag under it, reeling back from the stink when I tore it open.

I must be certifiable, pawing through gross, days-old kitchen garbage in this kind of weather. I turned my head, sucked in a deep breath and held it, then groped the contents, shoving aside rotten orange peels, fish bones, wilted salad, a liquefied tomato, grimy paper towels, and a dead bouquet of birthday flowers I'd given Irene almost two weeks earlier. I squatted there staring at those now-shriveled pink roses, recalling her smile of delight as I'd handed them to her. I felt the ghost of her warm kiss on my cheek. My eyes stung from more than the swirling snow.

You are not going to do this, I thought. *Blubbering will accomplish nothing. The best thing you can do for her right now is to find that stupid cup.*

The sensible part of me asked, *And then what?* I shushed her. Sensible Jane could be such a nag.

I worked my way to the bottom of the bag. No Janey's Place cup. The wind whipped my hair into my face. I tried shaking it back, tried nudging it back with my shoulder. I would become a godforsaken vegan before I touched my hair with those icky gloves. I lifted the ripped bag to place it back into the can, but the wind had other ideas and I found myself sprinting after tumbling eggshells and paper napkins.

I slammed the lid on the first can and started in on the second. Hold breath, tear bag, grope grope grope. I began to think the cup had entered an alternate universe when suddenly it appeared in my gloved hand. It was crushed, but clinging to the inside was the prettiest thing I'd seen all day: a residue of dried orange smoothie.

9
More Groping

WHERE THE HECK was Sten? I stood just inside the entrance to the ballroom of the Crystal Harbor Country Club, scanning the ten elliptical poker tables for the lawyer's distinctive tall frame. He had to be here. He always entered the annual charity tournament, even though, to my knowledge, he'd never come close to first place or even been one of the top five players, the lucky few who strolled out of there with serious swag and insufferably smug grins.

The prize for first place was always a luxury vehicle, which is how Irene came to own those three swell cars. Over the years she'd won a grand total of nine such pricey rides. Each time she'd had to sell one of the older ones just to make room in her three-car garage.

Speaking of which, I had to arrange a time for Patrick to pick up the vehicles he'd inherited. Considering my blossoming suspicions, I wasn't eager for another one-on-one with him. Maybe I'd ask Dom to be present when I unlocked the garage and handed over the keys.

Colette had come in first place almost as many times as Irene, which is the only reason she and Burt had been able to drive their

BMW. More often than not, they sold the prize, cash in hand being of more use to them than another car.

Second prize was most often a Rolex or something of that sort, and third prize was a paid vacation for two to Hawaii or the like. Third and fourth prizes were almost always generous gift certificates to Broadway plays and high-end restaurants.

The powers that be capped the number of players at one hundred, and invariably there was a waiting list. This tournament enjoyed quite a reputation, and players flocked to it from as far away as Connecticut and Pennsylvania. The buy-in was five thousand dollars. Eighty percent of the resulting haul went to the Historical Society for its work in landmark preservation and maintaining the town's little museum and botanical gardens. The rest went to the prizes.

The Historical Society didn't skimp on the amenities, starting with the elegant country-club venue. Professional dealers dealt the cards and narrated the play-by-play. Uniformed wait staff circulated with top-shelf drinks. Masseuses wandered from player to player, dispensing shoulder rubs. On the other side of the expansive ballroom, buffet tables groaned under a gut-busting assortment of your snootier snacks, everything from shrimp and avocado sushi rolls at one end to bourbon-pecan mini tarts at the other. In truth, the buffet served mostly as a consolation prize for those who wiped out in the first hour or two of play. The most serious, skillful players weren't thinking about sushi as they concentrated on the game and watched their stacks of chips grow.

There was always a buzz of excitement as players made their bets and won and lost hands, but this year the air crackled with an unprecedented energy. The players seemed more intense, more driven. It wasn't hard to figure out why. Within the past week, the tournament had lost its two most formidable players, Colette O'Rourke and Irene McAuliffe, long recognized as the practically unbeatable grande dames of the game in these here parts. Accomplished players who'd watched the coveted top prize go to one old lady or the other year after year now had a reasonable shot at taking home this year's tricked-out red Mercedes and the bragging rights that went with it.

The Wild West had come to Crystal Harbor, New York.

I didn't see Sten, but I did spy my ex-husband at a distant table. When I noticed who sat next to him, my heart tripped over its own aorta. Martin McAuliffe. Automatically my fingers slipped into my jacket pocket and felt the battered calling card Patrick had handed back to me an hour earlier. What was the padre doing here? I couldn't imagine where he'd gotten the dough for the buy-in.

On second thought, I could imagine it all too well. When you fenced a stolen bauble worth a hundred grand, you could afford to throw away a measly five thou on something like this. The tournament had started about an hour and a half ago and not only was he still in the game, but he had a respectable pile of chips in front of him. I frowned. Martin had more chips than Dom did, and Dom was a skilled player. I watched as the two men tossed some of those chips into the center. Martin said something and they both laughed.

Just then Martin glanced up, his blue eyes homing in on me like heat-seeking missiles. He lifted his glass of dark beer in a silent toast. Dom looked from Martin to me, his curiosity clearly piqued as he pondered the connection between his ex-wife and his new poker buddy.

Well, ponder away, I thought. *To hell with you both.* I skirted the tables, still hoping to find Sten. The other Posse members were present and accounted for. Jonah Diamond and Sophie Halperin shared a table with four other players and four empty seats representing folks who'd already bottomed out. Jonah appeared to be holding his own, but you wouldn't know it by his glum, preoccupied expression. Who knew? Maybe that was his revealing tell. If I perused Irene's exhaustive notes on her Poker Posse, the entry on him might read something along the lines of, *Jonah looks like his dog ran away when he's holding a full house or better.*

Nina Wallace, in her capacity as president of the Historical Society, basically ran the tournament. Her responsibilities kept her too busy to play, which I'd assumed would irk her. However, she appeared to relish her role as Empress of All She Surveyed. At that particular moment she was consulting a clipboard and taking stock of the players left at each table.

I made my way toward the buffet area, where a dozen or so people stood snacking and chatting. These were the players who'd forfeited all their chips, and their five grand, early in the game. Sten Jakobsen was easy to spot among this crowd. He was six four, his blond hair and trim beard now mostly white. Intelligent amber eyes gazed out through wire-rimmed glasses. Age had diminished neither his regal posture nor his sharpness of wit. In short, the man had presence.

Sten kissed my cheek and gave my hand a fatherly squeeze. I'd been about to ask if we could find a quiet place to talk, but he beat me to it, handing his empty wineglass to a passing waiter and leading me to a corner near some kind of potted tree.

"Is that…" He squinted at the sleeve of my suede jacket. "Coffee grounds?"

I looked. Well, wasn't that just lovely. I'd been in such a hurry to find Sten, I hadn't noticed. There could be a rotten banana peel clinging to my back, for all I knew. I brushed the grounds off into the potted tree.

"I did not expect to see you before our meeting next Friday," Sten said. He asked how I was doing, with his usual slow, measured delivery. "And the little dog?" he added.

I bit back a smile, knowing his aversion to uttering the little dog's name. "Sexy Beast is fine. I'm here to ask you a favor. You're the executor of Irene's estate. You're the one who can make decisions. Um, sensitive decisions."

"Let us cut to the chase," he said. "What is on your mind, Jane?"

"Has Irene been… Has the cremation occurred yet?" I held my breath.

"Possibly. It is scheduled for today."

"Oh God," I groaned. "Can you call them to stop it? If it's not too late?"

If this seasoned lawyer was surprised by my request, he didn't show it. "I could try if there is a compelling reason to do so."

Don't talk so damn slowly! I wanted to scream. In the time it took Sten to get to the end of a thought, Irene could go from being a hundred-thirty-pound dead person to a two-pound dead person.

"I have reason to believe someone might have poisoned Irene." There. I'd said it out loud for the first time. It didn't feel as weird as I'd thought it would. Sten didn't react. Either he had a high regard for my judgment or he was really good at hiding his disdain.

"You want an autopsy performed," he said.

I nodded, glancing around to make sure our conversation was still private. "I know Jonah signed the death certificate, I know he believes it was a heart attack. I'm not questioning his expertise, I just… There are things I can't ignore."

"What would these things be?" he asked.

I didn't like implicating Patrick without firm proof, but I had no choice. I told Sten all about why I suspected the smoothies in general and Patrick in particular.

He pursed his lips. "It is not an overwhelming amount of evidence."

"I know that, and it's why we need the autopsy. They'll check for chemicals that shouldn't be there, right? Isn't that part of it?"

"A toxicology screen is generally part of the process, yes," Sten said, "but results can take weeks to come back." He started to shake his head. "Jane, I do not think—"

"I have this, too." I pulled the crushed Janey's Place cup, securely double-bagged, out of my purse. I told him about my budding career as a dumpster diver. "This is what Patrick was looking for. So he could get rid of the evidence." In a small voice I added, "Maybe," and wondered how big a fool I was making of myself.

He sighed. "Well, if we are talking chain of evidence, there are definite problems with a cup pulled out of old garbage by a civilian."

"Meaning it could be contaminated," I said, "or deliberately messed with. I get that. But if you can get an autopsy done, and they find something suspicious in her system, they can compare it to what's in here."

I handed him the bag, and to his credit, he didn't shy away from taking it. He turned it in his hand, examining it and thinking. I saw the beginning of another negative head-shake.

"Sten." I took a step closer to him, lowered my volume. I wasn't beyond playing dirty. "I know I'm not the only one Irene cared about. I know you two had a close friendship."

His gaze snapped to my face. Suddenly he appeared even taller, if that was possible. I wondered if I'd gone too far, but I wasn't about to backpedal now. Too much was at stake.

"Maybe not so much in recent years," I continued, looking him right in the eye, "but for a long time you and Irene maintained a very close, very discreet… friendship."

Sten had been married to the same woman for more than forty years. I happened to know that for the last thirty-eight of those years she'd been in and out of mental institutions and required a full-time aide at home. Theirs hadn't been a marriage in the real sense for decades. Yet to his credit, he'd taken care of her in the most tender fashion the whole time. I didn't blame him for any happiness he'd found with Irene, and I had no desire to cause him trouble.

He said, "I fail to see what bearing that has—"

"It's only that I know how much she meant to you." I beseeched him with my eyes. "We owe her this, Sten. If there's even the smallest doubt." I paused to collect myself. "You can tell me what an idiot I am later, after they find nothing. In the meantime, we have to try."

He looked at me steadily. "You should have gone to law school."

"You'll do it?"

A ghost of a smile. "If I say no, I shall never hear the end of it."

From me or from his conscience, I knew, now that I'd sown the seeds of suspicion in his mind.

"Excuse me." Sten produced his cell phone, located a number

on his contact list, and had a short, pointed conversation with Lenny Ahearn. "Call me back either way, Lenny." He hung up and told me, "Irene has already been transferred to the crematory. He is going to cancel the cremation if it is not too late, and bring her back to the funeral home."

I nodded. "But why the funeral home? Shouldn't she be taken to the medical examiner's office?"

He shook his head. "The ME would not be interested. Irene's personal physician said she died of natural causes, and there is not enough evidence to the contrary. I can arrange for a private autopsy. I know a good pathologist who does this sort of thing. She can do it right at Ahearn's."

I chewed my lip. "But the toxicology results can take weeks, you said. Anything can happen in the meantime." Like the murderer cramming sixteen million bucks into his Samsonite and hightailing it to Venezuela.

"We would be using a private lab," he said, "and I can put a rush on it. At the very least, we should have preliminary results within a few days, even if the full report takes longer."

"Sten, I'm dying to know why Irene left nearly everything to Patrick O'Rourke. What's their connection?"

"I appreciate your curiosity," he said, "but I do not feel it is appropriate for me to answer that question."

Can't say I was surprised, but I plowed on. "She also gave him the cars and the contents of a safe-deposit box. Any idea what's in the box?"

"That is between Irene and Patrick."

I sighed. "Well, can you at least tell me whether Patrick knew he was going to inherit this enormous bequest? Do you know whether she mentioned it to him before she died?"

Sten nodded. "He knew."

Finally, an answer. And a helpful one at that.

His phone rang. My heart stopped. He listened for a few moments, thanked Lenny, and hung up. I could tell nothing from his maddeningly unreadable expression.

"Well?" I asked.

"She will be back at Ahearn's within the hour," he said, and I almost fainted with relief.

I grabbed his big, dry hand and squeezed it. I swallowed a lump of emotion. "Thank you, Sten."

It might have been my imagination, but his eyes looked suspiciously shiny. He cleared his throat. "I shall call Joyce Huang. She is the pathologist I mentioned." He indicated the bagged takeout cup. "And I shall get this to her."

I hugged Sten, feeling lighter of mind than when I'd entered the ballroom. I wasn't alone in this. Sten Jakobsen was in my camp, and he didn't think I was crazy.

I detoured to the buffet tables, suddenly ravenous, wondering if anyone would notice if I opened my big purse and shoveled in a platter of Thai spring rolls. I'd just popped a steak-and-Stilton appetizer into my pie-hole when a pair of long arms snaked around my waist from behind. *The padre!* The steak tried to lodge itself halfway down my gullet, resulting in a fit of coughing and eye-squirting, plus some pointless pounding on my back by the owner of the arms, who spun me to face him.

Dom grinned. "You okay? Went down the wrong way, huh?"

"I wasn't expecting to be grabbed like that." I also wasn't expecting to be held in a light embrace as my ex was now doing.

"There's another reason to avoid meat," he said. "Choking hazard."

"Really?" I started to move away and was surprised when he didn't let go. Which wasn't really a problem since it felt so nice. "And here I thought being groped while eating was the choking hazard."

His grin widened. "When I grope you, you'll know it." To illustrate, he slid a hand southward and squeezed my bottom.

I gave a little gasp. Where had that come from? In the seventeen years since our divorce, Dom had never stepped over the line. I'm not proud to admit I would have welcomed the occasional line-overstepping, but the man was perpetually in a relationship and he didn't stray.

Something in his dark gaze put me on alert. Outwardly his attention was wholly on me, yet I couldn't ignore a certain proprietary glint. I followed his brief glance and spied Martin McAuliffe at the other end of the buffet tables, hammering home a mini red-velvet cheesecake and studying us with an amused expression.

I shoved Dom away. A rush of angry blood scalded my cheeks. "Next time you want to put on a show, leave me out of it."

I started to move past him. He caught my arm. "What's wrong with you, Janey?"

"What's wrong with me?" I tried to wrench out of his grasp. He wasn't letting go. "I don't like being used."

"Used?" he said. "What's that supposed to mean?"

My eyes burned with fury and humiliation. All that pathetic yearning, for so long, watching helplessly as he moved from wife to wife. Knowing that when he thought of me at all, it was as a youthful mistake.

I forced calm into my voice. "That little ass-grab was for the padre's benefit, not mine."

"Who?"

I nodded toward Martin, whose attention was no longer on us. He was chatting up the caterer, Maia Armstrong, an attractive black woman in her mid-thirties. Maia and I often found ourselves in a position to refer clients to each other. It was a mutually beneficial relationship. They were both smiling.

"How do you know that guy?" Dom asked.

"None of your business. Let me go, Dom," I growled.

He glanced around, saw we were drawing stares, and released my arm. The possessive smirk was gone, replaced by a baffled frown.

I knew where the bafflement came from. He wasn't used to seeing me angry. Even back when we divorced, I wasn't angry. I was hurt. Inconsolable. Heartbroken. Maybe I should have gotten angry.

"You're wrong, Janey," he said. "I put on that 'show' for your sake. To protect you."

My bark of incredulous laughter brought him up short, but he recovered enough to add, "Martin McAuliffe is trouble. You shouldn't get mixed up with him."

"Oh please," I said. Dom's little display had been triggered by nothing more noble than male territoriality. The fact that the male in question had no desire for the territory being ass-grabbed was immaterial. It had been a reflex, like taking a crap.

"Your concern for my welfare stirs me deeply," I said. "Now, stay the hell away from me."

Seldom had I been blessed with such a righteous exit line, and I made good use of it. As I strode across the ballroom, I noticed that, due to player attrition, some tables were being consolidated. Players were taking advantage of the lull to stretch their legs, which explained Dom's and Martin's sudden interest in ass-grabbing and munchies, respectively.

A female voice called, "Jane!"

I halted in my tracks and saw Sophie Halperin hurrying toward me. My sudden stop caused someone to barrel into me from behind. It was Jonah, striding quickly toward the exit. He murmured an apology, but his distracted expression made me wonder if he even realized who he'd bumped into. Gee, maybe his dog *had* run away.

Sophie caught up to me, moving with surprising speed for someone so short and round. She was in her mid-fifties, with graying dark hair and a seemingly limitless wardrobe of colorful, flowing tunics and pants. I'd known Sophie almost as long as I'd known Irene. She was a longtime client as well as a friend.

"Didn't expect him to bust out so early," she said, watching Jonah's swiftly retreating form.

"He looked like he was doing okay a little while ago," I said.

"His mind was somewhere else. Played like a rookie the last few rounds. Almost like he wanted to get rid of his chips so he could get out of here. Half our table's gone now, so they're moving me."

"Jonah told me you were in the emergency room Wednesday evening," I said, "but that it was nothing serious?"

"Oh, that." She made a face. "Waste of time. Got these pains in my calf as I was leaving the office at five. Made the mistake of calling Jonah, who, *of course*, insisted I go to Harbor Memorial. Thought it might be deep vein thrombosis. Doppler ultrasound turned up zilch."

"Well, that's good."

"Just one of those unexplained things," she said. "Got to

hand it to Jonah, though. I was there for four miserable hours and so was he."

Yeah, I thought, *because unlike most of us lowly mortals, you can afford to have a concierge physician at your beck and call.* What I said was, "Hey, he's got to take good care of you. You're the damn mayor of this burg."

"And as the damn mayor, I want to congratulate the newest Crystal Harbor homeowner." She stuck out her hand and I shook it.

"Stumping for votes already?" I joked. "Next election isn't for a year."

"Never too early." I wasn't surprised Sophie knew about my inheritance. She was always the first to know anything in this town. She looked around and lowered her voice. "Looks like Nina Wallace is going to try to unseat me."

"But she just got elected president of the Historical Society," I said. "That's a two-year commitment."

She shrugged. "Does she care? I'll have to bring my A-game. That woman does not run a civilized campaign."

"I heard some things about last week's election," I said.

"Not to speak ill of the dead and all, but Irene gave as good as she got. Still, it wouldn't surprise me if there was something to her rumor about Nina."

"Which rumor would that be?" I said.

Sophie snorted. "If you have to ask, you never heard it."

Not being personally involved with the Crystal Harbor Historical Society, I had blessedly been spared the worst of the gossip. "I don't even want to know," I said.

"That's good, 'cause I don't spread unsubstantiated smears. I just listen to them," she snickered.

"You call the rumor unsubstantiated," I said, "yet you say there might be something to it?"

"Well, everyone knows Irene hired a private investigator to dig up dirt on Nina during the campaign."

My jaw dropped. "Irene did that?"

Sophie's expression said, *Get real.* "Come on, Jane, you knew her better than anyone. You going to stand there and tell me you're shocked?"

I wished I could. I said nothing.

"Anyway," she continued, "Nina won the election before the PI got very far in his snooping. He found out just enough to let Irene stir things up. Backfired on her, though—slinging dirt when she had no firm proof. Might've cost her the election."

"Well, Nina sure seems settled in to her new role," I said.

"Tell me about it." Sophie looked around as if to make sure the subject of our conversation was out of earshot. Nina was over by the buffet tables, obviously complaining about something to Maia. Maybe the caviar turned out to be lumpfish instead of beluga. "President for a week and already she's renaming the tournament."

"Renaming it?" I said. "To what?"

Sophie spread her plump arms and intoned with mock reverence, "The Colette O'Grady O'Rourke Memorial Poker Tournament."

"O'Grady *and* O'Rourke?" I said. "For real?" I knew Colette's maiden name was O'Grady, but I doubted she'd used it as a middle name during her married life. Talk about an inharmonious mouthful.

"I mean, Nina and Colette were good friends, sure," she said, "but everyone knows who this is really about."

"Irene," I agreed. "It's a slap in the face to her. To her memory." Irene and Colette had both been members of the Historical Society forever. They'd both served on the board, and both had been fixtures in the tournament. If anything, Irene's financial contributions to the organization should have tipped the scale in her favor. Not that there was a compelling reason to rename the tournament after either woman.

"Winning the election isn't enough for Nina," Sophie said. "She has to totally stick it to her opponent. Who died. I mean, yeah, Irene ran a nasty campaign and all, but she lost. And then she *died*." She spread her hands. "Like that's not enough?"

"Can Nina decide this on her own?" I asked.

Sophie shook her head. "She blindsided the other board members this morning before the tournament started, forced a vote. No one but me had the balls to stand up to her. Bunch of spineless wimps."

My eyebrows rose. "So the name change is really going through?"

"Madame President is going to announce it along with the winners later." She nodded to a dealer across the room. "Listen, they're waiting for me, I've got to go."

"Before you do," I said, "just something to keep in mind—if you know of anyone who needs a housekeeper, I think Maria Echevarría might be looking for work."

Her eyes widened. "Irene's Maria? *I'll* hire her, *and* her guacamole. My Danielle just quit. She's moving to London, where her boyfriend lives. They're opening an art gallery." Her eye-roll said, *Good luck with that.*

I managed to locate Maria's phone number in my cell. Sophie shot her insistent dealer the one-minute sign with her index finger, muttering, "Yeah, kiss my ass, I'm the damn mayor of this burg," and punched the number into her own phone.

No sooner had she joined her table than I noticed someone else sharing contact info on the other side of the ballroom. Martin scribbled something on a card—one of his gentleman's calling cards, no doubt—and handed it to Veronica Sheffield.

Veronica happened to be one of my most lucrative repeat clients, the center of a galactic network of friends, relatives, and business associates, a rewarding percentage of whom dropped dead each year, compelling Veronica to invest in the usual gravesite visits, cremains dispersal, and sympathy-card writing, plus a host of bizarre assignments only her inventive and bored little mind could devise. Remember the dildo crafted from the boyfriend's ashes? Yep. That was Veronica.

On top of all that, she required a chic new black outfit for each of the countless funerals she attended. I acted as private shopper for funeral finery and also peddled the worn-once outfits for her on eBay, earning a fee on both ends. Plus she regularly recommended my services to members of her book club, investment club, yacht club, beach club, and bowling league. Veronica was your basic Death Diva cash cow.

Once again, flirtatious smiles all around. Veronica was okay-looking, I supposed, and recently divorced, but she had to be ten years Martin's senior. It was easier to understand his interest in Maia.

Just then Veronica looked over and noticed me noticing. Her smile fled, replaced by a flurry of nervous blinking, which happened to be her signature poker tell. I didn't know how she'd lasted so long in today's tournament. She usually blinked her way out of it within twenty minutes.

Martin followed the direction of her gaze and sent me a chipper wave before pumping Veronica's hand and resuming his seat behind a veritable cordillera of chips. A pretty young masseuse pounced like a bobcat and started kneading his broad shoulders.

I scowled. Something about this stank.

"Don't do that, you'll get lines." Nina appeared at my side and tapped my forehead. She inspected me more closely and added, "Well, more lines," before mouthing, *Botox*.

Nina Wallace was the last person I wanted to see right then, the archetypal high school mean girl all grown up. I wrestled with my anger and disgust, recalling the syrupy false sympathy she'd extended to me yesterday at Janey's Place.

Where was a great big pot of vegetarian chili when you needed it? God help her if she mentioned Irene.

"It just doesn't seem the same without Irene, does it?" She produced a tissue and discreetly dabbed at her upper lip. Only then did I notice a sheen of perspiration and the pale cast of her skin.

"Are you all right?" I asked.

"Never better." Her grin was so bright and earnest, it was hard not to believe her. Still…

"You look a little green around the gills," I said. "Maybe you should sit down for a—"

Nina bolted out of the ballroom. I caught up with her as she sprinted down the hallway and into the ladies' room. She didn't have time to lock the stall door before her lunch said sayonara. I couldn't help thinking of Irene and her recent indigestion.

I was ready with wet paper towels when she staggered to a sink to rinse her mouth. She blotted her face and offered a crooked smile. "Well, that was fun."

The sumptuously appointed john had a separate seating area. I encouraged her to lie down on the couch. She waved off the suggestion.

"I'll be fine now." Gratefully she accepted a mint I fished out of my purse.

There weren't too many reasons a woman would recover so quickly and cheerfully from a bout of vomiting. I watched her check her makeup and thought I detected a hint of self-satisfaction. Any connection to Irene's malady instantly vaporized.

"Congratulations," I said. "When are you due?"

She looked at my reflection, then turned to face me. "Please tell me it's not that obvious."

"Not to anyone who didn't just watch you puke."

She took a deep breath. "I'm about six weeks along. We're not telling anyone yet, so I'd appreciate it if you wouldn't mention—"

"Of course not," I assured her. "It's nobody's business until you decide to share it."

She was visibly relieved. "Thanks." She shot one more glance at the mirror. "Do I look okay?"

"Perfect." I didn't doubt that Nina Wallace would look more fashionable and put together at full term than I could ever hope to be on my best day.

She returned to the ballroom. I used the facilities and headed out of the building, having no reason to linger now that I'd accomplished my mission. The snow had ended, but it was still cold. Two men stood on the portico, smoking and talking. I recognized one of them as Malachy Wallace, a richer-than-Croesus investment banker and Nina's much better half. He greeted me and introduced me to his pal Rich, who'd come down from Rochester for the tournament.

Unfortunately, Rich had already busted out. "I'm going to take out my indignation on that buffet table," he said, depositing his cigarette butt in the elegant, sand-filled receptacle provided for that purpose. "Think I can eat five thousand dollars' worth of hors d'oeuvres?"

"Start with those steak-and-Stilton thingies," I suggested. "They're to die for."

He gave me a mock salute and disappeared inside. I turned to Mal Wallace, who was on the tall side, with thinning dark hair and an incipient spare tire. His best features were a strong, square jaw and the patience to put up with his high-maintenance wife. "You're not playing?" I asked him.

"If Nina doesn't get to play, I don't." If that bugged him, you couldn't tell by his affable smile. "She put me to work today, helping out."

"Is that why you're hiding out here?"

He exhaled a stream of smoke. His smile widened and he shrugged.

I exchanged greetings with Lacey Vargas, the owner of UnderStatements, the lingerie boutique, as she exited the building. When she was out of earshot, I told Mal, "Congrats, by the way."

He gave me a perplexed look as he discarded his cigarette butt.

"About the baby," I said. "I sort of found out by accident. Nina just had a bout of morning sickness."

He stared at me wide-eyed for a long moment, then his face lit up in a mile-wide grin. "She's pregnant?"

I gasped. "You didn't know? Oh my God, Mal, I'm so sorry. I just assumed she told you. I didn't mean to beat her to it."

Mal chuckled, beaming. He patted my arm. "Don't worry about it. She did the same thing with the other two, waited to let me in on it. She likes to do it just right—make a romantic dinner, set the mood, all that nonsense I couldn't care less about."

"Well, I feel like the biggest dope."

"I won't tell her you spilled the beans," he said. "I just hope she doesn't wait too long to give me the good news. I'm going to have a hell of a time keeping this asinine grin off my face."

10
Motive for What?

"SO JONAH WAS right," I said. "Irene really did die of a heart attack."

Sten Jakobsen leaned back in his massive leather chair behind his massive mahogany desk which dominated his massive, wood-paneled corner office. He nodded. "That is what Joyce Huang reported."

"But a heart attack can be triggered by all sorts of things, right? Like being poisoned?"

"I am no physician," he said. "Joyce will let me know what, if anything, the laboratory tests reveal."

Irene's autopsy had been performed last Sunday, five days earlier. I'd set this thing in motion on the flimsiest of evidence, and I wondered what Sten would think of me if, when the lab tests came back, it turned out to be a simple case of an elderly woman with atrial fibrillation succumbing to a sudden and massive myocardial infarction.

Jonah was right. The respectful thing would have been to honor Irene's wishes for prompt, direct cremation. No embalming. Certainly no postmortem.

Suddenly I felt like changing the subject.

"So," I said. "Paperwork's done. Does this mean I can move into the house anytime?"

He nodded. "This very day if it suits you."

I shrugged. "I've got nothing else planned for today, and I'm mostly packed. My landlord offered his station wagon. I should be able to haul my stuff in one or two trips."

Which was kind of sad, to think that all my worldly possessions could fit into Mr. Franckowiak's battered old Chevy wagon. Although to be fair, I was leaving my furniture, such as it was, behind in the little basement apartment. Well, except for my precious antique student desk, which had sentimental value because of its connection with Dom. This despite the fact that even now, nearly a week after that little ass-grabbing display during the tournament, I was still indignant as hell. Dom had tried to call me twice since then. I hadn't picked up and he hadn't left a voice mail. Pushing him away was a novel experience, one I had to admit was long overdue.

I glanced at the heavy brass clock on Sten's credenza. It was ten-forty a.m. Our meeting had lasted almost an hour. He'd provided the name of a good investment advisor to handle the upkeep money. "I'm sure you have had some concerns about estate taxes," he'd said, and I'd restrained the impulse to respond, "Huh?" What did I know about rich people's problems? He'd explained that the state and especially the IRS would take a big, juicy bite out of Irene's estate, but that her will provided for the taxes to be paid out of Patrick's portion of the inheritance. Even so, in the end he'd still be a very wealthy man.

It was Sten's responsibility to monitor Sexy Beast's welfare and the condition of the property. After SB eventually shuffled off to doggie heaven, I would be free to sell the house, should I so choose, and keep the proceeds. I could dispose of Irene's personal possessions at any time, except for the furniture, rugs, artwork, appliances, and durable furnishings such as those hideously expensive ebony floors. All that stuff, or replacement stuff of equivalent value, had to remain in the house for the time being.

So much for my dream of gutting the place and turning it into a crack house.

"How does it feel," Sten asked, "to go from renting a small apartment to owning a four-million-dollar home?"

"It feels kind of unbelievable, though technically it isn't really mine yet."

We turned in unison to look at Crystal Harbor's latest millionaire landowner, who lay curled on the leather sofa in the sunlight streaming through the huge picture windows, lustily licking his nether regions.

"Did the groomer really have to do that to him?" Sten asked.

"You saw him before," I said. "He was a hairball on legs. Rocky told me he had no choice but to shave him down." Sexy Beast had been left with a fuzzy little cap and pompom tail. Unfortunately, the rest of him was now practically hairless. It was the canine equivalent of Martin McAuliffe's ultrashort buzz cut.

"I understand that," Sten said. "I am referring to the garment he is wearing."

I sighed. SB's doggie sweater was a pink chenille concoction covered with sparkly hearts and trimmed in fluffy pink boa-type feathers. "He needs something for warmth until the hair grows back—it's still chilly outside. And this was the only thing Rocky had in the shop in SB's size. I'll swing by a pet store when I can and get him something more butch. Anyway, I think it's a little late to worry about gender confusion in SB's case. About two and a half years too late if you get my drift." I turned my fingers into scissors and performed a midair snip-snip.

Sten crossed his legs. "How did you manage to secure an appointment with Rocky on such short notice? Penelope and Mister have been on his waiting list for ten months," he said, referring to his two ragdoll cats. Speaking of hairballs.

"A, um, friend intervened for me." Bonnie Hernandez could hardly be called a friend, but it was quicker and less awkward than saying, *My ex-husband's fiancée and don't even get me started.*

As it turned out, I couldn't have been more wrong about Rocky. I'd walked into his shop expecting Rambo on steroids, only to find myself getting a reassuring hug from Richard Simmons on sequins.

Rocky—no last name, à la Cher and Madonna—had promised he'd be very *gentle* with Sexy Beast and what a *fabulous* name for such a *messy* little poodle and oh my *goodness* this matted stuff has got to *go* I'm *sorry* darling but it has all just got to *go* and how *is* Bonnie and I always make her show me her *gun* and it must make her boyfriend incredibly *horny* to come home to this sexy *cop* who carries this *great big gun* and isn't her Frederick absolutely the most *gorgeous* dog ever and I mean talk about a *sexy beast!*

"Thank you for forwarding Irene's mail to me." Sten lifted a sheet of paper from a stack. "I am hoping you can shed light on this invoice. It is from Benjamin Ralston. Ben is a private investigator here in Crystal Harbor. I occasionally use him myself when a case requires the services of an investigator. I was unaware of Irene having hired him. She never mentioned it to me."

No doubt because she didn't want a lecture from her old

friend, erstwhile lover, and attorney. "Oh. Well… I believe this may be connected with the election for president of the Historical Society. Irene… well, she was trying to, um…"

"Dig up dirt on her opponent," he said.

"I'm afraid so."

He examined the bill. "Ben is a good man and these charges appear in order, now that I know what prompted them. I shall add it to her other bills for payment." He slid the paper into a folder. "It is just as well that Ben's investigation was cut short when Irene died. It is bad enough that everyone in town now knows Nina Wallace is cheating on her husband. Well, everyone but her husband—I doubt the gossip has reached Mal. We do not need to know the identity of the third party."

His matter-of-fact tone said he assumed Nina's affair was old news to me. I bullied my features into a neutral expression and murmured, "I couldn't agree more," while a voice in my head screamed, *Oh my God, who is Nina messing around with?*

Sten removed his wire-rimmed glasses and massaged the bridge of his nose. "I will not waste my breath spouting platitudes about Irene McAuliffe. You knew her as well as I, Jane. She was a mixed bag."

I returned his sad smile. "She was that."

Sten's intercom buzzed. He put his glasses back on and pushed a button, and I heard his secretary tell him Dr. Huang was on the line. My heart stuttered as he lifted the handset and greeted the pathologist. He listened for a minute or two while I mentally rehearsed ways to apologize for wasting his time, not to mention Irene's money and dignity, on a private autopsy and lab work. Actually, it was Patrick's money I'd wasted since he was Irene's major beneficiary, which, assuming he was innocent, added injury to insult. Sten had already received Dr. Huang's bill, and it was a whopper. At last he thanked her and hung up.

He looked me in the eye. "You were right."

The breath fled my lungs and all I could do was gape at him. Finally I croaked, "What?"

Sten shook his head slightly, as if loath to believe what could no longer be chalked up as a figment of Jane Delaney's robust imagination. "The toxicology screen revealed the presence of dangerous chemicals in Irene's stomach contents, blood, and urine."

I swallowed hard. "What kind of chemicals?"

"Insecticides. Two common types that are found in many household bug killers. This was just the initial findings. We will have more information when the final report is completed, but meanwhile Joyce was able to say with certainty that the quantity of insecticides in Irene's system is more than could be accounted for by accidental exposure."

"You said stomach contents," I began. "So…"

"So she ingested it." Sten yanked off his glasses and tossed them onto his desk in one harsh movement, making me jump. Color suffused his lined cheeks. I'd never seen him angry before, had never known this even-tempered man could get angry. "Needless to say, she did not consume it intentionally."

"The cup?" I said. "The smoothie?"

"The residue in the cup showed significant amounts of the same two chemicals," he said. "Someone deliberately poisoned Irene."

Someone, huh? We both knew who that someone had to be. But Sten was a man of law first and foremost. Innocent until proven guilty and all that.

He returned his glasses to his face and reached for the phone. "Who are you calling?" I asked.

"The police."

*

I PARKED ON the cobblestone courtyard in front of my new house, having somehow made it there in one piece in Mr. Franckowiak's rattletrap station wagon. The car sported a cracked windshield, multihued paint job, countless dents and dings, and bench seats that were more duct tape than fabric. The front end felt and sounded like an off-balance washing machine, and the rear end belched clouds of acrid exhaust. The good news was, by experimenting I found that if you stood on the brake pedal and bounced hard enough, you could bring the thing to a stop. At least the day was sunny and mild. I didn't have slippery roads to contend with.

I was grateful that Mr. F. had volunteered to keep an eye on Sexy Beast. The only thing that could have made the ride more hair-raising would have been a shaved poodle in a ridiculous boa-fringed sweater whining and scrabbling and dodging shifting boxes that outweighed him by eighty pounds.

You're a damn millionaire! I railed at myself. *You have no business being behind the wheel of a death trap like this.*

Not that my old Civic was much better. If the shiny Lexus SUV sitting in my garage belonged to me, I'd have loaded it up instead. But all three of Irene's lovely chariots now belonged to Patrick O'Rourke, and I found I didn't relish the prospect of accidentally crumpling the fender of a hellishly expensive vehicle belonging to a murderer.

I had not, in fact, been able to take all my stuff in one trip.

Once I'd wedged the kiddie desk into the trunk and crammed boxes and bags around it and in the backseat and passenger side of the front seat, I still had another full load sitting in Mr. F's backyard. I looped the handles of several shopping bags filled with office supplies over my wrists and grabbed a heavy cardboard carton crammed with business files, then kicked the car door closed and struggled up the steps to the portico. Balancing the box on my knee, I managed to unlock the massive double doors and swing them open. The box fell onto its side, disgorging files and papers, which I shoved back into it willy-nilly.

I managed to make it up the staircase and stopped at the top to catch my breath and rest the carton on the balcony railing.

A male voice rang out from the master suite. "Need help with that?"

I screamed and lost my grip on the box, which tipped over the railing and sailed down to the foyer floor far, far below. I very nearly made the same unscheduled trip as I flailed wildly, trying in vain to snatch it from the brink. File folders and papers flew in all directions, catching air currents and touching down on the glossy, brown and black macassar ebony floor.

"No?" The voice sounded bored. "Suit yourself."

I wheeled around and stalked into the master bedroom. Martin McAuliffe lounged on Irene's king-size sleigh bed, surrounded by his own assortment of papers. Lazily he perused the contents of a manila folder.

I parked my fists on my hips. "How did you get in here?"

"Did you know that Sten Jakobsen hums when he has a decent poker hand?" Martin was wearing his priest getup again, dog collar and all. At least he'd kicked off his shoes before climbing onto Irene's hand-woven silk-and-linen bedspread. "'The Battle Hymn of the Republic' when he's looking at a straight or a flush, and 'Dixie' for a full house or better."

"I installed new locks. *Unpickable* locks." I got in his face. "And a state-of-the-art alarm system."

He flipped a page. "And Nina Wallace taps her fingernails when she's bluffing."

Obviously he'd gotten ahold of Irene's notes about her friends' poker habits. I looked at the other folders strewn on the bed. Medical records. Bank statements. Income tax returns. "You have no shame."

"Sophie Halperin and Jonah Diamond possess outstanding poker faces, according to Irene," he said, "as did Colette O'Rourke."

"Wait, Jonah has a good poker face?" I asked. "As in a blank expression that gives nothing away?"

He thumped the folder. "Downright inscrutable, according to Irene. Why?"

Jonah had looked anything but inscrutable during the tournament. What was it Sophie had told me at the time? That he'd played like a rookie and burned through his chips, as if he couldn't get out of there fast enough. Of course, any number of things could have thrown him off his game. A bout of food poisoning. A fight with Rachel. A patient taking a turn for the worse.

I shook my head. "It's nothing."

"He was Irene's doctor, right?" Martin said. "I've never met the guy. Now, this is interesting. Your ex has a tell when he's holding four of a kind or better, but he knows about it and can usually control it. You get three guesses."

I didn't need them. "He bites his bottom lip." The revealing gesture I'd always thought of as sweet and sexy had been repurposed by Irene as a poker tell, letting her know when to fold 'em. Dom hadn't been so self-aware eighteen years earlier when he'd planned my surprise twenty-first birthday party. I'd had enough warning to put on makeup and a nice outfit, thanks to his unconscious lip-nibbling.

"Why aren't you cute kids still together?" he asked. "You must still care for the guy, to let him feel you up in public like that."

"Get out." I pointed to the door. "Get. Out."

"So where's your affectionate ex now? I'd have thought he'd want to help you move."

I didn't bother saying, *He would have if I'd asked him.* Instead I retrieved the shopping bags from the floor of the balcony and carried them down the hall into the office, where I dumped them on the rug. "I mean it, Padre," I called as I returned to the master suite. "I want you out or I'm calling the po—" I skidded to a halt when I saw what he was doing. "Stop that! Put your clothes back on."

"Not to worry." Martin had stripped off his clerical collar and black shirt, revealing a snug white undershirt. Now he sat on the edge of the bed to put on his shoes. "This is as far as I go without a steak dinner." He eyed me up and down, his gaze appreciative despite my glamorous moving-day attire of baggy jeans and faded SUNY Stony Brook sweatshirt. "Though I've been known to make exceptions."

My visceral response to his words annoyed me, so I offered a glower in response and escaped to Mr. F's station wagon. Martin caught up with me there as I attempted to wrestle a carton of books out of the trunk. My beleaguered back demanded to know why I'd chosen such a huge box for the books and such a teensy one for the kitchen sponges.

"The only thing missing from this vehicle," he said, "is Granny Clampett and her rocker."

A *Beverly Hillbillies* analogy. How droll.

He nudged me aside, shoved the box back into the trunk, and held out his hand. "Keys, Elly May."

"No." Logical Jane asked Paranoid Jane if she was worried about the padre making off with Mr. F's coffin on wheels and her antique kiddie desk—a particularly ludicrous scenario as it would require him to abandon the expensive motorcycle he'd no doubt left in the parking area by the garage.

He didn't wait for the internal debate to resolve itself but slid his fingers into my front jeans pocket and plucked out the car keys.

"Hey!" I smacked his bare forearm. This was why he'd stripped down to his undershirt—not to jump my bones but to help me unload the car.

"Open the garage." Martin got behind the wheel, got the engine started on the third try, and moved the station wagon while I went inside and did as he asked. He was right, it made more sense to bring stuff in through the garage.

Mr. F's monstrosity looked even more ludicrous next to Martin's big, gleaming Harley as he backed up to the open garage door and got out. He eyed the three vehicles parked inside. "When's O'Rourke coming for his cars?"

Just the mention of Irene's presumed killer made my stomach clench. I shrugged. I'd intended to get Dom to play bodyguard while I transferred the vehicles to Patrick. I'd be damned if I'd ask my ex for a favor now.

Martin strode past the Porsche, lifted a handcart off a wall bracket, and positioned it near the station wagon's trunk. "So do you believe that about O'Rourke?" he asked.

"He certainly had motive," I said, distracted by the sight of Martin lifting the box of books as if it were filled with feathers and setting it on the cart's base. The curious look he gave me focused my mind. "Wait," I said, "what are you talking about?"

He leaned on the cart. "I'm talking about Patrick O'Rourke and Nina Wallace engaging in illicit acts of sexual congress outside the bonds of holy matrimony, but gosh, your story sounds a lot more interesting. Motive for what?"

I started pulling smaller items out of the backseat. "Where did you hear that about Patrick and Nina?"

"Motive for what?" He stacked another heavy box on the cart.

Stall. Think. "I mean, I heard she was having an affair," I said, "but not who she was having it with."

His smile was wry as he dragged another carton from the trunk. "I know you're not talking about his motive for sleeping with a good-looking woman, never mind that this particular babe is a certifiable bitch on wheels."

"Yeah, yeah." I gathered an armload of shoeboxes, precariously balanced. "Men and their built-in excuse. 'My testosterone made me do it.' Whatever happened to personal responsibility? Marriage vows?"

"Motive for what?" He hefted the last box into place and stood staring at me, awaiting an answer.

"Congratulations on winning the tournament, by the way," I said. "I'm surprised you're not driving that gorgeous Mercedes today." That had sent shock waves through the snooty town: Arthur and Anne McAuliffe's bastard grandson, not just entering the tournament but walking away with the top prize. As little use as I had for Martin, I couldn't suppress a frisson of glee at his triumph.

I stepped around him and led the way through the garage to the house. I took a few steps down the hall to the maid's room— I really should stop thinking of it as the maid's room—and set the boxes on the dresser, then turned back to help Martin lift the ponderous cart up the two steps from the garage. As it happened, he didn't need my help. He'd already pulled it up the first step. The muscles of his back bunched and flexed in the most interesting way as he got the thing up the second step and into the house. He didn't appear the least bit winded.

"Um, just put everything in there." I pointed to the maid's room. "I'll sort it out later."

He indicated the lettering scrawled in black marker on the cartons. "Most of these go upstairs." He lifted the top two boxes, filled with books and clothes, and headed in the other direction. I grabbed the shoeboxes and followed him through the kitchen to the foyer, still strewn with papers and files.

"No, really, you've done plenty already. I appreciate it." Did my ears deceive me? Was I actually thanking Martin McAuliffe for something?

He glanced over his shoulder as I trailed him up the stairs. "Motive for what?"

"I don't believe it's Patrick," I said. "Who Nina's doing it with. I saw them together just last week at Janey's Place. They acted perfectly normal toward each other. There was none of that, you know, sexual chemistry or whatever." I'd already learned that Patrick O'Rourke was lousy at hiding his feelings, yet I'd seen nothing revealing in his attitude toward Nina. Then again, the two of them hadn't really spoken, they'd just exchanged a friendly greeting before Patrick had to get back to work.

"I have it on good authority." He entered the master suite and left the carton of clothes in one of the walk-in closets.

"Whose good authority would that be?" I deposited the shoeboxes next to the carton and followed him to the office at the far end of the hallway.

"Veronica Sheffield for starters."

"Yeah, I noticed you two getting chummy at the tournament," I said. "She doesn't seem your type."

"Is that right?" He offered a crooked grin. "What's my type?"

I wasn't going to touch that one. "What did Veronica say about Patrick and Nina?"

"Well, before your ex gave O'Rourke the job at Janey's Place, he did a lot of handyman work for Nina." He set the carton of books on the office floor near the bookshelves, which were completely filled.

I'd have to go through all of Irene's books and decide which ones to keep. And then there were her clothes and other personal possessions. I would need to research the best charities to donate them to and make time to sort and pack them all. I'd heard of an organization that provided poor women with nice outfits for job interviews. That seemed a good place to start.

"I knew that Nina and Colette were good friends," I said. "I didn't know that Nina had hired her son to do... what? Repairs around the house?"

He nodded. "Painting. Woodwork. Plumbing. Whatever needed doing. She kept him busy." He offered a smile full of meaning, which I answered with a disgusted shake of my head. "Of course, now I expect she'll dump him," he added.

"Why?"

"Guy's rich now. Fifteen point nine million and change."

I was about to ask how he knew the precise amount Irene had left Patrick, before I remembered he'd been all through her private financial records. "Minus the estate taxes," I said, trying to sound like I knew something he didn't.

"Yeah, he'll lose about seven mil. Don't ask me to feel sorry for the guy."

"Why would his coming into money make Nina want to dump him?" I asked.

He shrugged. "She already has a rich husband. O'Rourke was her working-class boy toy. Her bad-boy ex-con. The allure of the forbidden and all that."

I had a hard time envisioning sixty-year-old Patrick O'Rourke as any kind of boy. "You gossip like an old woman, Padre."

"Hey, I'm just trying to make conversation," he said. "We could talk about your ex instead and why you let him molest you in public."

"Maybe I liked it." I crossed my arms and tried to look defiant.

"Didn't look that way from where I was standing."

"Really?" I said. "I didn't think you noticed. You were pretty busy chatting up Maia Armstrong."

"How do you know I wasn't talking with her about a catering job?"

I let my expression ask him how much of an idiot he thought I was.

"Not that I blame Faso for sneaking a feel," he said. "It takes moral fortitude to resist an ass as fine as yours. I know."

"Oh, here we go." My BS meter was edging into the red.

"I almost blew my cover that night at Ahearn's." he said, "watching you get up from the kneeler in that tight skirt."

Embarrassed heat flooded my cheeks as I recalled ogling the sexy priest's buns during Colette's wake. Talk about a mutual-admiration society. Martin gave my jeans-clad derriere a playful smack and strode past me back to the staircase. I caught up with him at the bottom of the steps as he started back up with more boxes.

"Get all that picked up—" he nodded at the mess of papers on the foyer floor "—before I slip and break my neck."

"Yes, Father."

I stopped trying to talk him out of helping. Why look a gift hunk in the mouth? The truth was, just the thought of doing all that schlepping by myself exhausted me. I would have waited for the weekend and asked a couple of friends to help, but I'd assumed that moving my meager stash of stuff would be a piece of cake. Yeah, a piece of beefcake, I thought as I watched Martin climb the stairs with his ponderous load.

With him taking the heavy stuff and me lugging the smaller items, we had the car emptied in twenty minutes. When I held out my hand for the car keys, he answered by getting behind the wheel. He once more looked the part of Father Martin, complete with black shirt and collar.

"There's more stuff at your place, right?" he said. "Get in. I have to be somewhere, but it can wait."

I slid into the passenger seat and buckled my shoulder strap, giving him pointers on how to start, turn, and stop this particular vehicle. Martin pulled around the house and down the cobblestone drive. His nose wrinkled and he eyed the upholstery with suspicion. "What's that smell?"

"I decided I'd rather not know."

"That works for me," he said.

"Take the expressway south to—"

"I know how to get to your place."

My gaze shot to his maddeningly placid profile. "How do you know where I live?"

"Where you lived," he corrected. "I know a lot about you, remember?"

I was determined not to let him get the better of me. The work orders. He knew my address from all those work orders he'd swiped from Irene's office.

"Where do you have to be," I asked, "dressed like that?"

"A boy needs some secrets."

Yeah, right. This boy was all secrets, whereas I appeared to be an open book. The unfairness of it grated on me.

Our disreputable vehicle drew stares as Martin negotiated the spit-polished side streets of Crystal Harbor. When folks spied a man of the cloth behind the wheel, their expressions of frosty disdain thawed. He rewarded them with pope waves and saintly smiles, while I slid lower in my seat and hid my face. Heck, the padre was still a relative stranger in town, but I *knew* some of these people.

Through assertive driving, he managed to shave almost ten minutes off the forty-minute drive, even after swinging through a Burger King drive-through to get us lunch. He entertained himself the whole while by attempting to fill in the blanks inherent in the Death Diva's provocative yet unexplained statement: *He certainly had motive.* I tuned out his wild guesses and tuned in the car's staticky radio, which was permanently stuck on a station that broadcast Caribbean music. I cranked it loud and sang along.

I refrained from offering local directions once we were off the Seaford-Oyster Bay Expressway—SOB for short. I assumed Martin would have to ask, despite his boast that he knew the way.

I waited. He knew the way. He turned onto Mr. F's weed-choked gravel driveway and parked at the far end, near the detached garage with its sagging roof.

The small, two-story house had once been white, but over the past aeon or so it had dulled to a grimy gray. Many of the shingles were broken or missing. An abandoned washing machine sat rusting in the compact backyard. Mr. F had placed it there sometime during the Clinton administration, with every intention of repairing it someday. A black cat reclined on the washer, soaking up the early spring sunshine. Several more cats lounged around the yard. Mindy, a yellow, three-legged mutt, chased a squirrel away from the food and water bowls set on the little concrete patio. A pair of fluffy bantam chickens, one gray and one rusty orange, pecked in the scrubby grass near their tumbledown coop.

I opened the car door. "Welcome to Dogpatch."

11
Father Martin's Naughty Ramblings

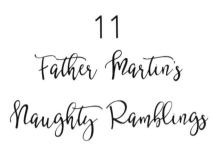

SB RAN UP to me, barking a greeting. I gave him the obligatory scritches and he ran off to rejoin the menagerie.

The rest of my belongings were piled in boxes and leaf bags near the wide-open cellar doors. Martin stepped out of the car and opened the trunk, unable to drag his gaze from Sexy Beast and his glamorous new look.

"I'm going to get him a new sweater as soon as I have time," I said, "so just shut up."

"I didn't say a thing." He lifted a leaf bag crammed with my blankets and bed linens, and lobbed it into the trunk.

"You didn't have to." I wedged a box of toiletries next to the bag. "Don't stare at him like that, you'll give him a complex."

Sexy Beast approached Luba, the orange chicken, and assumed the doggie play stance, chest down and butt high in the air. He gave a sharp *Play with me!* bark. Luba inspected him with jerky nods, then started pecking at the pink boa fringe of his sweater.

The side door of the house slammed and Mr. Franckowiak appeared, carrying a partially filled casserole. I estimated his age at somewhere between ninety and a hundred thirty. He hadn't changed after his morning jog, I noticed. Orange gym shorts showed off his skinny white legs, while a white wife-beater, open bathrobe, and gigantic hearing aid completed the elegant ensemble.

I made introductions. Martin's priest getup wasn't lost on Mr. F. "I got no use for religion," he declared. "Meaningless mumbo-jumbo designed to keep the proletariat in their place. Read your Karl Marx!"

"Yes, sir," Martin said. "I'll relay your message to the pope."

Mr. F shuffled over to the big steel food bowl and shoveled the remains of the casserole into it. The cats made a beeline for it, as did the chickens and Sexy Beast. The animals shoved one another and jockeyed for position. Mindy yawned and scratched her flank. The plump dog didn't need to compete with the rabble for kitchen scraps. When Mr. F prepared his meals, he always filled two plates. If he got Hamburger Helper and canned peas, with a Fudgsicle for dessert, so did Mindy, who sat on a kitchen chair across from him.

Martin watched the animals gobble food from the bowl. "What are they eating?"

"You're not going to like this," I warned. "Chicken stroganoff."

I saw the instant my words registered, saw his helpless dismay as he watched the two hens attack Mr. F's leftovers with gusto. "That is so wrong," he murmured.

Within fifteen minutes the car was packed and we were back on the road, this time with Sexy Beast on my lap, secured with a safety strap connecting his harness to my seat belt.

Martin negotiated the side streets of Sandy Cove, shooting irritated looks at the dog. "Does he have to do that?"

The instant SB gets in a car, he begins to whine—a high-pitched mewling sound from deep in his throat. I'd long ago learned to tune it out.

"He gets excited in cars." I stroked SB's silky, newly detangled ears. "Just ignore it."

"How do I ignore something like that?" he demanded. "When's he going to stop?"

"When we get there."

Martin shook his head and grumbled something I was just as happy I couldn't make out. He turned onto Route 109, a four-lane leading to the expressway. "You'll be happy to know I have an answer to the big question of the day," he said.

"I neither know nor care what you're talking about."

"Oh, sure you do," he said. "It's the question you tantalized me with for hours, you coy vixen. As in, What does Patrick O'Rourke have a motive for? Answer: Why, murder, that's what. Old lady croaks, he rakes in millions. I'd call that motive." One glance at my face and he crowed, "Yes! I knew it," prompting an answering howl from Sexy Beast.

So it had been an educated guess on his part, which my expression had conveniently verified.

In case you were wondering why I don't play poker, you have your answer.

I blew out an exasperated breath, wishing I'd stranded the padre at Mr. F's and driven myself back to Crystal Harbor.

He said, "Hard to believe someone despised that old bitch more than I did."

"I don't think he despised her," I said. "I think he was just... greedy, I guess. Impatient for that inheritance."

"Then he knew Irene was leaving her fortune to him?"

"That's what Sten said."

"Have they arrested him yet?" he asked.

"Not yet," I said. "Well, maybe. The cops must have questioned him by now. Sten called them this morning after the tox screen came back."

"Tox screen?" Martin frowned. "He poisoned her?"

"You know, I really don't think we should be talking about—"

"Sure we should," he said in a soothing tone. "Tell Father Martin all about it, child. Unburden yourself."

I rolled my eyes. "Next you're going to tell me gossip is good for the soul."

Oh, what the heck. It would be all over town at the speed of light, if it wasn't already. So I told Martin about Irene's unprecedented indigestion and the daily smoothies hand-delivered by Patrick, whose connection to her remained a mystery. I told him about that last smoothie cup and the autopsy and the insecticides.

He grinned. "I missed seeing you paw through garbage? You should've called me to come over."

"You would have helped me?" I asked.

"Hell no, I'd have paid to watch."

I chewed back a smile. "How much?"

"Fifty bucks. American."

"Just fifty?" I asked, with mock indignation.

"A hundred if there was a bikini involved. A little topless action and we could be talking serious bread."

I shook my head. "You have no shame, Padre."

"I believe this has been established." He turned onto the entrance ramp to the northbound SOB. The afternoon rush was an hour or so away and traffic was moving well on the six-lane expressway.

"Patrick didn't have to do that," I said." Kill Irene, I mean. She was in her seventies. She had a heart problem. If he'd just been patient, he could have gotten his inheritance without the risk. Now all he has to look forward to is a life behind bars. I feel so sorry for Barbara and the kids."

What would become of Cheyenne now, with her dad in the hoosegow? I tried to reconcile Patrick the murderer with Patrick the concerned father trying to keep his daughter from reliving his mistakes. It was not a good fit.

I leaned toward Martin's side of the car, trying in vain to glimpse the speedometer. "You know, we don't need to set any land speed records. You can let up on the accelerator."

"The sooner we get there, the sooner my brain will stop hurting." He jerked his head toward Sexy Beast, whose incessant whining formed a nerve-jangling duet with the engine of Mr. F's jalopy as it thunk-thunked through the spin cycle.

"After I found Irene's will," Martin said, "I went all through her papers looking for a connection between her and O'Rourke—besides him being her former friend's son. Nada. And this was a woman who kept meticulous records. I mean, I found a receipt for golf balls she bought Arthur in 1986. I searched the house, top to bottom. I kept thinking, there's got to be a clue here somewhere. Drove me crazy. It doesn't make sense."

"Sten knows," I said, "but he's not telling. Lawyer-client confidentiality. And I asked Patrick outright, but his lips are sealed. Out of respect for Irene, he claims."

"Taking the patient, wait-for-her-to-die approach might not have paid off for O'Rourke," he said. "Irene was in decent shape for someone her age. Yeah, she took digoxin for a hinky heart rhythm, but according to her medical records, she was doing pretty well."

"Jonah told me she was overdue for a pacemaker."

"Well then, maybe she just put on a good act," he said. "She certainly seemed indestructible."

"That's how I always thought of her too." I offered a sad smile.

"Look at it from O'Rourke's perspective," he said. "The guy's getting on in years. He's, what, around sixty? And not in the best shape. Lived a hard life, did a lot of drugs when he was younger."

"Maybe he was afraid Irene would outlive him," I said. "Maybe that's what sent him over the edge."

"And where does Nina fit in to all this?" he asked.

"What do you mean?" I fluffed the boa fringe on SB's sweater.

"She's banging O'Rourke. He kills Irene. She despised Irene."

I stared at him. "You think she could be involved?"

"Those two women were on the outs even before Irene started that rumor about Nina," he said.

"Yeah, but come on. It's one thing to hate someone. It's another to hate someone so much you're willing to commit murder."

"What if Irene was on the verge of discovering who Nina was screwing?" he asked. "What if she taunted her with it? Like, 'As soon as I know who you're getting it on with, the whole town will know.' I could see her doing that."

Unfortunately, so could I.

Martin exited the expressway and merged with traffic on a busy four-lane artery. "Think about it, Jane. A vague rumor about an affair is one thing. If that gets back to Mal, Nina could always claim it was a case of dirty politics. He's such an agreeable guy he'd probably buy it."

"But if her mystery lover is identified," I said, "she stands to lose Mal and maybe even the kids. The thing is, I know you think she's going to dump Patrick, but I don't necessarily agree. I think she might be planning to make a new life with him." And the baby they were expecting.

"What do you base that on?"

"It's just a feeling," I said.

I tried to recall Nina's exact words after she'd tossed her cookies during the tournament. Hadn't she used the word *we*? She'd said something like *We're not telling people yet*. Her husband hadn't known she was pregnant, but maybe the real father did. Patrick. I chose not to share Nina's condition with Martin. She asked me to keep mum, and unless our idle speculation about her involvement in Irene's death turned out to be true, I saw no reason to go back on my word.

"Let's not forget," he said, "O'Rourke's married too. Though as motives for murder go, inheriting sixteen mil beats saving a marriage."

"You're an incurable romantic."

"That's one thing I've never been accused of." He zipped around slow-moving traffic, seemingly oblivious to the posted speed limit. "So is it true that Irene hired a PI to get the goods on Nina?"

I nodded. "Sten already received his bill."

"My guess is that she had no intention of calling off the

investigation just because she lost the election," he said. "If I knew Irene, the defeat would make her even more determined to seek revenge—to find out who Nina's mystery man was so she could wreak maximum havoc."

"But if the mystery man turned out to be someone Irene was close to?" I asked. "She must have cared deeply about Patrick to leave him all that money."

Martin nodded. "If she even suspected he was the one Nina was sleeping with, she would've found some other way to attack her—some way that didn't involve O'Rourke."

"What was that you said earlier," I asked, "about Nina's poker tell? She taps her fingernails?"

"Yep. When she's bluffing. Why?"

I'd seen Nina do that nail-tapping thing not too long ago. I struggled to recall the circumstance. "It's nothing, I guess. I can't remember."

He gave me a searching look. "What was she saying when she did it? Think."

I closed my eyes and took a deep breath. I thought back to that day at Janey's Place when Nina and I were talking, before she got doused with chili. We were discussing Irene's death. She was offering cloying false sympathy.

My eyes flew open. "*Jaws*. She said Irene was watching *Jaws* when she died."

"Was she?"

"Yes, but no one knew that but me," I said. "Well, Jonah knew, but I asked him not to spread it around. I didn't want everyone in town talking about it, you know? He said he wouldn't, and I believed him. Still do. Nina told me she didn't remember where she heard it. That's when she did that nail-tapping thing."

"She was lying," he said. "So the question becomes, how could Nina Wallace know what Irene was doing at the time of her death?"

"Unless she was there." My breath caught. "Maybe those were her wet footprints."

Martin glanced at me, a question in his pale blue eyes. I told him about the footprints in the laundry room the night Irene died. "I thought maybe Irene went outside for something after the rain started," I said, "but they could have been left by someone entering through the back door."

"Since when does Nina Wallace know how to pick locks?" he asked.

"Nina *Hannigan* Wallace," I said. "You're forgetting her illustrious family heritage."

"Oh, right, she's Hokum Hannigan's, what, granddaughter?"

"Great-granddaughter," I said. "You know, Hannigan's criminal activities didn't stop at bootlegging and rum-running. That guy was one scary dude."

I thought of the framed black-and-white photo of Hokum that held a place of honor in the Prohibition museum Nina had constructed in the basement of the Historical Society. He'd stared right into the camera. Everything about the image, from the angle of his fedora to the way he held his cigar to his menacing sneer, said, *You don't want to mess with me.*

"You think Nina got the bad gene?" Martin asked. "Three generations later?"

"It's just something to keep in mind. I'm brainstorming here."

"I thought Irene was poisoned by something in the smoothies Patrick brought her."

"She was," I said, "but maybe Nina really was in cahoots with him, like you said. Maybe she went there to deliver some kind of coup de grâce." I entertained a mental image of Nina slipping in through Irene's back door, wearing a black ski mask and carrying a plate of yummy baked goods. She never visited anyone without bringing yummy baked goods. "You know…" I waved away the thought. "Nah, forget it, it's nothing."

"Nothing's nothing at this point." He shot me a commanding look. "What is it?"

"It's just that, you know, Nina's always baking. She brought homemade cookies and stuff to the Poker Posse games all the time. It would have been easy for her to… No, that's stupid," I said. "I've been eating those cookies. So has everyone else. No one but Irene got a stomachache."

"Okay, but that gets me thinking about the assumptions we're making." He turned onto the road that would take us into Crystal Harbor.

"What do you mean?"

"Well, we know that O'Rourke brought Irene smoothies," he said. "We know that the smoothies contained poison. Who's to say he's the one who poisoned them?"

"Well, I suppose Nina could have done it without his knowledge, but—"

"You're ignoring the obvious," he said.

It took a few moments for the implication to sink in. "Maria?"

"She had access to all of Irene's food," he said. "Hell, she *made* all of Irene's food. Did they get along?"

"Well, outwardly they did, but privately Irene treated her like crap and she resented it." I saw what Martin was getting at. "If

Maria poisoned her employer's food, everyone would know it was her. But if she poisoned the smoothies that someone else brought her…"

"Then the deed gets blamed on the someone else." He blew past a traffic light as it turned red.

I frowned, mentally grasping at something that kept skittering away. "Oh," I said when I caught up with it. "Hmm."

"'Oh hmm' what?" he asked. "And don't tell me it's nothing."

"I don't know how thoroughly you searched Irene's house. Which is my house now," I added, "so you can just stop it."

"Why? What did you find?"

"Well, I saw something under the kitchen sink," I said. "I didn't think anything of it at the time. Wasp spray."

"Which is a kind of insecticide."

"Yeah, but… well, everyone has bug spray and stuff like that lying around."

"Irene left Maria zilch in her will," he reminded me. "Well, almost zilch, which is worse. After how many years of service?"

"Twenty-eight," I said. "But the thing is, Maria thought Irene was leaving her a wad of cash. Enough to retire on. That's what Irene told her."

Martin emitted a low whistle. "Good reason to want her dead. She could have dosed the smoothies with wasp spray and made sure there were leftovers sitting in the fridge."

I followed his train of thought. "So that in case anyone got suspicious, the evidence would point away from her and toward Patrick."

"Imagine," he said. "Maria murders her employer for the inheritance, and then finds out the old woman left her enough for a couple of fill-ups at the gas station."

I glanced out the window and jerked upright. I'd been so absorbed in our conversation I hadn't noticed where Martin was taking us. "What are we doing at the cemetery?"

"A little detour." He drove along the narrow main road, past rows of headstones. "This won't take long. Where's Seventh Street? Okay, there's Sixth."

I knew Martin's grandparents weren't here. They'd been cremated. "Are you looking for relatives?"

"Why would I?" he asked. "They never looked for me. Anyway, Clan McAuliffe is over in the north section. Green Valley, they call it." His mouth twisted. "You see any valleys around here?"

Valleys, no, but there were a few stretches of open lawn and more than a few willow trees sheltering stone benches. Whispering Willows Cemetery was a pleasant, well-maintained boneyard, for which I was grateful since my chosen career brought me here on a regular basis.

Martin turned left onto Seventh and slowed to a crawl, peering at section markers. Finally he stopped and got out of the car. He gestured for me to follow.

"I'll stay here," I said, trying to control Sexy Beast, who was excited by the fact that we'd reached some sort of destination and also by the interesting aromas that had him sniffing to beat the band. Considering where we were, I chose not to think about what his turbocharged nose detected that mine didn't. "Anyway," I added, "I'm pretty sure dogs aren't allowed here."

He bent to grin at me through the open window, his blue eyes luminescent in the sunlight. "And you always follow the rules, don't you, Jane?"

I sighed, looking around the cemetery. Other than an elderly couple in a distant section, the place was deserted.

"Come on." Martin thumped the car hood. "I need an assistant." He turned and strolled among the headstones, looking for one in particular, clearly confident I'd follow.

Which made me want to stay put to spite him, but SB was scrabbling at the door and barking, and curiosity gnawed at me. Assistant for what?

I exited the car with SB, who strained at the leash, wild to investigate this wonderful new playground. I indulged him until he started to lift his leg on a headstone. "No!" I cried. "SB, no! Hold it in!" I shortened the leash and trotted him to the nearest willow tree. Anxiously I peered around while SB watered the tree, expecting at any moment to be busted by a cemetery employee.

By the time I joined Martin, he was standing before a granite headstone, studying a small index card he held which was covered in scribbled notes. I looked at the stone. Roberta Lynton Montero, who'd died five years earlier at age sixty. The name was familiar, though I couldn't place her. The stone next to hers belonged to a Roberto Alejandro Montero—her husband, I assumed. Roberto and Roberta. How adorable is that? He'd died seventeen years ago.

After a minute Martin nodded to himself, slid the card into his pocket, and retrieved his cell phone. "All right, let's get started."

"Why are you talking like that?" I asked.

"Like what?"

"You know darn well like what," I said. "Like an Irishman. From Ireland."

"Well now, I'm just getting into character, aren't I?" He tapped the screen on his cell and handed it to me. Another smart phone. Good grief, was I the last holdout?

"What am I supposed to do with this?" I asked.

"Stand here." Martin positioned me off to the side. "You're going to be shooting video. Start with an establishing shot. Do a sweep of the whole graveyard, then home in on Roberta's headstone for a few seconds, make sure it can be read, then move out to frame me and the stone in the shot. Try to keep the dog quiet." He adjusted his clerical collar and brushed lint off his black priest's outfit.

"'Establishing shot,' huh?" I was tempted to remind him his last name wasn't Scorsese. "I don't even know how to work this thing."

"Nothing to it." He indicated a little red icon on the phone. "Just touch that. As long as it's blinking, it's recording. Let's go." He circled his finger as if to say, *Roll 'em.*

What the heck. I looped the leash handle over my wrist and told SB to lie down and then stay. He looked like he had other plans, but he obeyed. "Good boy." I reached into my purse for a slender, pepperoni-style dog treat that I hoped would keep him busy for a while.

I started the video and did as Martin had instructed, getting a sweeping view of the rows of tombstones before zeroing in on Roberta's. Martin cleared his throat and I realized I'd lingered a little too long on her stone, still trying to remember how I knew this woman.

I backed up until I had both Martin and the stone framed in the shot. The little red dot was blinking. So far, so good. Then the padre started to speak.

"Oh, Roberta, my beautiful, sexy darlin', how I have missed you." If anything, the Irish brogue got thicker. "When I close my eyes, I imagine I can still taste your luscious lips, your silken shoulders…"

He went on to list the other parts of Roberta he could still taste, in XXX-rated detail. My mouth sagged open.

"You were the only woman who could make me forget my vow of celibacy, my darlin' Roberta," he went on, with feeling. "From the very moment we met, all I could think about was the wicked, sinful things I yearned to do to you."

He commenced to describe those wicked, sinful things, one by one, as my face heated. And yeah, that wasn't my only physical response. There, I said it. You happy?

Part of me wanted to stop the recording, to demand what in the world was going on. Another part of me wanted to hear what other dirty stuff Father Martin intended to tell the corpse moldering under our feet. Guess which part won.

He continued, "I'll never forget that time we slipped away from the potluck supper and made savage love in the church coatroom. I know I was rough with you then, my darlin', but I couldn't help myself. You always brought out the beast in me."

To hear the padre tell it, their rough coatroom sex involved a variety of inventive acts and acrobatic positions.

My brain chose that moment to slide the pieces together. Roberta Montero. I'd helped arrange her funeral reception five years earlier. The client who'd hired me? Roberta's good friend Veronica Sheffield, my Death Diva cash cow.

The very same Veronica Sheffield I'd watched Martin chat up at the poker tournament.

My gasp of outrage brought an answering yip from SB but had no effect on Martin, who was in the process of wrapping up his filthy little monologue.

"Memories of that last time," he said, "in the church school bus, are what keep me going during the long, cold nights—"

"You bastard!" I stalked up to him with the phone, framing a close-up of his hatefully handsome face. Sexy Beast jumped up, barking excitedly at this new game. "You raided my client!"

He plucked the phone out of my hand and shut off the video camera. "No need for a second take. I can delete that last bit before Veronica sees it."

"You copied my business model." I shoved his chest. Hard. He didn't seem to notice. "*I'm* the Death Diva, Padre. I've been doing this for more than twenty years. You can't just waltz in and… and make off with my idea. My clients."

I'd spied him talking to Maia Armstrong, too, at the tournament. The caterer. Maia and I had been referring clients to each other for years. Obviously he intended to horn in on that action as well. I thought Martin had just been taunting me that night at the bar when he'd said he might try his hand at what I did for a living. *Doing sick things to dead people* was how he'd put it.

He jerked his head toward Roberta's tombstone. "Veronica's pal here had a thing for Irish priests. She wanted to give Roberta a little something to keep up her spirit in the afterworld."

That certainly sounded like flaky Veronica. "She should have come to me," I said.

"Roberta was into priests, not nuns." His grin was salacious. "Although if you ever take a job that calls for hot lesbian action, give me a call. I'll hold the video camera."

"Can you be serious for one second?"

"Hey." He spread his hands, all innocence. "I'm just offering to return the favor."

"I didn't mean I'd have, you know, stood here and…" I made a vague gesture toward Roberta's grave. "But I could have… well, I could have subcontracted it out. Found a guy to dress up like a priest and put on an accent and all that."

"It wouldn't have been the same. Admit it." He slathered on the brogue. "You got yourself all hot and bothered listening to Father Martin's naughty ramblings, now didn't you, lass?"

"Oh, good grief." I turned and headed for the car so he wouldn't see how on the mark he was. "Come on, SB, we're done here."

He kept pace with me. "It was Veronica's script, not mine. Well, I embellished a bit."

"I'm sure you did," I said. "That's not even anatomically possible. That last position. In the, um, school bus."

"Is that so?" His voice held the hint of a dare.

I picked up the pace, jerking poor SB away from this and that fascinating thing he paused to sniff. I grabbed him up, hurled us into the passenger seat, and slammed the door. It felt darn good and I got a chance to do it again when I realized I'd caught the leash in the door.

Martin took his place behind the wheel with exasperating calm. He reached across my body and I shouted, "What are you doing?" just before he pulled the seat belt and buckled me in.

"What's got you so jumpy all of a sudden?" His silky half smile made me want to beat him with Mr. F's tire iron.

"This is the worst possible time for you to horn in on my business," I said, as he drove toward the exit. "A lot of my jobs came from Irene. With her gone, my income's going to take a big hit."

"You talk like you haven't just inherited a big-ass house worth millions." Before I could speak, he added, "And spare me that crap about how it really belongs to the dog."

"Well, technically—"

"My grandmother's dream house does not belong to any damn poodle!"

His outburst caused the damn poodle in question to stop car-whining. Martin's features were rigid, his knuckles pale on the steering wheel.

After a few moments I said, "Of course it doesn't. That's just a… it's a legal device." I watched him take a deep breath and slowly exhale. I wondered about his mysterious past, about the experiences that had shaped him and taught him to control his anger. "Your grandma McAuliffe chose that house?"

He didn't answer right away and I wondered if he'd shut me out. He turned out of the cemetery onto the town's main road and said, "They had it built as soon as they could afford to. Their sons were grown by then—it was the mid-sixties—but Grandma had wanted a house like that her whole life, and Grandpa was finally in a position to give it to her."

"Yeah, but when they divorced about twenty years later," I said, "Arthur ended up with the house."

"Irene was on the lookout for a rich old husband, and he fit the bill," he said. "So the old bitch pried him away from Grandma, but that wasn't enough. She knew how much Grandma loved that house, how she'd built it to her specifications. Grandpa was still in thrall to Irene at that point, and she persuaded him to fight for the house and put her name on the deed. It was all too much for Grandma."

"Anne died not long after Irene and Arthur married, as I recall."

"Eight months," he said. "That's when Grandpa realized what a monumental mistake he'd made. He never got over it."

He died a few years later, and Anne McAuliffe's dream house went to the scheming second wife. And eventually to Jane Delaney, Death Diva. And a neurotic little poodle.

"Are you thinking the house would have gone to you," I asked, "if your grandparents had remained married?"

He shrugged, as if that were of no concern. "It would've stayed in the family, that's all that matters."

"I thought you hated the McAuliffes."

"That's not the point." He wore an enigmatic smile as he added, "The younger generation aren't so bad."

The younger generation? Was Martin in touch with Anne and Arthur's grandchildren? Or was he referring to the great-grandchildren? I didn't even know how far the McAuliffe dynasty had spread.

"So that's why you're doing this to me?" I asked. "Sabotaging the business I worked two decades to build because I happened to end up owning your grandmother's house? I don't know what you think, but I never asked for it or… or schemed to get it. I was stunned when I got the news."

"Oh, I forgot," he sneered. "You're just a helpless pawn in all this. You are in no way responsible for any part you might have played in Irene's malignant little games."

Malignant game. An apt description for loading the ashes of anti-firearms activist Anne McAuliffe into shotgun shells. I was tempted to remind him I was just following orders, but it would have sounded as lame to him as it did to me. Hadn't I already decided I wasn't off the hook for trying to steal the brooch for Irene? I should have challenged her all along instead of doing her bidding without question for all those years.

And if I had, would she have left me her house?

Martin glanced at me and I knew he read it on my face. The doubt, the self-recrimination. Instinct told me to go on the attack.

"Speaking of games," I said, "you deliberately flirted with Veronica Sheffield just to get this sex-talk gig. Deny it."

"What's your point?"

I sat up. "Wait a minute. Hold on." I'd been so outraged by Martin's raiding my clients, it hadn't occurred to me to ask the obvious question. "How did you know about Veronica?"

"What do you mean?"

"You know what I mean." I twisted in my seat to face him. SB perched on my hip to whine out the window. "How did you find out she's one of my clients? And Maia too—that we throw business each other's way?" These were things he couldn't have learned from Irene's files.

"Have you always been this suspicious?"

It hit me like an anvil. "You broke in to my apartment!"

"You need better computer passwords," he said. "Your anniversary? Really?"

"You got into my *computer*?" I thought of my out-of-date laptop, sitting there all vulnerable on my rickety kitchen table.

"It took me less than a minute, literally, to guess it," he said. "I mean, your *anniversary*? How long has that marriage been over?"

"I've been meaning to change it," I muttered. "Wait, how do you know the date Dom and I got married?"

"It's printed right there on the invitation. Page one in your wedding album."

"You went through my wedding album? You were in my bedroom?" I'd kept the album on a closet shelf, in a box with other memorabilia. Pictures of Dom. Pictures of me and Dom. Little gifts from Dom. Birthday cards from Dom. Love letters from Dom.

I couldn't decide whether to throw up or faint, imagining Martin reading Dom's youthful, lustful letters to me.

"When…" I could barely speak. "When did you do this? When did you break in to my place?"

"Last Friday. I waited till you left." He turned onto my street. "You looked totally hot, by the way. You should wear that green dress more often."

That was the day I'd gone to Ted Seabrook's funeral, playing the part of his sexpot mistress. I'd left my bedroom strewn with clothing and shoes, after trying on practically every item in my closet in an attempt to find an outfit sexy enough for the gig. And then there was the matter of choosing the right underwear to go with the slinky dress. I groaned, recalling the thongs and push-up bras I'd left littering the bed.

I narrowed my eyes at him. "Did you finish my tequila?"

"There was a sip left."

"There was a good, solid shot left in that bottle. I was saving it." I could have used it right then. "So who else?" I demanded. "What other clients of mine have you gone after?"

"Well, Sophie Halperin's uncle Morty just kicked the bucket," he said. "She has me ordering a bunch of food for the folks sitting shivah. What do you think? Nova or belly lox?"

"That job was supposed to be mine!" I said. "Morty's been teetering on the edge for months. I had the menu picked out and everything."

"You snooze, you lose." He turned onto the long, tree-lined drive to my new home. "Sophie had doubts about trusting the job to some shaygetz she'd just met, but I assured her I've catered plenty of kosher events. And that I'm half-Jewish."

"You lied, in other words."

"Plus I undercut your prices by twenty percent," he said. "Plus I'm cute as all get-out."

"Who's that?" I squinted at the dark sedan parked in the courtyard. I didn't recognize it.

Martin frowned. "Plainclothes."

"What?"

"A cop." He pulled in behind it.

"How can you tell?" I asked, then realized I probably didn't want to know.

The occupant of the unmarked vehicle got out at the same moment we did and I found myself standing face-to-face with Detective Bonnie Hernandez.

Dom's fiancée wore a smart burgundy pantsuit and heels. Her dark hair was cut short and feathery around her face, and she was as pretty as I remembered from Dom's Christmas party last December when he'd introduced us. If Bonnie was surprised to see me in the company of a priest, she hid it well.

Of the many thoughts vying for attention at that moment, the one that whined loudest was, *I hope she doesn't think this heap is my car.*

Sexy Beast, the anti-Frederick, strained at the leash, barking ferociously at the interloper. I picked him up and hushed him, causing him to mutter indignantly about not being allowed to do his job.

"Bonnie. Hi. This is a, uh, surprise." I forced myself to smile.

She made no such effort. "Listen, I want to thank you for getting SB that appointment with Rocky."

"You're welcome. This isn't a personal visit." She retained a slight accent from her native Dominican Republic, from which she'd emigrated with her family as a small child. She stuck out her hand to Martin. "Detective Bonnie Hernandez, Crystal Harbor PD."

They shook. "Martin Kade."

How convenient. A middle name that sounded like a last name. I found myself wondering whether impersonating a priest is a crime.

"I have some questions that I'm hoping you can help me with, Jane." Bonnie indicated the front door. "This shouldn't take long."

"Um, okay," I said. "This is about Irene, I assume? I mean, I know Sten Jakobsen told the police—"

"Why don't we discuss this inside." She dismissed Martin with a curt "It was nice to meet you, Father Kade."

"Jane, don't talk to her without a lawyer," he said. "You don't have to talk to her at all."

"What? No," I said. "Bonnie just wants me to tell her what little I know—the same stuff I told Sten. Right?" I asked her.

"We're wasting time standing around out here," Bonnie said. "I'm sure you're as busy as I am. The sooner we get started—"

"I know someone." Martin tipped my face up, his gaze locked on mine. "He can be here in half an hour."

"That's… it's insane. I don't need a lawyer just to answer a few routine questions." I turned to Bonnie, feeling my insides tighten. "Do I?"

At last, something that could almost be called a smile. "Not if you haven't done anything wrong."

12
You Never Told Me What a Ditz She Is!

"SO YOU HAVEN'T arrested Patrick yet?" I asked. Bonnie and I were perched on matching linen-upholstered armchairs. Martin sat across the glass coffee table from us on the big, cushy living room sofa. His posture was indolent, one arm draped on the sofa back as he lazily stroked Sexy Beast, but I knew he was anything but relaxed.

When the meddlesome Father Kade had followed us into the house, Bonnie had told him to make tracks. He'd told her no. Just like that. "No." In the end it was up to me, and I'd decided to trust his instincts and let him stay. It was a good bet he knew more about the perils and pitfalls of chatting with the cops than I did. I'd drawn the line, however, at calling in a lawyer. I mean really—how could I possibly be considered a suspect?

"No one is under arrest at this point," she said.

"But you interrogated him, right?" I said. "I mean, I know Sten shared all the facts with you, the toxicology report and all—"

"I spoke with Patrick this morning at Janey's Place," she said.

"He confirmed that he'd been bringing Irene those special drinks from the shop to settle her stomach."

"See?" I leaned toward her, jabbing the air. "He lied to me. He said they didn't come from him. But Maria—that's Irene's housekeeper—"

"I know Maria."

"She told me they did," I said. "Why would he have lied about that if he had nothing to hide?"

"When did you and Patrick have this conversation?"

"Last Saturday," I said, "when I caught him snooping through the fridge looking for that last remaining smoothie cup. The cup that could incriminate him."

"The cup you later found in Irene's garbage."

"Right."

"Patrick says he was never here that day."

"Well, that's just another whopper," I said.

"And no one else was here then?" she asked. "You're the only one who saw him going through the fridge?"

"Yeah. So?"

"So the thing that makes this awkward, Jane, is that I have only your word to go on." Bonnie gave me an apologetic little smile. Out of the corner of my eye I saw Martin go very still.

"Why would I fabricate something like that?" I asked.

"No one's accusing you of fabricating anything," she said, "but I can't make any progress here when it's just your word against Patrick's. He insists he hasn't been in this house since before Irene died."

"Well, isn't there some way you can prove he was here?" I said. "I mean, he had to have left fingerprints on the fridge."

"I'm sure he did," Bonnie said, "since he brought her those

smoothies every day. He told me she didn't drink them right away. He'd put them in the fridge and she'd sip them a little at a time whenever her stomach was acting up."

"Great, and meanwhile the stuff that was supposed to be helping her was slowly killing her." Yet Irene hadn't mentioned the chronic pain to her doctor until it was too late. If she were alive, I'd give her hell for being such a stubborn old fool.

"Your fingerprints are probably on that fridge, too," Bonnie said.

"Well, sure they are." My guts knotted again. "This is my house now. And even before then, when Irene was alive, I was here all the time. At least two or three times a week."

Martin caught my eye and sent a wordless command. *Shut up. Stop volunteering information she didn't ask for.*

"I need to consider every possibility, Jane, no matter how outlandish it might sound." Bonnie gave me another of those benign little smiles that were beginning to seem anything but. "You can understand that, right? It's my job." She spread her hands. The four-karat diamond on her left ring finger ignited in the sunlight streaming through the towering window. Good grief, the thing was the size of an M&M. Plain, not peanut, but still.

When Dom had married me, I'd gotten a plain silver band. He'd promised to replace it with a gold one as soon as the money started coming in, as soon as Janey's Place was out of the red. It was all right because I loved him. We loved each other. And wasn't that worth more than gold and diamonds and all that shallow stuff?

Bonnie's shallow stuff threatened to blind me every time she moved her left hand. Of course, I happened to know she was getting another little wedding present from Dom that I didn't get back then either—a prenup. Pretty standard nowadays when one party comes to the marriage with significantly more wealth than the other, but that doesn't take away the ick factor. I was dying to know the details of the contract Sten had drawn up at Dom's request—who walks away with what, and under what circumstances, in the all-too-likely event Mrs. Faso Number Four turns into The Former Mrs. Faso Number Four.

Then again, Bonnie Hernandez was what Irene used to call a smart cookie. I couldn't see her compliantly signing any old thing Dom shoved under her nose before her own lawyer had checked it over and negotiated more favorable terms.

Ah, romance.

"So just bear with me here," Bonnie said, "while I work through the various what-ifs."

Why did I get the feeling this smart cookie had already worked through the various what-ifs long before she pulled up to my door? I sensed it would be all too easy for me to step in a big, steaming pile of what-if.

I glanced at Martin and saw my thoughts reflected on his face. I could stop answering questions at any time, he silently reminded me. But wouldn't I look guilty then? Like I had something to hide?

"The insecticides they found in that cup, and in Irene," she said, "they're pretty common."

I nodded. "That's what the pathologist told Sten. They're found in a bunch of different bug killers."

"Patrick says he has no idea how the poison got into those drinks," Bonnie said. "Or to be more precise, how it got into the cup you gave to Sten, because that's the only thing connecting the smoothies with the poison."

"Of course he doesn't," I scoffed.

"So the question I have to ask myself is, who had access to those drinks?" she said. "Obviously Patrick did while he was making them and transporting them here."

"Not to mention his sneaking into my house and lying—"

She stopped me with a raised palm. "We're talking opportunity here, Jane. Who else could have messed with those smoothies?"

"You know, I did wonder about Maria, but the more I think about it..." I shook my head.

"She was here every day," Bonnie pointed out. "It would have been easy enough for her to do it."

"She tasted one of them once," I said. "She told me it was awful and she didn't know why anyone would drink them."

"Yet her boss did. Willingly."

"Well, Irene despised health food," I said. "To her, the poisoned smoothie probably tasted exactly like she expected a healthy drink to taste, and she choked it down because it was supposed to make her stomach feel better. My point is, why would Maria come right out and say that to me, just volunteer how terrible the stuff tasted, if she was the one who poisoned them?"

"I see what you mean," Bonnie said. "It would be in her interest to let everyone keep thinking Irene died of a simple heart attack. No autopsy, no investigation. Saying that to you about the smoothies is like waving a red flag."

"Exactly." I sent Martin a smug look that said, *See? I have this under control.* He did not appear convinced, especially when I added, "There's actually a can of wasp spray under the kitchen sink, but everyone has stuff like that lying around, right?"

"Do you mind if I take it with me for testing?" Bonnie asked.

I opened my mouth to say, "Knock yourself out," but Martin spoke first.

"No." He sat up straight. "Jane, don't let her remove anything from this house."

I wanted to argue with him. I wanted to ask why on earth I shouldn't cooperate if it would help the cops apprehend Irene's killer. But the look on his face told me I had my foot poised over that stinky old pile. He could see it even if I couldn't.

"Well, um," I said, "maybe it's not such a good idea for you to do that, Bonnie. Not right now, anyway."

"Don't you want to know whether the ingredients in the wasp spray match up with what they found in the tox screen?" she asked, the soul of reason.

If they did, it would be coincidence. I was certain Patrick had poisoned the smoothies before bringing them into this house and that Irene's wasp spray had nothing to do with it. "It can, you know, wait. Like I said."

Detective Hernandez treated the pesky priest to a long, suspicious stare. "Tell me, Father, do you belong to the diocese? I know you're not with the local parish."

"You know, I'm really very busy today," I blurted, hoping to deflect her attention from Martin. "I'm in the middle of moving. So if that's all…"

"That's not all," Bonnie said. "Maria isn't the only one who had unimpeded access to Irene's refrigerator."

It took a few seconds for her meaning to sink in, and when it did, the blood drained from my head in a sickening rush. I glanced at Martin, who said, "Now would be a good time to stop talking."

"I'm sure Father Kade thinks he's doing you a favor," Bonnie said, "but refusing to cooperate with the police does not send a favorable message."

My mouth felt dry. I licked my lips. "That's just... crazy. I could never hurt Irene."

Martin stood, and SB immediately curled up on the nice warm spot he'd just vacated. "Jane. Listen to me." He leaned on the arms of my chair, his face inches from mine. "Talking to the cops can never help you. It can only hurt you."

I tore my gaze from his. I had to make Bonnie understand. "Ask Dom. He'll tell you how I felt about Irene. She was like a grandmother to me. I loved her."

Martin straightened with a sigh of resignation.

"What possible reason would I have to hurt her?" I continued. "Okay, she gave me this house in her will, but I didn't even know about that until after she died. Now, Patrick *knew* he was in her will. He knew ahead of time that she was leaving him sixteen million bucks. That's a motive for murder if ever there was one."

Martin slumped back onto the sofa, displacing SB, both of them looking thoroughly disgruntled. Well, what could it hurt to point out the obvious? To remind Bonnie that what Patrick had to gain by killing Irene was a heck of a lot more than what I had to gain?

"I agree," Bonnie said. "That kind of money would definitely qualify as motive for murder."

"Thank you." I tossed my hand as if to say, *There! Some common sense.* Martin did not appear to share my relief. The grump.

Bonnie smoothed a wrinkle out of her pants leg. "Of course, if

Patrick O'Rourke were convicted of murdering Irene McAuliffe, he would be disqualified from inheriting her fortune."

"Well, I should hope so," I said.

"I take it you've read Irene's will?" she asked.

"Of course."

"Then you know that if Patrick is disqualified," she said, "his inheritance will go to you."

I started to nod, then said, "Wait, what? It'll go to me?" I looked at Martin, who glumly nodded. Unlike me, he'd apparently made it past the first few paragraphs of legalese. I experienced another head rush and slumped back against my chair.

"It works in reverse," Bonnie said. "If you were disqualified from inheriting, Patrick would get the house. I mean, it's a nice house, but it can't compare with what he's getting, am I right? Plus the money comes with no strings attached." She nodded toward Sexy Beast, as if he were some kind of unwanted obligation.

As I struggled to formulate a response, she added, "But you know all this, because you read the will."

"Yes," I murmured, then, "No! I didn't read that far. I didn't know about that part. Plus I didn't even come across her will until after she was dead."

"Where did you come across it?" Bonnie asked.

I pointed upstairs. "Her file cabinet."

"Did she keep the cabinet locked?"

Absently I nodded. "The key is behind the O'Keefe painting."

Martin's gruff exhalation shook me out of the stupor that threatened to hijack my brain.

I got to my feet. "Okay, we're done here. This conversation is over."

"And you're telling me you never borrowed that key and sneaked a peek at Irene's will?" Bonnie asked. "Coming here two or three times a week like you did, for how many years?"

I didn't bother telling her that Irene had shown me where she hid the key in case of an emergency, because she trusted me. I didn't tell her that I'd never opened that file cabinet while Irene was alive and that when I finally did, I hadn't needed the key because Martin had left it unlocked after breaking into it.

Too late, I remembered what the smart murderers always told the detectives on the ten million episodes of *Law & Order* I'd sat through. *I'm not saying anything until my lawyer gets here.*

Gee, if only someone had given me good advice like that.

I imagined Bonnie entertaining Dom with a blow-by-blow of this whole wretched conversation. She'd tell him how I kept opening my yap and digging myself in deeper, all the while ignoring Father Kade's commonsense warnings. They'd laugh and she'd say, You never told me what a ditz she is! And he'd say, Why do you think I never wanted to have kids with her?

Bonnie didn't budge from her seat. "You do see how it looks, don't you, Jane? You, who have the most to gain from Patrick O'Rourke's conviction for Irene's murder, have pulled out the stops to incriminate him." She ticked off points on her fingers. "You claim you found Patrick searching the victim's fridge, a claim that cannot be corroborated. You 'discover' a contaminated cup that links him to the crime. You pressure the victim's executor to halt her cremation and order an autopsy, which, sure enough, reveals the presence of toxins matching those found in the cup. And for some inexplicable reason, you refuse to allow me to test a can of bug spray that might be connected to the crime."

Martin rose and stood next to me. "Jane ended this interview, Detective. It's time for you to leave."

She sighed, stood, and produced a business card from her pocket. "We got off to a bad start, Jane. If you truly had nothing to do with Irene's death, I know you'll want to help the investigation any way you can. I'll be in touch, but in the meantime, please call me if you decide you're ready to talk." She flicked an irritated glance at Martin. "Just the two of us."

When I didn't take the card, she set it on the coffee table, just as the doorbell rang. Sexy Beast flew off the sofa and ran into the foyer, barking. He built up so much steam he skidded the last few feet on the wood floor and nearly beaned himself on the doorframe.

I left Bonnie and Martin in the living room and went to open the front door. Dom stood on the porch, offering a sheepish smile and a crystal vase crammed with more tulips than I'd ever seen in one place in my life. My favorite flower in my favorite color assortment: peach, cream, and pale pink, with a scattering of butter yellow. He tipped his head to the side in that charmingly apologetic way he had.

SB stopped barking and went into the submissive, I-am-unworthy posture he adopts when greeting one more alpha than he—a category that includes any human he knows and trusts. Head down, tail tucked in, scraping toward the object of his adoration, basically pleading for a scrap of recognition. But only if it's not too much trouble. I was grateful Bonnie was in the other room and not witness to this embarrassingly un-Frederick-like display.

Dom bent to give SB a few pats and said, "I figured if I delivered these myself, there'd be less chance of you sending them back."

In a whisper I said, "This is not a good time, Dom."

He managed to slip into the house before I could slam the door shut. "One minute, that's all I ask." He closed the door behind him. "Hear me out."

"This is *not* a good time," I growled, sotto voce. "Trust me, you do not want to be here right now." I tried to reach around him for the doorknob, a move he deflected by wrapping his free arm around me.

"Janey, I'm sorry. Sincerely sorry. I never meant to disrespect you, especially in public."

I tried in vain to push him away. "Dom—"

"Am I forgiven?"

"Yes! Yes!" I hissed. "You're forgiven. Now, go."

"That's my Janey. Next time I grab your ass," he joked, while grabbing my ass, "I'll make sure there are no witnesses."

"Good idea," Martin said.

Dom looked toward the entrance to the living room, where the padre stood next to a grim-faced Bonnie. If I'd morphed into a giant, radioactive scorpion, he couldn't have shoved me away any faster, while losing his grip on the vase. Water, glass shards, and about a million tulips erupted in all directions on the gleaming ebony. SB shrieked and bolted for the dining room. I ran after him and scooped him up as Dom tried to make his mouth work.

"B-Bonnie—what are—I didn't—this isn't—"

Her frigid gaze traveled from his stricken face to the tulips carpeting the foyer to his left hand, the one she'd just witnessed giving his ex-wife's posterior a merry squeeze. Brick red splotches crawled up her throat and into her cheeks, but to her credit, she kept it together.

"I'm here on business," was all she said.

"Business?" His eyebrows pulled together. "What kind of business?"

"*Police* business, Dom?" Her expression said, *You do recall what I do for a living?*

Martin wore a cream-lapping grin, the first smile he'd offered since before Bonnie showed up. Dom seemed to notice him for the first time.

"What's he doing here?" he demanded, as though his fiancée weren't wondering the same thing about him.

"Spiritual support," Martin said.

Watching Dom squirm was the second most entertaining thing I'd done all day—after hearing Martin talk dirty to a corpse—but my schadenfreude was dampened by the knowledge that if Detective Hernandez didn't have it in for me before, she sure as shootin' did now. Based on the preponderance of evidence, she doubtless considered Dom's presence in my home an open-and-shut case.

Before Dom could pounce on that "spiritual support" line and out the faux padre, I jumped in with, "I'll tell you what Bonnie's doing here. She thinks I killed Irene and framed Patrick O'Rourke for the murder."

I don't think I'd ever seen Dom do a classic double-take before. He looked, as the Brits so eloquently put it, gobsmacked. He wheeled on Bonnie. "Are you insane?"

"Dom, this is official police business," she said. "It's none of your concern."

"None of my concern? This is about Janey. Of course it's my concern."

Hoo boy, it was going to be a fun time in the Faso-Hernandez household that night. And okay, I wasn't exactly broken up at the thought. Does that make me a bad person?

Shut up, it was a rhetorical question.

Bonnie said, "We can discuss this later—"

"You couldn't be bothered giving me a heads-up?" he asked. "Considering who we're dealing with here?"

Bonnie folded her arms and treated Dom to a scary dead-eye stare. She hadn't looked at me that way, and she thought I was a coldblooded murderer.

Dom plowed ahead. "Plus Patrick is an employee of mine. Just when were you planning to let me in on all this, *Detective*?"

"Best not to let the water sit on that nice floor," Bonnie told him as she strode toward the front door. "Your Janey will show you where she keeps the mop."

She reached for the knob just as we heard a key scrape in the lock. After a few fruitless jabs from the other side, Bonnie pushed open both double doors, knocking Patrick O'Rourke onto his keister.

"Detective!" Patrick got his feet under him and stumbled over the threshold. His gaze flicked over the tulip carnage, but he paid it no mind. "I can't let you arrest Jane. She didn't do it. Cheyenne made up all that stuff about her framing me."

Cheyenne concocted that story? Was I the only one who couldn't be bothered reading the fine print in Irene McAuliffe's will?

"I came here as soon as I found out she called you," he told Bonnie. "Don't blame my daughter. She's just trying to protect me, but I can't let an innocent person take the rap for something I did."

"Patrick, shut up." Dom pushed past the rest of us to place his hands on his employee's shoulders and look him in the eye. "Don't say anything else without a lawyer."

"Oh, for crying out loud." Bonnie threw up her hands. "Dom, back the hell off and let me do my job."

"Yeah, Dom," I said, "let her do her job." He was supposed to be on my side!

Patrick shook off his boss and faced Bonnie. "It was me. I killed Irene. I did it for the inheritance."

She placed a soothing palm on his back. "Let's go down to the station, away from this crowd, and—"

Martin calmly interrupted her. "That car's going to end up in the living room."

We followed his gaze through the open doorway and saw a compact red sedan race up the drive and fishtail into the courtyard. We held our collective breath as it headed straight for Patrick's Hyundai. At the last second it turned and sideswiped all four of our vehicles lined up in front of the house. Groans and curses filled the foyer. Finally the car spun a three-sixty and came to rest smack-dab in the center of the courtyard.

"Cheyenne, no!" Patrick cried as his daughter lurched out of the car and ran toward the house.

"He didn't do it!" she shouted, tottering up the steps on sparkly five-inch platform pumps. "Daddy didn't kill her. He had nothing to do with it."

"Cheyenne, stop it." Patrick grabbed his daughter's arms and gave her a little shake. "I took care of it, do you hear me? I told the detective the truth—"

"Don't send Daddy to jail!" Her face was red and tear-streaked. "I did it, not him! I murdered my grandma!"

13
Add 2 Tbsp. Insecticide and Stir Well

"YOUR GRANDMA?" I glanced at the others, who appeared just as befuddled. All except Patrick, whose expression, as he gazed at his daughter, was heartbreakingly sad. Colette O'Rourke had officially died of natural causes. If she'd been murdered, it was news to me.

Cheyenne's gaze zeroed in on Martin's clerical collar. "Father!" She dropped to her knees in front of him and grasped his hands, sobbing. "You have to hear my confession. *Please*, Father. I did a terrible thing. I'm gonna go to hell!"

For the first time since I'd known him, Martin was at a complete loss for words. He lifted his stunned face to mine. What could I tell him? *Is it still fun impersonating a priest, smart-ass?*

Bonnie moved to take control of the situation. "Cheyenne, you and your dad are going down to the station with me—"

"No! I have to make confession." She clung tighter to Martin. "Bless me, Father, for I have—"

"Whoa! Whoa!" Martin pulled her to her feet. "Don't do that, Cheyenne. This, uh, this isn't the place."

"Plus," Dom said, "this guy isn't really—"

He broke off with a grunt as my elbow found his ribs. The look I gave him might not be as scary as Bonnie's, but it did the trick. His mouth snapped shut.

Clearly, neither Cheyenne nor her father recognized Martin as the phony priest who'd swiped Colette's brooch—which wasn't surprising considering that for the minute or two that he'd stood at her casket, Patrick had been busy chatting with me, and Cheyenne had been preoccupied with her iPad.

"I won't say anything without him." Cheyenne squeezed Martin's hands so hard, I half-expected to hear bones crack. The knees of her skintight jeans were soaked with tulip water. By some miracle, she'd avoided getting gouged by the broken glass littering the foyer.

I could see Bonnie debating the wisdom of hauling Cheyenne down to the station. By the time they got there, the girl might decide to clam up. "Everyone into the living room," she ordered. "Get away from this mess before someone gets hurt."

"Mop's in the laundry room," I told Dom. He looked ready to object until Bonnie and I gave him a double dose of The Stare. He went to fetch the mop while the rest of us got settled in the living room.

Sexy Beast snugged himself between my right side and the upholstered arm of my chair, one of his favorite snoozing spots. Cheyenne sat on the sofa, flanked by Patrick and Martin, who looked very much like he wanted to stop playing Father Kade. Doing so, however, might have caused Cheyenne to rescind her confession and once again point the finger at me. He was continuing this charade for my sake, I knew.

Bonnie started by reciting Cheyenne's rights, the whole Miranda thing. Patrick wanted her to hold out for a lawyer, but his daughter was determined to get her crime off her chest.

"So, Cheyenne." Bonnie took a small notebook from her jacket pocket. "You say you murdered Colette O'Rourke."

The girl reared back. "What, are you nuts? Grandma O'Rourke had, like, a stroke."

"Well, you said it was your grandma, so…"

Bonnie and I frowned in unison as we mentally wrestled the facts into a new and intriguing reality. Patrick's inheritance. His key to the house. His daily visits.

"Oh," she said.

"Oh," I said.

"Seriously?" Martin looked at Patrick.

Patrick said, "I kinda expected someone would figure it out before now."

I examined Patrick with fresh eyes, looking for some physical similarity to Irene—and found it, in the shape of the mouth and the light brown eyes.

I'd wondered why she'd asked Dom to hire Patrick. Mystery solved.

"Sten Jakobsen's the only one who knew?" Bonnie asked.

Patrick nodded. He squeezed his daughter's hand. "I never even told my family that Irene was my real mom, not until after Sten called to tell me she was gone. I didn't know myself until last June after Dad passed. Mom let it slip then," he said, referring to Colette. "She didn't mean to, she meant to take the secret to her grave."

"But why did Irene give you up?" I asked. "How did Colette

and Burt end up raising you as their own?"

Patrick sighed. "Irene had plans, big plans, from the time she was a kid. No way was she gonna follow in her mom's footsteps, marry some blue-collar guy from the neighborhood and raise a bunch of brats in Bay Ridge. That might be good enough for the other girls, but she wanted something more."

"A rich husband," Dom called from the foyer, where he could hear the whole conversation as he cleaned up the mess.

I looked at Martin and knew he was thinking about his grandparents, whose marriage Irene had wrecked to fulfill her goal.

"But then Irene got pregnant," Bonnie said, and Patrick nodded.

"She was only seventeen," he said. "Mom was her best friend. They were closer than sisters back then. Mom wasn't holding out for a sugar daddy, though. She and Dad were in love. He gave her a ring before he went to Korea. But he got wounded over there and, well, they told him he could never father kids. He offered to let Mom go, to let her find a man that could give her a family, you know? But her and Irene, they came up with a different plan."

"Colette would take care of Irene's problem," I said, "and Irene would take care of Colette's."

Martin spoke up. "By giving her the child she and her husband couldn't have."

Patrick said, "Mom and Dad get married quick. Irene goes away for a few months and Mom pads her dresses. Then she supposedly gives birth, and no one the wiser."

"I didn't know Mrs. McAuliffe was my real grandma. Not until after I—" Cheyenne choked back a sob. "I didn't mean to, I swear. She wanted me to make her sick, not dead."

"Who, Cheyenne?" Bonnie reached across the coffee table to hand the girl tissues. "Who wanted you to make Irene sick?"

Cheyenne looked at her father, who glumly nodded. "Go on," he murmured.

"Grandma O'Rourke." The girl honked into the tissues. "She… she wanted Mrs. McAuliffe to get sick so she'd stay home from the poker tournament and Grandma would win. She—" Another sob racked her. "She paid me to help her. She gave me some of the money from Grandpa's life insurance."

Well, that explained the fancy new purchases. Not drug dealing, after all, but murder for hire. Or rather, indigestion-gone-bad for hire.

"Mom wasn't herself," Patrick said, "ever since Dad died. In some ways she kinda went a little nutty. I didn't know about this scheme of hers till a couple of days after Irene passed. That's when Cheyenne finally told me what she did."

"That would be last Friday, right?" I asked. "After she ran out of Janey's Place so upset?" The result, I now realized, of a guilty conscience.

Patrick and his daughter said, "Yeah," in unison.

"So the next day," I said, "when I found you going through the fridge here, you were searching for that last smoothie cup. You wanted to get rid of anything that could link Cheyenne to Irene's death."

Patrick nodded. "The damage was done. There was nothing I could do for Irene. I had to protect my daughter."

I caught Bonnie's eye. *See? He really was here that day.*

Patrick addressed Cheyenne. "You never shoulda called the cops with that BS about Jane trying to frame me. I had everything under control."

"I got so scared when the detective came to the shop to talk to you," Cheyenne said. "I didn't want them to throw you in jail. They woulda done it, too, 'cause you got a record. My story was solid, it was totally believable. But then you had to run over here to confess. I couldn't let you take the blame for me."

Martin spoke up. "But you had no problem letting Jane take the blame."

The glance Cheyenne flicked my way was unreadable. I couldn't tell whether she felt contrition for falsely implicating me or frustration that her father had ruined her plan.

"Not to mention," Patrick added, "you spin a lame tale like that to the cops, nine times outta ten it falls apart. And then who do you think they're gonna be taking a real close look at?"

She stared at him long seconds as if the question were a stumper. "The person that told the tale?"

Dom joined us in the living room, prompting his fiancée to peer into the foyer to assess the job he'd done. The floor was spotless. She might have been surprised, but I wasn't. Among my ex-husband's many impressive talents—okay, I'll wait till you stop snickering—is the ability to make a floor sparkle in record time. It took years for Janey's Place to take off and spread like organic kudzu through the tri-state area. Meanwhile, the founder and CEO was also chief cook and bottle washer. You should see him balance a ledger sheet—the pencil is a blur.

"We'll get back to the various tales that were spun," Bonnie promised, giving Cheyenne's lying dad a significant look, "but for now, I want you to tell me exactly what happened, Cheyenne. Start at the beginning."

"Whaddaya mean?" Cheyenne sat twisting a strand of hair.

"When did your grandma O'Rourke first talk to you about Irene McAuliffe?"

"She was always talking about her," Cheyenne said. "Mrs. McAuliffe was, like, this really snotty rich bitch. I mean, I'm sorry I killed her and everything, but she made Grandma so upset. Always showing off how much money she had, all her fancy stuff." She tossed her hand to indicate our elegant surroundings. "Rubbing Grandma's nose in it."

"But that's nothing new," Bonnie said. "That situation had been going on forever."

"I'm not finished," Cheyenne said. "After Grandpa died, Daddy started spending a lot of time with Mrs. McAuliffe. I didn't know she was his real mom then or anything, and Grandma didn't tell me, she just said Mrs. McAuliffe was, like, lying to him and stuff to get him to love her and not Grandma."

"It was nothing like that," Patrick said. "When I found out Irene was my real mom—my whatchamacallit, biological mother—her and me connected, you know? Well, not at first. At first she was pissed that Mom let the cat out of the bag. But then she kinda loosened up and we got close. Like long-lost relatives."

"But Grandma raised you, Daddy," Cheyenne said. "She's the one that used to bail you out and make you go to rehab and stuff. And then Mrs. Rich Bitch McAuliffe comes along after all the bad stuff is over and, like, steals you from her."

He scrubbed a hand over the back of his neck. "I know that's how Mom saw it. I think it's what tipped her over the edge. She was so... fragile after Dad passed." To Bonnie he said, "I just don't want you thinking my mom was some kinda crazy lady going around poisoning anybody that looked at her wrong."

"Noted," Bonnie said.

"Did you know that Mrs. McAuliffe used to cheat at poker?" Cheyenne gave a confident nod. "It's true. That's how she won all those tournaments."

Dom and I exchanged a look. No one who'd known Irene would believe that. In many ways she'd been a hard woman to love, but she was no card cheat. I was sure Colette hadn't believed it either, no matter what she'd told her granddaughter.

"So me and Grandma were talking about how to keep Mrs. McAuliffe out of the tournament this year," Cheyenne continued, "and Grandma says she can't play if she's sick. And I say how do we get her sick ha ha, like a joke, you know, but Grandma, she takes it serious. Maybe we can put something in her food, she says."

"Then what?" Bonnie asked.

"Well, Daddy would bring Mrs. McAuliffe stuff from the shop once in a while when he was going to her place straight from work. Like soup and stuff—nothing too, you know, health-foody, 'cause she wasn't into that. So one day he, like, packs up some soup for her and then he, like, goes to the bathroom. So I, like, grab the can of roach powder from the back and stir some of it into the soup. Mushroom barley flavor. The soup, not the powder. I don't know what flavor the powder was."

"Did you measure the roach powder?" Bonnie asked.

Cheyenne's expression asked how dumb the detective was. "It wasn't, like, a recipe. I just used, you know, enough."

Okay, I'll bite, I thought. What's "enough" insecticide when you're trying to make someone sick but not dead?

"What then?" Bonnie said.

"Then the next day after the soup, Daddy says Mrs. McAuliffe's stomach was bothering her. So I, um, I say let me make her one of those, like, stomach smoothies. With ginger and stuff? And I did and he brought it to her."

"And you put roach powder in the smoothie, too?" Bonnie asked.

"Yeah. When Daddy wasn't looking."

Patrick closed his eyes briefly, hearing the sad tale of his unwitting complicity in Irene McAuliffe's murder.

"When was this?" Bonnie asked. "When did you start poisoning her?"

"It was, like, the Sunday before Easter," Cheyenne said.

"And every day your father brought Irene a smoothie that you'd doctored?"

"'Doctored'?" Cheyenne said. "You mean poisoned?"

"Yes. Poisoned."

"Uh-huh." More hair twisting. "Well, not after Easter. Grandma told me to stop on Easter. I think she felt, um, bad about what we were doing. And then she passed the next day."

I wondered if Colette's fatal stroke had been triggered by the stress of a nagging conscience.

Cheyenne turned to Martin. "Grandma called it off before she passed, so God can't be too mad at her, right? I mean, she's not in hell now, is she?"

"Umm…" Martin awkwardly patted Cheyenne's hand. "Why don't you talk to your parish priest about that."

"Cheyenne," Bonnie said, "how much did your grandma O'Rourke pay you to poison Irene?"

"Two thousand bucks. In advance. More than I take home from Janey's Place in a month." She stood. "Can I go now? I left Bradley alone at the shop, and he loaned me his car." The very car that had left red paint and gouges on all of our vehicles. Bradley was about to learn that no good deed goes unpunished.

Dom said, "Bradley the trainee? Isn't this his first day?"

"Yeah. So?"

Bonnie started to speak—no doubt to inform Cheyenne that the only place she was going was the police station—but was interrupted by vigorous pounding on the front door. Whoever was there had dispensed with the knocker and was using his fist. SB woke with a yip. I held him close to keep him from hurtling himself at the door.

"Patrick O'Rourke!" *Boom! Boom! Boom!* "Get the hell out here, you son of a bitch!" It was a man's voice. "The kid at the shop told me you're here, so don't try sneaking out the back."

I stepped into the foyer, followed by the others, and opened the door. Mal Wallace, Nina's husband, stood on the porch, his features dark with fury. He spied Patrick and bulled past me into the house.

"Where is she?" He threw himself at Patrick, who stumbled back, arms raised.

"I don't know what you're talking about," Patrick said. "Where's who?"

"You know who—my wife!" Mal shoved Patrick against the wall with bone-rattling force. "What did you do to her?"

"I didn't do any—"

Mal's fist connected with Patrick's jaw.

Cheyenne screeched, "Leave my dad alone!"

Dom, who was nearest to them, tried to intervene, but Mal threw him halfway across the room, pumped with adrenaline as he was. SB barked nonstop, trying to squirm out of my grasp and join the brawl.

"Back off, Mal." Bonnie yanked at his arm. "Now!"

Patrick tried to squirm away and Mal threw him to the floor. "What have you done with Nina, you bastard?" He landed a couple of savage punches to Patrick's ribs before Martin was able to wrestle him off of him.

"That's enough, man," Martin huffed, pinning Mal facedown on the floor with his arms behind him. Mal struggled but couldn't break Martin's hold. "Settle down and tell us what the hell's going on."

Mal was flushed, breathing hard. "Nina's missing. I haven't seen her since yesterday and I can't get ahold of her."

As Cheyenne helped Patrick sit up, he asked, "What's that got to do with me?"

"I know about you and Nina. I know about the baby." Mal tried again to get at Patrick, but Martin had him immobilized. "I never should've let a junkie ex-con like you anywhere near my family."

"My dad's not a junkie." Cheyenne tried to kick Mal, but Patrick restrained her. "That was a long time ago."

"What," Patrick said, "you think there's something going on between me and Nina? That's nuts."

"I was the last to find out. It's all over town. Let me up," Mal told Martin. "I won't kill him. Not yet."

Martin looked to Bonnie, who nodded. She said, "They teach you those moves at the seminary, Father?" Her wry smile told me she was on to him. Fortunately, she had more urgent concerns at the moment than a counterfeit priest.

Martin released Mal and placed himself between the two combatants as they got to their feet.

Bonnie turned to Mal. "Did Nina tell you she's having an affair with Patrick?"

"She didn't mention him by name. She said she's in love with someone else and that she…" He paused to gather his composure. "She's having his baby. She said she's leaving me and taking the kids."

"Daddy?" Cheyenne gave her father a look that said, *Eww, you didn't, did you?*

"It's not me, I swear," Patrick said. "We're friends. Her and my mom were friends. Nina gave me work when I needed it. That's all."

Mal tried to get in his face. Martin blocked him. Mal said, "Yeah, well, everyone in town seems to think it's you, O'Rourke. I only learned that after I started asking around today, trying to track her down." He stabbed a finger toward Patrick. "If you hurt my wife, I promise you I will find you and I will kill you."

"All right, Mal, dial it back a notch." Bonnie got her notebook out again. "When did Nina tell you all this?"

"Wednesday night, after the kids were in bed."

"That must have come as a shock," she said.

"To put it mildly. But I didn't lose control, if that's what you're getting at. It was all very—" he made a face "—civilized."

"When did you last see her?"

"The next morning, before I left for work. That was yesterday, around six-forty. I take the seven oh-two train to the city. She was getting the kids up for school."

"Did you speak with her after that?" Bonnie asked.

He shook his head. "The girls got home from their after-school activities at four-thirty. Julia called me—she's my fifteen-year-old. She said Nina wasn't there, and I figured, I don't know, I thought maybe she was with him." He gave Patrick a disgusted look. "She probably was, but not by choice."

"When did you get home yesterday?" Bonnie asked.

"Around eight," he said. "I had a meeting that ran late. Nina still wasn't home, but that didn't worry me because her book club meets the second Thursday of every month. Only… well, she always bakes something for book club and it didn't look like she'd done any baking yesterday."

"What does it look like when she's been baking?"

"It's more like how the house smells," he said. "Like fresh-baked whatever. But not yesterday. Plus there were no baking pans in the dishwasher, no crumbs."

Bonnie might not comprehend the significance of Mal's words, but I did. Nina wouldn't go for so much as an oil change without bringing home-baked goodies.

"No sign of a struggle, I take it?" Bonnie asked.

"No, nothing like that."

"Was her car there? Her wallet and purse?"

He shook his head. "Her car's not parked at the Historical Society or in a municipal lot. Sometimes Nina and a couple of the others go out for drinks after book club. I was beat, so I went to bed early. I didn't begin to panic until this morning when I saw she still hadn't come home."

"Didn't you think that maybe she went ahead and left you," Bonnie asked, "without waiting for a formal separation?"

"No way." Mal shook his head. "Absolutely not. Nina would never have left her girls. She wouldn't have done anything that could be construed as abandonment or jeopardize her getting custody. Plus she didn't take any clothes or jewelry or even her damn toothbrush."

"Have you called her relatives," Bonnie asked, "her friends?"

He started nodding before she finished the question. "I called everyone. I've spent the whole day driving around and making calls. No one's seen her or heard from her since early yesterday." He ran his fingers through his thinning hair. "Bonnie, I don't want to lose my wife. She's having another man's baby, I get that. I'll raise it as my own. I just want her back home, safe."

"Under the circumstances, Nina's absence doesn't look all that unusual." Bonnie spread her hands. "I mean, try to look at it objectively, Mal. Your wife tells you she's leaving you for another man, then spends the night away from home. Isn't that almost to be expected?"

"Nina wouldn't have stayed away for even one night without saying something to her girls," he said. "She's in trouble, Bonnie. The police have to do something."

"I'll tell you what," Bonnie said. "If you still haven't heard from her by tomorrow, come in and file a missing-person report."

"By then it might be too late." Mal gave Patrick a venomous look. "This bastard was happy enough when Nina was just a convenient piece on the side. But now it's gotten complicated. Right, O'Rourke? The inheritance, the baby. Maybe he didn't want to leave his family for her. Maybe that was all her idea, not his. Maybe it was time to make the whole problem of Nina Wallace go away."

14
Delicate, Schmelicate

SOPHIE HALPERIN LIVED in one of Crystal Harbor's historic homes, a nineteenth-century farmhouse located in a quiet residential neighborhood on the far west end of Main Street. Nevins House had been built in 1832 by Charles Rutherford Nevins, a member of the town's "first family," whose illustrious ancestor Jeremiah Nevins had founded Crystal Harbor in the 1650s by purchasing the land from a Native American chief.

The last remaining member of the first family, a reprobate snake-oil salesman named "Doctor" Archibald Nevins, had been run out of town in 1903 for treating the mayor's rheumatism with a patent medicine that was a tad heavy on the arsenic, while treating the mayor's comely young bride to vigorous and inventive rounds of physical therapy.

Nevins House was a symmetrical building with a front-facing central gable and chimneys on either end. The colonnaded porch extended the width of the house, each column topped with lacy fretwork brackets. The narrow clapboards were painted yellow, the shutters dark green, and the front door a deep, rich red. The picket fence was—you guessed it—white.

To me, this old place had about a thousand times more charm and appeal than the contemporary mini-mansion I'd inherited from Irene. This was a warm and welcoming home, made all the more so by its current owner and her outsize personality.

I rang the bell. After a few moments the door swung open and I faced Sophie's new housekeeper. I counted on her being too polite to slam the door in my face.

"Hi, Maria," I said. "May I come in?"

"The mayor isn't home."

"I know that." It was Monday morning and Sophie was at work, busy performing whatever mayoral duties demanded her attention. "I came to see you."

"What about?"

"I'd really like to come inside," I said. "It'll only take a minute."

She hesitated, then stepped aside and led the way to the front parlor, with its high ceilings and eclectic furnishings. The aroma of fresh-brewed coffee was overlaid with the tang of cilantro, and I knew I'd interrupted her cooking. I suspected Sophie had hired Maria for the express purpose of ensuring a steady supply of her locally famous guacamole.

Maria didn't invite me to sit or offer any of that coffee, which was okay because I had no desire to prolong the encounter.

"Irene left a note, Maria. She wanted you to have this." I pulled three heavy velvet bundles out of my straw tote bag and set them on a hand-hewn maple console table.

She frowned, looking from me to the bundles. She loosened the tie on one of them and unrolled it to reveal the glint of gold, platinum, and precious stones. "She gave me her jewelry?"

I nodded. "She was very clear. All of it is to go to you. To show her deep gratitude for your many years of service."

Her expression didn't soften. "Where is this note?"

"I left it at home."

We stared at each other for long moments. Behind her dark eyes, I watched pride duke it out with self-interest. Finally she said, "I appreciate what you're doing, but Mrs. M would not have written a note like that."

I hadn't expected this to go smoothly. "Irene wasn't good at expressing affection. You took such good care of her, and we both know she didn't make it easy." When she didn't respond, I added, "I can show you the note if you really need to see it." Silently I prayed she wouldn't force me to compound my lie with forgery.

Maria lifted an elaborate emerald-and-diamond earring and let it dangle from her fingers. She was familiar with Irene's jewelry collection, though she probably wasn't aware that, according to the latest insurance appraisal, it was worth close to three hundred grand.

Full disclosure: Right about now you're thinking, Oh, that Jane Delaney, what a noble, selfless person she is. Okay, I'll just say it. The original artwork on Irene's walls is worth twice what her jewelry is. Of course, I'm not yet free to sell the artwork or give it away, and I might choose never to do so, but I just wanted to, you know, set the record straight.

"I'm not taking this back with me, Maria," I said. "It's yours. Sell it and use the money for your retirement. Or if not for yourself, spend it on your grandchildren."

I watched that tough woman. I watched her stony features begin to crumple. I watched her eyes fill and felt the answering sting of tears in my own. I swallowed them back. Maria composed herself with an obvious effort and carefully replaced the earring on the velvet.

She cleared her throat and looked me in the eye. "Thank you, Jane."

"Don't thank me," I said, "I'm just the delivery girl."

The hint of a smile told me Maria wasn't buying it for an instant. "Would the delivery girl like a cup of coffee?"

I grinned. "You read my mind." I set my tote on the floor and followed Maria into the homey country kitchen, with its white-painted walls and cabinets. Daisies sprouted from a cluster of mismatched bud vases in the center of the big, rustic pine table. Guacamole ingredients sat out on a counter. Déjà vu.

She poured coffee into two mugs and handed me one, remembering I take it black.

I asked, "Any news from Sophie about Nina Wallace?" I assumed the mayor was in regular contact with the cops, who'd begun a full-blown investigation over the weekend. Plus Sophie always seemed to be the first to know anything about anything in this town.

Maria shook her head, stirring cream and sugar into her coffee. "She's been missing for four days. It doesn't look good."

"You're assuming she didn't just run off," I said.

"And leave her kids? Mrs. Wallace is not my favorite person, I'll admit it, but she's a devoted mother." She lifted the metal dome of an old-fashioned cake keeper, revealing half of a coconut layer cake. She pulled a small china plate from a cabinet.

"Breakfast of champions," I said, watching her cut a slice.

"None for me," she said. "I need to lose a few pounds."

"Oh, do you really think so?" I said, out of politeness. As long as I'd known Maria, she could stand to lose a few.

She joined me at the table. I lifted my fork and stared at the slice of cake while a memory shimmered, just out of reach.

"What, you don't like coconut?" she asked. "I have brownies."

"No, it's not that. It looks delicious. I just…" A mental image coalesced, of another piece of cake in another kitchen. "Maria, do you remember the morning I told you that Irene had died?" I asked.

"How could I forget?"

"Well, there was a piece of carrot cake." I saw it clearly now in my mind's eye. The nut-studded layers, the cream-cheese frosting decorated with a little orange frosting carrot, all of it enclosed in a clear plastic clamshell bearing the familiar white-and-gold label of Patisserie Susanne, a popular bakery and café on the ground floor of the Crystal Harbor Town Hall building.

"It was in the fridge the night she died," I continued. "I saw it when I spilled that smoothie. But by the time I returned the next morning, the cake was gone." My subconscious mind had registered that something was absent, but my conscious mind had been unable to fill in the blanks. Until now.

"I didn't move it." She shrugged. "I never even knew it was there."

"I didn't know Irene liked carrot cake."

"She hated carrot cake." Maria smiled. "It was the carrot thing more than the cake thing. She must have been expecting Dr. Diamond."

"Jonah?"

She nodded and sipped her coffee. "Susanne's is his favorite lunch spot, and he can never get enough of their carrot cake. Whenever he was coming over, Mrs. M would send me out to buy a piece for him. The day you're talking about, it was a

Wednesday, my day off. She must have picked it up herself."

"But Irene wasn't expecting Jonah the day she died," I said. "He told me he hadn't heard from her since the poker game six days earlier. Could she have bought the cake for someone else?"

Maria shook her head. "Dr. Diamond was the only one. It was kind of a tradition with them, you know? He comes over and examines her, checks her BP or whatever, and then he sits down and has his carrot cake and a cup of coffee. Mrs. M would have a dish of ice cream or a martini, depending on the time of day."

"Right, she was very strict," I said. "No booze before ten a.m."

Maria offered a rare grin. The two of us had known Irene better than anyone. Nevertheless, since her death, I'd begun to feel that I hadn't known her nearly as well as I thought I had.

"I'm sure you were upset the night Mrs. M died," Maria said. "Could it be that you just imagined seeing the cake?"

"Could be," I said, though I hadn't imagined seeing it. Nor had I imagined lifting the clamshell container from the fridge shelf and wiping spilled smoothie off it, before abandoning the cleanup effort. "Let's make sure I'm not imagining this one." I forked a bite of Maria's coconut cake into my mouth and gave her a rapturous thumbs-up.

*

BEFORE TODAY, Sexy Beast and I had never visited the town dog park. Irene hadn't believed in it. She'd envisioned a flea-infested medical-waste dumpsite where marauding packs of rabid pit bulls preyed on small, helpless poodles with buckfangs and silly names. My arguments in favor of canine socialization, not to mention regular play and exercise, had fallen on deaf ears.

Sexy Beast was not what one would call a well-socialized animal. He simply hadn't had adequate opportunity to interact with other dogs. He started barking well before I led him through the entrance gate, and didn't seem to know what to make of the four-legged creatures running around and wrestling one another and generally having a swell old time.

The dog park turned out to be a lovely field carved out of the southeast corner of Nevins Park, the town's waterfront playground. There were benches and shade trees, not to mention a poop-bag dispenser and a water station. A mild breeze carried the welcome scent of new green things. It was late afternoon, close to dinnertime, but the day was unseasonably warm for mid-April, and the mild weather had brought about a dozen dogs and their owners to the park.

I was glad most of them were on the other side of the fence that separated large dogs from small. SB had only to deal with a Pomeranian and a French bulldog. He answered their friendly butt-sniffing with furious barking, followed by an attempt to scale my legs. I sighed and picked him up. Well, baby steps, right? I smiled and waved at the little dogs' owners, who sat chatting on a bench and ignored me.

I gazed longingly over the fence, where the popular kids hung out. Medium-size and big dogs happily chased one another, occasionally sprinting up to their owners for a pat before resuming their play. It was hard to ignore the largest dog, a black Great Dane you could have saddled. A lavender bandana was tied jauntily around her neck. I'd never met her before, but I was willing to bet this was Daisy, Jonah and Rachel Diamond's pet. How many black Great Danes could there be in a town the size of Crystal Harbor?

Okay, the truth? I knew the Diamonds often came here. I was hoping to run into Jonah so I could ask him about the magical disappearing carrot cake. It had been bothering me all day since my conversation with Maria.

I scanned the dogs' owners, who stood chatting in groups. Sure enough, the Diamonds were among them. Rachel and I spied each other at the same moment. She jogged over to me and we exchanged air kisses across the chain-link fence. Rachel was a pretty woman in her late thirties. Her glossy chestnut hair was clipped back today, exposing simple pearl earrings. Though she was dressed casually, I suspected her designer jeans cost more than I could get for my car on a good day. Ditto for the Kate Spade diaper bag she set on the grass at her feet.

"I've never seen this young gentleman here before." Rachel scratched behind SB's ears and was rewarded with a lick.

"Well, we're trying some new things." I didn't need to add, *Now that Irene's not around to stop us.*

"Including a trip to the groomer's, I see." She tipped her head, admiring SB's new do. I'd swung by the local canine boutique and bought him a military-styled camo dog jacket. If possible, he looked even more preposterous in the überbutch GI Joe outfit than he had in the frilly pink sweater.

There was a sudden commotion in the small-dog section. A white Chihuahua in a rhinestone-studded halter strutted through the gate as if she owned the place, tiny head and tail held high. Her exuberant barking needed no translation: *Let's get this party started!* The Pomeranian and French bulldog were all over that. *OMG, look who's here! I'm so excited I don't know what to do with myself! If I don't sniff another butt right now, I'll explode!*

Sexy Beast growled low in his throat. I shifted to block his view of the action. The newcomer's human, a young woman in a crisp business suit, nodded to us and joined the other owners on the bench. Apparently the regulars were well acquainted.

"That can't be Gabe." I squinted toward Jonah, who wore a baby backpack currently occupied by a sturdy-looking one-year-old with blond curls. "He's gotten so big. When's the last time I saw him?"

Rachel pondered that as she caught her husband's eye and waved him over. "Probably a few weeks after he was born. We ran into you at Janey's Place around then, remember?"

"That's right. You had all the kids with you that day." The Diamonds had two other children, ages six and ten. Before they were born, Rachel was a professional fund-raiser. Not that she needed to work, having chosen her parents wisely. But her lofty social connections and persuasive personality made her darn good at transferring truckloads of cash from the fat cats who didn't need it to the charities that so desperately did. I knew she planned to resume her career once Gabe was in school.

Jonah joined us at the fence. We exchanged greetings and I oohed and ahhed over the pink-cheeked baby in his backpack carrier. Jonah appeared happy and relaxed, in contrast to the last time I'd seen him, just over a week ago at the tournament. I recalled thinking then that he looked like his dog had run away. Obviously she hadn't.

When Gabe spied SB, he bounced excitedly and reached for him. I lifted the poodle within petting distance as Jonah reminded his son, "Gently, gently." The stubby little fingers gently, gently patted SB's fluffy topknot, before seizing a fistful and yanking hard. SB emitted ear-splitting yelps as Rachel pried open the baby's fingers.

SB continued to whine pitifully and Rachel fell over herself apologizing.

"Oh, please, he's fine," I said. "Sexy Beast is the original drama queen. He'll milk this atrocity for every scrap of pity he can get." I tipped his chin up and stared into his dark little doll eyes. "Where's your pride, dog?" He licked my nose and offered a few more halfhearted whimpers.

"Isn't it terrible about Nina Wallace?" Rachel handed Gabe a teething biscuit from the diaper bag. It looked disconcertingly like the dog biscuits I carry around for SB. "How many days has she been missing now? Three?"

"Four," I said. "Mal last saw her Thursday morning."

"I know the husband is usually the first person they look at in cases like this," she said, "but I can't believe Mal would do anything to Nina, even under the circumstances."

"The circumstances?" I asked.

"Well, you know. The affair. Patrick O'Rourke."

"Patrick denies they were involved," I said.

"Well, he can deny it all he wants," she said, "but it's true. Nina told Jonah all about it. Patrick wasn't happy about the baby."

Jonah gave his wife a gently chiding look. "She told me all that in confidence, honey, as a patient speaking privately with her doctor."

She glanced around and lowered her voice. "Well, you told Bonnie Hernandez, didn't you?"

"That's different," he said. "I want Nina's disappearance solved."

"That doesn't sound like a recipe for romantic bliss," I said. "I mean, why would Nina have been leaving Mal to start a new life with her lover if he was upset about her pregnancy?"

"Maybe he pretended to change his mind," Rachel said, "to lure her away and… do whatever he did to her. What a family." She shook her head, incredulous. "First the O'Rourke girl kills Irene, and it turns out that Colette, of all people, put her up to it. And now Patrick… well, we can't know for sure, not yet, but I'd be shocked to find out he's not behind Nina's disappearance."

"Woops, time to call in the backhoe." I pointed toward Daisy some distance away, hunched with unmistakable purpose.

Jonah and Rachel both blurted, "Not *it*!" but he beat her by a nanosecond. His wife gave him a wry look as she reached into his jacket pocket for a couple of latex medical gloves and headed for the poop-bag dispenser. As I watched Daisy daintily sniff the elephantine pile she'd deposited, I decided that if they let animals that size in this place, they should provide a hazmat-suit dispenser.

Now that I had a moment alone with Jonah, I found myself doing mental backflips trying to decide how to ease into a delicate subject. Then I thought of Irene. She'd never eased into a subject in her life. Delicate, schmelicate. I'd always admired that about her.

"Irene was expecting you the day she died," I said.

His pleasant expression never faltered, but he hesitated a split second too long before shaking his head. "I don't know where you got that idea," he said. "Last time I saw her was the Poker Posse almost a week before."

"Yeah, you said that. You also said you hadn't spoken with her since that game." I offered a wide-eyed shrug. "Yet for some reason, she thought you were coming over."

"What makes you think that?" he asked.

"In going through her stuff, I discovered she made an appointment with you for that day. It's been bugging me, so I figured I'd ask you about it."

The teething biscuit slipped from Gabe's gooey fingers. A sharp-eyed beagle snapped it up the instant it hit the ground. Jonah reached into the diaper bag for another cookie before the outraged baby could work up a full head of steam.

He sighed. "I was less than honest with you, Jane. I felt guilty about her death, if you must know."

My heart lurched. "What do you mean?"

Jonah curled his fingers into the chain-link fence and glanced over his shoulder as if to ensure his wife was out of earshot. Rachel was scooping like a champ. If I'd ever yearned for a large dog, I was officially over it.

He said, "Irene called me that morning and said her stomach had been acting up and could I swing by. She had things to do during the day, so we agreed on six p.m."

"But then you ended up at Harbor Memorial with Sophie," I said. "All evening."

He nodded. "I called Irene and asked if she wanted to see my covering physician, but she insisted it wasn't urgent. We rescheduled for the next morning. If only I'd managed to make it over there…" He gave a miserable shake of his head. "I keep thinking I might have been able to save her."

"Jonah." I waited until he met my eyes. "Only one person is responsible for Irene's death, and she's currently out on bail." In truth, two people had been responsible, but Colette O'Rourke was beyond the law—six feet beyond, to be precise.

"It was never my intention to mislead you," he said. "I just didn't want to think about how I'd failed her, much less talk to anyone else about it. I didn't realize she'd written down the appointment."

"She didn't." I quirked an eyebrow. "You were busted by a slice of carrot cake."

Jonah blinked in surprise. "But I—" He cut himself off.

"Yeah, I know, you got rid of it." I'd figured out this part. "You found the cake after I left and you knew it was meant for you, so…" I mimed tossing the thing, which made SB snap to attention. "No cake, no awkward questions from me or Maria. What you didn't know is, I'd already spied it in the fridge."

That night had been stressful for me. Until now, I hadn't realized it had been just as stressful for Jonah, due to his misplaced feelings of guilt.

Rachel rejoined us. "That's it, our next pet is going to be a goldfish."

15
Wrong Side of the Blanket

I TURNED ONTO Jefferson Street and slowed the car, peering at house numbers. Rocky Bay, Long Island, is only twenty-six miles from Crystal Harbor, but it's light-years away in all other respects. I passed a few dozen modest, cookie-cutter houses on lots about forty feet wide. The properties were decently maintained for the most part. Serviceable sedans and minivans occupied the driveways. I spied a few kids walking home from school, and two young moms with strollers chatting on the sidewalk. It was another sunny spring afternoon.

I'd already made the long drive to Tierney's Publick House way out in Southampton. Tommy, the grumpy owner, remembered me from my first visit two weeks earlier. He gave Sexy Beast, my "service animal," the stinkeye as he informed me Martin was off that day. I asked him for the padre's home address.

He frowned in intense cogitation. "Am I allowed to do that?"

"Absolutely," I replied without hesitation.

That had been good enough for Tommy, who'd scrawled the address on a cocktail napkin.

I'd often wondered where Martin lived, my overactive

imagination conjuring one mysterious man cave after another. A gloomy abandoned warehouse in Brooklyn. A slick penthouse apartment in Manhattan. A sleeping bag that traveled from beach to woods to friends' floors as the mood struck.

I had to admit, a one-and-a-half-story Cape in working-class Rocky Bay had never been in the running.

I pulled up in front of 2639 Jefferson and sat staring at it. White paint, light blue trim. A patched roof. A few azaleas fronted by a straggle of daffodils. I tried in vain to picture the padre on his knees planting bulbs. And next to the front stoop, a cluster of big-eyed lawn ornaments: a lop-eared mama rabbit and three baby bunnies.

Oh, and? A big, gleaming red Mercedes in the driveway. I recognized the first prize in the recent Crystal Harbor Historical Society Poker Tournament. It was parked behind a bodacious black Harley which I also recognized.

All right then. I settled Sexy Beast in a comfortable football hold, grabbed my tote bag, and traversed the short distance to the front door, which was adorned with an Easter wreath—pastel eggs, baby chicks—that should have been taken down a couple of weeks earlier. I had to ring twice, but eventually the door swung open.

I wasn't surprised to see a woman on the other side of the threshold. That girlie wreath was the clincher. The padre did not live alone. She had longish blond hair, the top section wrapped around some of those fat Velcro rollers, the kind I could never quite master. She was barefoot and wore faded jeans and a logo tee-shirt featuring a band I'd never heard of. The woman was in the process of putting on her face. The way I knew this? She held a blush compact and makeup brush in one hand and a portable, lighted mirror in the other. Plus one cheek was rosier than the other. See? I could have been a detective.

"Yes?" she asked, not rudely but with an unmistakable *I don't want whatever you're selling* vibe.

"Um…I'm here to see Martin?"

"Marty!" she hollered over her shoulder. "Look sharp, you have company." She stepped aside and beckoned me to enter. "I'm Stephanie. Everyone calls me Stevie."

"Hi, Stevie. Jane Delaney." I stuck out my hand, then retracted it when she apologetically indicated her full hands. "I'm a, um, friend of Martin's," I added.

"And yet you look so respectable. *Marty!*" Stevie had a good figure. From the neck down, she could have been thirty. Her face was unlined, but her throat and hands told a different story— this lady was no spring chicken. I supposed that said something good about the padre, that his live-in wasn't some airhead half his age.

"And who's this cutie?" she asked, bending to admire SB, only to jerk back with a startled laugh when he tried to lick her freshly made-up eye.

"His name is Sexy Beast." I braced for the usual snort of derision.

Instead she said, "Loved the movie. Go on, sit." She nodded toward the matching sofa and love seat. "Just shove the newspapers onto the floor." The living room was cluttered, but in a normal, lived-in way, not a *Buried alive in their home! Story at six!* way. SB sniffed avidly, taking inventory.

A Siamese cat strolled into the room, prompting him to stiffen and growl. I tightened my grip, certain that a showdown between the two animals would not end well for my runty pet.

The cat growled right back, long tail twitching, blue eyes skewering SB like lasers.

Stevie wagged a finger. "Miss Persephone, you behave yourself." She offered me a drink, which I declined. I heard feet pounding down the stairs, then Martin appeared, pulling a black tee-shirt over his torso. Just like at the bar that time, he showed zero surprise at seeing me. He was altogether the most irritating man I'd ever met.

"Don't mean to be rude," Stevie said as she headed for one of the rooms off the small central hallway, "but I'm running late."

Martin stalked over to the cat and unceremoniously lifted it by the scruff. He stared it down as its growls intensified. "I hate this thing." Following in Stevie's tracks, he opened the door she'd disappeared behind, flung the animal inside, and slammed the door shut.

He said, "You gonna sit or what?" and threw himself on the love seat.

I shifted the stacks of newspaper on the sofa and sat on the end nearest Martin. SB curled up next to me. "So," I asked. "How long have you and Stevie been together?"

"Forty-two years."

It took my wee brain a couple of seconds to figure it out, then I muttered a bad word as my face warmed.

"Mom!" he yelled toward the hallway. "Jane thought you were my girlfriend."

Peals of delighted laughter rang out from behind Stevie's closed door. She called out, "I like Jane."

"Wow," I said. "She looks good for her age. Whatever that is."

"Sixty-one," he said. "Mom's a poster child for good genes and an active lifestyle. She still dances."

That triggered a memory. At Tierney's, Martin had mentioned the married deacon who'd sired him: Arthur and Anne McAuliffe's middle son, Hugh. *My mom was an exotic dancer he was screwing on the side.*

He smiled, watching my expression. "She long ago retired from that kind of dancing."

"Of course," I said. "I didn't think…" I hated how smug he looked. I decided to do something about that. "So does this work for you? Being a middle-aged man living with his mom?"

"It's temporary. And it beats being a middle-aged woman living in Mr. F's basement," he replied smoothly. "Oh, but wait. You fixed that."

I bit my tongue to keep from blurting, *I didn't fix anything, I didn't even know Irene was leaving me the house.* He already knew that. Instead I said, "I consider the lower threshold for middle age to be forty. That gives me ten months before I have to start shopping for mom jeans."

"Let's agree on forty-five and I'll never mention Dogpatch again."

"Deal," I said.

"And you'd look good in anything." A flirtatious smile. "Even mom jeans."

Good grief. And just when the heat in my cheeks had begun to cool. Martin hadn't asked why I'd come looking for him. Maybe he thought I just couldn't stay away. I said, "I was noodling around the internet and came across something interesting." I pulled a folded sheet of paper out of my tote bag and handed it to him. I watched him unfold it and examine the image I'd printed out.

It was a silver shield topped with a gold boar's head. Three blue stars decorated the shield, along with three blue mermaids, each holding a comb and mirror.

The McAuliffe family coat of arms.

He tossed the paper onto the coffee table. "Took you long enough to make the connection."

"You could have made it for me and saved me the research," I said.

"Where's the fun in that?" He stood. "You want a beer?"

"No, thanks."

I left SB on the sofa and followed him into the kitchen, where he grabbed a Guinness from the fridge and popped the cap with a gargoyle-shaped opener screwed into a knotty-pine cabinet. I parked my buns on a counter stool and watched him expertly pour the dark brew down the side of a glass, resulting in a thick, creamy, downright sexy head.

"You could have been a bartender," I said.

"So I've been told." He tipped back the glass and took a deep gulp.

I was dying to know what other occupations he'd had, or still had, in addition to bartender, but I didn't waste my breath asking. "So I already knew that the mermaid brooch is a family heirloom," I said, "made by some famous jewelry artist over a century ago. What I didn't know is that the mermaid design is based on the McAuliffe coat of arms."

He leaned back against the sink. "What's your point?"

"I'm curious, is all," I said. "Have you fenced the brooch yet?"

"Don't tell me you're still trying to get her back for O'Rourke."

"I don't think you have any intention of selling her," I said. "I'm beginning to think you weren't BS'ing Irene, or me, about why you swiped her. She belongs in the family." Just as his grandmother Anne's dream house, now my home, belonged in the family. Martin McAuliffe had a complicated love-hate relationship with his father's people. Theirs was a blood connection, almost tribal. He despised most of the McAuliffes, yet he was inescapably one of them.

"That's why Grandma returned the mermaid to Grandpa when they divorced," he said. "Because she's a McAuliffe heirloom. He gave her to Grandma when they got married and she could have kept her—would've been well within her rights after he dumped her for Irene—but she did the right thing. Answer me," he said. "Is that why you're here? To get your hands on the mermaid?"

I puffed out a conflicted sigh. "Technically she belongs to Patrick. He's Colette's heir."

Martin turned his hand into a stop sign. "He's the heir of the woman who persuaded her granddaughter, *paid* her granddaughter, to poison her old friend Irene, who herself was so protective of her dead husband's heirloom that she threw it into the pot during a poker game. Just to put the whole thing into perspective. Proceed."

"None of that changes the fact that Patrick is the legitimate owner, strictly from a legal standpoint."

Martin sensed my reservations. "But…" he prompted.

I took a deep breath. "But the thing is, he's super-rich now. He doesn't need the brooch to, you know, elevate his lifestyle." Or to send his daughter to college, as I'd originally hoped. Cheyenne was going nowhere but prison. "And he has no sentimental attachment to it. I mean, he's not a McAuliffe. The brooch means zip to him."

"While you're working so hard to justify stiffing the 'legitimate owner,' there's something else you might want to take into consideration. O'Rourke is suspect numero uno in Nina Wallace's disappearance. He might be off the hook for Irene's murder, but until his pregnant mistress turns up…" He spread his hands.

"Yeah, well, innocent until proven guilty and all that," I said. "It bugs me that the cops are concentrating so hard on Patrick. I mean, I haven't known him that long, but he just doesn't seem capable of anything really awful."

"That's not what you were saying a few days ago."

"Only because the evidence seemed so compelling," I said, "linking him to Irene's death. Even then I had a hard time picturing him as a murderer."

"Why, because he's a good family man?" Martin offered a crooked half smile. "Because he loves his wife and kids?"

"Okay, so I'm hopelessly naïve. Better that than being hopelessly cynical."

"If you say so."

From somewhere far away came a familiar tune and Isaac Hayes's mellifluous voice inquiring as to the identity of the African-American private detective who reliably provides satisfying carnal relations to all the young females of his acquaintance. Except not in those words.

It was the "Theme from *Shaft*," which just happened to be Irene's ring tone. I leapt off the stool. "You have Irene's phone! No wonder I couldn't find it." I followed the music out of the kitchen and up the carpeted stairs. Not until I stood staring at Martin's crisply made bed did I realize where my indignation had taken me.

I let out a startled yip as he brushed past me to get to Irene's cell phone, which was on his chest of drawers. He answered it, listened for a moment, then said, "Mrs. Storch, this is Irene's grandson, Martin. Step-grandson. I'm sorry to be the bearer of sad news. Irene died two weeks ago."

He listened some more while I scanned his surprisingly neat and clutter-free room, which had nothing in common with either the abandoned Brooklyn warehouse or the swanky Manhattan penthouse of my imagination. Or any variety of man cave, however that term might be defined.

"I know," he told Mrs. Storch in soothing tones, "it was a shock to everyone. Very sudden… I agree, we can be grateful for that." His eyes never left me as I roamed around his room, taking in the small desk with laptop and reading lamp, a pair of guitars in a stand, a stack of plastic milk crates crammed with CD's and paperbacks: thrillers, sci-fi, dog-eared classics.

The walls were bare—no art or posters. No curtains covering the blinds.

"No, ma'am," he said, "my dad is Hugh, Arthur's middle son… Don't blame your memory. I'm sure Irene never mentioned me. I was born on the wrong side of the blanket, to use a quaint old expression."

He watched me lift a framed photograph from his chest of drawers, an outdoor shot of Arthur and Anne sitting on a picnic blanket with a boy about twelve years old. The boy had shaggy blond hair and blue, blue eyes. I recognized the rear of my house, Anne's dream house, in the background. About three years after this photo was taken, Arthur would divorce his wife of fifty years to marry Irene Hardy, a well-preserved forty-nine-year-old home wrecker who'd probably passed herself off as thirty-nine.

"Well, that's a very enlightened attitude, Mrs. Storch," he said. "I wish everyone shared it." He gave her the where and when of the memorial mass that would be held at the end of the month and said good-bye.

"Have you been doing that a lot?" I asked. "Answering Irene's phone and telling complete strangers about the 'wrong side of the blanket' thing?"

"Every chance I get."

"I wonder how your father the deacon feels about that," I said. "It has to be getting back to him."

"I know how he feels about it. It makes him nuts. To hell with him." He sat on his bed and idly punched buttons on Irene's phone. "I spent too many years being that man's dirty little secret."

It seemed to me that Martin had far more reason to be ashamed of Hugh than Hugh had to be ashamed of Martin.

He casually patted the bed next to him, an invitation to sit. I hesitated, but after all, I told myself, the door was open and his mom was right downstairs.

Good grief, this man turned me into a nervous teenager. I sat, not too close, and leaned across to look at the phone. "What are you doing?"

"Checking out the calls she made and received." He scrolled to the top of the list, which displayed names, phone numbers, and the date and time of each call. "Here's the day Irene died. Looks like you were the last person to talk to her."

I took the phone and saw *Jane, cell,* on the screen, along with my number. Apparently I'd made the call at 8:07 p.m., not long before she died. My throat tightened with emotion. I recognized the names of a couple of her friends who'd phoned her earlier in the day.

Martin peered at the list over my shoulder. He'd moved closer. I found I didn't mind. "Jonah Diamond called, too," he said.

The call from *Jonah, cell*, had come in at 5:12 p.m. "I know what this is. He was supposed to be at Irene's at six, but he had to cancel." I filled Martin in on the carrot-cake drama and Jonah's unwarranted conviction that he'd let Irene down.

"So he throws away the cake?" he said. "Doesn't that strike you as a little suspicious? I mean, the guy's patient croaks and he takes pains to make sure no one knows he was supposed to be there that day?"

"Stress makes people do dumb things," I said. "And speaking of dumb things, we already know who killed Irene."

"By accident, supposedly. I can't help it, though, the cake thing just seems fishy." He took the phone from me and swiped his finger up the screen, swiftly scrolling through Irene's calls in the last weeks and months of her life.

"You aren't going to give that back to me, are you?" I asked.

"No, I don't think that's going to happen. Hey, I know this guy," he said, peering at the screen. "Ben Ralston. His name comes up a few times."

I frowned. "Why does it sound familiar?"

"I've known Ralston for years," he said, "since before he took his police pension and set up shop as a PI."

"Oh, right. Sten mentioned him. Ben Ralston's the guy Irene hired to get the goods on Nina during the election." I could only imagine what sorts of dealings Martin might have had with a cop turned PI.

"Wonder if he called to tell her he found out who Nina was getting it on with," he said.

"I suspect that if Irene had lived long enough to find out that said mystery lover was none other than her own beloved son Patrick, she'd have paid Ben's bill and added a big bonus to keep his mouth shut."

"Marty!" Stevie called up the steps. "Shake a leg. We're supposed to meet Lexie at the caterer's at three-thirty."

Martin rose and lazily descended the stairs, leaving me to follow. "We've been through this," he told his mother. "Maia just wants to go over the final menu. You two don't need me for that."

Stevie had finished her hair and makeup. Her colorful outfit—dress and leggings, suede boots, and unconstructed blazer—was funky and flattering. Young looking, but not *too* young. "Lexie wants you there," she said, as if that settled it.

"I don't know why," he said. "I'd just be in the way. Women are better at that stuff." This from the man who'd recently catered Uncle Morty's shivah spread for Sophie.

Stevie gave me the fed-up look women have been giving one another for millennia: *Men!*

When I'd spied Martin chatting with Maia Armstrong at the tournament, I'd naturally assumed it was a boy-girl thing. Then later I'd just as naturally assumed he was using her to horn in on my business. Now it appeared the two of them had indeed been discussing a catering job, as he'd claimed. I suppose stranger things have happened.

But what kind of catering job? And who was Lexie? My imagination readily filled in the blanks, and in a way I didn't particularly care for, but hadn't I just learned the folly of making assumptions?

"Anyway," Martin said as he grabbed SB and ushered me out the door, "Jane and I have an urgent appointment." He pinched my arm before I could say, *We do?* "Piggies in a blanket," he called to a fuming Stevie as he slid into the passenger side of my Civic. "You can never go wrong with piggies in a blanket."

I stopped Martin from tossing Sexy Beast into the backseat and instead attached the dog's safety strap to his seat belt. SB settled on his lap and commenced car-whining. As I pulled away from the curb, I asked Martin why we weren't taking his lovely new Mercedes instead. Turned out it now belonged to Stevie. The man who had no use for family had given his mother a brand-new, bells-and-whistles Mercedes Benz.

"Anyway, I prefer my bike," he said. "If you want, we can take that. I have an extra helmet."

"Right," I snorted, "that'll happen."

Will you be shocked if I admit I entertained a momentary fantasy of clinging to the padre's sinewy flanks as his big, bad motorcycle ate up the miles and the engine vibrations did unruly things to my body?

Yeah, that's what I thought. Already you know me too well.

"So who's this 'urgent appointment' with?" I asked.

"Here's a hint." Martin lowered his voice to a rumbling baritone and crooned the opening lines of Irene's ring tone.

"We're on our way to see John Shaft?"

"Wrong black private dick."

"Ben Ralston?" I said. "What can we learn from him? Except maybe that Patrick is the guy Nina was sleeping with, and Ben never got that far in his investigation before Irene died."

"I want to hear it from him." Martin muzzled SB with his fingers, commanding him to shut up. The dog wrenched his snout free and whined louder. "Ralston's a tenacious SOB. I can't see him just dropping an investigation."

"His client died."

"Let's just see what he has to say."

"You know," I said, "you could just pick up the phone and call him."

"Face-to-face is always better."

I realized that our dropping by unannounced might not be the swiftest move. I didn't know much about the PI biz, but I was willing to bet Ben was bound by some sort of confidentiality rule. At the very least, he wouldn't want it getting around that he blabbed about sensitive investigations to anyone who asked. So I pulled over, called Sten, and persuaded him to phone Ben and grant permission, as Irene's executor, for him to discuss his investigation with me.

Ralston Investigations occupied a modest office on the top floor of a venerable three-story brick building on Main in Crystal Harbor. It was just him, no receptionist. Ben was a black man in his late forties, just under average height and fit looking if you didn't count the slight paunch beneath his red polo shirt.

He'd been expecting me, thanks to Sten's call, but was surprised to see his old pal Martin tagging along. He made friends with SB and gestured for us to sit on the well-worn, leather-upholstered guest chairs. "What's a seemingly decent girl like you doing hanging with a bum like this?" he wanted to know.

"Funny," I said, "someone else said pretty much the same thing today."

"Who?" he asked.

I jerked my head toward Martin. "His mother."

Ben laughed. "Well, I guess Stevie knows her boy. So." He thumped his desk, signaling an end to the small talk. "I'm going to go out on a limb here and guess that our very own Marty McAuliffe—" he tossed his hand toward the padre "—is somehow related to the Crystal Harbor McAuliffes, seeing as you guys are here to discuss the assignment that Irene Hardy McAuliffe hired me for. How am I doing so far? Do my powers of deduction thrill and amaze?"

Martin might have known Ben for years, as he claimed, yet he'd never bothered to fill him in on his connection to the "Crystal Harbor McAuliffes." I wasn't surprised.

"Irene was my step-grandma," Martin said. "Her late husband's son Hugh had an extramarital fling with Mom way back when."

Ben said, "So that means I have to get married and/or win the Lotto to have a chance with Stevie?"

"Don't worry, she got over the rich-family-man thing," Martin said, "around the time Hugh McAuliffe sicced a squad of high-priced lawyers on a pregnant, homeless teenager."

I spoke up. "Stevie was homeless?"

"When Mom started showing, her folks kicked her out of the house." To Ben he said, "Give her a call. She thinks you're cute."

"Hey." Ben indicated himself with a flourishy gesture. "It doesn't get much cuter than this. So." He pulled a large brown envelope off a stack of folders. "You guys know why Irene hired me, right?"

The padre and I answered in the affirmative.

"Then you also know that before her death," Ben said, "I was able to report that there was compelling evidence that Irene's election opponent, Nina Wallace, was doing the nasty with a man who was not her husband."

"By now the whole town knows that," I said, "which I guess

was the point. Now that Nina's gone missing, we thought you might—"

"Hold on." Ben straightened. "Nina's missing?"

"You didn't know?" Martin asked.

"I've been out of the loop for a few days. Had to fly out to Chicago to see my mom. Medical emergency."

"Oh no," I said. "I hope she's okay."

"She's fine." Ben waved away my concern. "Audrey Ralston is the queen of the fake stroke. And fake pneumonia. And fake sudden-onset paralysis. One time she decided to mix it up and give herself a case of fake flesh-eating virus."

"Let me guess," Martin said. "By the time you rush out there…"

Ben spread his arms. "An immediate and miraculous cure, Lord be praised! It's not like I never visit, but when that woman takes it into her head that she wants to see me, she means *now*. You'd think I'd stop falling for it. I mean, people pay me to tell them when other people are lying, and I'm very good at it."

I chewed back a smile. "But it's your mom."

A frustrated growl rumbled in the PI's chest. Sexy Beast lifted his head and offered a halfhearted response, then snuggled back into my lap.

"Anyway," Ben said, "I just got back to town about an hour ago. So Nina Wallace is MIA?"

"For five days now," Martin said. "Since last Thursday."

"I flew out Wednesday night," Ben said. "Missed all the excitement. Who's handling the investigation?"

"Bonnie Hernandez," I said.

Ben gave an approving nod.

"I thought you two had issues," Martin said, "from when you were on the force together."

"We don't always see eye to eye, but Bonnie's a capable detective," Ben said. "Is she leaning on the husband?"

"Mal's the one who sounded the alarm," I said. "He's really broken up over it."

Ben looked skeptical. "I'm betting he knew his wife was stepping out on him."

"Not until Nina told him she was leaving him for the other guy," I said. "Mal still wants to salvage his marriage."

"That's what he says. Bonnie's talking to the boyfriend, too, I assume?"

"Patrick O'Rourke's at the top of the suspect list," I said.

Ben frowned. "What's O'Rourke got to do with it?"

Martin and I exchanged a look. "That's who she was screwing," Martin said.

"I don't know where you got that," Ben said. "Sure, the guy was at her house a lot, doing odd jobs, but the most intimate thing he did was nibble her muffins—and no, that's not code."

I said, "Then who…?" and watched the hint of a smug smile form.

"Nina and her boyfriend took great pains to keep their affair under wraps," Ben said. "They were good, but I'm better, and just before I left town, I was able to get these." He slid a stack of eight-by-ten photos out of the envelope and pushed them across his desk.

Martin and I leaned forward. The top photo was an expanse of gray interspersed with thin horizontal slivers revealing the interior of a room. It took me a moment to realize the shot had been taken at a downward angle through the narrow gaps between closed window blinds. Anyone viewing the window straight on or from street level would never see past the blinds.

I was just able to recognize Nina Wallace. She appeared to be setting her purse on a chair near the window. I saw a tile floor and the edge of a utilitarian cabinet.

I was about to ask where the picture was taken when Ben said, "I was on the rooftop across the street with a telephoto lens. Here's a better angle." He slid the top photo aside. The next one showed Nina unbuttoning her blouse.

"Now it's getting interesting." Martin lifted the picture, and that's when I noticed it.

"She's in a doctor's office." I squinted at the sliced-up image. That certainly looked like an exam table, partially shrouded with white paper.

"Bingo," Ben said.

In the next shot Nina was stepping out of her slacks, leaving her in a black-and-ivory lace demi-bra and matching thong.

"Damn blinds," Martin grumbled.

"Wait," I said. "You can't take pictures of someone at the doctor."

"I told you," Ben said. "I'm good."

"No, I mean it's an invasion of privacy."

Martin had moved on to the next shot. He said, "Whoa," and tried to show it to me. The pig. I pushed it away and crossed my arms.

"It's just wrong," I told Ben. "It's a violation."

"Jane." Martin waggled the picture. I refused to look.

"There have to be limits." I was all hopped up on moral outrage. "You can't just invade someone's—"

Martin grabbed my head, turned it, and shoved the photo in my face.

In this shot Nina had been joined by a second person. She sat perched on the exam table, her arms and legs wrapped around the man. Even at the downward angle, and with most of the image obscured by the window blinds, and with the couple tangling tonsils as he reached around to unhook her bra, there was no mistaking the identity of Nina's mystery lover.

Dr. Jonah Diamond.

16
Employees Only

"I KNOW THE guy's a concierge doctor," Ben said, "but this brings personalized service to a whole new level."

"Nina and *Jonah*?" My overtaxed brain struggled to make sense of this new reality, to fit it into what I knew about Nina's disappearance.

"Didn't I tell you Ben's tenacious?" Martin said as he pored over the rest of the photos, squinting to fill in the blanks behind the window blinds. I myself had seen more than enough. "He's a regular pit bull."

"If that's a compliment," Ben said, "I'll take it."

I yanked the photos away from Martin and shoved them back at Ben. "So you continued the investigation Irene hired you for even after her death?"

"She paid me a hefty retainer," Ben said. "I felt a responsibility to see it through."

"With no one to report the results to?" Martin asked.

Ben shrugged. "The truth? I'm not used to throwing in the towel. Gives me hives." He held his thumb and forefinger a half inch apart. "I was this close."

"Nina and Jonah had to be meeting somewhere besides his

medical office," I said. "How many doctor visits can a healthy woman like her have before it begins to look suspicious?"

"Oh, they were definitely hooking up somewhere else," Ben said, "but I was never able to catch them at it until they decided to play doctor. During the day when her kids are in school, Nina runs errands and visits friends. She spends a lot of time at the Historical Society, of course, but Jonah's not a member and I never saw him go in there."

"Did the two of them ever leave town at the same time?" Martin asked. "Like for a secret weekend getaway?"

"Never," Ben said. "There's something else. I did a little digging into Jonah's background. It seems he and his wife Rachel signed a prenup when they got married."

"I'm not surprised," I said. "As I understand it, he couldn't even pay back his med-school loans when they met, and her family is made of money."

Ben nodded. "Rachel's daddy got his lawyer to craft an airtight contract."

"Let me guess," Martin said. "There's a cheating clause."

"Is there ever. If he strays, she cuts him loose without a dime. He can kiss the big, fancy house goodbye."

"Ditto for the country club," I said, "the luxury cars, high-stakes poker games, all of it."

"Nina was pregnant," Martin pointed out. "She told Mal she was leaving him for the baby's father."

"Her parents were fairly well off, but they're gone now and so is their money," Ben said. "She owes her lavish lifestyle to hubby's successful career as an investment banker."

"So Jonah's looking at a drastic lifestyle change if he leaves Rachel for Nina," I said. "Or if Rachel even finds out he's been getting some on the side."

I was surprised and kind of touched when the padre added, "Not to mention, he'll for sure lose custody of his kids."

I recalled how rattled Jonah had appeared during the poker tournament. He might have an excellent poker face, as Irene had noted, but you try looking serene when your secret lover has just told you she's pregnant. I envisioned Nina taking him aside right before the tournament started, sharing the exciting news, telling him the time had come for the two of them to leave their spouses and start a new life together. If that's what had Jonah upset on the day of the tournament, he seemed to have gotten over it by the time Ben took his dirty pictures four days later. Then I remembered something else.

"Jonah told his wife that Nina was involved with Patrick," I said. "He says she confided in him as her doctor."

"Who tells their doctor who they're shtupping?" Ben picked up his phone. "Bonnie's been talking to the wrong guy about Nina's disappearance."

The officer Ben spoke with said Detective Hernandez was testifying in court and would return his call when she was free.

Martin and I thanked the PI and took our leave. No sooner were we on the sidewalk than my cell rang. I handed SB to the padre and answered it as we strolled the half block to my car. In his unhurried way, Sten Jakobsen informed me that he'd just received the final toxicology report from Joyce Huang, the pathologist he'd hired to perform the autopsy.

"Irene died of a heart attack," he said.

"Right, we've been over this," I said. "A heart attack brought on by ingesting poison."

"What I mean to say is, she died of a, shall we say, garden-variety heart attack, presumably brought on by… well, by the usual causes. There was not enough poison in her system to do her in, only enough to give her indigestion."

"Wait, what?" I stopped in my tracks. Martin and Sexy Beast cocked their heads in tandem.

"I am as surprised as you," Sten drawled, "but relieved at the same time. At least now we know she was not the victim of murder. Naturally, that young lady, the O'Rourke girl, will have to answer charges of second-degree assault."

"Wow," I said. "I assume you've shared this with Detective Hernandez?"

"I attempted to phone her, but she is—"

"I know, she's in court." I told him about our visit with Ben Ralston and the surprising news about Jonah.

"If I hear from the detective first," Sten said, "I shall ask her to contact Ben posthaste."

I told Martin about the tox report as we got into the car and merged with late-afternoon traffic on Main Street. I figured I'd drop the padre back at his place, grab a couple of slices of Sicilian and an orange soda, and watch a funny movie—perhaps in my basement home theater, where I hadn't set foot since Irene had died there two weeks earlier. The time had come to reclaim the room, if I could do so without weeping all the way through *Blazing Saddles*. Thinking about the home theater triggered another memory.

"Jaws!" I smacked the steering wheel.

"Where?" Martin glanced around.

"Remember I told you that Nina somehow knew that Irene was watching *Jaws* when she died?"

"And you didn't know how that was possible since the only

person besides you who knew about it was… Ah," he said.

"Exactly. Jonah promised not to spread it around, but it's a scientific fact that the rules of discretion don't apply to pillow talk."

"You think Jonah told Nina about *Jaws*?" he asked.

"It certainly explains how she came by that tidbit, assuming she wasn't there herself."

"You know, a guy who's capable of offing his mistress—"

"We don't know that he did that," I said. "I don't want to jump to conclusions. Jonah's always seemed like, well, a decent person." Maybe a little less decent now that I knew he was cheating on Rachel.

"Isn't that what the neighbors always say after the cops dig a dozen corpses out of some guy's flower bed? 'He seemed like such a nice man. Quiet. Mowed his lawn.' Anyway, my point is that a man who, for the sake of argument, would kill his mistress to keep the gravy train chugging along, that man wouldn't be above offing some nosy old biddy who'd hired a PI to snoop into his illicit love affair. He'd assume that with the paying client out of the picture, the PI's investigation would grind to a halt and his secret would be safe." Martin watched me, gauging my reaction. "You were thinking the same thing."

I blew out a heavy sigh, not wanting to admit it. "But Sten just told us Irene died of a heart attack. 'Garden variety.' That's how he put it."

"Jonah's a doctor, Jane. He'd know what drugs to give her so it looks like natural causes. You know, like those angel-of-death nurses that get away with murder."

"The pathologist didn't find anything except the pesticides," I said.

"Aren't there drugs that are undetectable?"

"You're asking me?" I did not like where this conversation was going. Yet I couldn't help adding, "Jonah had a key."

"To Irene's house?"

I nodded. "So he could let himself in for house calls. Irene trusted him."

He said, "So those wet footprints you told me about…"

"Were probably Irene taking SB outside, like I said. But still."

Sexy Beast's ears twitched when he heard his name, but his car-whining continued unabated as I negotiated the side streets, heading for the parkway.

"Maybe Jonah didn't cancel his appointment with Irene," he said. "Maybe he parked in some out-of-the-way spot and let himself in through the back door so no one would see him enter the house. Maybe he tracked rainwater in the laundry room. Maybe he went downstairs to Irene's home theater, and maybe he gave her a shot of some nasty stuff that he knew wouldn't show up during a tox screen."

"And maybe you're letting your imagination run away with you," I said, but my heart wasn't in it. I felt a little sick recalling how Jonah and I had hung out in Irene's kitchen the night she'd died, waiting for Ahearn's people to arrive. I'd shown Jonah the wet footprints, insisted that her death was suspicious. Could he have…?

Then I remembered something else and nearly laughed with relief. "I'll tell you why your neat little theory doesn't hold water, Padre. Jonah was at Harbor Memorial Hospital for four solid hours that evening, till a little after nine. Sophie Halpern had to go to the ER, and she said he was with her the entire time."

Martin offered an annoyed frown. "When did you get to Irene's that night?"

"Quarter past nine. I found her about ten minutes later. When I called Jonah on his cell, he was on his way home from the hospital."

"Turn the car around," he said.

"What?"

I was about to turn right onto the entrance ramp to the parkway. Martin grabbed the wheel and jerked it to the left, making us veer into the wrong lane. I smacked his hand away as drivers around us leaned on their horns. Sexy Beast responded to the excitement with nonstop barking in my ear.

"What the hell?" I yelled.

"Turn around there." He pointed to an upcoming intersection with a big *No U-Turn* sign.

"This better be good," I said as I made a legal left and went around the block.

*

WE FOUND A parking space in front of the Town Hall building. I lowered Sexy Beast into my straw tote bag, still lined with Irene's old blue sweater, his favorite napping surface. I didn't know whether dogs were allowed in the building, but SB had exhausted himself with all his barking in the car, and as soon as he hit the sweater, he curled up and conked out.

The ground floor of the building housed Patisserie Susanne, and as we passed the open entrance to the bakery, the ambrosial aromas of la-dee-da pastries and coffee made me lightheaded.

"We're swinging by there on our way out," I told Martin, who did not object.

Sophie's office was on the top floor of the four-story building, which had been a hotel during the 1920s and '30s. When we stepped out of the elevator, there was no trace of the old speakeasy and gambling den that had once occupied the space. The décor of the mayor's office suite was ultramodern, furnished in pale earth tones with brass and marble accents.

I'd anticipated a struggle getting in to see Her Honor without an appointment, but there she was in the reception area, shooting the breeze with her secretary, Amanda, and a young male intern. It was close to quitting time. Sophie was tossing back M&M's from a bowl on Amanda's desk and choking with laughter at something the intern had said.

Sophie greeted us with hugs. I asked if we could speak with her in private. She escorted us into her office and shut the door, then peeked into my tote. "Thought so. Glad you got that animal trimmed. Poor little thing looked like a tribble on meth. Sit, sit. What can I do you for?"

"It's about your trip to the emergency room a couple of weeks ago," I said. "The day Irene died."

Her eyebrows rose. "What about it?"

"Well, you told me Jonah was there with you the whole time. For four hours, you said?"

She nodded. "Thinking about signing up for his concierge service? Don't do it. You're young and healthy. Wouldn't be worth the gigundo fees he charges."

Martin spoke up. "What brought you to the ER, if I may ask?"

"Calf pain," Sophie said, "which—surprise, surprise—was completely gone by the time I got to the hospital. Eventually they did a Doppler ultrasound and found zip. Monumental waste of time."

"When you say 'they' did an ultrasound," Martin said, "do you mean Jonah?"

"Nah, they have technicians for stuff like that," she said. "Mine was a hottie from Brazil named Lucas. There I lay in that darkened room while Lucas gently massaged my legs—with cold gel and an ultrasound thingie." She cackled. "I can dream, right?"

"How long did the scan take?" I asked.

Sophie looked from Martin to me. "Okay, what's this about?"

I took a deep breath. I had no intention of slandering Jonah on such thin evidence. Hadn't I already done that to Patrick? "It's… complicated. Can I ask you to trust me for now? I'll fill you in later, I promise."

Sophie gave me a long, serious look. "I'll hold you to that. The scan took about forty-five minutes."

I could tell Martin was thinking the same thing I was. Jonah's forty-five-minute window of opportunity, in and of itself, did little to bolster the padre's theory. I was glad I hadn't mentioned our suspicions to Sophie.

"What time did Lucas finish?" I asked.

"Around nine. Jonah looked at the results, declared my veins to be A-okay, and walked me to my car. I felt bad for tying up his evening, but hell, that's what I pay him for."

"You only tied up the first half of his evening," I said. "I ruined the rest of it." Or rather, Irene did, by dying. "So the two of you left the hospital when? Around a quarter past nine?"

"Nine-twelve on the dot. Checked my watch to see precisely how much time I'd wasted hanging around the ER when I should've been down at Murray's Pub playing bar trivia. My team nailed the local-history category last week. 'What was the name of Charles Rutherford Nevins's last horse?'" She shook her head, snickering. "Amateurs."

"One last question," Martin said, as we prepared to leave.

"Make that two. What was the name of Charles Rutherford Nevins's last horse?"

"Lucifer the Fourth. I can show you his grave. Next question."

"You don't happen to know what Jonah was doing while you were getting the ultrasound?"

"Out sneaking a cigarette." Sophie made a face. "You'd think an M.D. would know better. Plus he's a runner."

I frowned. "I've never seen Jonah smoke."

"Neither have I," she said, "but when he put on his trench coat, I noticed it was wet, and it wasn't raining earlier when we got to the hospital."

My heartbeat accelerated. "The rain started around eight."

"He admitted going outside for a smoke while I was with the handsome and debonair Lucas," Sophie said. "Made me promise not to tell Rachel."

The instant Martin and I were behind closed elevator doors, I said, "Jonah would have known how long that scan was going to take." The padre's theory was back in the running.

"Harbor Memorial is a fifteen-minute drive from Irene's house," he said. "He would've had just enough time to quietly slip out of the hospital, drive to Irene's in the rain and give her the angel-of-death treatment, then slip back into the ER around the time Sophie's scan ended."

I pictured Jonah entering Irene's home theater. I pictured her using the remote to pause the movie and bring up the room lights. Greeting him. Smiling at him. Then I pictured the rest of it. Jonah going through the motions. Asking about her stomachache. Filling a syringe with "medicine." Watching her die. Then lowering the room lights, restarting the movie, and letting himself out of the house—at about the time I was strolling into Ahearn's to liberate the mermaid.

I didn't want to believe it. Jonah had been her doctor for years. Could salvaging his marriage, and his elevated lifestyle, be worth committing murder? Possibly double murder, depending on Nina's fate.

"He called Irene a little after five," I reminded Martin, lowering my voice as we exited the elevator. Several Town Hall employees passed us in the lobby, leaving for the day. "To cancel her appointment, I assumed, but maybe it was to tell her he was going to be late. He'd be figuring that once Sophie went in for her scan, he could sneak out and do the deed."

"It's a great alibi if anyone questions death by natural causes," he said. "Everyone would assume he was at the hospital the whole time."

"He had to know Wednesday was Maria's day off. All things considered, it was the perfect opportunity." I pulled out my phone. "I wonder if Bonnie's back at the station yet."

He snatched the phone out of my hand and shoved it back into my tote bag. "Face-to-face, Jane. We're going to the PD. If she's not there, we wait."

"Okay, but first things first." I steered him toward the entrance to Susanne's. "I'm about to faint from hunger."

Sexy Beast still snoozed in the tote. I hoped he'd remain asleep and unnoticed until after I'd procured my sugar fix. I suspected Susanne would not take kindly to the presence of an animal in her pristine cafe.

"What's good here?" Martin asked as we entered the shop and perused the sweet and savory dainties arranged behind glass.

"Everything. If you're in the mood for a sandwich, try the

croque-monsieur. Or the duck." I had my heart set on a chocolate croissant, in particular the plump specimen in the front of the case that was winking and whispering my name.

The joint was jumping with after-work customers. All the round bistro tables were occupied. We joined a short queue of folks waiting to place their orders. Idly I glanced around, and heard myself gasp.

"That's him!" I whispered into Martin's ear. "That's Jonah Diamond."

He followed my gaze to the man now paying Susanne and accepting a small white sack in return.

"He comes here a lot," I murmured.

"Right, the carrot-cake guy. But why bring his medical bag in here?" he asked as Jonah deposited the bakery sack in his black leather satchel.

"Beats me." I was afraid Jonah would notice me on his way out, which would have been awkward under the circumstances. But instead of heading for the exit, he moved toward the opposite side of the room and the staircase that led to the basement.

"What's down there?" Martin asked.

"Restrooms." The woman in front of us picked out a gorgeous little cake made to resemble a gift-wrapped box. "I hope we're out of here before he comes back up."

"We're going to wait for him," he said. "I want to meet this guy. Introduce us when he comes through."

"No way! I don't want to talk to him. I might, I don't know, give something away."

We continued to argue about it as we placed our order—Martin got a pâté sandwich—and grabbed the first available table. Several minutes later, when I was licking the last of the chocolate filling off my fingers, Jonah still hadn't returned.

"Is there an exit down there?" Martin asked.

"I don't think so," I said. "I mean, it's a basement. I'm sure this is the only way out."

He stood. "Come on."

Good, he had come to his senses. I shouldered the tote—carefully so as not to wake Sexy Beast—stuffed our trash into the nearest bin, and started for the doorway. The padre seized my elbow and propelled me toward the staircase.

"Oh, for heaven's sake." I couldn't wrench free without creating a scene and waking SB. Whatever indisposition had caused Jonah to linger in the bathroom, I'd just as soon remain in ignorance.

Martin pulled me down the steps and we found ourselves in a pretty foyer with pale floral wallpaper, potted plants, and white-painted doors adorned with porcelain signs: *Hommes* and *Femmes*.

"Wait here." He disappeared into the men's room and reappeared seconds later, shaking his head. "He's not in there."

"What do you mean he's not in there?" I asked. "That's impossible. Where else could he be?"

"Check the women's john."

"Why on earth would Jonah go into the women's john?"

He pulled an exasperated face and walked into the *Femmes* before I could stop him. From behind the closed door I heard a squeak of alarm and the padre explaining, "Sorry, miss, I don't read French. Thought this was the men's." This was followed by muted conversation I couldn't make out, punctuated by feminine giggles.

When he finally rejoined me, he was slipping a scrap of paper into his pocket. Only Martin McAuliffe could invade a ladies' restroom and emerge with a phone number.

I tamped down my irritation and tried the knob of the only other door, which bore a sign that read *Employees Only*. Locked. "I don't get it," I said. "Who is he, Houdini? There are no windows down here and no other exit besides the staircase. What are you doing?"

He'd slipped a credit card out of his wallet. Or rather, something that was the size and shape of a credit card, but slightly thicker and solid black. He slid the back off the card to reveal five slim steel objects. He selected one that had a ninety-degree bend near the tip and another that had several squiggles at the end.

Realization dawned. "Put those things away," I hissed. "You're going to get us both arrested." I kept one eye on the door to the ladies' room, through which his giggly new friend could materialize at any moment.

He inserted the bent thingie into the keyhole and held it there while he stuck the squiggly one in and yanked it out a couple of times. *Voilà.* The knob turned. The whole process took less time than pouring a bowl of Fruity Pebbles.

Martin pulled me inside the *Employees Only* and closed the door. The room was about twelve by twelve feet with brick walls and exposed pipes overhead. Cobwebs abounded and a musty, dusty smell pervaded the room, which appeared to serve as a catchall for unused furniture and equipment. Desks. Filing cabinets. Lamps. Bakery racks. A cluster of fat, outdated computer monitors. A tall metal storage locker. We immediately ascertained that we were alone.

"Someone left the light on." I nodded toward the bare light bulb dangling from a ceiling joist. It emitted a weak glow that failed to penetrate the corners of the room. Neither of us had flipped the switch by the door, so the last person in here must have failed to turn it off. Judging by the neglected look of the place, that could have been weeks ago.

I detected movement in my straw tote as Sexy Beast yawned and stretched. His front paws and sleepy face appeared over the top edge of the bag, nose twitching as he catalogued the contents of the room. He whined to be set down on the floor so he could explore—which would never, ever happen. Not in this dirty, gloomy place. As a consolation, I offered him scritches and a treat from one of the bag's inside pockets.

Martin, meanwhile, poked around the room. He pushed aside a stack of folding chairs and examined a small wooden door set halfway up the wall. "This looks like a dumbwaiter." He shoved upward on the brass handle and managed to slide the door partway up. He stuck his head in and peered upward.

His voice echoed. "Looks like the shaft goes all the way up. For room service, I guess, when this place was a hotel."

"More like booze service," I said. "During Prohibition there was a speakeasy where Sophie's office is now."

He straightened and plucked a cobweb off his ear. "I guess they used the dumbwaiter to sneak bottles up and down."

"Hokum Hannigan owned the building," I said. "Also the Historical Society building, only it was a boardinghouse and brothel back then. Supposedly they were connected by a secret tunnel where they stored and transported the stuff."

That got the padre's attention. "Yeah? There's a tunnel down here?"

"Well, not anymore, if it even existed. They say the entrances were boarded up."

He looked crestfallen but still curious. "Wonder where it was."

"Who knows? Let's go." I'd had enough of that creepy room. I paused with my hand on the doorknob, listening for activity on the other side. It wouldn't do to be seen leaving the *Employees Only*. SB gave a sharp bark, impatient to explore. I shushed him and urged him to settle down on his sweater-nest.

"Where's the Historical Society?" Martin asked. "What direction?"

"You mean from where we're standing? Uh…" I pointed to the closed door. "Well, the front of this building is thataway. It faces west. And the Historical Society is a few blocks directly north of here, so…" I pointed northward.

He turned to face the north wall. "So the mouth of the tunnel could be right behind these bricks."

"Or it could be behind plaster and wallpaper out there." I jerked my head toward the door and the prettily decorated foyer beyond. "Or it could've been some kind of trapdoor in the floor and was cemented over decades ago. Or the whole thing could be BS."

He stood in the one spot where no clutter blocked the north wall and ran his fingers over the bricks, cast in shadowed relief by the anemic overhead light, which seemed to obscure more than it revealed. In truth, I shared his fascination. What child has never fantasized about a secret passageway? But I was relieved when he roused himself with a little shake and said, "Let's go find Detective Hernandez."

He crossed the room and reached for the doorknob, but I didn't relinquish it. Now I was the one standing there staring.

Not at the wall but at the floor directly in front of the wall—the space Martin had just occupied.

"What?" he said, watching me.

I squinted through the long shadows and slowly approached the spot, a paler rectangle in the filthy cement floor. The patch measured about eighteen inches by three feet. "It's cleaner here. Something was moved." I glanced around. "That thing."

I indicated the dented metal storage cabinet standing nearby, six feet tall with the same footprint as the pale spot.

He gave the cabinet a shove, and we discovered it was on wheels. "So what?" he said. "Someone did a little rearranging."

I looked from the north wall to the other three. "It's hard to tell in this dim light, but do the bricks here look different from the rest? A little more uniform maybe? I wish I had a flashlight."

Martin produced his key ring and freed something from it. A small, bright circle of light illuminated the bricks in front of us. The mini flashlight couldn't have been more than two inches long, but it was powerful.

"Were you a Boy Scout?" I asked.

"Until I earned my Criminal Mischief badge." He directed the light at the brickwork, concentrating on the room's corners. "You know, I think you're right. Also, the mortar looks neater on the north wall. I bet it was built more recently."

"Maybe the tunnel wasn't just local legend." I took the flashlight from him and peered closely at the bricks. The differences were subtle, but they were there if you looked hard enough. "Maybe it really existed and this is where they bricked up the entryway."

"Or maybe it's old Hokum Hannigan they bricked up back there."

"Hokum died quietly in his sleep at age ninety-three," I said, standing on the clean patch of cement and running the light over the bricks.

"Sure, that's what they want you to believe," he said. "Give me the flashlight."

I battcd his hand away. "I'm not finished."

"What are you looking for?"

"I'll know when I find it," I said.

Then I found it.

"Do you see this gap?" I ran my finger over the end of a brick where the mortar didn't seem to adhere.

He examined the spot. "That can happen when mortar shrinks over time, usually because it was improperly mixed. Or when the foundation settles. Also, variations in temperature can cause moisture to infiltrate. And don't even get me started on expansion joints."

"You have no idea what you're talking about, do you?"

"Sure I do." He puffed out his chest. "I'm a guy."

"Okay, does this look like random shrinkage to you?" I moved the light upward from the floor, tracing a connected pattern of nearly invisible gaps between bricks and mortar. When the pattern continued over my head, Martin commandeered the flashlight and traced its path as it made a ninety-degree turn and ran horizontally for about four feet before turning again and continuing to the floor. It was the size and general shape of a wide door.

"Hmm…" he said.

"Hmm…" I said.

Holding the flashlight between his teeth, he placed both palms on the bricks and pushed. Nothing. He pushed again, harder. Then he handed me the light and gave the wall a bone-jarring slam with his shoulder. I heard the breath hiss between his teeth and suspected that if I hadn't been there, he'd have howled and cursed up a storm.

"Well, that's it," he said, rotating his shoulder. "Whatever caused that crack, it's not budging. Let's go."

"In a second. Hold on to this. Don't let SB get down." I handed Martin the straw tote, then pressed my fingertips to the inside edge of the crack and gently pushed, alert for the subtlest sign of movement. I felt like a safecracker as I slid my fingers downward a couple of inches and tried again.

The padre said nothing, but I sensed him losing patience. What effect could my puny efforts have after his manly display of brawn?

I worked my way down the right side, then shifted my attention to the left, palpating the inside edge of the gap.

He sighed. "Jane—"

"Sh! Be quiet and let me concentrate."

He brought his mouth close to SB's ear and stage-whispered, "Mommy's lost it."

I gave another small push at waist level and felt a brick depress slightly beneath my fingers. "Uh, Martin?"

"What?"

I lifted my hand away. The entire brick "door" popped forward several inches, with a metallic murmur. We leapt back. Sexy Beast lost his cool, and it was long seconds before I even thought of shushing him.

"Whoa," Martin said. "Whoa." I'd dropped the flashlight. He retrieved it and ran the light around the edges of the protruding bricks, which were backed by a wooden panel that barely cleared the surrounding wall. We couldn't see what was behind it.

A finger pull had been installed in the edge of the panel. Martin gave me an impish smile. "You want to do the honors? You earned it."

"It's all yours, Padre." All I could think of was Hokum Hannigan's grinning, rag-draped skeleton falling on me in a clatter of cobwebbed bones.

Okay, you can just shut up right now. You weren't there.

He gave the finger pull a tug and the brick door swung wide. We would have paused to admire the fancy hardware that made such a cunning thing possible, but our attention was fixed on something else.

No, not on Hokum's ghastly remains, which were blessedly absent, but on a heavy steel door that had been concealed under the false wall. It was an old door, battered and rusty, with a tubular push bar and a big, serious-looking padlock hanging open on a big, serious-looking hasp. The door was set into the original brick wall, which was partially visible behind the false one.

Discussion would have been pointless. We both knew that walking away at that moment was not an option. He handed me the tote bag, then reached out and depressed the push bar. We watched the door swing open on grumpy hinges.

17

Not if the Death Diva Has Anything to Say About It

THE TUNNEL EXHALED moist, earth-scented air. A dozen plank steps led down to a brick-walled passage with a tamped dirt floor and wooden ceiling. The reason we could see all this is that the lights had been left on here as well. However, while the bulb in the storage room was the old-style incandescent type, forty pathetic watts at most, the one hanging in the tunnel was a modern, energy-efficient fluorescent bulb that emitted lumens galore.

Sexy Beast growled softly, his dark little gaze unblinking as he stared into the underground passage. I decided I'd rather not know what manner of critter his high-powered nose detected.

Next to the staircase was a scarred wooden ramp. My overstressed brain flashed on an image of wheelchair-bound smugglers before it came to me. Hokum's men probably slid cases of liquor down this ramp.

We began speaking in whispers. We both knew Jonah Diamond might be somewhere in that tunnel, if he hadn't already exited from the other end about a quarter mile away. We had no desire to alert him to our presence.

The padre said, "Boarded up, huh?"

"That's what everyone believes," I said. "Looks like someone wanted to keep the tunnel to themselves."

"Yeah, someone who had access to this building long enough to erect a fake wall and an invisible doorway," he said. "Not to mention enough bread to get the job done and buy the workers' silence. You said Hokum Hannigan owned the place?"

I nodded. "After he died, Nina's parents donated both buildings to the town—this one and the Historical Society. For tax purposes."

"When was that?"

"Sometime in the nineties. Nina's folks were well off, like Ben said. I never met them, but I heard stories about how eccentric and secretive they were. I wouldn't put something like this past them." I gestured toward the clever brick door, which I now saw had an interior latch so it could be opened and closed from the inside.

"So they deed the buildings to the town but keep the cool smuggling tunnel in the family," he said.

"Looks that way. Which would mean that Nina knows about the tunnel and how to get into it. She probably inherited the keys." I indicated the open padlock. "And I know that she's in charge of the Prohibition museum, which is in the basement of the Historical Society. That has to be where the second entrance is hidden."

"So she and Jonah were getting it on in the tunnel," he said. "Their own secret trysting spot."

"You think so?" I made a face. "How romantic."

"It would explain why Ben could never track them down. Nina gives Jonah the key to this door so he can sneak into the tunnel during trips to the bakery. Meanwhile she goes into the Historical Society a few blocks away—"

"Which she does practically every day," I said.

"—and all anyone sees is two people entering two different buildings."

"They slip into the tunnel separately," I said, "meet somewhere in the middle, and what, make whoopee in some dark, disgusting corner?"

"Maybe not so dark and disgusting. Remember, this place is all theirs. They can fix it up any way they want. Maybe there's some kind of underground honeymoon suite back there." He descended the steps, which creaked alarmingly under his weight.

"Don't do that. He might be in there." I didn't add what we both had to be thinking: that if Nina had been murdered, her body could be stashed somewhere in there. The hairs on my nape stood up and saluted that possibility. "Let's go find Bonnie."

"In a minute. I just want a quick look." He took a few steps into the passage and gestured for me to join him. "Come on, we'll probably never get another chance."

Gingerly I walked down a few rickety steps, peering into the murky recesses beyond the reach of the light, clutching SB's tote to my chest. I shivered, whether from excitement or fear, I couldn't say—probably a heart-thumping mixture of both. "They say it's not safe." I was still whispering.

"Who's 'they'?" He strolled a little farther, looking around. "The same folks who claimed the entryways were boarded up?"

I took the last steps but stayed put at the bottom of them. Loose bricks lay scattered on the dirt floor. "The walls aren't holding up too well. And look." I pointed to the ceiling where the wooden planks that held back thousands of tons of earth were rotting and even missing in places. Massive vertical timbers had been placed along the sides for support, but they, too, had seen better days.

"Don't you know? That's part of the allure of doing it in a place like this." He wagged his eyebrows. "A little danger to spice things up."

I had one hand inside the tote, restraining a squirming Sexy Beast, who was all too curious about this strange new place. "I'm out of here, Padre. And I'm locking the door behind me." Never mind that I didn't have the key.

He lifted a piece of wood with some kind of writing on it— probably part of an old liquor crate. "Where's your sense of wonder, Jane?"

"It's cowering behind my sense of self-preservation, if you must know."

He tossed the artifact and ambled back to me, shaking his head in regret at the lost opportunity. "All right, let's go get the cops up to speed on all this." His mouth quirked. "Never thought I'd hear myself say those words."

I turned to go back up the stairs just as a supersized rat ran across my foot. I screamed and flailed my legs, losing my balance and landing on my butt in the dirt. SB leapt out of the tote with a ferocious bark and took off after the rat, both animals swiftly disappearing into the tunnel.

"*SB!*" I ran full tilt after him, my legs moving before my brain could catch up. "SB, you get back here right now, do you hear me?"

"SB, *come!*" Martin shouted, sprinting past me into the near darkness beyond. Unlike me, he had the presence of mind to use a command the dog would understand, if SB even heard us. With each passing second, his shrill barks became fainter and fainter. He might be a runty toy poodle, but those little legs could eat up the ground when he was motivated.

I kept running, sweating now, concentrating on Martin's footfalls ahead as the passage curved and the inky shadows succumbed to the glare of another fluorescent bulb. The lights were strung at regular intervals along the length of the tunnel, I discovered as we ran deeper and deeper into it. Prohibition-era detritus littered the route: empty bottles, the remains of wooden crates, a rusted handcart lying on its side.

I caught up with Martin when he stopped where a side tunnel branched off the main passage. He was breathing hard, listening intently, trying to ascertain which direction the dog had gone. We heard no barking, no rat squeals, no nothing.

"Oh God oh God oh God," I muttered, imagining Sexy Beast catching up to the rat and wondering how much damage the disgusting, disease-ridden beast was liable to inflict. Then my imagination turned it into a swarm of rats, then a veritable tidal wave of rats ganging up on my poor SB. There's never just one rat, right?

"Stop it," Martin said.

"What?"

"We're going to find him. He's not going to get eaten by rats. So just stop it."

I took a deep breath, my heart still banging from exertion and fear. I nodded. It was disorienting being underground. I wondered how far we'd gone and which end of the tunnel was now closest. A light bulb hung nearby, so I had a good view of the sagging and broken ceiling planks, the dirt and rubble that had sifted down from the gaps between them, and the half-rotted support timbers.

The mouth of the side tunnel was in the worst shape, partially blocked by fallen bricks and ceiling debris, and held up only by a pair of heavy, tall timbers. A cluster of tools stood propped against a wall. Sledgehammer. Ax. Shovel.

A body could be buried in the dirt under my feet and who would ever know?

Martin cupped his mouth and in a booming, alpha-male roar, commanded, *"SB! Come!"*

From deep within the side tunnel came a response, only it wasn't SB. The voice was decidedly human, but muffled behind something. We looked at each other.

He said, "You stay here in case the dog comes this way."

I gave another shaky nod. I knew it made sense for us to separate, though I wasn't happy about it. I watched him sidestep the pile of bricks and enter the side tunnel, which was in total darkness and extended who knew how far. I saw a small, bright light and knew he'd switched on his little flashlight.

"Hello?" he called. "Can you tell me where you are?"

I heard the faint voice again, shrill and agitated. It was definitely female. One person came immediately to mind and I felt a glimmer of hope. Nina Wallace might not be my favorite person, but she didn't deserve to be murdered. As for the other missing creature…

"SB!" My voice cracked. Sweat dried on my skin, chilling me. "Come, boy. Come to Mommy so I can wring your little neck."

Martin's voice reverberated off the brick walls. "Keep talking," he told whoever was back there. "I'll find you."

The response was a hysterical outburst, still muted.

Less than a minute later, which felt like an hour as I continued to plead with Sexy Beast, I jumped at the sound of some kind of impact deep within the side tunnel. Then another. I cupped my mouth. "Martin? What's going on?"

He yelled something, but he was too far away for me to make it out. I ventured about twenty feet into the dim passage, glancing constantly in the other direction in case SB ran past, and called out for him to repeat his words.

"Call nine-one-one," he said. "Nina's locked up in here."

She was alive! Automatically I reached for my tote bag before remembering that I'd left it back at the stairs. I told him I didn't have my phone.

"Come get mine," he hollered. "I'm busy with the lock."

I forced myself to forget about Sexy Beast for the time being. Freeing Nina took priority. I made my way down the side passage, which quickly went from murky to pitch-black. No lights here. I felt fallen rubble underfoot and suspected the ceiling was in even worst shape here than in the main tunnel.

Nina's voice became progressively louder. She was sobbing, cursing, screaming hoarsely over and over, "Get me out of here!"

I picked up my pace and promptly tripped over an unseen rock. Gravel bit into my palms, and I didn't want to think about how many rat turds now adhered to my jeans and shirt. I found my feet and hurried ahead, my eye on the firefly glow of Martin's flashlight.

The side tunnel was about fifty yards long. When I reached the end, I found Martin crouched in front of a rough wooden door set into the bricks. His compact lock-pick set lay on the ground and he held the flashlight between his teeth, illuminating an antique-looking lock. Both hands were busy manipulating two of the slim steel tools inside the keyhole.

He spoke around the flashlight. "Tried to kick it in. Almost caused a cave-in. This rusty old lock's a bitch."

"Where's your phone?"

"Right front pocket."

He shifted his weight to give me access to the pocket. I slipped my hand in and felt around. It was a pretty deep pocket and I found myself groping the padre in a most unladylike manner before I finally managed to grasp the phone and pull it out. The scrap of paper with the giggler's phone number came out with it. I accidentally dropped the paper and then accidentally ground it into the dirt under my shoe.

Nina, meanwhile, never ceased her caterwauling from behind the thick wooden door.

"Nina, it's Jane. Jane Delaney." I pushed random buttons on the phone until the screen lit up, displaying a close-up of a beautiful young woman. Who the heck was that? Meanwhile I kept talking. "We're going to get you out of there, but you have to calm down so Martin can concentrate on the lock."

The door rocked under three savage kicks from the other side, which caused a hail of dirt and gravel from overhead and made one of the picks slip from the lock and land in the dirt. Martin felt around for it, muttering ripe curses under his breath. Something told me this wasn't the first time Nina had been called those particular names.

I swiped my finger on the smart phone and was rewarded with a display of icons. "How did you end up in there?" I asked Nina. If I could get her talking, maybe there'd be less kicking.

"How do you think?" she screeched through the door. "Jonah tricked me."

"Tricked you how?"

"By pretending to change his mind, that's how. When I first told him about the baby, he was all upset. Wanted me to let Mal believe it was his and go on like nothing happened. Didn't want to leave his insipid wife and her money."

After some trial and error, I located the icon for making a phone call and tapped in 911. Then it was my turn to say a bad word. "No phone service," I told Martin, as he abandoned one lock pick and selected another. "We must be too far underground." His response was a growl of frustration. I shoved the phone back into his pocket, took the flashlight out of his mouth, and aimed it squarely at the keyhole.

"Don't leave me here!" Nina sounded on the verge of a breakdown.

"I'm here, Nina," I said. "We both are. We're not going anywhere until we get you out of there, I promise. Have you been here since last Thursday?"

"Yes! Jonah brings me food and water every day, otherwise I wouldn't even know how long I've been here. There are no windows, no clock, nothing."

A sliver of light shone under the door, so at least she hadn't been in darkness this whole time.

"So Jonah pretended to do an about-face?" I asked her. "He said he wanted to leave Rachel and marry you?"

"It was all lies to keep me quiet," she said through sobs. I heard her slide down the door and pictured her slumped against it, exhausted, betrayed, terrified for her life.

I whispered to Martin, "What's taking so long? You had that

other lock open in about five seconds."

"I'm almost there," he muttered. "Keep that light steady."

To Nina I said, "When was this? That he said he was leaving Rachel?"

"Wednesday," she said. "He had me come in for an office visit. Acted all apologetic. Said the news about the baby freaked him at first but that he thought about it and was ready to leave Rachel. Said he wants to be with me for the rest of his life. And I believed him."

I thought of the sexy surveillance photos Ben had taken through the blinds of Jonah's exam room. Jonah had been putting on a lovey-dovey act for Nina, making her think he was with the program.

"And he told you to meet him down here the next day as usual?" I asked.

"Yes. He told me not to say anything to Mal yet, that we had to wait for the right time. But I was so excited, Mal could tell something was up. So I told him I was leaving him, and about the baby. He wanted to know who the other man was, but I wouldn't say."

"Nina… how long does Jonah intend to keep you here? Did he mention?" It was better than asking, *Why are you still alive?*

"I don't *know*! I thought he wanted me to change my mind, to tell him that everything would stay the way it was. So that's what I did. But he could tell I was lying. Plus Mal already knows about the baby, that it isn't his. Jonah can't let me go now. He knows I'd run to the cops, no matter what I told him." After a few moments she said in a trembling voice, "Jane?"

"Yes, Nina. I'm here."

"He's acting weirder every day. I think he's really losing it. I think he's trying to work up the nerve to kill me." Her voice broke. "He doesn't want to because of the baby. I think that's the only reason I'm not dead yet."

I took a deep breath and let it out. What was I supposed to say? That she had to be mistaken? That the man she'd loved, the father of her unborn child, would never do such a thing?

Before I could figure out how to respond, Martin said, "Yes!" He turned the knob and the door swung outward.

I blinked against the sudden glare from inside the room as Nina spilled through the open doorway. Martin steadied her and helped her to her feet. Never had I imagined Nina Wallace could look so bedraggled: her clothes a wrinkled mess, hair lank and greasy, no makeup to conceal her pallor or the dusky circles under her eyes.

I returned the mini flashlight to Martin and gaped at the love nest turned prison cell, complete with whitewashed brick walls, a colorful area rug, and a plank ceiling showing signs of recent repair. The light source was another bare, dangling bulb. A king-size air mattress dominated the room, its covers rumpled. The only other furnishings were two folding chairs matching those we'd seen in the storage room, a bakery rack, and last and indisputably least, a tin bucket in the corner. Yeah, you know what the bucket was for. You don't need me to spell it out.

Some honeymoon suite.

Martin poked his head into the room, clearly fascinated by the cavelike refuge. A wrapped deli sandwich lay unopened on the bakery rack, along with boxes of cereal and crackers, spray cheese, three bottles of water, and the white paper sack from Susanne's. Jonah had been taking good care of his pregnant mistress while he summoned the backbone to do what needed to be done: eliminate her just as he'd no doubt eliminated Irene.

Obviously Jonah had been there minutes earlier, dropping off the food. He had to know we were in the tunnel, considering the racket we'd made trying to find Sexy Beast. A chill scampered down my spine. "Guys, let's get out of—"

I yelped as a muscular arm whipped around me from behind, dragging me a few stumbling steps from the others and pinning my arms.

Nina whimpered, her eyes huge. Martin started to lunge toward us but stopped short. That's when I felt what they'd both seen: the tip of a needle nudging the side of my neck. I cut my eyes in that direction and saw a hand holding a hypodermic syringe filled with a clear liquid.

"You called it right, Nina," Jonah said as his arm tightened around me. "I let maudlin sentiment sway me for too long. I should've buried you five days ago."

Through tears Nina said, "Jonah, I love you—"

"You love yourself," he barked. "This is all your fault—you gave me no choice. Get back in there." I felt him nod toward the room's open doorway. "You too," he told Martin. "But I'll take those lock picks first."

"Listen, man." Martin raised his palms. "So you kept your girlfriend here for a few days. Sounds to me like some kind of kinky sex game. That's how anyone would see it—if Nina even told anyone about it, which she's not going to do, and neither are we. Right, Nina?"

"I won't tell anyone, I swear," she sobbed. "Please don't put me back in there."

"Nice try, sweetheart," Jonah sneered. "I heard you tell them you'd run straight to the cops."

I wondered how long he'd been silently creeping up the dark side tunnel, sneaking up on us. He'd probably heard our whole conversation.

To Martin he said, "I'm not going to ask how you tracked us down here. I'm not in the mood for more lies. The lock picks?" He gave the needle a little jab, making me gasp. "Don't make me say it again."

"Here." Martin quickly retrieved the set from his pocket.

Jonah loosened his hold on me long enough to catch the card-sized set as Martin tossed it. The presence of the needle tip pricking my neck was enough to keep all of us under control as Jonah thumbed open the small case one-handed. He shook the five miniature picks into his palm and pitched them over his shoulder. I heard one of them ping against a rock.

He repeated his order for Martin and Nina to get into the room.

Martin and I locked eyes as he pushed a sobbing Nina into the room and backed in after her. In his gaze I read a plea for forgiveness, though we both knew he had no choice. If he went for Jonah, the contents of that syringe would be racing through my veins before he took a single step.

But there was more than apology in Martin's grim features. It was the most candid I'd ever seen him, the message clear and unambiguous. *Save yourself. Do whatever you have to, but get out of this place alive.*

Somewhere along the line, I'd gotten under his skin. The thought shouldn't have warmed me, considering our dire situation, but it did. The last thing I wanted to do was let him down.

He turned to Jonah. "Put Jane in here, too."

I wasn't surprised when Jonah said, "Not a chance." In the

short time he'd been in Martin's company, he'd obviously sized him up and knew better than to underestimate him. Jonah would never be able to shove me into the room and lock the door before Martin charged him.

Nina collapsed on the bed, hugging herself and crying. Martin backed up to the far wall and knelt on the rug. "I'm not going to try anything, man, I swear. You're better off leaving Jane with us." He must have figured that my chances of survival were better inside a locked room with him and Nina than outside the room with Jonah and his needle.

In response, Jonah marched me to the door and kicked it shut, plunging us into pitch darkness. He immediately turned the lock and pocketed the key, then banded his arm even tighter around me.

"Let her go, Jonah!" Martin yelled from behind the door. "She's not going to give you any trouble."

"It's t-true." The velvet blackness before my eyes only compounded my terror. "I have nothing to tell anyone. Nina's okay. You didn't do anything that bad."

"Treating me like an idiot is not in your best interest, Jane." He traced the tip of the needle over the tender skin of my neck, making me stiffen. "I can make your death much more unpleasant than it needs to be."

This was my cue to turn on the juice and fight like hell. I'd run out of options, and I'd be damned if I was going to passively stand there and wait for Jonah to snuff out my life. I twisted and kicked, but I was no match for his superior size and strength.

"Don't do it, Jonah!" Martin pounded the door, bellowing a promise. "If you hurt her, I'll make you wish you'd never been born."

Jonah ignored him. "You're a meddlesome bitch, just like Irene." I felt him adjust the needle's angle against my neck and knew he was positioning his thumb on the hypodermic's plunger. "And you're going to die the same way she did."

I squeezed my eyes shut and braced myself for the stab of the needle.

A frenzy of barking erupted at our feet, startling us both and causing Jonah to loosen his hold for a split second. It was all the time I needed to knock his hand away from my neck, drive my elbow into his solar plexus, and break free. As I turned to run, I heard the hypodermic bounce on gravel.

Jonah was in great shape and he was a runner. I had scant hope of making it out of the side passage, much less all the way to the bakery to get help, but I had to try. I assumed SB was sprinting with me toward the distant light of the main tunnel— until I heard his sharp yelp echoing off the bricks.

"Say goodbye to your dog," Jonah yelled, as SB emitted yips of fear or pain or both.

I stumbled to a halt. "*No!* Jonah, please don't hurt him."

"Get back here now or I'll bash his brains out on the wall," he said.

"I'm coming, just... please don't do anything to SB." I retraced my steps back to Jonah. I couldn't see him, but I could hear his harsh breathing and SB's whimpers. The only light was the faint glow at the bottom of the door.

I pictured Sexy Beast squirming against Jonah's hold. Hot rage rose up within me like some relentless force of nature. With effort, I reined it in. An impotent display of emotion would solve nothing and could tip him over the edge. Nina had said he was losing his grip on reality, and from what I could see, she was right.

"Where are you?" he growled. "Get over here."

Before I could move toward his voice, his free hand found my arm in the dark, gripping it with bruising force. I cried out as he flung me like a rag doll against the wooden door. I slid to the ground as pain exploded in my back.

"Jane!" Martin called from inside the room. "Are you okay?"

I fought to suck in air. "Yes," I croaked, pretty sure I was lying.

At least Jonah was now unarmed. I doubted he'd get on his hands and knees to search for his hypodermic in the dark, and I was right. His voice was already retreating toward the main tunnel. "If you move from that spot, if I see you or hear you trying to come out, this animal is dead. Understand?"

"Jonah, leave SB with me. We'll stay right—"

"Do you understand?" He was officially unhinged.

"Yes. I won't move. You have my word."

I listened to SB's whimpers grow fainter as Jonah jogged out of the side tunnel. *I'm sorry, SB. Please forgive me.*

Martin said, "Is he still there?"

"No. He's gone." I choked back a sob. "Martin, he has SB. I think he's going to kill him no matter what."

"Is he out of earshot?"

He didn't try to console me or offer lame reassurances, and for that I was grateful. As heartbroken as I was over the prospect of my precious Sexy Beast meeting a grisly end, his fate was now out of my control. I had to keep it together for all our sakes.

"Yes," I said. "He can't hear us as long as we keep our voices down. How's Nina?" I asked.

"Practically catatonic. I assume Jonah took the key?"

"Of course. I'm going to give him a few minutes to get out of the tunnel, then I'll go for help." And pray I wouldn't encounter

SB's lifeless corpse along the way.

I remembered the padlock on the door to the tunnel. Jonah would no doubt lock it on his way out, but as long as he didn't make off with my tote bag, which contained my cell phone, I should be able to get a signal there and call 911. If not, I'd pound on the door and holler until someone heard me.

Jonah's voice suddenly reverberated down the side tunnel, hurling vile curses at my dog. This was followed by vigorous barking, which grew louder as SB raced to return to me.

He leapt on me in the dark and I scooped him up and rained kisses on his furry little head. Never in my life had I been happier to have a dog lick and lick and lick my face.

"What did SB do?" Martin asked through the door. "Take a chunk out of his hand?"

"That would be my guess," I said, "but he's never bitten anyone in his life."

"Maybe he never had a reason until now. Do you hear Jonah coming back?"

"No." I heard something else, though, something that made me forget to keep breathing. I stood on wobbly legs, clutching SB to my chest. "Martin? Do you hear that?"

Thunk. Thunk. Thunk. A series of percussive blows, the sound ringing off the brick walls.

"Yeah," he said. "What's happening?"

"I think…" My mouth was desert dry. I thought about the ax I'd seen earlier. "I think he's chopping down the supports at the entrance to the side tunnel."

Martin was ominously silent.

My voice climbed a couple of octaves. "This place is already on the verge of collapse."

I saw it clearly now, Jonah's simple strategy: cave in the mouth of the side passage. It was all too easy to imagine such a cave-in cascading down part or all of the passage's deteriorated length. Meanwhile Jonah would escape through the main tunnel, and the three of us—or four of us including Sexy Beast—would never be heard from again.

With Martin and Nina locked up, I alone would be trying to dig us out. In complete darkness. With my bare hands. That is, if we were lucky and the collapse didn't kill us outright.

On second thought, that would be the lucky thing, dying quickly under tons of earth and rock rather than facing slow suffocation or starvation. At least Martin and Nina had spray cheese.

"I have to try and stop him," I said.

"Jane, no!" Martin said. "What are you going to do, tackle a man with an ax?"

"I refuse to just stand here and wait to die." I squeezed SB so tightly he yelped. I gave him an apologetic nuzzle. "Do you have a better idea?"

"I know how we can make it a fairer fight," he said. "You're going to pick this lock."

After a startled pause, I said, "I don't know how to pick locks."

"I'll walk you through it. First you have to find those picks that Jonah tossed."

"It's pitch black out here," I said.

"I know that. Hurry up. This tunnel could implode at any moment."

It was true. The chopping sounds continued unabated, along with the occasional falling plank or brick.

I didn't waste another second. As unrealistic as Martin's plan was, it was the only one we had. I put SB down and fell on my hands and knees in the area where I thought the lock picks had landed. I pushed all thoughts of rat turds out of my mind as I swept my hands over dirt and rocks, searching for the tiny steel tools. I wished I'd held on to Martin's flashlight.

"Ow!" Something stabbed my hand. I groped in the dark and discovered Jonah's hypodermic attached to me, the needle deeply embedded in the base of my thumb. Careful not to touch the plunger, I pulled it out and hurled the thing toward the nearest wall. It clattered against the bricks, followed by the squeal of a rat and the shuffle of tiny feet scampering directly in front of me.

Sexy Beast growled, but I managed to grab him before he could take off again. I ordered him to sit and stay, and something in my tone must have told him I meant business. He griped about the one that got away, but he stayed put.

"What happened?" Martin asked. "Are you all right?"

"Never better. Can't remember when I've had this much fun. Hey, I found one!" I ran my fingers over the slender piece of metal. It was definitely one of his lock picks.

"Which one?"

"How do I know which one?" I said.

"What does the end of it feel like?" he asked. "You're looking for the torsion wrench and the hook."

"This one has a bunch of bumps. You used it on the storage-room door."

"That's the rake. It's useless with this lock. Keep looking."

"Terrific," I muttered, and shoved the rake into my pocket. Less than a minute later I found another one. "The wrench—is that the one with the *L*-shaped end? I've got that."

"Great. Hurry up."

I discarded the occasional extraneous find: a cork, a bottle cap, a crushed cigarette pack. Several hefty insects took an interest in me and I bravely shook them off. It's amazing the salutary effect one's imminent demise can have on one's maturity level.

The next two picks I found were the diamond and the snake, according to Martin. I'd found every pick in the set except the one I needed.

"It has a little rounded hook on the end. It's the only one I could get to work in this lock," he said. "Come on, Jane, it's got to be there."

I expanded my search area, clawing my fingers through dirt and rubble. My hands were raw and scraped, but I ignored the pain.

The regular *thunk* of Jonah's ax-blows abruptly ceased. I heard distant thuds and pictured him kicking the timber he'd just hewn, urging it to split in two. More likely, he was using the sledgehammer I'd spied earlier. This was followed by the creak of splintering wood, then the crash of a huge support timber toppling, along with portions of the wall and ceiling at the entryway. Before the racket had settled, he started chopping the second timber.

"Jane?" Martin's voice sounded different. Subdued. "I just want you to know something. You know, in case we don't—"

"Save it, Padre." I refused to entertain an *in case we don't* scenario. I couldn't think that way if I was going to get us out of there alive.

That scalding surge of anger once again threatened to engulf me, and this time I let it. That sick bastard was not going to get away with this—not if the Death Diva had anything to say about it. I was going to find that damn lock pick. Then I was going to pick that damn lock. Then the three of us were going to get that damn ax away from that damn psycho and run like hell out of that damn tunnel. Damn it.

I redoubled my efforts to find the last pick, crawling in an ever-widening circle, tossing aside rocks, sifting dirt and gravel through my sore fingers. "I've got it!" I raised the pick in triumph, though I couldn't see it in the inky dark. Then I dropped it. I cursed, groped, found it again.

Martin was already barking orders, instructing me to insert the bent tip of the wrench into the lower part of the keyhole and turn it clockwise, holding it with slight pressure while I slid the hook pick into the top part.

"There are five spring-loaded pins in the cylinder." He spoke quickly. "You'll need to push each pin up, working from back to front. Keep pressure on the wrench, but not too much pressure."

How much was too much? I tried not to think about how even Martin, with all his experience, had found this lock a beast to open.

"Can you feel the pins?" he asked.

"Umm…" I wiggled the pick in the lock. How was I supposed to tell what was in there? "There's something bumpy along the top."

"That's them. You'll feel a bit of give when each pin sets. You might even hear a little click." His voice seemed to come right through the lock. It comforted me to know he was sitting mere inches away. If not for the thick wooden door, I could touch him.

With his ear so close to the action, he heard every scrape of the pick. "You're being too aggressive," he said. "You need to use a real soft touch. Feel for the slightest movement."

Panic threatened to overtake me. "I told you, I don't know how to do this!"

"Try to relax," he said. "Take a moment and breathe."

"I don't have time to breathe!" I didn't have time to throw up, either, so I forced myself to put that one on hold. My hands were now shaking so badly, I couldn't have picked my nose, let alone a cranky antique lock.

"Trust me, Jane." His voice was warm and smooth and steady as a rock. "I will help you do this, I promise. But you have to trust me. Now, breathe."

My chest had never felt tighter. I forced myself to drag in a lungful of stale, grave-scented air. Then another. Moisture pooled in my eyes and made silent tracks down my cheeks. I would not let him hear me cry.

The only sound was the unrelenting *thunk thunk thunk* of Jonah's ax.

"Okay," I whispered. Then louder. "Okay, Padre. Let's do this."

Through stubborn force of will I gained control over my trembling fingers. I exerted the slightest pressure on the wrench and gently probed with the pick.

I'd seen a photo once of a kind of lemur called the aye-aye. This strange creature possesses a long, thin middle finger which it uses to dig grubs out of trees. I imagined the lock pick was just such a finger, a living extension of my hand and just as sensitive to touch.

"That's good," Martin murmured from the other side, listening. "Just keep— You got one! Did you feel that?"

I nodded stupidly, afraid to speak, afraid to break whatever spell had allowed me that little victory.

He said, "You're a natural, baby. Pin number two—let's go."

My armpits were drenched. He had to remind me again to breathe, but eventually I pushed the second pin up. Only, it didn't stay up.

"It's all about the wrench," he said. "You need to turn the cylinder just enough to hold any pins you've already set, but not enough to keep the next pin from setting. You have to finesse it."

I groaned. Finesse it? My fingers were so slippery with sweat, just keeping a grip on the slim little picks was a challenge. Sexy Beast decided that would be an excellent time to jump on me and beg for scritches. I told him to lie down and he did, with a huff of disappointment, smooshing his warm little body against my leg.

I pushed the second pin again. I was beginning to visualize what was going on inside that corroded lock, and why setting the pins and keeping them set was so tricky. Martin was right. It really was about what my left hand was doing with the tiny wrench.

This time when I set the pin, it stayed set.

"I'll turn you into a first-class burglar yet," he said. He didn't need to tell me to keep going. I was already working on pin number three.

The sound of ax-blows stopped and I almost wet myself. The remaining support timber was about to fall.

"Come on, come on, come on," I murmured, forcing myself to concentrate on the lock and push everything else out of my head. It wasn't just my life on the line. Two other people were relying on me, not to mention Sexy Beast.

"Jane, run!" Martin said. "Save yourself. *Go!*"

I said nothing, just teased the third pin into place and went to work on the fourth.

"Jane, I mean it. If Jonah's still there, hit him on the head with a brick or something, but get out of here while you still can."

"Shut up and get Nina ready to run." My hands were shaking again and beginning to cramp. I couldn't tell how much pressure I was putting on the wrench. One slip and the three pins I'd already set would fall.

Again I heard distant thuds: Jonah sledgehammering the support timber he'd just chopped.

I expected Martin to keep insisting I run. Instead he started yelling at Nina, trying to jolt her out of her stupor. In my mind's eye I saw him pulling her up off the bed and shaking her.

He didn't consider it hopeless. He believed in me.

I felt the fourth pin lift and stay there. One more to go. My senses were on overdrive. In the impenetrable darkness I saw the fifth and final pin as if blessed with X-ray vision. I knew that lock by now. I felt like I'd gone twelve rounds in a boxing ring with it. I positioned the curved tip of the lock pick directly under the pin and pushed upward.

Nothing.

At the mouth of the side tunnel, I heard one final hammer blow and then the sound of wood splintering.

The hell with finesse. I wiggled the pick. I jabbed it. I put elbow grease into it. "Move!" I commanded that rusty old pin. *"Move, damn you!"*

Click.

I turned the wrench like a key and felt the cylinder fully rotate. *I did it!*

Martin shoved the door open, knocking me on my butt and flooding the area with light. SB barked excitedly at all the commotion. I grabbed him as Martin yanked me up by the arm and started running.

Adrenaline gave me wings. Even Nina managed a decent speed, with Martin pulling her along. We covered the fifty yards in seconds, sprinting toward the resounding crash of the entryway's last remaining support timber.

Ahead of us, the light of the main tunnel dimmed under clouds of roiling earth as the entryway began to cave in. I didn't think it was possible for us to run faster, but we did, reaching the end and clambering blindly up the accumulated rubble, choking on the billowing dirt. Rocks and ceiling planks pelted us from above. The side tunnel was beginning to collapse around us, shuddering in its death throes.

I felt more than saw a small opening, rapidly filling with rubble. I propelled SB through it, and Martin did the same for me. I wriggled into the main tunnel—which remained untouched, thank goodness, the lights still blazing—then turned back to pull Nina through as he gave her a shove from behind. Blessedly, Jonah was nowhere to be seen.

Martin started to shimmy through just as the entryway collapsed completely, burying him under an avalanche of earth and rock. Frantically I began trying to dig him out, even as falling debris pummeled me and undid all my efforts.

"Help me!" I screamed at Nina, who responded by fleeing down the tunnel and disappearing from sight. Sexy Beast was more loyal. He stood at a safe distance from the cave-in, barking nonstop.

If I relied on my hands alone, Martin would soon suffocate. *Think!*

Wildly I glanced around, recalling the tools I'd seen earlier leaning against a wall. The ax and sledgehammer were missing, having been pressed into service by Jonah, but the shovel was still there. I grabbed it and started digging like a maniac. I couldn't say how long I kept at it. The muscles in my back and shoulders screamed as I shoveled without pause, sending soil and rocks and bricks flying. My mind was empty, my entire being focused on getting to Martin.

My heart nearly seized up when a hand shot out of the dirt. I gave it a reassuring squeeze and continued to dig, taking care not to clobber him with the shovel. He worked with me, gradually freeing his head and shoulders. Finally I dropped the shovel and grabbed hold of him, pulling hard as he laboriously hauled himself out of the pile of debris.

We fell to the ground in a filthy heap, our lungs pumping like bellows. SB hovered over me, warm dog breath fanning my face, as if searching in vain for a clean spot to lick. Martin and I turned our heads and just looked at each other. He was covered head to toe in dirt, bleeding from myriad deep scratches, and I wasn't much better.

"Nina booked on you?" he asked.

I shrugged. What was there to say?

Martin managed to get to his feet. He pulled me up and I wobbled, grateful when he steadied me against his side. As we began to shuffle down the tunnel toward civilization and an interesting conversation with Detective Hernandez, I noticed Sexy Beast wasn't with us. I turned back to see him avidly sniffing at the mountain of fallen debris.

"SB." I barely had the energy to form the words. "Come."

He whined.

"Come on, be a good boy for Jane." I stumbled over and picked him up. I kissed his grotty head. "You need a bath almost as badly as I do."

I looked down to see what he'd found so fascinating. It was the sledgehammer, poking out of the rubble. The more I stared at it, the more my eyes played tricks on me. I looked at Martin. He saw it too.

He knelt by the sledgehammer and brushed dirt and gravel off the wooden handle and the human fingers clutching it. I heard a low moan and belatedly realized it had come from me.

He pushed aside detritus and exposed part of a massive timber, one of the pair that had supported the mouth of the side tunnel. When I saw what lay under it—Jonah's head, crushed— I took a reflexive step back. The top section of the timber must have toppled on him when he split it.

Martin placed his fingers on Jonah's neck and shook his head, confirming what I already knew. He stood. "Let's get out of here."

18

Inseparable

"DOM, I DON'T have time. I'm on my way out." I shouldn't have answered the door. I was already running late.

"You going to let me in?" He produced that impish smile I'd once found so irresistible and held out a crystal vase overflowing with tulips.

"You sure you want to do this? Remember what happened last time." I took the vase and moved into the living room, setting it on the glass-topped coffee table. It was a balmy Saturday afternoon in mid-May. Sunlight streamed through the tall Palladian window. I heard Dom close the front door and follow me.

Over my shoulder I said, "Thanks for these. I'm sorry I'm in such a rush." I turned to find his arms circling my waist. He went in for a lip-lock, which I deflected by turning my head. I shoved him away and put a little distance between us. "Where's this coming from, Dom? This isn't like you."

He looked sweet and serious and heartbreakingly earnest as he said, "Marry me, Janey."

"What?"

"We never should have split up. It's taken me all these years to realize that." He shrugged, a wry smile on his handsome face. "What can I tell you? I'm a slow learner."

I struggled to form words. "What about Bonnie?"

"That's over. I broke up with her." He nibbled his lower lip—his signature tell—and I knew it hadn't gone down that way. She'd broken up with him.

It had been nearly five weeks since Martin and SB and I had tracked tunnel dirt across the immaculate black-and-white tile floor of Patisserie Susanne, collapsed on a pair of delicate bistro chairs, and phoned Dom's then-fiancée at the Crystal Harbor PD.

Since that day, I'd neither seen nor heard from Martin… until an hour ago when I'd received a text telling me to be at a certain North Fork winery at three o'clock. Oh yeah, and to "dress nice."

He waits five weeks? After what we'd been through together in that tunnel? *Five weeks?* He hadn't even shown up for Irene's memorial mass. And okay, I shouldn't have been surprised by that, but still.

I would have called him and given him what for, but his number was blocked from caller ID—his default setting, no doubt. By contrast, and as has already been established, he knew everything about me, so there you had it. I could either get dolled up and show up for this… Was it a date? Would have been nice to know. Or I could sit home and stew in my outrage, watching *Family Feud* and muttering darkly to SB about the male of the species.

I chose the slinky green halter dress I'd worn to Ted Seabrook's funeral, the dress Martin had said I looked "totally hot" in.

You know what? You can just keep it to yourself. I don't want to hear it.

And now that I was running late for this… this whatever it was that felt an awful lot like a date, here was Dominic Faso, the man I'd spent my entire adult life obsessing about, the man I'd recently decided I was finally *over,* standing in my living room asking me to marry him.

"You don't look happy," Dom said. "I thought you'd be happy."

"I don't know what I am. This is…" I groped for words.

"Sudden?" There was that mischievous smile again, the smile that used to melt my innards like Jell-O on a griddle. "Long overdue is more like it." He parked himself on the sofa and beckoned me to join him.

I stood my ground. "Um… seriously, Dom, it's not that I'm not, you know, blown away by all this, but I have to be somewhere."

Only then did he appear to notice that I wasn't in jeans and a tee. "Where are you off to?" When I didn't answer right away, he said, "You have a date." His tone was neutral, but I knew this man. He didn't feel neutral at all about my seeing another man, particularly after he'd just opened his heart to me.

I relented and sat next to him. "Things have changed, Dom. I'm not the same person I was."

"I know that, I—"

I interrupted him with a raised palm. "I don't think you do. I don't think I can reverse direction and…" I shook my head, at a loss for words.

He took my hand. His felt as big and warm and reassuring as it always had. He stared at me until I returned his gaze. "I want to have a family with you, Janey. I want the kids we should have had a long time ago."

I swallowed hard. I wasn't going to say it.

"I know," he said. "I didn't want them back then. I wasn't ready."

And yet, not being ready hadn't kept him from becoming a daddy a mere year after we'd split. His second wife, Svetlana, was eleven years older than he. A successful M.D. with a nagging biological clock and a commanding personality, she'd given birth to Karina and Ivan in quick succession. A few months after their divorce, he got Meryl pregnant with Jonathan and married her.

At the time I'd wondered if that's what I should have done when we were still married: been more assertive, put my foot down and insisted on children, despite his strenuous objection. And if that didn't work, maybe conveniently forget to use birth control. Ready or not, he'd been overjoyed with the arrival of each child. Dom was the epitome of the proud, doting papa.

But I couldn't turn back the clock, and I meant what I'd told him. I'd moved on. It might have taken a ridiculously long time, but his Janey was no longer the heartsick divorcee dreaming about a reconciliation with the one true love of her life.

I tried, at that moment, to ignore the ticking of my own biological clock, which had long since gone from nagging to deafening. Good Lord, how I wanted a baby. I'd wanted a baby two decades ago, and the passage of time had done nothing to dampen that overpowering, instinctual need. I'd never allowed myself to remarry for the simple reason that whenever I'd fantasized about being a mommy, only one man had played the role of daddy.

That man now sat next to me, eager to fulfill that fantasy. And here I was saying no.

I closed my eyes and took a steadying breath, willing myself to be strong, willing myself to remember that Dominic Faso, while a tender and devoted husband, never remained tender and devoted for long. Could I endure another divorce and single motherhood while Dom moved on to the next wife? My storybook plan to grow old with this man had been flawed from the start. As much as he loved being married, he'd never gotten the whole till-death-do-we-part thing down.

As if reading my mind, he said, "I've changed too."

Not in the way I need. In truth, my doubts went beyond his reliability as a life partner. At that point in our lives, and after everything I'd been through, I no longer felt the gut-deep certainty that Dominic Faso was my soul mate. I didn't say it, I simply shook my head.

He squeezed my hand harder. "You need time to think about it."

"My mind's made up, Dom."

He turned to face me fully and spoke with startling vehemence. "I respect your decision, but I don't accept it. I'm not going to give up, Janey. Somehow I'm going to prove to you that we belong together."

*

THE FARTHER EAST you travel on Long Island, the more rural and spread out it becomes. An hour's drive from Crystal Harbor brought me to the Island's wine country, a strip along the North Fork that's home to numerous vineyards. Maybe Martin had an afternoon of wine tasting planned, going from winery to winery sampling the Island's best vintages. It would have been gentlemanly for him to pick me up, perhaps in that tasty red Mercedes he'd given his mom.

Wait, did I just use *gentlemanly* with reference to Martin McAuliffe? I must have gotten walloped on the head in that tunnel and not realized it.

That thought opened the door to a memory I would pay dearly to expunge from my brain: Jonah Diamond lying under that massive timber with his head smashed in. One could argue that he'd deserved his fate, but I didn't deserve to have that image burned into my retinas when I stared at my bedroom ceiling each night.

I wondered how long it would take poor Rachel to recover from the shock and put her life back together. Losing her husband in such a bizarre and grisly fashion had been bad enough, but the revelation of what he'd done to keep his philandering under wraps—murder, attempted murder, and kidnapping—had magnified the tragedy and turned it into headline news and juicy fodder for the town gossip mill. She'd taken their kids and moved into her parents' home in Greenwich, Connecticut. The elegant Crystal Harbor mini-mansion she'd shared with Jonah was now on the market.

I'd half expected Nina and Mal to move away too, but they were staying put—and married. After everything that had happened, I could only assume he was sticking with her for the sake of the kids, the two daughters they already had plus the baby she was expecting next winter. Jonah's baby. I'd always thought Mal was a certifiable saint for putting up with Nina. By all accounts, he truly loved her. Knowing that he intended to raise this newest addition as his own put a fresh gloss on his halo as far as I was concerned.

Several days after we rescued Nina from the tunnel, her car was found in a chop shop in New Jersey. It seemed Jonah had driven it from the Historical Society, where she'd parked it, to a sketchy part of Newark and removed the plates.

And speaking of cars, Patrick finally took possession of the three luxury vehicles Irene had left him. My enormous garage now housed nothing but my eleven-year-old Civic. Maybe I could make the case that I needed to spend some of SB's maintenance funds on a newer, safer vehicle to transport him to the vet and the dog park. I'd have to run that one past Sten.

Patrick also emptied Irene's safe-deposit box, which contained family mementoes she'd held on to since childhood, including airmail letters from her grandparents in Ireland, a girlish pink diary with a busted lock, a yellowed scrapbook with pictures of movie stars she'd cut out of magazines, and most poignantly, a black-and-white, scallop-edged snapshot of thirteen-year-old Irene Hardy and her best friend in the world, Colette O'Grady, sitting on the front stoop of their apartment building in Bay Ridge, Brooklyn. They sat cheek to cheek, arms around each other's skinny waists. Inseparable.

Patrick showed me the keepsakes the day he and I planted Irene. Okay, "planted" sounds kind of cold, so let me explain. For someone who possessed a limitless imagination when it came to disposing of other people's cremated remains, Irene had been conspicuously closemouthed regarding what to do with her own. She'd left no written or verbal instructions. Sten had presented her ashes to her son, Patrick, who'd promptly sought my advice since I was the one "with the experience."

Which is how we'd ended up digging a hole in my backyard last week, depositing her ashes in the hole, and planting a pink dogwood sapling on top of them. Her favorite tree.

Later, over beer and burgers at Murray's Pub, I brought up

the subject of the mermaid brooch. I told him about its significance to the McAuliffes and why Martin felt so strongly about keeping it in the family. I was betting Patrick could identify with Martin's motives if not his means. After all, hadn't Patrick been willing to take the rap for Irene's murder, sacrificing a $16 million inheritance into the bargain, to protect his daughter from prosecution? The man knew a little something about family loyalty.

"Don't you worry about all that," Patrick said. "Me and Marty already worked it out."

This was not what I was expecting to hear. "Martin got in touch with you?"

"Uh-huh," he said around a mouthful of French fries. "He's not that bad a guy, you get to know him. What do I need that old brooch for? The design's from the McAuliffe coat of arms, for cripes sake. Mom never shoulda got her hands on it in the first place."

As I wondered which mom he meant, he added, "Irene neither. I got Sten to help me sign it over to Marty, all legal. He can do whatever he wants with the thing."

I'd bought him a piece of cheesecake to celebrate. I'd had the fruit cup. And half of his cheesecake.

The ornate sign for Zuccaro Cellars now loomed ahead. I turned off Sound Avenue and followed a tree-lined drive to the winery's parking area, which was practically filled—unusual for this early in the season. I spied Stevie's red Mercedes, which meant the padre had indeed borrowed her car but couldn't be bothered swinging by my place to pick me up. Gee, maybe he'd even invited his mom along on this thing that felt less like a date with each passing second.

Suddenly I wished I'd stayed home. Or at least worn something less totally hot.

Neat rows of grapevines stretched into the distance, a balm for the eyes and spirit, reminding me why I love this part of the Island. A large white event tent occupied a clearing in the vineyard. I parked, slipped out of my ballet flats and into a pair of wretchedly uncomfortable but oh-so-awesome four-inch heels, and click-clicked my way across the parking lot to the charming, Tuscan-style stone building. I was about to go inside when I spied a pretty, hand-painted wooden sign on a post. It bore the names *McAuliffe* and *Kovac*, separated by a pair of wedding rings. An arrow pointed to the rear of the property.

My stomach did a sickening flip. I recalled Martin's conversation with Stevie about meeting with the caterer. Lexie wanted him there, she'd said. A mental picture of the padre exchanging *I do's* with this Lexie had popped into my brain and I'd ordered my dumb self to stop leaping to conclusions. Now it looked like that particular conclusion had been worth leaping to, after all.

His wedding. Martin had invited me to his wedding and he hadn't even had the decency to send an invitation. I'd heard of A-list guests and B-list guests. I decided I didn't want to know how far down the alphabet you had to be to receive a last-minute text.

As I followed a stone path around the building, an enormous expanse of emerald lawn came into view, extending a couple of hundred yards to the edge of the vineyard. About eighty people milled about amid rows of white chairs that faced the vines. The chairs were bisected by an aisle which ended in a graceful grapevine arch decorated with clusters of purple, pink, and white flowers. Matching flowers filled tall galvanized bucket vases flanking the aisle.

You'd be hard-pressed to find a prettier spot to get married.

The guests were being urged to take their seats. I hurried across the lawn and slid into an empty chair on the aisle, then turned with the others to view the processional.

Stevie exited the building arm in arm with a gray-haired woman who appeared several years older but could very well have been the same age. They beamed as they strolled up the aisle to their seats in the front row. The other woman wore your typical dumpy mother-of-the-bride frock, while Stevie showed off her figure in a 1960s-style coral-colored cocktail dress. They were followed by two middle-aged couples. As I watched them settle in their seats up front, I realized I must be the only person there who had no idea who these people were.

The woman next to me murmured, "Isn't he handsome?"

I looked over my shoulder, expecting to see the padre coming down the aisle. Instead it was a tall man in his late twenties with an auburn ponytail, accompanied by a fortyish woman wearing a conservative blue jacket dress and carrying a folder. The two took up position under the grapevine arch. The woman was clearly the officiant—not a priest, obviously, but a minister or justice of the peace.

Three bridesmaids came next, wearing charmingly mismatched pastel dresses and escorted by suit-clad groomsmen. The attendants lined up on either side of the arch as the maid of honor and best man joined them. The flower girl, who looked to be about three years old, seemed to have trouble with the concept of strewing petals from the basket she carried. Halfway down the aisle, she dumped the petals in a heap and sprinted for the comforting arms of a relative. Everyone got a chuckle out of that.

The front-row guests stood, prompting the rest of us to follow suit. We turned to welcome the bride, now beginning the traditional trek down the aisle with her dad.

My heart somersaulted and I had to grab the chairback to remain on my feet. The bride was in her mid-twenties with dark blond hair and striking pale blue eyes. Her father's eyes.

I'd failed to note the family resemblance when I'd seen her picture on Martin's phone as I'd tried to call 911 in the tunnel. To be fair, I'd been somewhat distracted at the time. But now, as I watched him proudly walk this lovely young lady down the aisle, there could be no doubt.

She whispered something and he grinned, giving her fingers a loving squeeze where they curled over his elbow. For those few magical moments as he escorted his daughter to her waiting bridegroom, there was nothing the least bit mysterious or dangerous about Martin Kade McAuliffe.

He spied me and gave a little wink. He wore an impeccably tailored dark charcoal suit. His daughter's gown was a flowing sheath of pale yellow silk. Sunlight glinted off something colorful pinned to her bodice. When I saw what it was, I stifled a gasp.

The last time I'd seen the mermaid brooch, it had been pinned on a dead woman lying in her coffin. The artful arrangement of platinum, diamonds, and precious stones looked far better on this vibrant young bride than it had on Colette O'Rourke. And now that I knew it had been inspired by the McAuliffe coat of arms, the effect was… perfect.

I swear the mermaid winked at me, too.

*

MARTIN SWIRLED THE ICE in his glass of Jameson's as we strolled between rows of grapevines, each vine bearing clusters of tiny green buds. "They say the scent of these flowers is an aphrodisiac."

"Is that so." I smirked even as I wondered whether it could be true. More likely, the yummy hum of awareness I felt was the result of my third glass of champagne. Or the romantic setting. Or how ruthlessly sexy Martin looked in semiformal attire.

"Would I lie?" he said.

"You don't really expect me to answer that."

"Haven't you noticed that Ben and my mom can't keep their hands off each other? It's this." He inhaled deeply, drawing the delicate, earthy perfume of the vines into his lungs.

"Or it might be the fact that he's her date to this shindig." I recalled Martin informing Ben Ralston, during our meeting at his office that fateful day, that Stevie thought he was cute and urging him to go for it. I liked them both and was glad to see that one or the other of them had made a move.

The sun had recently set, painting the western sky salmon and gold. We were some distance from the big white tent where the wedding guests lingered over dessert, but the music carried on the breeze, a lovely classical piece being played by the string quartet Martin had hired. Earlier I'd slipped away to my car and changed back into the ballet flats. I mean, four-inch heels in a vineyard? Please.

"Ben's the reason you're here today." Martin sipped his drink.

"Do I want to hear this?" I was still steamed about the text.

"Lexie and Dillon wanted to keep the guest list under control, and her mom and I were fine with that," he said. "It's their day and we figured they should invite their own friends, not ours."

I'd met Lexie's mother during the reception. Erin and Martin had been seventeen when Lexie was born, more like high school friends with benefits than sweethearts. Martin had worked hard to support his daughter and be a real father to her, even after Erin got married a few years later and gave Lexie two siblings. The one thing he'd insisted was that she share his last name.

"So how did Ben get me invited?" I asked.

"By telling Lexie and Stevie what went on in that tunnel."

I stopped walking. So did he. I said, "They didn't know?"

He shrugged. "They had a wedding to plan. They didn't need all the grisly details."

"Let me get this straight," I said. "You told Ben all about it, but not your mother and daughter."

"Ben found out from Bonnie." He flung his half-melted ice into the vines. "He was there this morning when the women were getting ready, and I guess he thought they already knew about it."

"I still don't get it," I said. "Why would that make Lexie invite me? She never even met me."

His pale eyes appeared to glow in the fading light of dusk. "She insisted on meeting the woman who saved her dad's bacon. Twice."

Apparently, picking the lock and digging him out of the cave-in counted as two separate heroic gestures. I must be one hell of a gal.

"I can't hog all the credit," I said. "If SB hadn't snuck up on Jonah and startled him into dropping that syringe, you and I would still be down there, taking the big dirt nap."

His features grew serious. Quietly he said, "Thank you for saving my bacon twice, Jane."

"You're welcome." I couldn't help adding, "But a *text*, Padre?"

Another shrug. "We were busy. I knew you'd figure it out once you got here."

We started walking again. "You did a fine job raising Lexie. She's terrific," I said, and meant it.

He smiled softly. "If I did one thing right in my life, it's that girl."

"The mermaid brooch looks beautiful on her."

"She belongs to Lexie now," he said. "A link to her great-grandparents. Lexie was two when Grandpa died. I wish Grandma could have met her."

We walked in silence for several minutes. Finally I asked, "Did you know that Sten had the funeral home hold on to Irene's body after the autopsy?"

"I thought she was cremated right after."

"So did I," I said, "but he had a feeling she might have more to tell us. Turned out he was right."

"In other words, the pathologist missed something the first time around," he said.

I nodded. "In the tunnel, Jonah basically admitted to me that he killed Irene by injecting something. So Dr. Huang examined her body again and found an almost invisible needle mark. Apparently they can be difficult to spot, especially in loose and wrinkled skin like Irene had. Plus Jonah had deliberately used a tiny needle."

"Were they able to discover what drug he used?"

"Epinephrine," I said. "It can trigger a heart attack, especially when the victim is taking digoxin, like Irene was. The thing is, the human body naturally produces epinephrine, so when they did the initial toxicology test, there were no red flags."

"So how did they find it?" he asked.

"Once Dr. Huang discovered the injection site, she tested that patch of skin and there it was."

After a moment he said, "Angel of death."

"There was nothing angelic about Jonah Diamond. The cops are looking into his past to see if they can link him to any other unexplained deaths."

We paused and gazed back toward the tent, now a distant, glowing oasis amid endless rows of grapevines. The western sky had turned dusky plum, with one lingering streak of fire at the horizon. The breeze picked up and I shivered. Martin shrugged out of his suit jacket and settled its delicious warmth over my goose-bumped shoulders.

A gallant gesture. Just when I thought I had him figured out.

He said, "They're going to send a search party after us." Reluctantly we reversed direction and headed for the tent.

I studied his profile in the semidark. "You tried to tell me something in the tunnel."

"I did?"

"When it looked like we weren't going to get out. You said you wanted me to know something in case we didn't make it."

Martin was silent for long moments. "Did I say that? I don't remember."

I smiled at the lie. "Well, maybe it'll come back to you."

About the Author

Pamela Burford comes from a funny family. You may take that any way you want. She was raised in a household that valued laughter above all, so of course the first thing she looked for in a husband was a sense of humor. Is it any wonder their grown kids are into stand-up comedy and improv? Oh, and here's another fun fact: Pamela's identical twin sister, Patricia Ryan, aka P.B. Ryan, is also a published novelist. Patricia is the Good Twin, and yeah, Pamela knows what that makes her. But hey, Evil Twins have more fun!

It should come as no surprise that everything Pamela writes is infused with her own quirky brand of humor, from her feel-good contemporary romance and romantic suspense novels to her popular Jane Delaney mystery series, featuring snarky "Death Diva" Jane, her canine sidekick Sexy Beast, and a fun love-triangle subplot. Pamela's own beloved poodle, Murray, wants you to know that any similarities between himself and neurotic, high-strung Sexy Beast are purely coincidental.

Pamela is the proud founder and past president of Long Island Romance Writers, Inc., a chapter of Romance Writers of America. Her books have won awards and sold millions of copies, but what excites her most is hearing from readers. Swing by and say hi at pamelaburford.com.

Made in the USA
Middletown, DE
06 May 2018